Mr Clarinet

Mr Clarinet

NICK STONE

MICHAEL JOSEPH
an imprint of
PENGUIN BOOKS

MICHAEL JOSEPH

Published by the Penguin Group

Penguin Books Ltd, 80 Strand, London WC2R ORL, England

Penguin Group (USA) Inc., 375 Hudson Street, New York, New York 10014, USA

Penguin Group (Canada), 90 Eglinton Avenue East, Suite 700, Toronto, Ontario, Canada M4P 2Y3
(a division of Pearson Penguin Canada Inc.)

Penguin Ireland, 25 St Stephen's Green, Dublin 2, Ireland (a division of Penguin Books Ltd)

Penguin Group (Australia), 250 Camberwell Road,
Camberwell, Victoria 3124, Australia (a division of Pearson Australia Group Pty Ltd)

Penguin Books India Pvt Ltd, 11 Community Centre,
Panchsheel Park, New Delhi – 110 017, India

Penguin Group (NZ), cnr Airborne and Rosedale Roads, Albany,
Auckland 1310, New Zealand (a division of Pearson New Zealand Ltd)

Penguin Books (South Africa) (Pty) Ltd, 24 Sturdee Avenue,
Rosebank, Johannesburg 2196, South Africa

Penguin Books Ltd, Registered Offices: 80 Strand, London WC2R ORL, England

www.penguin.com

First published 2006

1

Set in 13.5/16pt Monotype Garamond
Typeset by Palimpsest Book Production Limited, Polmont, Stirlingshire
Printed in Great Britain by Clays Ltd, St Ives plc

A CIP catalogue record for this book is available from the British Library

ISBN-13 978-0-718-14855-3
ISBN-10 0-718-14855-X

For Hyacinth and Seb

And in loving memory of Philomène Paul (Fofo),
Ben Cawdry, Adrian 'Skip' Skipsey and my grandmother,
Mary Stone

Yo byen konté, Yo mal kalkilé.
Haitian saying

Prologue

New York City, 6 November 1996

Ten million dollars if he performed a miracle and brought the boy back alive, five million dollars if he came back with just the body, and another five million if he dragged the killers in with it – their dead-or-alive status was immaterial, as long as they had the kid's blood on their hands.

Those were the terms, and, if he chose to accept them, that was the deal.

Max Mingus was an ex-cop turned private investigator. Missing persons were his specialty, finding them his talent. Most people said he was the best in the business – or at least they had until 17th April 1989, the day he'd started a seven-year sentence for manslaughter on Rikers Island and had his licence permanently revoked.

The client's name was Allain Carver. His son's name was Charlie. Charlie was missing, presumed kidnapped.

Optimistically, with things going to plan and ending happily for all concerned, Max was looking at riding out into the sunset a millionaire ten to fifteen times over. There were a lot of things he wouldn't have to worry about again, and he'd been doing a lot of worrying lately, nothing but worrying.

So far, so good, but now for the rest:

The case was based in Haiti.

'*Haytee?*' Max said as if he'd heard wrong.

'Yes,' Carver replied.

Shit.

He knew this about Haiti: voodoo, AIDS, Papa Doc, Baby Doc, boat people and, recently, an American military invasion called Operation Restore Democracy he'd seen on TV.

He knew – or had known – quite a few Haitians, ex-pats he'd had regular dealings with back when he'd been a cop and worked a case in Little Haiti, Miami. They hadn't had a decent thing to say about their homeland, 'bad place' being the most common and kindest.

Nevertheless, he had fond memories of most of the Haitians he'd met. In fact, he'd admired them. They were honest, honourable, hard-working people who'd found themselves in the most unenviable place in America – bottom of the food chain, south of the poverty line, a lot of ground to make up.

That went for *most* of the Haitians he'd met. When it came to people there were always plenty of exceptions to every generalization, and he'd come face to face with those. They hadn't left him with bad memories so much as the kind of wounds that never really heal, that open up at the slightest nudge or touch.

The whole thing was already sounding like a bad idea. He'd just come out of one tough spot. Why go to another?

Money. That was why.

Charlie had disappeared on 4 September 1994, his third birthday. Nothing had been heard or seen of him since. There had been no ransom demands and there were no witnesses. The Carver family had had to call off its search for the boy after two weeks because the US army had invaded the country and put it on lockdown, imposing curfews and travel restrictions on the whole population. The search hadn't resumed until late October, by which time the trail, already born cold, had frozen over.

'There's one other thing,' Carver said when he'd finished talking. 'If you take the job, it's going to be dangerous . . . Make that *very* dangerous.'

'How so?' Max asked.

'Your predecessors, they . . . Things didn't turn out too right for them.'

'They dead?'

There was a pause. Carver's face turned grim and his skin lost a little of its colour.

'No . . . not dead,' he said, finally. 'Worse. *Much* worse.'

PART ONE

I

Honesty and straightforwardness weren't always the best options, but Max chose them over bullshit as often as he could. It helped him sleep at night.

'I can't,' he told Carver.

'Can't or *won't?*'

'I won't because I can't. I can't do it. You're asking me to look for a kid who went missing two years ago, in a country that went back to the Stone Age about the same time.'

Carver managed a smile so faint it barely registered on his lips, yet let Max know he was being considered unsophisticated. It also told Max what kind of rich he was dealing with. Not rich, *riche* – *old* money, the worst; connections plugged in at every socket, all the lights on, everybody home – multi-storey bank vaults, fuck-off stockholdings, high-interest offshore accounts; first-name terms with everybody who's anybody in every walk of life, power to crush you to oblivion. These were people you never said no to, people you never failed.

'You've succeeded at far tougher assignments. You've performed – *miracles*,' Carver said.

'I never raised the dead, Mr Carver. I only dug 'em up.'

'I'm ready for the worst.'

'Not if you're talking to me,' Max said. He regretted his bluntness. Prison had reformed his erstwhile tact and replaced it with coarseness. 'In a way you're right. I've looked for ghosts in hellholes in my time, but they were *American* hellholes and there was always a bus out. I don't know your

7

country. I've never been there and – no disrespect meant – I've never *wanted* to go there. Hell, they don't even speak *English.'*

That was when Carver told him about the money.

Max hadn't made a fortune as a private detective, but he'd done OK – enough to get by and have a little extra to play with. His wife, who was a qualified accountant, had managed the business side of things. She'd put a fair bit of rainy-day money away in their three savings accounts, and they'd had points in the L Bar, a successful yuppie joint in downtown Miami run by Frank Nunez, a retired cop friend of Max's. They'd owned their house and two cars outright, taken three vacations every year, and eaten at fancy restaurants once a month.

He'd had few personal expenses. His clothes – suits for work and special occasions, khakis and T-shirts at all other times – were always well cut but rarely expensive. He'd learnt his lesson after his second case, when he'd got arterial spray on his five-hundred-dollar suit and had to surrender it in to forensics, who later handed it in to the DA who recycled it in court as Exhibit D. He sent his wife flowers every week, bought her lavish presents on her birthday, and at Christmas and on their anniversary; he was also generous to his closest friends, and his godson. He had no addictions. He'd quit cigarettes and reefer when he'd left the force; booze had taken a little longer, but that had gone out of his life too. Music was his only real indulgence – jazz, swing, doo-wop, rock 'n' roll, soul, funk and disco; he had five thousand CDs, vinyl albums and singles he knew every note and lyric to. The most he'd ever spent was when he'd dropped four hundred bucks at an auction on an autographed original double ten-inch vinyl copy of Frank Sinatra's 'In The Wee

Small Hours Of The Morning'. He'd framed it and hung it in his study, opposite his desk. When his wife asked he lied and told her he'd picked it up cheap at a house repo-sale in Orlando.

All in all, it had been a comfortable life, the sort that made you happy and fat and gradually more and more conservative.

And then he'd gone and killed three people in the Bronx, and the wheels had come off and everything had skidded to a loud, ungainly stop.

Post-prison: Max still had the house and his car in Miami, plus $9,000 in a savings account. He could live on that for another four or five months tops, then he'd have to sell the house and find a job. That would be hard. Who would employ him? Ex-cop, ex-PI, ex-con – three crosses, no ticks. He was forty-six: too old to learn anything new and too young to give in. What the fuck would he do? Bar work? Kitchen work? Pack shopping bags? Construction? Mall security?

True, he had some friends and people who owed him but he'd never called in a favour in his life, and he wasn't about to start now that he was on his knees. It would be tantamount to begging, and that went up against his every rule. He'd helped people out because he could at the time, not for what they could do for him later, not for points in the karma bank. His wife had called him naïve, marshmallow soft under the concrete and razor wire carapace he showed the world. Maybe she'd been right. Maybe he should have put self-interest before others. Would his life have been any different now? Probably, yes.

He saw his future, clearly, a year or two from now. He'd be living in one of those one-room apartments with stained wallpaper, tribes of warring roaches, and a set of dos and don'ts on the door, handwritten in semi-literate Spanish. He'd hear his neighbours arguing, fucking, talking, fighting; upstairs, downstairs, left and right. His life would be one chipped plate, a knife, a fork and a spoon. He'd play the lotto and watch the results go against him on a portable TV with a shaky picture. Slow death, gradual extinction, one cell at a time.

Take Carver's job or take his chances in the post-con world. He had no other choice.

Max had first spoken to Allain Carver over the phone in prison. They didn't get off to a good start. Max had told him to fuck off as soon as he'd introduced himself.

Carver had been pestering him pretty much every day of the last eight months of his sentence.

First came a letter from Miami:

'Dear Mr Mingus, My name is Allain Carver. I greatly admire you and everything you stand for. Having followed your case closely . . .'

Max stopped reading there. He gave the letter to Velasquez, his cellmate, who used it to make a joint. Velasquez had smoked all of Max's letters, except for the personal ones. Max nicknamed him 'The Incinerator'.

Max was a celebrity prisoner. His case had been on TV and in all of the papers. At one point almost half the country had had a strong opinion about him and what he'd done, a sixty–forty split, for and against.

During his first six months behind bars he'd had fan mail by the sackful. He'd never replied to any of it. Even the sincerest well-wishers left him cold. He'd always despised strangers who corresponded with convicted criminals they'd seen on TV, or read about in the papers, or met through those fucked-up prisoner penpal clubs. They were the first to demand the death penalty when the boot was on the other foot and that foot had stomped one of their loved ones to death. Max had been a cop for eleven years. There was a lot of it left over in him. Many of his closest friends were still on the force, keeping these very same people safe from the animals they wrote to.

When Carver's first letter arrived, Max's mail was down to letters from his wife, in-laws and friends. His fanbase had moved on to more appreciative types like OJ Simpson and the Menendez brothers.

Carver met Max's silence over his first letter with a follow-up two weeks later. When that too elicited no response, Max received another Carver letter the next week, then two more the week after that and, seven days later, two more again. Velasquez was pretty happy. He liked Carver's letters because the paper – thick watermarked cream stationery, with Carver's name, address and contact numbers embossed on the right-hand corner in emerald foil letters – had something in it that reacted fantastically with his weed and got him more stoned than usual.

Carver tried different tactics to get Max's attention – he changed paper, wrote longhand and got other people to write in – but no matter what he tried everything went by way of the Incinerator.

So the letters stopped and the phone calls started. Max guessed that Carver had bribed someone high up because only inmates with serious juice or imminent retrials were allowed to take incoming calls. A guard fetched him from the kitchens and took him to one of the conference cells where a phone had been plugged in, just for him. He spoke to Carver, long enough to hear his name, think he was English from his accent and tell him what was what and never to call him again.

But Carver didn't give up. Max would be interrupted at

work, in the exercise yard, at meals, in the shower, during lockdowns, after lights-out. He dealt with Carver as he always did: 'Hello', hear Carver's voice, hang up.

Max eventually complained to the warden, who thought it was the funniest thing he'd ever heard. Most inmates griped about hassles on the *inside*. He told Max not to be such a pussy and threatened to put a phone in his cell if he bothered him again with such bullshit.

Max told Dave Torres, his lawyer, about Carver's calls. Torres put a stop to them. He also offered to dig up some information about Carver, but Max passed. In the free world he would have been curious as hell; but in prison curiosity was something you gave up with your court clothes and your wristwatch.

The day before his release, Max had a visit from Carver. Max refused to see him, so Carver left him his final letter, back on the original stationery.

Max gave it to Velasquez as a going-away present.

After he got out of jail, Max was all set to go to London, England.

The round-the-world tour had been his wife's idea, something she'd always wanted to do. She'd long been fascinated by other countries and their cultures, their histories and monuments, their people. She was always going off to museums, queuing up to get into the latest exhibitions, attending lectures and seminars, and always reading – magazines, newspaper articles and book after book after book. She tried her best to sweep Max along with her enthusiasms, but he wasn't remotely interested. She showed him pictures of South American Indians who could wear pizza plates in their bottom lips, African women with giraffe-like necks fitted with industrial springs and he really couldn't begin to see the attraction. He'd been to Mexico, the Bahamas, Hawaii and Canada, but his world was really just the USA and that was a world big enough for him. At home they had deserts and arctic wastes and pretty much everything in between. Why go abroad for the same shit, only older?

His wife's name was Sandra. He'd met her when he was still a cop. She was half-Cuban, half-African–American. She was beautiful, clever, tough and funny. He never called her Sandy.

She'd planned for them to celebrate their tenth wedding anniversary in style, travelling the globe, seeing most of the things she'd only read about. If things had been different Max would probably have talked her into going to the Keys for a week, with the promise of a modest foreign trip (to Europe or Australia) later in the year, but because he was in prison when she told him her plans, he wasn't in a position to refuse. Besides, from where he was, getting as far away from America as possible seemed like a good idea. That year out would give him time to think about the rest of his life and what best to do with it.

It took Sandra four months to organize and book the tour. She arranged the itinerary so they'd arrive back home in Miami exactly a year to the day they'd left, on their next wedding anniversary. In between they would see all of Europe, starting with England, and then they'd move on to Russia and China, followed by Japan and the Far East, before flying on to Australia and New Zealand, and then on to Africa and the Middle East, before closing out in Turkey.

The more she told Max about the trip during her weekly visits, the more he started looking forward to it. He took to reading up about some of the places they'd be visiting in the prison library. It was initially a way of getting him out of one day and into the next, but the more he began to delve into the stuff of his wife's dreams, the closer he got to her, perhaps closer than he'd ever been.

She finished paying for the trip the day she died in a car crash on US 1, which she appeared to have caused by inexplicably and quite suddenly switching lanes straight into the path of an oncoming truck. When they performed the autopsy they found the brain aneurysm that had killed her at the wheel.

The warden broke the news to him. Max was too stunned to react. He nodded, said nothing else and left the warden's office and went about the rest of his day pretty much as normal, cleaning the kitchen surfaces, serving at the counter, feeding the trays through the dishwasher, mopping the floors. He didn't say anything to Velasquez. You didn't do that. Showing grief or sadness or any emotion unrelated to anger was a sign of weakness. You kept those things well hidden, bottled up, out of sight and sense.

Sandra's death didn't sink in until the next day, Thursday. Thursday was her visiting day. She'd never missed one. She'd fly in the night before, stay with an aunt who lived in Queens, and then, the next day, she'd drive up to see him. At around 2.00 pm, when he'd usually be finishing off in the kitchen or bullshitting with Henry the cook, he'd be called out to the visiting room over the tannoy. Sandra would be waiting for him on the other side of the booth, behind the glass partition and the wall between them. She'd always be immaculately dressed, a fresh layer of lipstick on her mouth, big smile on her face, eyes lighting up, just like she was on a first date. They'd talk about this and that, how he was feeling, how he was looking, then she'd give him back-home news, tell him about herself, tell him about the house, talk about her job.

Henry and Max had an arrangement. Henry would work around Max on Thursdays, giving him things he could finish up quickly so he could get out as soon as his name was called. Max always helped Henry out in the same way on Sundays, when Henry's family – his wife and four kids – came to see him. They got on well enough for Max to ignore that Henry was doing fifteen to life for an armed robbery that had left a pregnant woman dead, and that he ran with the Aryan Bund.

On the outside it was business as usual that Thursday. Only, Max had woken up with a heavy, aching feeling in his chest and a sense of emptiness that opened up into a numb void as the morning went on. He kept on hearing a peculiar rush of air in his ears, as though he was stuck in a wind tunnel, and the vein in his forehead began to wriggle and twitch under his skin. He wanted to tell Henry his wife wasn't coming that week and then let him know the why the following week, but he couldn't bring himself to say anything because he knew the minute he did he'd lose control of his words and most likely crack up.

He didn't have enough to do in the kitchen to keep his mind busy. He had the almost spotless cooker to wipe down. The cooker had a clock set in the middle of its controls. He tried to stop himself, but he kept on staring at the clock, watching the black hands move in clicks, stepping up to 2.00.

He replayed the previous week's visit in his mind, every single second of the last time they were together. He recalled every word she'd said to him – about the surprise discount she'd managed to get from one airline, the free nights at a luxury hotel she'd won in a competition, how impressed she was with his knowledge of Australian history. Had she ever said anything about migraines, or headaches, or dizzy spells, blackouts, nosebleeds? He saw her face again through the bulletproof glass partition they met through; the glass was smeared with the ghostly fingerprints and lipmarks of where a million convicts had touched and kissed their loved ones by proxy. They'd never done that. They agreed it was pointless and desperate. It wasn't as if they'd never get to do the real thing again, was it? He wished they had now. It would have been better than the absolute nothing he was left with.

'Max,' Henry called over from the sink. 'Time to play husband.'

It was a few clicks away from 2.00. Max started taking off his apron, right on cue, then stopped.

'She's not coming today,' he said, letting the straps of the apron fall to his side. He felt a hot surge of tears geyser up to his eyes and mass around the edges.

'Why so?'

Max didn't answer. Henry came over to him, wiping his hands on a dishcloth. He saw Max's face, about to crack wide open and spill. He looked surprised. He even backed off a step. Like almost everyone else in the joint, he thought Max was a tough motherfucker – an ex-cop in General Population who'd held his head up and hadn't once flinched from meeting violence with violence.

Henry smiled.

He could have smiled out of mockery, or the sadistic delight in the misfortune of others that passes for happiness in prison, or plain simple confusion. Tough guys didn't cry – unless they were pussies all along, or worse, in mid-meltdown.

Max, buried fifty feet deep in grief, read mockery in Henry's face.

The roaring in his ears fell still.

He punched Henry in the throat, a straight short jab powered in with his full weight that went directly to the windpipe. Henry's mouth dropped open. He gasped out for air. Max smashed a right hook into his jaw and busted the bone in two. Henry was a big tall guy, a daily freeweight freak who could press 350 clean without breaking a sweat. He went down with a huge thud.

Max fled the kitchen.

It was a bad move, the worst. Henry was high up in the Bund, and their main source of income. They dealt the best drugs in Rikers. Henry's kids smuggled them in for him in the cracks of their asses. The Bund would want blood, a face-saving kill.

Henry was in the infirmary for three days. Max deputized in his absence, all the while waiting for payback. The Bund weren't stray killers. They liked to come in packs of four or five. The guards would know about it in advance. Tipped off and paid off, they'd look the other way, as would everyone in the vicinity. Inside, where he hurt most, he prayed they stuck him clean, straight through a vital organ. He didn't want to wind up a free man in a wheelchair.

But nothing happened.

Henry claimed he'd slipped on some stray grease on the kitchen floor. He was back running the kitchen by Sunday, his jaw tightly wired. He'd heard about Max's loss and the first thing he did when he saw him again was shake his hand and pat him on the shoulder. This made Max feel worse about hitting him.

Sandra's funeral was held in Miami, a week after her death. Max was allowed to attend.

She was laid out in an open casket. The undertaker had dressed her in a black wig that didn't suit her. Her real hair had never been that straight or that black; she'd had a russet tinge to it in places, brown in others. The make-up was all wrong too. She'd never needed much when she was alive. He kissed her cold rigid lips and slipped his fingers between her folded hands. He stood there staring down at her forever, feeling her a million miles away. Dead bodies were nothing new to him, but it was very different when it was the most important person in his life.

He kissed her again. He desperately wanted to flick her eyes open and see them one last time. She'd never closed her eyes when they kissed, ever. He reached out and then noticed that the overhanging white lilies from the massed display had shed their pollen on to the collar of the dark-blue pinstriped business suit she'd been dressed in. He wiped it clean.

At the service her youngest brother Calvin sang 'Let's Stay Together', her favourite song. The last time he'd sung it was at their wedding. Calvin had an incredible voice, mournful and piercing like Roy Orbison's. It busted Max up. He cried his fucking heart out. He hadn't cried since he'd been a kid. He cried so much his shirt collar got wet and his eyes swelled up.

On the way back to Rikers, Max decided he'd take the trip Sandra had spent the final part of her life organizing. It was partly to honour her wishes, partly to see all the things she never would, partly to live her dream, and mostly because he didn't know what else to do with himself.

His lawyer, Dave Torres, picked him up outside the prison gates and drove him to the Avalon Rex, a small, cheap hotel in Brooklyn, a few blocks away from Prospect Park. The room was functional – bed, desk, chair, closet, bedside table, lamp, clock-radio and phone – and there was a communal bathroom and trough-like sink on the top floor. He was booked in for two days and nights, after which he was taking a plane to England from JFK. Torres handed him his tickets, passport, three thousand bucks in cash and two credit cards. Max thanked Torres for everything and they shook hands and said goodbye.

First thing Max did was open his door, step out of his room, walk back inside and close it behind him. He liked it so much he did it again and again half a dozen times until he'd taken the shine off the novelty of being able to come and go as he pleased. Next thing he did was take off his clothes and check himself out in the wardrobe mirror.

Max hadn't seen himself naked in a mirror since he'd last been a free man. Eight years on, he looked good from the neck down, dressed in just his two tattoos. Big shoulders and bulging biceps, chunky forearms, a short wide neck, cobblestone abs, thick thighs; put him in a posing pouch and body oil and he could have won a Mr Penitentiary trophy. There was an art to working out in prison. It wasn't about vanity and fitness, it was about survival. It was wise to be big – if you cast an impressive shadow people thought twice about fucking with you, and usually kept out of your way – but you didn't want to get *too* big in case you stood out and became a target for young first-timers out to get a rep; there was nothing more ridiculous-looking than a cell-block hulk dying from a toothbrush shiv rammed in his jugular. Max was very fit before he'd gone into prison. He'd been a three-times Golden Gloves middleweight boxing champion in his teens, and he'd stayed in shape running, swimming and sparring at a local boxing gym near Coral Gables. Exercise wasn't a quantum leap to him; he had the in-built discipline that comes from learning to swallow a punch whole. He'd been allowed half an hour a day in Rikers. He'd hit the weights six days a week, upper body one day, legs the next. He'd done three thousand push-ups and crunches in his cell, every morning, five hundred at a time.

Although still handsome in the blunt and brutal sort of way that deceptively appealed to women and gays with a taste for rough sex and kamikaze relationships, his face wasn't too good. His skin was tight, but it was wrinkled and waxy pale, almost ghostly from the lack of sunlight. The needlepoint scars around his lips had faded. There was a new meanness in his blue eyes and a sour downturn to the ends of his mouth he recognized from his mother who, like him, had been left alone at the onset of her autumnal years. And as had happened to her at the same age, his hair had gone completely grey. He hadn't noticed the transition from the dark brown he'd been on the day of his incarceration, because he'd stayed bald in the joint to appear more forbidding. He'd let his hair grow out in the last few weeks leading up to his release – a mistake he intended to rectify before he left town.

The next morning he went out. He needed to buy a warm winter coat and jacket, and a hat too if he was going to lose his old man's hair. It was a bright, freezing cold day. The air burned his lungs. The street was swarming with a multitude of people. Suddenly he was lost and didn't know what he was doing or where he was going. He'd walked slap bang into the middle of rush-hour, everybody on their way to earn money and take shit with a thank you and a smile and build up a tailback of grudges and resentments in the process. He should've known better and prepared himself for it, but he felt as if he'd been beamed in from another planet against his will. Seven years of time slipped its leash and rushed at him, jaws wide open, belly empty. Everything had changed – clothes, hairstyles, walks, faces, brands, prices, languages – too much to take in and absorb and break down and analyse and compare. Too much too soon after prison, where everything stayed the same and you were on at least face terms with everyone you saw. Now he was straight in at the deep end. He could float but he'd forgotten the strokes. He plodded along, keeping two steps behind the people in front of him and two steps in front of those behind, chain-gang style. Maybe no matter how free we think we are, we're all prisoners in our own way, he thought. Or maybe he just needed time to wake up and get with the programme.

He slipped out of the crowd and snuck into a small café. It was packed with people getting a caffeine fix before hitting their offices. He ordered an espresso. It came in a cardboard cup with a holder and a warning printed on the side that the drink was VERY HOT. When he tasted it it was lukewarm.

What was he doing in New York? It wasn't even his town. What was he doing even thinking of travelling the world when he hadn't been home, got his bearings and readjusted himself to freedom?

Sandra wouldn't have wanted him to do this. She would have said it was pointless, running away when he'd have to come back eventually. True. What was he scared of? Her not being there? She was gone. He'd just have to get over. And the way you got over was by walking across the absence, embracing your loss, and moving on.

Fuck it. He'd go back to Miami on the first plane out.

In his hotel room Max called up the airlines. All flights booked solid for the next two and a half days. He got a seat for the Friday afternoon.

Even though he didn't have a clue what he'd do when he

got to Miami, he felt better now that he was heading some-where familiar.

He thought about taking a shower and getting something to eat, and maybe that haircut if he could find somewhere.

The phone rang.

'Mr Mingus?'

'Yes?'

'Allain Carver.'

Max didn't say anything. How had he found him here?

Dave Torres. He was the only one who knew where Max was. How long had he been working for Carver? Probably when Max had asked him to stop the calls he was getting in prison. Instead of going to the authorities, Torres had gone to the man himself. Double-dealing scumbag never missed an opportunity to make a buck.

'Hello? Are you still there?'

'What's this about?' Max said.

'I have a job you might be interested in.'

Max agreed to meet him the next day. His curiosity was back.

Carver gave him an address in Manhattan.

'Mr Mingus? I'm Allain Carver.'

First impressions: imperious prick.

Carver had stood up from behind an armchair when Max had walked into the club. Instead of coming over, he'd taken a few steps forward to identify himself and then stood where he was, arms behind his back, in the style of royalty meeting an ambassador from a former colonial state, now hopelessly impoverished and in dire need of a handout.

Tall and slender, dressed in a well-tailored navy-blue wool suit, light-blue shirt and matching silk tie, Carver might have strolled in off a 1920s-set musical where he'd been cast as an extra in a Wall Street scene. His short blond hair was slicked back from his forehead and parted down the middle. He had a strong jaw, long pointed face and tanned skin.

They shook hands. Firm handshake, soft smooth skin, unperturbed by manual labour.

Carver motioned him to a black leather and mahogany tub chair set in front of a round table. He waited until Max had sat down before he took his place opposite him. The chair was high-backed and finished some two feet above his head. He couldn't see to his left or right without leaning all the way forward and craning his neck out. It was like being in his own booth, intimate and secretive.

Behind him was a bar that stretched the width of the room. Every conceivable spirit seemed to be lined up there – green, blue, yellow, pink, white, brown, clear and semi-clear bottles glinting as gaily as plastic bead curtains in a well-heeled brothel.

'What would you like to drink?'

'Coffee, please. Cream, no sugar.'

Carver looked over to the far end of the room and raised his hand. A waitress approached. She was camera-lens thin, with high cheekbones, pouting lips and a catwalk strut. All the staff Max had seen so far looked like models: both the barmen had that slowburn stubbled seducer look advertisers employed to sell white shirts and aftershave, while he could have easily wished up the receptionist from a clothes store catalogue, and in another life the security guy monitoring the CCTV screen in a side office might have been the Diet Coke break guy on the construction site.

Max had almost missed the club. It was in an anonymous five-storey townhouse in a cul-de-sac off Park Row, so anonymous that he'd walked past it twice before he'd noticed the number 34 stamped faintly into the wall near the door.

The club was three flights up in a mirrored elevator with polished brass handles running around the middle and reflections accordioning to infinity. When the doors opened and he'd stepped out, Max thought he'd arrived in the lobby of a particularly luxurious hotel.

The interior was vast and very quiet, like a library or a mausoleum. All over the thickly carpeted floor the same black tub chairs sprouted like burned-out oak stumps in a desecrated forest. They were arranged so you only saw their backs and not the people in them. He'd thought they were alone until he saw clouds of cigar smoke escaping from behind one of the chairs, and when he looked around more closely he saw a man's foot in a beige slip-on beyond another. A single framed painting adorned the wall nearest to them. It was of a young boy playing a flute. He was dressed in a ragged, Civil War-era military uniform a good ten years too big for him.

'Are you a member here?' Max asked, to break the ice.

'We own it. This and several similar establishments around the world,' Carver replied.

'So you're in the club business?'

'Not particularly,' Carver answered, with an amused look on his face. 'My father, Gustav, set these up in the late fifties to cater for his best business clients. This was the first. We have others in London, Paris, Stockholm, Tokyo, Berlin – and elsewhere. They're a perk. When individuals or their companies do over a certain amount of net dollar business with us they're offered free lifelong membership. We encourage them to sponsor their friends and colleagues, who of course pay. We have a lot of members, turn a good profit.'

'So you can't just fill in a form?'

'No.' Carver chuckled.

'Keep the peasants out, huh?'

'It's just the way we do business,' Carver said, dryly. 'It works.'

There were traces of East Coast WASP wrinkling Carver's otherwise crisp English accent, an unnatural reining in of some vowels and an over-exaggeration of others. English school, Ivy League diploma?

Carver: matinee idol manqué, looks fading agreeably. Max placed him as his age, maybe a year or two younger; balanced diet – healthy. There were frowns on his neck and crow's feet etched at the ends of his small, sharp blue eyes. With his golden skin he could have passed for white South American – Argentinian or Brazilian – bloodlines all the way back to Germany. Untouchably handsome, but for his mouth. That let him down. It resembled a long razor cut where the blood has just started to bubble but not yet run over.

The coffee came in a white porcelain pot. Max poured himself a cup and added in a measure of cream from a small jug. The coffee was rich and strong and the cream didn't leave a greasy slick on the surface; it was connoisseur stuff, the kind you bought by the bean and ground yourself, not the mongrel brews you picked up in the supermarket.

'I heard about your wife,' Carver said. 'I'm sorry.'

'Me too,' Max countered curtly. He let the subject die in the air, then got down to business. 'You said you had a job you wanted me to look at?'

Carver told him about Charlie. Max heard the basics and told him flat out no. Carver mentioned the money and Max quietened up, more out of shock than greed. In fact greed didn't even enter into it. While Carver was talking numbers he handed Max a brown A4 envelope. Inside were two glossy black-and-white photographs, a headshot and a full-length bodyshot – of a little girl.

'I thought you said your *son* was missing, Mr Carver?' Max said, holding up the picture.

'Charlie had a thing about his hair. We nicknamed him Samson because he wouldn't let anyone go near it. He was born – somewhat unusually – with a full head of the stuff. It covered his face like a caul. I remember when they tried to cut it in hospital, he *screeched* – this *deafening* howl of pain. It was terrifying. And it was like that afterwards, whenever anyone tried to sneak up on him with a pair of scissors. We left it alone. He'll outgrow the phobia eventually,' Carver said.

'Or not,' Max said, bluntly, deliberately.

Max thought he saw Carver's face change for an instant, as a shadow of humanity stole away a fragment of his all-business composure. It wasn't enough to make him warm to his potential client, but it was a start.

Max studied the headshot. Charlie didn't look anything like his father. His eyes and hair were very dark and he had a large mouth with full lips. He wasn't smiling. He looked pissed off, a great man interrupted in the middle of his work. It was a very adult look. His stare was intense and stark. Max could feel it prodding at his face, humming on the paper, nagging at him.

The second photograph showed Charlie standing in front of some bougainvillea bushes with almost the same expression on his face. His hair was long all right, bow-tied into two drooping bunches that poured over his shoulders. He was wearing a floral-patterned dress, with frills on the sleeves, hem and collar.

It made Max sick.

'It's none of my business and I ain't no psychologist, but that's a sure as shit way to fuck a kid's head up, Carver,' Max said, hostility upfront.

'It was my wife's idea.'

'You don't seem the henpecked kind.'

Carver laughed briefly, sounding like he was clearing his throat.

'People are very backward in Haiti. Even the most sophisticated, well-educated sorts believe in all kinds of rubbish – superstitions –'

'Voodoo?'

'We call it *vodou*. Haitians are ninety per cent Catholic and a hundred per cent *vodouiste*, Mr Mingus. There's nothing sinister about it – no more than say, worshipping a half-naked man nailed to a cross, drinking his blood and eating his flesh.'

He studied Max's face for a reaction. Max stared right back at him, impassive. Carver could have worshipped Safeway carts for all he cared. One person's God was another person's idea of a good joke, as far as he was concerned.

He looked back at the photograph of Charlie in his dress. You poor kid, he thought.

'We've looked everywhere for him,' Carver said. 'We ran a campaign in early 1995 – newspaper and TV ads, billboards with his picture on them, radio spots – everything. We offered a substantial reward for information, or, better still, for Charlie himself. It had predictable consequences. Every lowlife suddenly came out from under a rock and claimed they knew where "she" was. Some even claimed they'd kidnapped "her" and made ransom demands, but it was all – the sums they wanted were trivial, *way too small*. Obviously I knew they were lying. These peasants in Haiti can't see past the ends of their noses. And their noses are *very* flat.'

'Did you follow up on all the leads?'

'Only the sensible ones.'

'First mistake right there. Check everything out. Chase every lead.'

'Your predecessors said that.'

Bait and hook, Max thought. Don't go there. You'll get drawn into a pissing contest. Still he *was* curious. How many people had already worked on the case? Why had they failed? And how many were out there now?

He played indifferent.

'Don't get ahead of yourself. Right now we're just having a conversation,' Max said. Carver was stung, brought down to a level he usually didn't frequent. He must have been surrounded by the sort of people who laughed at all his jokes. That was the thing about the very rich, the rich born and bred: they swam in their own seas and didn't breathe the same air as everybody else; they lived parallel, insulated lives, immune to the struggles and failures that shape character. Had Carver ever been forced to wait until next month's pay cheque for a new pair of shoes? Been turned down by a woman? Had repo men knocking on his door? Hardly.

Carver told him about the danger, brought up the predecessors again, hinted that bad things had happened to them. Max still didn't rise to it. He'd gone into the meeting thirty per cent decided he wasn't taking the job. Now he was almost at the fifty per cent mark.

Carver clocked his indifference and switched his talk to Charlie – when he'd taken his first steps, how he had an ear for music – and then he went into a bit more detail about Haiti.

Max listened, feigning interest with a fixed look, but behind it he was going away, back into himself, delving, working out if he could still cut it.

He came up strangely empty, unresolved. The case had two obvious angles – financial motive or some possible voodoo bullshit. No ransom, so that left the latter, which he knew a bit more about than he'd let on to Carver. Or maybe

Carver knew about him and Solomon Boukman. In fact, he was certain Carver *did* know about that. Of course he did. How couldn't he, if he had Torres on his payroll? What else did Carver know about him? How far back had he gone? Did he have something stored up, ready to spring on him?

Bad start, if he wanted to take it further. He didn't trust his future client.

Max ended their meeting telling Carver he'd think about it. Carver gave him his card and twenty-four hours to make up his mind.

He took a cab back to his hotel, Charlie Carver's photographs on his lap.

He thought about ten million dollars and what he could do. He'd sell the house and buy a modest apartment somewhere quiet and residential, possibly in Kendall. Or maybe he'd move out to the Keys. Or maybe he'd leave Miami altogether.

Then he thought about going to Haiti. Would he have taken the case in his pre-con prime? Yes, certainly. The challenge alone would have appealed to him. No forensics to fall back on and cut corners with, just pure problem-solving, brain work, his wits pitted against another's. But he'd mothballed his talents when he'd gone to prison and they'd quietly wasted away with inattention, same as any muscle. A case like Charlie Carver's would be up the hill backwards, the whole way.

Back in his room, he propped the two photos up on his desk and stared at them.

He didn't have any children. He'd never cared for kids all that much. They tried his patience and fried his nerves. Nothing would piss him off more than being stuck in a room with a crying baby its parents couldn't or wouldn't shut up. And yet, ironically, many of his private cases had involved finding missing children, some mere toddlers. He had a hundred per cent success rate. Alive or dead, he always brought them home. He wanted to do the same for Charlie. He was worried that he couldn't, that he'd fail him. Those eyes, sparkling with precocious rage, were finding him again, all the way across the room. It was stupid but he felt they were calling out to him, imploring him to come to his rescue.

Magic eyes.

Max went out and tried to find a quiet bar where he could have a drink and think things through, but everywhere he passed was full of people, most of them a generation younger than him, most of them happy and loud. Bill Clinton had been re-elected President. Celebrations everywhere. Not his scene. He decided to buy a bottle of Jack at a liquor store instead.

While he was looking for a shop he bumped into a guy in a white puffa jacket and ski hat pulled down almost to his eyes. Max apologized. Something fell out of the man's jacket and landed at the man's feet. A clear plastic ziplock bag with five fat joints rolled tampon-style. Max picked it up and turned to give it to the man but he was gone.

He slipped the joints into his coat pocket and carried on walking until he found a liquor store. They were out of Jack. They had other bourbons, but nothing came close to a hit of Jack.

Of course there was always the reefer.

He bought a cheap plastic lighter.

Back in the day, Max Mingus and his partner Joe Liston had liked nothing better than to unwind with a little reefer they got off a snitch dealer called Five Fingers. Five'd feed them certified busts and throw in a few free ounces of Caribbean Queen – a very potent strain of Jamaican grass he used himself.

It was the best shit Max had ever had, way better than the year-old garbage he'd just smoked.

An hour later he was sat on his bed, staring intently at the wall, vaguely aware of the lurchy feeling in his stomach.

He lay back and closed his eyes.

He thought of Miami.

Home sweet home.

He lived near Hobie Beach, on Key Biscayne, off the Rickenbacker Causeway. On a good evening he and Sandra used to sit out on the porch and watch Downtown Miami in all its hypnotic, neon-lit splendour, the smell of Biscayne Bay wafting in on the cool breeze, fish and boat oil mixed in. No matter how many times they took in the view it was always different. Manhattan had nothing on his hometown on a good day. They liked to talk about the future then, right then when life was good and promised to get better. The future to Sandra meant starting a family.

Max should have told her about the vasectomy he'd had a few months before they'd met, but he'd never had the – yeah, he'd never had *the balls*.

How could he bring children into the world after seeing what was left of the ones he found in his line of work, the ones he had to pick up and reassemble piece by piece? He couldn't. He'd never let his kids out of his sight. He'd lock them up and throw away the key. He'd stop them going to school and playing outside and visiting friends in case they got snatched. He'd run background checks on all his relatives and in-laws in case they were hiding paedo convictions.

What kind of life would that be – for them, for his wife, for him? None at all. Best to forget having a family, best to forget continuing the cycle; best to shut it down completely.

Nineteen eighty-one: that had been a bad time for him, a shit era. Nineteen eighty-one: the year of Solomon Boukman, a gang leader from Little Haiti. Nineteen eighty-one: the year of the King of Swords.

Sandra would have understood, if he'd been honest with her from the start, but when they'd first started dating he was still in confirmed bachelor mode, lying to every woman he met, pretending he was a long-term prospect, telling them whatever they wanted to hear so he could fuck them and flee. He'd had plenty of opportunities to come clean with her before they got married, but he thought he'd lose her. She came from a big family and loved children.

Now he regretted not reversing the vasectomy when he'd had the chance. He'd thought about it a year into his marriage, when being with Sandra had started changing him for the better and with it, little by little, his attitudes to starting a family. It would have meant everything to him to still have something of her left behind, even a trace he could love and cherish as he had loved and cherished her.

He thought about their house again.

They had a large kitchen with a counter in the middle. He used to sit there at night, trying to get his head around a case that was keeping him awake. Sometimes Sandra would join him.

He saw her again now, dressed in a T-shirt and slippers, hair pillow-frazzled, a glass of water in one hand, Charlie's headshot in another.

'I think you should take this case, Max,' she said, looking across at him, her eyes all puffed up with broken sleep.

'Why?' he heard himself ask.

'Because you got no choice, baby,' she said. 'It's that or you know what.'

He woke up with a start, fully dressed on the bed, staring at the blank ceiling, his mouth dry and tasting of rotted beef.

The room stank of stale reefer, taking him right back to his cell after Velasquez had taken a nightcap hit before saying his prayers in Latin.

Max stood up and staggered over to the desk, twenty jack-hammers busting out of his cranium. He was still mildly stoned. He opened the window and the freezing cold air tore into the room. He took a few deep breaths. The fog in his head retreated.

He decided to take a shower and change his clothes.

'Mr Carver? It's Max Mingus.'

It was 9.00 am. He'd gone to a diner and eaten a big break-fast – four-egg omelette, four pieces of toast, orange juice and two pots of coffee. He'd thought things through one more time, the pros and cons, the risk factor, the money. Then he'd found a phone booth.

Carver sounded slightly out of breath when he answered, as if he was cooling down from a morning run.

'I'll find your son,' Max said.

'That's great news!' Carver almost shouted.

'I'll need the terms and conditions in writing.'

'Of course,' Carver said. 'Come by the club in two hours. I'll have a contract ready.'

'OK.'

'When will you be able to start?'

'Assuming I can get a flight, I'll be in Haiti on Tuesday.'

2

Back in Miami, Max took a cab from the airport to his house. He asked the driver to take the longer way round, down Le Jeune Road, so he could check out Little Havana and Coral Gables to get a feel for how far his hometown had come in seven years, check the pulse beating between the poles, from *barrio* to billionaires' row.

Max's father-in-law had been looking after the house. He'd picked up the bills. Max owed him $3,000, but that wasn't a problem because Carver had given him a $25,000 cash advance in New York when he'd signed the contract. He'd played dumb and brought Dave Torres with him to read through it and witness it. It had been funny watching Torres and Carver pretend they'd never met. Lawyers are great actors, second only in talent to their guilty clients.

Max stared out of the passenger window but not much was getting through. Miami: Eight Years Later ... was passing him by in a glistening blur of cars, more cars, palm trees and blue sky. It had been raining when the plane touched down, one of those almighty Sunshine State soakings where the raindrops hit the ground so hard they bounce. The downpour had stopped a few minutes before he'd walked out of the airport. He couldn't focus on the outside when there was so much going on within. He was thinking about returning to his old home. He hoped his in-laws hadn't decided to spring a surprise welcome-back party for him. They were good-hearted, always well-intentioned people and it was just the sort of good-hearted, well-intentioned shit they'd pull.

They'd passed Little Havana and Coral Gables and he hadn't even noticed. Now they were on Vizcaya's main highway and the Rickenbacker Causeway turn-off was indicated.

Sandra had always met him at the airport when he'd been away on a case, or out of town to meet a potential client. She'd ask him how it had gone, although she could always tell, she said, by looking at him. They'd walk out of the Arrivals section and she'd leave him waiting outside the terminal while she went and got the car. If things had gone well, he'd do the driving. On the way home he'd tell her what had happened and what he'd done to make it so. By the time they'd reached the front door he'd have talked the case dry and the subject would be closed, never to be mentioned again. Sometimes he'd come out into Arrivals beaming, triumphant, vindicated, having flown out someplace on a wild hunch that had turned up one of those golden leads that brings a case to a swift and happy conclusion. Those occasions were few and far between, but they were always Occasions. They'd go out dancing, or to dinner, or down the L Bar if there were other people to thank. But two times out of three Sandra did the driving because she'd have read failure in Max's body language, resigned despair in his face. She'd make light smalltalk while he sat and brooded in silence, staring out at the sky through the windscreen. She'd sprinkle domestic trivialities in his thought stream, stuff about mended curtains and cleaned carpets and new household appliances, stuff to let him know that their life went on, despite the deaths he'd uncovered and had to report back to a hope-against-hope spouse or relative or friend.

She'd always been there, waiting at the barrier, the face for him.

He'd looked for her, of course, when he'd come through

35

Arrivals. He'd looked for her in the faces of women who might have been waiting for men, but none of them looked as she always had.

He couldn't go back to the house. Not now. He wasn't ready for that museum of happy memories.

'Driver? Keep driving, don't take the turn,' Max said, as he heard the indicator lights go on.

'Where we goin'?'

'The Radisson Hotel, North Kendall Drive.'

'Hey, Max Mingus! Wassappenin'wit'chu?' Joe Liston's voice boomed down the phone when Max called him from his hotel room.

'Good to hear your voice, Joe. How you been?'

'Good, Max, good. You home now?'

'No. I'm staying at the Radisson in Kendall for a few days.'

'What's wrong wit' your house, man?'

'Sandra's cousins are there,' Max lied. 'I thought I'd give them the run of the place a while longer.'

'Yeah?' Joe said, chuckling. 'They got ID?'

'*ID?*'

'You're a big fuckin' hero round here, Mingus, don't you go spoilin' it,' Joe said, losing the chuckle. 'Ain't *no one* at your house, man. I've been sendin' a patrol car up and down your street on the hour every hour since Sandra passed.'

Max should have known better. He felt embarrassed.

'I ain't gonna be thinkin' more or less of you 'cause you're hurtin'. I *will* think less of you if you start playin' me for some fool that just got off the bus from Retard City, Ohio,' Joe said, admonishing him as he probably did his children, cutting the reproach with a guilt-inducer.

Max didn't say anything. Neither did Joe. Max heard the sounds of office life going on through the receiver –

conversations, phones ringing, doors opening and closing, pagers. Joe was probably used to his children apologizing about now, and then crying. Joe would pick them up and squeeze them and tell them it was OK, but not to do it again. Then he'd give them a kiss on the forehead and put them down.

'I'm sorry, Joe,' Max said. 'It's been hard.'

'*No es nada, mi amigo,*' Joe said, after a deliberate pause meant to make Max think he was evaluating his sincerity.

'But it's gonna *stay* hard for you as long as you keep runnin' away. You got to go to the mountain otherwise that sucker's gonna go for you,' Joe said. Probably what he told his kids when they complained about their homework being difficult.

'I know,' Max said. 'I'm working on it right now. In fact, that's one of the reasons I was calling. I need a couple of favours. Records, old files, anything you've got on an Allain Carver. He's Haitian and –'

'I know him,' Joe said. 'Missin' son, right?'

'Yeah.'

'Came in here a while back and filed a report.'

'I thought the kid went missing in Haiti?'

'Someone reported they'd seen him here in Hialeah.'

'And?'

'That someone was some crazy old lady claimed she had visions.'

'Did you check it out?'

Joe laughed – big and hearty laughter, but dry and cynical too – classic cop's laugh, the way you got after more than two decades on the job.

'Max? We started doin' *that* we'd be lookin' for little green men in North Miami Beach. That ole lady's from Little Haiti. That kid's face is every place – stuck on everythin' – walls, doors, stores – I bet it's in the water they drink too – his face and the fiddy thousand dollar reward for information.'

Max thought about Carver's initial campaign in Haiti. The Miami version had probably yielded the same results.

'You got an address for the woman?'

'You takin' the case, right?' Joe said. He sounded worried.

'Yeah.'

'Main reason Carver came to see me was he wanted to get in touch wit'chu. I hear you played hard to get? What changed your mind?'

'I need the money.'

Joe didn't say anything. Max heard him scribbling something down.

'You'll need a piece,' Joe said.

'That was the second favour.'

Max was banned from owning a gun for life. He'd expected Joe to refuse.

'And the first?'

'I'll need a copy of everything you've got on the Carver kid, plus his family.'

He heard more scribbling.

'No problem,' Joe said. 'How about we meet at the L tonight, say round eight?'

'On a *Friday*? How about someplace quiet?'

'The L's got this new lounge bar? Away from the main one? It's *so* quiet you can hear a flea fart.'

'OK,' Max laughed.

'It'll be good to see you again, Max. *Real* good,' Joe said.

'You too, Big Man,' Max said.

Joe was going to say something and then stopped. Then he tried again and stopped again. Max could hear it in the slight sucking noises he was making as his mouth opened and he took in the right amount of air to launch the words massed at the back of his throat.

They still had it, their old couple's telepathy.

Joe was worried about something.

'What's bugging you, Joe?'

'You *sure* you wanna go to Haiti?' Joe asked. "Cause it ain't too late to back out.'

'Where's this coming from, Joe?'

'It ain't gonna be too safe for you out there.'

'I know about the country's situation.'

'It ain't *that*,' Joe said slowly. 'It's Boukman.'

'*Boukman*? *Solomon* Boukman?'

'Uh-huh.'

'What about him?'

'He got out,' Joe said, his voice dropping close to a mumble.

'*What*?! He was on *death row*!' Max shouted, standing up as his voice rose. His reaction surprised him: seven years in prison and he'd mostly kept his emotions in check, his expressions to a bare minimum. You couldn't afford to let people see what got you up or down in jail because they'd use it against you. He was already adjusting to the free world, finding his left-behind self again.

'That re-elected asshole Clinton gave him a free pass home,' Joe explained. 'We're shippin' the criminals home. Happenin' all over – state and fed.'

'Do they know what he *did*?' Max said.

'That ain't the point, as far as they see it. Why waste taxpayers' money keepin' him in prison when you can send him back home?'

'But he's *free*.'

'Yeah, but that's the Haitians' problem now. And now it's yours too – you meet him out there . . .'

Max sat himself back down.

'When did this happen, Joe? When did he get out?'

'March. This year.'

'Mother-*fucker*!'

'There's more to tell –' Joe started and then he broke off to talk to someone. He put the receiver down on his desk. Max heard the conversation get louder. He couldn't make out exactly what was being said, but someone had fucked up. Dialogue turned to monologue, Joe's voice crushing everything in its path. Joe grabbed the phone. '*MAX?!!? I'LL SEE YOU TONIGHT! WE'LL TALK SOME MORE THEN!*' he roared and slammed the phone down.

Max laughed, imagining the poor subordinate getting the trade end of one of Joe's tirades. He had a way of using every inch of his towering frame to win an argument, leaning his face right over yours and looking down into your eyes like you were a piece of dog shit he'd trodden in on his way to church. And then he'd start talking.

He suddenly stopped laughing when he remembered the first child sacrifice victim, the way the body had looked on the morgue slab.

Solomon Boukman: child killer. *Free.*

Solomon Boukman: mass murderer. *Free.*

Solomon Boukman: cop killer. *Free.*

Solomon Boukman: gang-leader, drug baron, pimp, money launderer, kidnapper, rapist. *Free.*

Solomon Boukman: his last case as a cop, his last collar, the one that almost killed him.

Solomon's words to him in court: 'You give me reason to live,' stage-whispered with a smile that chilled Max to the core. Those words had made the whole thing between them very personal.

Max's words back: *'Adios, motherfucker.'* How wrong he'd been.

Boukman had headed up a gang called the SNBC – short for Saturday Night Barons Club, adapted from Baron

Samedi, the voodoo god of death. Its members swore their leader had supernatural powers, that he could read minds and predict the future, that he could be in two places at once, materializing in rooms just like they did in *Star Trek*. They said he got his powers through some demon he worshipped, some *méchant loa*. Max and Joe had caught him and shut down the gang.

Max was shaking with anger, fists balled up, heat rising up in his face, the vein in his forehead twitching and wriggling like a worm in a frying pan. Solomon Boukman was someone Max had taken great pride in catching – and great joy in working over with his fists and a sap before he'd booked him.

Now Boukman was free. He'd beaten the system. And he'd beaten Max and pissed in his face. It was too much – too much to have to come back to.

3

Max had known Joe for twenty-five years. They'd started out as partners in Patrol and moved on up through the ranks together.

The pair were known as 'Born to Run' within the Miami PD. Their boss, Eldon Burns, coined the nickname because he said the two of them standing together reminded him of the cover of Bruce Springsteen's famous album, where the pale, scrawny singer is propped up against Clarence Clemons, his gargantuan, pimp-hatted sax player. It wasn't a bad comparison. Joe dwarfed everyone. Built like a linebacker who's swallowed the team, he was six foot five in his socks and had to duck to get through most doors.

Joe dug the nickname. He loved Bruce Springsteen. He had all his albums and singles, and hundreds of hours of live shows on cassette. It was virtually all he seemed to listen to. Whenever Springsteen toured, Joe would have front-row seats for all the Florida concerts. Max dreaded having to share a car with his partner after he'd seen his hero in the flesh, because Joe would describe the experience in excruciatingly precise detail, song by song, grunt by grunt. Springsteen's shows averaged three hours. Joe's reports would go on for six. Max couldn't stand Springsteen, didn't know what all the fuss was about. To his ears the voice of the so-called 'Boss' was stuck somewhere between throat clearing and throat cancer – and the perfect soundtrack for white guys who drove station wagons in motorcycle jackets. He'd once asked Joe what the attraction was. 'It's like everything that moves one person and leaves another standing still: you either get it or you don't. Ain't just about the music and the voice with Bruce. It's about a whole lotta *other* things. You get me?' Max hadn't, but he'd left it at that. Bad taste never hurt anybody.

That said, he had no problem with their nickname. It meant they were being noticed. After they'd both made detective, Max had the album image and title tattooed on his inner right forearm. A year later he had a traditional cop tattoo – a shield bearing a skull and crossed six-guns, surrounded by the legend 'Death IS Certain – Life Is NOT' – inked into his left arm.

The L was named after the shape of its building, although you'd have to see it from above to know. Detective Frank Nunez had first spotted it from a police helicopter while giving chase to a vanload of bank robbers across Downtown Miami. He got some of his friends to come in with him in return for points, including Max and Sandra, who put in $20,000. Until they'd had to sell their share to help pay Max's legal bills, the bar had made them double their investment back every year. It was a big hit with the Downtown business and banking crowd, who packed it out Monday to Saturday.

From the front the L resembled a fairly typical bar, with its wide black-shuttered windows and flashing beer signs spelled out in bright neon squeezed-toothpaste lettering. There were two entrances. The right took you straight to the bar, a big high-ceilinged space with varnished wooden floors and a maritime theme in the ship wheels, anchors and shark harpoons mounted on the walls. The left entrance led up a long flight of stairs to the L Lounge. The Lounge was screened off from the bar by a tinted wall-window which allowed its patrons to see the goings-on down below unobserved. It was ideal for first dates and clandestine office affairs, because it was sectioned off into intimate booths, each softly lit with red-and-gold Chinese-style lamps. The Lounge had its own bar and served some of the best cocktails in Miami.

When Max walked in he saw Joe sitting on the outside of a middle booth close to the window. He was in a blue suit and tie. Max felt underdressed in his loose sweatshirt, khakis and running shoes.

'Lieutenant Liston?' Max said as he drew up to his friend.

Joe smiled broadly, a capsized quarter moon of teeth that glowed across the bottom of his dark face. He got up. Max had forgotten quite how immense he was. He'd put on a few pounds around the waist and his face was a little rounder, but he still looked like every suspect's interrogation room nightmare.

Joe gave Max a big hug. Despite his prison work-outs, Max's shoulders didn't make either side of Joe's chest. Joe patted Max's arms and stood back a couple of steps to look him over.

'See they fed you,' he said.

'I worked the kitchen.'

'Not the barbershop?' Joe said, patting Max's bald head.

They sat down. Joe took up most of his side of the booth. A ring-binder file was on the table. A waiter came over. Joe ordered a Diet Coke and a shot of bourbon. Max asked for a Fat Coke.

'You dry?' Joe asked.

'Dry-ving. You?'

'Slowed drinkin' down so much I might as well *have* quit. Middle age is beatin' my ass. Can't shake a hangover like back in the day.'

'You feel better for it?'

'Nope.'

Joe's face hadn't aged much – not in the Lounge light at any rate – but his hairline had been beaten back from his forehead and he wore his hair longer than before, which led Max to suspect he was thinning in the middle.

There were a few couples in the Lounge, all still in their office suits. Anonymous piano muzak tinkled from corner speakers, the tune so indecipherable they might as well have been playing the sound of a horse pissing on wind chimes.

'How's Lena?' Max asked.

'She's good, man. Sends her love,' Joe said. He reached into his suit jacket, pulled out some photographs and handed them to Max. 'Mugshots. See if you recognize anyone you know.'

Max looked through the pictures. The first was a family shot with Lena in the middle. Lena was tiny, next to Joe almost foetal. Joe had met her at his local Baptist church. He hadn't been particularly religious, but church was a better and cheaper alternative to trawling bars and clubs or dating fellow cops; he'd called it 'the best singles spot outside of heaven'.

Lena had never liked Max. He didn't blame her. The first time they'd met he'd had blood on his collar from where a suspect had bitten his earlobe. She'd thought it was lipstick, and from then on she'd always looked at him like he'd done something wrong; relations, like their conversations, had stayed the polite side of functional. Things hadn't improved between them after he'd left the force either. His marrying Sandra had appalled her. Even God didn't cross the colour line in her world.

The last time Max had seen Joe he'd had three children, all boys – Jethro, the eldest, then Dwayne and Dean, one year apart – but there were two baby girls on Lena's lap.

45

'Yeah, that's Ashley on the left and on the right is Briony,' Joe said proudly.

'Twins?'

'Double trouble. Stereo.'

'How old?'

'Three. We wasn't plannin' on havin' no more kids. They just happened.'

'They say the unplanned ones are the most loved.'

'"They" say a lot of things, most of 'em bullshit. I love all my babies equally.'

They were cute-looking kids, took after their mother, same eyes.

'Sandra never told me,' Max said.

'You two's had more pressin' bidnis to talk over, I'm sure,' Joe said.

The waiter brought the Cokes and bourbon. Joe took the shot glass, quickly checked around him and tipped the drink on the floor.

'For Sandra,' he said.

Pour out a little liquor for the dead, spirit for spirit. Joe always did that every time someone close to him died. Right then solemnity threatened to invade their space, get the better of the moment. Max didn't need it. They had things to talk over.

'Sandra didn't drink,' Max said.

Joe looked at him, read the traces of humour left over on his lips and burst out laughing. He had a big laugh, a rolling rumble of joy that filled the room and made everyone look their way.

Max stared at the photograph of his godson. Jethro was holding a basketball up on splayed fingertips. The boy was twelve but already tall and broad enough to pass for sixteen.

'Takes after his daddy,' Max said.

'Jet loves his ball.'

'Could be a future there.'

'Could be, but best let the future be the future. Besides, I want him to do well in school. Kid's gotta good head on him.'

'You don't want him to follow in your footsteps?'

'Like I said, the kid's gotta good head on him.'

They clinked glasses.

Max handed him back the photographs and looked over at the main bar. It was packed. Brickell Avenue bankers, businessmen, white-collar workers with loosened ties, hand-bags on the floor, jackets draped carelessly over the backs of their chairs, hems trailing on the ground. He homed in on two executive types in similar light-grey suits, both clutching Bud bottles and talking to a pair of women. They'd just met, exchanged first names, broached common ground, and now they were searching for the next conversation lead-in. He could tell all that from the tensed-up body language – stiff-backed, alert, ready to run off to the next best thing. Both men were interested in the same girl – navy-blue business suit, blonde highlights. Her friend knew this and was already looking around the bar. Back in his bach-elor days Max had specialized in going for the ugly friend, reasoning that the better-looking one would be expecting attention and would play hard to get and leave him holding his dick and a big tab at the end of the night. The woman who wasn't expecting to get hit on would be more likely to give it up. It had worked nine times out of ten, sometimes with the unexpected bonus of the good-looking one making a play for him. He hadn't liked most of the women he'd dated. They were challenges, notches, things to be possessed. His attitudes had changed completely when he'd met Sandra, but now she was gone all those old thoughts were coming back to him like the ghost of an amputated limb, sending him feelings out of nowhere.

He hadn't had sex in eight years. He hadn't thought about it since the funeral. He hadn't even jerked off. His libido had shut down out of respect.

He'd been faithful to Sandra, a one-woman man. He didn't really want anyone else, someone new, not now. He couldn't even imagine what it would be like again, going through all that bullshit conversation, pretending to be a sensitive guy when the only reason you'd gone up to her was to see if you could fool her into a fuck. He was looking at the whole scene below him with the pioneer's distaste for the copyist.

Joe pushed the file over to him.

'Dug up a little on the Carvers of Haiti,' Joe said. 'Mostly back story, nothing current. The video's got a load of news footage about the Haitian invasion. Allain Carver's in there somewhere.'

'Thanks, Joe,' Max said, taking the files and putting them down on the seat beside him. 'Anything on them here?'

'No criminal records, but Gustav Carver, the dad? He's got a mansion in Coral Gables. Got B & E'd six years back.'

'What they take?'

'Nothing. Someone broke in one night, took one of their fine china dinner plates, shit on it, put it on the dining-room table and left without a trace.'

'What about the security cameras?'

'*Nada.* I don't think the case got followed through. Report is but two pages – looks more like a complaint than a crime. Probably some pissed-off ex-servant.'

Max laughed. He'd heard of far stranger crimes, but the thought of Allain Carver finding that on the table when he came down to breakfast was funny. He started to smile, but then he thought of Boukman and his expression wilted.

'So, you wanna tell me what happened with Solomon Boukman? When I went to New York he was sitting on death row, one last appeal away from the needle.'

'We ain't in Texas,' said Joe. 'Things take time in Florida. Even *time* takes time here. A lawyer can take up to two years to put in an appeal. That stays in the system for another two years. Then you got yet another two years before you get in front of the judge. Add all that up and it's 1995. They turned down Boukman's last appeal, like I knew they would, only –'

'But they fucken' set him *free*, Joe!' Max said, raising his voice to a near shout.

'Do you know how much a one-way ticket to Haiti costs?' Joe said. 'A hundred bucks, give or take – plus tax. Do you know how much it costs the state to keep a man on death row? Hell – forget *that*. Do you know how much it costs the state to *execute* a man? Thousands. See the logic?'

'The victims' families "see the logic"?' Max said bitterly.

Joe didn't say anything. Max could tell he was angry about it too, but there was something else eating away at him.

'You wanna tell me the rest, Joe?'

'They cleaned out Boukman's cell the day he left. Found this,' Joe said, handing Max a sheet of school-exercise book paper sealed in an evidence bag.

Boukman had cut out a newspaper picture of Max at his trial and stuck it in the middle of the paper. Underneath it, in pencil, in that strange childlike writing of his – capitals, all letters bereft of curves, strokes linked by dots and drawn so straight he appeared to have used a ruler – he'd written: 'YOU GIVE ME REASON TO LIVE'. Below that he'd drawn a small outline of Haiti.

'Fuck's he mean by that?' Joe asked.

'He said that to me at his trial, when I was givin' evidence,'

Max said, and left it at that. He wasn't going to spring the truth on Joe. Not now. Not ever, if he could help it.

He'd come face to face with Boukman twice, before his arrest. He'd never been so terrified of another human being in all his life.

'I don't know about you, but there *was* somethin' genuinely scary about Boukman,' Joe said. 'D'you remember when we busted in there – that zombie palace place?'

'He's just a man, Joe. A sick, twisted man, but a man all the same. Flesh and blood like us.'

'He didn't so much as *groan* when you laid into him.'

'So? Did he fly off on a broomstick?'

'I don't care how much Carver's payin' you, man. I don't think you should go. Give it a pass,' Joe said.

'If I see Boukman in Haiti, I'll tell him you say hello. And then I'll kill him,' Max said.

'You can't afford to take this shit lightly,' Joe said, angry.

'I'm not.'

'I got your piece.' Joe lowered his voice and leaned over. 'New Beretta, two hundred shells. Hollow point and regular. Gimme your flight details. It'll be waitin' for you in Departures. Pick it up before you get on the plane. One thing: don't bring it back. It stays in Haiti.'

'You could get into serious shit for this – arming a convicted felon,' Max joked, hiking up the sleeves of his sweatshirt to just below his elbows.

'I don't know no felons, but I do know good men who take wrong turns,' Joe smiled. They clicked glasses.

'Thanks, man. Thanks for everything you did for me when I was away. I owe you.'

'You don't owe me shit. You're a cop. We look after our own. You know how it is and always will be.'

Depending on what they'd done to get there (most rapes

and all kiddie sex crimes were out, but everything else was permissible), cops who went to jail were protected by the system. There was an unofficial national network where one state police department looked out for a felon from another state police department, knowing that the favour would be returned in spades sometime down the line. Con-cops would sometimes be kept in a maximum-security prison for a week or two and then quietly transferred out to a minimum-security white-collar jail. That was what happened to those who'd killed suspects, or got caught taking back-handers or stealing dope and selling it back on the street. If they couldn't swing a transfer, a fallen cop would be segre-gated, kept in solitary, have his meals brought to him by the guards from their own canteens and allowed to shower and exercise alone. If solitary was all booked up, as it frequently was, the cops would be put in General Population, but with two guards watching their backs at all times. If a con did make a move on a jailbird cop he'd get thrown in the hole long enough for the guards to put the word out that he was a snitch, and let out just in time to get shanked. Although Max was arrested in New York, Joe had had no trouble making sure his friend got five-star security treatment at Rikers.

'Before you leave you should go see Clyde Beeson,' Joe said.

'*Beeson?*' Max said. Out of all the Florida PIs, Clyde Beeson had been his major competition. Max had always despised him, ever since the Boukman case.

'Carver employed him before you. Didn't work out too good, way I heard it.'

'What happened?'

'Best you hear it from him.'

'He won't talk to me.'

'He will if you tell him you're going to Haiti.'

'I'll see him if I got the time.'

'*Make* time,' Joe said.

It was close to midnight and the bar crowd below was peaking. They were drunker, looser, their walks to and from the bathroom unsteady, their voices raised to shouting pitch above the music threading through a hundred different conversations. He could hear the muffled din through the glass.

Max checked on how the executives were doing with the women. He saw the blonde and one of the men at a table near the back. Their jackets were off. The man had rolled up his sleeves and taken off his tie. The woman had on a sleeveless black halterneck. From her well-toned and proportioned arms, Max guessed she might have been a personal trainer or a fitness magazine model. Or maybe an exec who worked out. The man was making his move now, leaning closer to her across the table, touching her hand. He was making her laugh too. It probably wasn't even that funny, but she was interested in him. Her friend was gone, so was the man's competition – probably separately; losers rarely left together.

Max and Joe talked some more: who'd retired, who'd died – three: cancer, bullets, drunk and drowned – who was married, divorced, what the job was like now, how things had changed post-Rodney King. They laughed, bitched, reminisced. Joe told him about the fifteen Bruce Springsteen concerts he'd seen while Max had been away. Mercifully, he kept the details to a minimum. They drank more Cokes, scoped out the Lounge couples, talked about getting older. It was good, it was warm, time passed quickly and Max forgot about Boukman for the whole while.

By two o'clock the bar had emptied of all but a few drinkers. The couple Max had been following had left.

Joe and Max made their way out.

It was cool and slightly breezy on the street. Max took in a deep breath of Miami air – sea, mixed with swamp and mild traffic fumes.

'How does it feel? Bein' out?' Joe asked.

'Like learning to walk and finding out you can still run,' Max said. 'Tell me something? How come you never came to see me?'

'Did you expect me to?'

'No.'

'Seein' you in there would've messed with my moral compass. Cops don't go to jail,' Joe said. 'Besides, I felt kinda responsible. Not teachin' you some restraint back in the day, when I could've.'

'You can't teach a man his nature, Joe.'

'I hear that. But you can teach him sense from none-sense. And some of that shit you pulled back then, man? That was some *senseless* none-sense.'

Those parental tones again. Max was close to fifty, two thirds of his life as good as gone. He didn't need a lecture from Joe, who was only three years older than him, but had always acted like it was ten more. Anyway, it wouldn't make the slightest bit of difference. What had happened had happened. There was no undoing any of it. Besides, Joe was no saint. When they'd been partners there had been as many brutality complaints against him as there were against Max. No one had given a flying fuck or done anything. Miami had been a war zone. The city had needed to meet violence with violence.

'We cool, Joe?'

'All-ways.'

They hugged.

'See you when I get back.'

'In one piece, man – the only way I wanna see ya.'

'You will. Give my love to the kids.'

'Take care, brother,' Joe said.

They went their separate ways.

Opening the door of his rented Honda, Max realized that Joe had called him 'brother' for the first time ever in all of the twenty-five years he'd known him. They might have been best friends, but Joe was a segregationist when it came to his terms of endearment.

That's when Max guessed things were going to be bad in Haiti.

Driving back to Kendall, Max thought about Solomon Boukman and his blood began to boil again. He started shouting and cursing and smacking the wheel.

He pulled over and killed the engine.

He breathed deep, calmed himself down, told himself to concentrate on Charlie Carver, focus on that and leave the rest to the side. Boukman was in Haiti. He'd gone back after Charlie's disappearance so he wasn't involved.

Didn't matter, Max thought. If he found him he'd kill him. He'd have to. Otherwise Boukman would kill him.

4

At the hotel Max took a shower and tried to catch some sleep, but it wouldn't come.

He kept on thinking of Boukman walking free while he'd still been in prison, Boukman laughing in his face, Boukman slicing up more kids. He didn't know what pissed him off more. He should have killed him when he had the chance.

He got up, turned on the light and grabbed Joe's file on the Carvers. He started reading and didn't stop until he'd finished it.

Nobody seemed particularly sure where the Carvers originated from, nor when they'd first appeared in Haiti. One rumour stated that the family were descendants of Polish soldiers who deserted Napoleon's army en masse to fight alongside Toussaint L'Ouverture's insurgents in the 1790s. Others linked the family to a Scottish clan called the MacGarvers, who lived on the island in the eighteenth and nineteenth centuries, where they owned and ran corn and sugarcane plantations.

What is known is that by 1934 Fraser Carver, Allain's grandfather, had become a multi-millionaire – not only the richest man in Haiti, but one of the wealthiest men in the Caribbean. He'd made his fortune by flooding the island with cheap essential foods – rice, beans, milk (powdered or evaporated), corn meal, cooking oil – bought for him at huge discount by the American military and shipped into the country for free. This very quickly drove many traders out of business and eventually led to Carver having the monopoly on virtually every imported foodstuff sold in the country. He opened the country's second national bank – the Banque Populaire d'Haïti – in the late 1930s.

Fraser Carver died in 1947, leaving his business empire to Allain's father Gustav. Gustav's twin, Clifford, had turned up dead in a ravine in 1959. Although the official cause was given as a car accident, no vehicle, wrecked or otherwise, was found near the body, whose every bone appeared to have been broken at least once. The CIA report quoted an unnamed witness who saw members of the militia – the FSN or Tonton Macoutes, as they were more commonly known – grab Clifford off a residential street and bundle him into a car. The report concluded that Gustav Carver had had his brother killed with help from his friend and close associate, François 'Papa Doc' Duvalier, the country's President.

Gustav Carver had first met François Duvalier in Michigan in 1943. Duvalier was one of twenty Haitian doctors sent to the city's university to train in public health medicine. Carver was in town on business. They were introduced by a mutual friend, after Duvalier, who knew of the family by reputation and legend, insisted on meeting Gustav. Carver later told a friend about this meeting and said he was convinced that Duvalier was bound for greatness, a future President of Haiti.

By then three quarters of the country's population was plagued by yaws, a highly contagious and crippling tropical disease, which ate away at limbs, noses and lips. Its victims were invariably the shoeless poor, as the disease entered their bodies through their bare feet in the form of a spirochaete.

Duvalier was sent to the most infected area of Haiti, the Rural Clinic of Gressier, fifteen miles southwest of Port-au-Prince. He quickly ran out of the penicillin he needed to cure the sick and sent for more supplies from the capital, only to be told that their stock was almost depleted and that he would have to wait another week for supplies to come in from the United States. He sent a message to Gustav Carver for help. Carver immediately dispatched ten truck-loads of penicillin, as well as beds and tents.

Duvalier cured the entire region of yaws and his reputation spread among the poor, who hobbled great distances on crumbling legs to be cured. They nicknamed him 'Papa Doc'. Thus 'Papa Doc' became a popular hero, a saviour of the poor.

Gustav Carver funded Duvalier's 1957 Presidential election campaign, and supplied some of the muscle to bully voters who couldn't be bribed into supporting the good doctor. Duvalier eventually won by a landslide. Carver was rewarded with a sizeable chunk of the country's lucrative coffee and cocoa businesses.

Haiti entered another dark age when Papa Doc declared himself 'President for Life' and went on to become the most feared and reviled tyrant in the country's history. Both the army and the Tonton Macoutes killed, tortured and raped thousands of Haitians – either on the orders of the government or more often than not for personal reasons, usually to steal a plot of land or take over a business.

Gustav Carver continued to make a vast fortune, thanks to his cosiness with Duvalier, who not only rewarded him with more monopolies – including sugarcane and cement – but he also had accounts in the Banque Populaire d'Haïti, where he regularly deposited the millions of dollars in US aid he received every three months. Most of it was quietly transferred to Swiss bank accounts.

Papa Doc died on 21 April 1971. Jean-Claude took his father's place as 'President for Life' at the age of nineteen.

Although nominally in power, Baby Doc had absolutely no interest in running Haiti and left it all to his mother, and later his wife Michele, whose wedding made the 1981 Guinness Book of Records as the third most expensive ever; while, in the same year, an IMF report rated Haiti the poorest country in the Western hemisphere.

Miami dawn. Max finished reading and stepped out on to the balcony. Like the best business people the Carvers were ruthless opportunists. And like the best business people they'd have a phone book of enemies.

The feeble sunlight had yet to fade out most of the stars and the breeze still had the chill of night about it, but he was sure it was going to be a nice day. Every day out of prison was a nice day.

5

Clyde Beeson had fallen far. Life hadn't just kicked him in the teeth; it had plugged the gaps with papier-mâché. He couldn't even afford a house. He lived in a trailer park in Opa-locka.

Opa-locka was a shithole, one of Dade County's most derelict areas, a small grey wart on Miami's toned, bronzed, depilated, hedonistic ass. It was a nice day, with clear light-blue skies and unbroken sunlight drenching the landscape, which made the area, with its neglected and crumbling Moorish-inspired architecture, seem all the more desolate.

Max had got the address off the receptionist who manned the lobby of Beeson's heyday home – a luxury apartment complex in Coconut Grove, overlooking Bayside Park with its joggers, yachting clubs and postcard-perfect views of Florida sunsets. The receptionist thought Max was a debt collector. He told Max to break both the *puta*'s legs.

Depending on their dwellers and location, some trailer parks make a good go at suburban drag, masking their identities behind white-picket fences, rose bushes, clean, close-cropped front lawns and letterboxes that aren't filled with dog shit. They even go as far as calling themselves cute homely things like Lincoln Cottages, Washington Bungalows, Roosevelt Huts. Most trailer parks don't go that far. They don't bother. They hold up their hands, admit what they are and pick their spot out in the scrapheap to the left of destitution.

Beeson's neighbourhood looked like it had been hit by

bombs dropped through the eye of a passing hurricane. There was wreckage – cookers, TVs, gutted cars, fridges – and rubbish strewn everywhere, so much that it had been incorporated into the landscape; some enterprising soul had built some of the waste into hillocks and then planted these with arrow-shaped wooden signs painted with the house numbers in large, semi-numerate digits. The trailers were in such bad shape on the outside, Max mistook them for torched and abandoned wrecks, until he glimpsed the shadows of lives through the windows. There were no working cars in sight. No dogs, no kids. The people who lived here were off the radar and staying there – welfare drop-outs, junkies, petty criminals, terminal no-hopers, born losers.

Beeson's trailer was a battered and flaking off-white oblong with two shuttered windows set either side of a sturdy-looking brown door with three locks on it, top, middle and bottom. The trailer was mounted on red brick blocks, permanently going nowhere. Max drove right up to it and parked his car.

He knocked on the door and stepped back so he could be seen from the window. He heard deep barks, the scratching of claws behind the door and then a thud, followed by another thud. Beeson had himself a pitbull. The shutters blinked behind the left window, then spread a little wider.

'*Mingus*?! *Max* Mingus?' Beeson shouted from inside.

'Yeah, that's right. Open up, I need to talk.'

'Who sent you?'

'No one.'

'If you're lookin' for a job, the toilet here needs emptyin',' Beeson chuckled.

'Sure, after we talk,' Max said. Wise-ass motherfucker

hadn't lost his ability to laugh at the misfortunes of others. Still spoke in that same voice, part growl, part squeak, caught between pitches, like he was losing his voice or waiting on his other ball to drop.

The shutter lifted and Max got a glimpse of Beeson's face – round, pudgy, blood-drained pale – staring left and right of where he was standing, checking the background.

A few moments later he heard the sound of maybe half a dozen chains being taken off hooks behind the door, followed by a tattoo of dead bolts thunking back, and all three Yale locks springing open. The inside of the door must have looked like a bondage corset.

Beeson stood in a sliver of cracked open doorway, squinting into the light. He'd left a thick chain on the door, level with his neck. At his feet the dog stuck his snout out into the open and barked and slobbered at Max.

'Waddayawant, Mingus?' Beeson said.

'Talk about Charlie Carver,' Max replied.

He could tell from the way Beeson was standing, half forward, half back, that he had a gun in one hand and the dog's lead in the other.

'The Carvers send you?'

'Not to you, no. But I'm looking into the case now.'

'You goin' to Haiti?'

'Yeah.'

Beeson pushed the door closed, undid the chain and pulled it back open. He motioned to Mingus to come in with a tilt of the head.

It was dark inside, even darker after the bright day, and this made the stench all the more overpowering. A huge acrid blast of baked ordure rushed up and smacked Max in the face and forced its way down his nostrils. He staggered back a couple of steps, his stomach contracting, the hint of

61

a heave brushing the edge of his throat. He clamped a handkerchief over his nose and breathed through his mouth, but he tasted the evil smell on his tongue.

There were flies everywhere, buzzing past his ears, bumping into his face and hands, some settling and sampling him before he shrugged them away. He heard Beeson drag the pitbull away into a corner and strap it to something.

'Better watch that car you came in,' Beeson said. 'Lil' fuckers here will strip the paint off a pencil if it stays out there too long.'

He opened the left blinds and stood away squinting. The flies in the room all darted for the bright white light that split through the darkness in a loud whizzing drone.

Max had forgotten quite how short Beeson was – he barely scraped five feet – and how disproportionately large his spoon-shaped head was.

Unlike many a Dade County PI, Beeson had never been a cop. He'd started his working life as a fixer for the Florida Democratic Party, gathering dirt on rivals and allies alike and moulding it into political currency.

He'd quit politics for private investigations after Carter's nomination in 1976. He was reputed to have made millions out of ruining lives – marriages, political careers, businesses – bringing down everything he snooped around in. He'd worn, driven, eaten, fucked and lived in the fruits of his success. Max remembered the sight of him when he was king of the hill: designer suits, gleaming patent-leather tasselled loafers, shirts so white they virtually glowed, storm clouds of cologne, manicured hands, and a thick pinkie ring. Unfortunately, given his gnomic stature, pomp- and prime-era Beeson hadn't cut quite the dash he assumed a few thousand dollars' worth of tailoring would give him;

instead of looking like some Florida hotshot, he'd always reminded Max of an overeager kid on his way to first communion in Sunday clothes his mom had picked out for him.

Now here he was, wearing a grubby vest under an open cheap black beach shirt with orange and green palm trees splashed over it.

Max was shocked at the sight of him.

It wasn't the shirt or the vest . . .

It was the *diaper*.

Clyde Beeson was wearing a diaper – a thick white greyish-brown towelling diaper, held together at the waist by large blue-tipped baby safety pins.

What the fuck had happened to him?

Max looked around the trailer. It seemed empty. Between him and Beeson was a linoleum-covered floor, an olive-green leather armchair with the stuffing popping out near the rests and an upturned packing crate he used as a table. The floor was filthy, covered in an oily-looking black grime, its original yellow colour apparent through the pitbull's claw gouges and pawprint streaks. There was dogshit everywhere, fresh, dried and semi-dried.

How had Beeson let himself go like this?

Max saw cardboard boxes stacked against the wall, from the floor to the ceiling, covering the windows to his right. Many of the boxes were damp and sagging at the middle, their contents about to rip out.

The light coming through the blinds sliced through air that was hung heavy with layered cigarette smoke and dotted with bluebottle flies hurtling past them and smacking into the exposed window, thinking it was the great outdoors. Even the flies wanted out of this pathetic cesspit.

The dog growled in Max's direction from a murky corner

where the darkness had retreated and bunched up on itself. He could just about make out its eyes, glinting, watching.

He guessed the kitchen behind him was stacked with filthy dishes and rotting food, and he hated to think of what lay in Beeson's bedroom and bathroom.

It was roasting hot. Max was already covered in a thickening film of sweat.

'Come on in, Mingus.' Beeson beckoned him over with his gun-holding hand. He had a long-barrelled .44 Magnum with solid steel cast, the identical six-shooter Clint Eastwood used in *Dirty Harry* – no doubt a major influence on its buyer. The gun was almost as long as the arm that held it.

Beeson noticed that Max hadn't moved. He was staying put, with his handkerchief clamped over his nose and a disgusted stare in his eyes.

'Suit yourself,' he shrugged and smiled. He looked at Max through sticky, toad-like brown eyes propped up on puffy cushions of greyish flesh. He couldn't have been sleeping much.

'Who are you hiding from?' Max asked.

'Just hiding,' he replied. 'So Allain Carver has got you looking for his kid?'

Max nodded. He wanted to take the handkerchief away, but the stench in the room was so thick he could feel particles settling on his skin in a fine dust.

'What d'you tellim?'

'I told him the kid was probably dead.'

'I never knew how you ever made a buck in this town wearin' an attitude like that,' Beeson said.

'Honesty pays.'

Beeson laughed at that. He must have been smoking three or more packs a day because his mirth triggered a loud,

64

raucous chugging cough that tore chunks out of his chest. He hawked a tongue-load of phlegm up on to the floor and rubbed it into the filth with his foot. Max wondered if there was tumour blood mixed in with the spit.

'I ain't doin' your spadework, Mingus – if that's what you come for – 'less you pay me,' Beeson said.

'Some things haven't changed.'

'Force-a habit. Money ain't no use to me now anyways.'

Max couldn't stand it any longer. He stepped back to the door and threw it open. Light and fresh air stormed the trailer. Max stood there for a second breathing in deep, cleansing breaths.

The pitbull was barking, yanking at the chain and the thing that held it, probably desperate to flee the cesspool it had been living in.

Max walked back to Beeson, side-stepping a slalom path of dog turds leading into the kitchen. He'd narrowly missed standing in a tepee of turds that looked too deliberately arranged to be natural. Beeson hadn't moved. He didn't seem to mind that the door was open.

The flies were all fleeing past Max, tearing through the air to freedom.

'How d'you end up like this?' Max said. He'd never believed in fate or karma or that God – if there was one – really got involved in individual cases. Things happened for no particular reason, they just happened – and rarely to the right people. You had dreams, ambitions, goals. You worked for them. Sometimes you succeeded, most times you failed. That was Max's take on life. No more complicated than that. But standing there, looking at Beeson, gave him pause for thought; made him question his beliefs. If this wasn't what divine retribution looked like, then there was no such thing.

'What? You feel *sorry* for me?' Beeson asked.

'No,' Max said.

Beeson smirked. He studied Max, running his eyes up and down him.

'OK – what the fuck? I'll tell ya,' Beeson said, moving away from the window, sitting down in his armchair with the gun rested across his lap. He took a pack of untipped Pall Malls from his shirt pocket, shook one out and lit it. 'I went out to Haiti September last year. I was there three months.

'See? I knew the case was a no-er from the moment Carver told me the specifics. No ransom, no witnesses, nothing seen, nothing heard. But what the fuck? I tripled my fee, seeing as Haiti ain't exactly the Bahamas. He said fine, no problem. Plus he mentioned the same dead-or-alive bonus thing he probably told you.'

'How much did he say?'

'A cool mil if I dug up the body. A cool *five* if I found the kid alive. That what he's promised you?'

Max nodded.

'Now, I know this guy's a businessman and you don't get to the kind of money tree the Carvers live in by spending it on hope. I told myself the kid is as dead as Niggertown cop chalk, and the dad just wants to bury the body or burn it or whatever shit they do to the dead out there. I figured it'd be an easy mil, plus I'd have myself a little vacation. Two weeks' work max.'

Beeson smoked his cigarette to the brand name then lit another off the end. He dropped the butt on the floor and ground it out with his bare heel without showing any sign of pain. Max guessed he was on some serious dope, hard-core painkillers that put the body on ice but kept the brain in a candlelit bubblebath.

All the while he was talking, Beeson hadn't stopped staring Max dead in the eye.

'Didn't work out that way. First three weeks I was out there, showin' the kid's picture around, I keep hearin' the same name – Vincent Paul. I find out he runs the biggest slum in the country. And because of that people are sayin' he's the real power in the land. He's meant to have built this whole modern town no one's ever been to or knows where it is. They say he's got people working there naked in his drug factories. He's got 'em wearin' Bill and Hillary Clinton masks. Like a fuck you to us. Forget Aristide or whatever monkey puppet Clinton is putting in there. This guy Paul? He's a major league gangster. Makes all these nigger gangbangers we got out here look like Bugs Bunny. Plus he hates the Carvers. Never found out why.'

'So you guessed he snatched the kid?'

'Yeah, clear as day. He's got motive and muscle.'

'Did you talk to him?'

'I tried, but you don't talk to Vincent Paul. *He* – talks – to – *you*,' Beeson said the last slowly.

'And did he?'

Beeson didn't reply. His eyes shifted downward, and then his head followed. He fell silent. Max stared at his front scalp, bare but for a few strands of long reddish-brown hair. The rest was massed up behind in a rusty halo, like half an Elizabethan collar. He stayed like that for a long minute, not making a sound. Max was about to say something, when he raised his head up slowly. Before his eyes had been defiant pinpricks, daring in his squalor. Now the look was gone and his eyes had widened, the sacks below them deflated. Max saw fear creeping into them.

Beeson glanced out of the window and dragged on his Pall Mall until he started coughing and spluttering again. He let the fit pass.

He moved himself up to the edge of the chair and leaned forward.

'I never thought I was getting close to nothing, but maybe I was, or maybe someone *thought* I was. Anyway, one day I'm sleeping in my hotel. The next day I'm wakin' up in some strange room with these yellow walls, no idea how I got there. I'm tied to this bed, naked, face down. These people come in. Someone gives me a shot in the ass and – kapow! – I'm gone. Out like a light.'

'Did you see these people?'

'No.'

'What happened next?'

'I woke up again. Obviously. I thought I was dreamin'. 'Cause I'm on a plane. American Airlines, mid-air. I'm flying back to Miami. No one looks at me like there's anything strange. I asked this stewardess how long I'd been there and she told me an hour. I asked the person behind me if they'd seen me get on, and they say no, I was lying there asleep when they got on.'

'You don't remember getting on the plane? Going to the airport? Nothing?'

'*Nada.* I went through Miami airport. I picked up my bag. Everything was there. It's only when I'm on my way out that I notice Christmas decorations. I grabbed a paper and saw it was 14 December! That freaked the shit outta me! That's two fuckin' months I can't account for! – *two whole fuckin' months*, Mingus!'

'Did you call Carver?'

'I woulda done, except . . .' Beeson took a deep breath. He touched his chest. 'I had this pain here. Like a tearing, a hot tearing. So I went to the airport bathroom and opened my shirt. This is what I found.'

Beeson stood up, slipped off his shirt and lifted up his

68

grimy vest. His torso was matted with thick curly dark-brown hair which spread out in a vague butterfly shape, starting below his shoulders and finishing at his navel. But there was a place where the hair parted and didn't grow – a long, half-inch-thick pink scar that ran from the edge of his neck, down the middle of his chest, passed between his lungs, and rode over his round stomach before ending at his guts.

Max got the chills, a sinking feeling in his stomach, as if the ground had opened up right there in that fucked-up trailer and he was falling into an endless abyss.

Of course, it *wasn't* Boukman's handiwork, but it all looked so familiar, so like those poor children's bodies.

'They did this to me,' he said, as Max looked on horrified. 'The *mother*-fuckers.'

He dropped his vest and fell back on the chair. Then he buried his head in his hands and started crying, his fat-like body shaking like Jell-o. Max reached into his pockets for his handkerchief but he didn't want Beeson getting his pestilential hands on it.

Max hated seeing men cry. He never knew what to say or do. Comforting them as he might a woman seemed to violate their masculinity. He stood there, feeling awkward and idiotic, letting Beeson weep himself out, hoping he'd finish up quick because there was a lot he needed to know.

Beeson's sobbing gradually broke up into diminishing puddles and sniffs and snorts. He scraped the tears off his face with his hands and wiped the damp off on the hairy back of his head.

'I checked myself straight into hospital,' he continued, once he'd gained control of his voice. 'There was nothing missing, but' – he pointed two fingers down at the diaper – 'I noticed after I ate my first meal. Went straight through.

Them Haitians fucked up my sewage works full time. No one could fix 'em here. I can't hold nothin' in too long. Permanent dysentery.'

Max felt a twinge of pity. Beeson reminded him of those cellblock bitches he'd seen in the exercise yard, waddling around in diapers because their sphincter muscles had been permanently loosened by multiple gang-rapes.

'You think it was this Vincent Paul who did it?'

'I *know* it was him. To warn me off.'

Max shook his head.

'That's a hell of a lotta trouble to go through just to warn someone off. What they did to you takes time. Besides, I *know* you, Beeson. You scare easy. If they'd burst into your room and stuck a gun down your throat you would have been outta there like a fart on a match.'

'You say the sweetest things,' Beeson said, sparking up another cigarette.

'What were you close to?'

'Whaddayamean?'

'Had you turned up something on the kid? A lead? A suspect?'

'Nothin'. I had *nickts* – that's old lady kike for shit.'

'Are you sure?' Max asked, searching Beeson's eyes for signs of lying.

'*Nickts*, I'm tellin' ya.'

Max didn't believe him, but Beeson wouldn't give it up.

'So why d'you think they fucked with me like this? Send a message to Carver?'

'Could be. I'll need to know more,' Max said. 'So what happened afterwards? With you?'

'I fell apart. Up here,' he said, matter of factly, tapping the side of his head. 'I had this collapse, this breakdown. I couldn't work no more. I quit. Gave it up. I owed clients for jobs I didn't finish. I had to pay 'em all back, so I don't have that much left, but what the fuck? At least I'm still alive.'

Max nodded. He knew all about the place Beeson was in now. Going to Haiti was about the only thing that was stopping him from finding his own shit-covered trailer to live in.

'Don't go to Haiti, Mingus. There is some *bad shit* out there in that place,' Beeson said, his voice a steady, even whine of cold wind passing by a warm house, whistling through the cracks, trying to get in.

'Even if I didn't want to, I haven't got much choice,' Max said. He took a last look around the trailer. 'You know, Clyde, I never liked you. I still don't. You were a two-bit Seamus, a greedy, double-dealing traitor scumbag with a morals bypass. But you know what? Even *you* don't deserve this.'

'Take it you don't wanna stay for dinner?' Beeson said.

Max turned and made for the door. Beeson picked up his Magnum and stood up. He padded over to Max, squishing a fresh turd on his way.

Outside the trailer, Max stood in the clean air and sunlight, breathing deeply through his nose. He hoped the stench hadn't stuck to his clothes and hair.

'Hey! Mingus!' Beeson shouted from the door.

Max turned around.

'They fuck you in jail?'

'What?'

'Was you some nigger's bitch? Some nigger call you "Mary"? You get some o' that ole jailhouse *lurve* from the booty bandits, Mingus?'

'No.'

'Then what the fuck special happened to you, make you

come over all sympathetic? Old school Max Mingus woulda said I got what I deserved, woulda kicked me in the teeth and wiped his foot on my face.'

'Take care of yourself, Clyde,' Max said. 'No one else will.'

Then he got in his car and drove away, feeling numb.

6

Max drove back to Miami and headed for Little Haiti.

When he was a kid in the 1960s, he'd had a girlfriend called Justine who lived in the area. It was called Lemon City back then, and was mostly white, middle class and great for shopping. His mother would often go there for Christmas and birthday presents.

By the time Max had become a cop a decade later, all but the poorest whites had moved out, the shops had closed or relocated, and the once prosperous neighbourhood had gone to seed. First the Cuban refugees had moved in, and then the more prosperous African-Americans from Liberty City had bought up the cheap houses. The Haitians started arriving in significant numbers in the 1970s, refugees from Baby Doc's regime.

There was a lot of tension between African-Americans and Haitians, often spilling into bloodshed – most of it the latter's – until the newly arrived immigrants began to organize themselves into gangs and look out for one another. The most notorious of these was the SNBC, aka the Saturday Night Barons Club, led by Solomon Boukman.

Max had last come to the neighbourhood when he was investigating Boukman and his gang in 1981. He'd driven through street after trash-choked street, past boarded-up stores and derelict or tumbledown houses without seeing a soul. Then there'd been the riot he and Joe got caught up in.

Fifteen years later, Max was expecting more of the same only worse than before, but when he got on to NE 54th

Street he thought he'd come to the wrong place. The area was clean and full of people walking streets lined with shops painted in bright, vivid pinks, blues, oranges, yellows and greens. There were small restaurants, bars, outdoor cafés and stores selling everything from clothes and food to wood sculptures, books, music and paintings.

Max parked, got out of his car and started walking. He was the only white face on the block but he had none of the anticipatory edge he would have had in a black ghetto.

It was late afternoon and the sun had started to set, giving the sky its first tinge of purple. Max walked down to a place his mother and father had taken him to in his teens, a furniture store on 60th Street they'd bought their kitchen table from. The store was long gone, but in its place stood the imposing Caribbean Marketplace which had been built as an exact replica of the old Iron Market in Port-au-Prince.

He went inside and walked past small stalls selling more food, CDs and clothes, as well as Catholic ornaments. Everyone spoke Kreyol, the Haitian dialect comprised of part-French and part-West African tribal tongues. The speech patterns sounded confrontational, as if its two composite parts were on the verge of full-scale argument with each other. Kreyol wasn't spoken, it was half-shouted, the pitch edgy and intense, everyone sounding like they were getting the last word in before the fists started flying. Yet when Max checked the speakers' body language he realized they were probably doing nothing more threatening than gossiping or bartering.

Max walked out of the Marketplace and crossed the road to the Church of Notre Dame d'Haïti and the neighbouring Pierre Toussaint Haitian Catholic Center. The centre was closed so he went into the church. He might not have had much time for any notion of God in his life, but he loved

74

churches. He always ended up going into them whenever he needed to think. They were the quietest, emptiest places he knew. It was a habit he'd picked up when he was in Patrol. He'd cracked many a case sitting in a pew with just the sound of his thoughts and a notebook for company. Churches had helped him focus. He'd never told anyone about this — including his wife — in case they'd thought he was a secret Jesus freak with a messianic identity complex, or in case they turned out to be Jesus freaks themselves.

The church was empty, save for an old woman sitting in the middle pews, reading aloud from a Kreyol prayerbook. She heard Max walk in and turned to look at him without breaking off from her recital.

Max took in the wall of stained-glass windows and the mural depicting the journey of Haitians from their homeland to South Florida, watched over from the skies by the Virgin Mary and the infant Jesus. The air reeked of stale incense and cold candles and of the scented pink and white lilies pouring out of vases mounted on metal stands either side of the altar.

The woman, still reading aloud, never left Max with her gun-barrel black eyes. He could feel her stare like you can feel a security camera following you around a bank vault. He looked her over — small, frail, white-haired, with liver spots sprinkled on a sagging, deeply lined face. He tried the smile he used on potentially hostile strangers — broad, well-meaning, open, all lips and cheeks — but it fell flat on her. He retreated slowly down the aisle, feeling for the first time awkward and unwelcome. Time to go.

As he was leaving he glanced over at a bookcase in the corner near the door. There were Kreyol, French and English Bibles, as well as a variety of books about the Saints.

Next to the bookcase was a large cork noticeboard, which

took up most of the remaining wall. The board was covered with small pictures of Haitian children. On the bottom of each photograph was a yellow sticker bearing the child's name, age and a date. The children were all colours, aged between three and eight, boys and girls, many in school uniforms. Charlie Carver's image caught the corner of his eye. A smaller print of the picture he had was tucked away in a right-hand corner, a face among dozens, easily lost. Max read the small print: 'Charles Paul Carver, 3 ans, 9/1994'. It was the month and year he'd disappeared. He inspected the dates on the other photographs. They went back no further than 1990.

'Are you the police?' a man's voice asked behind him, French-American accent, black intonation.

Max turned and saw a priest standing in front of him, his hands behind his back. He was slightly taller than Max, but slender and narrow about the shoulders. He wore round silver wire-rimmed glasses whose lenses reflected the light and hid his eyes. Salt and pepper hair, salt and pepper goatee. Late forties, early fifties.

'No, I'm a private investigator,' Max said. He never lied in church.

'Another bounty hunter,' the priest snorted.

'Is it that obvious?'

'I'm getting used to your type.'

'That many?'

'One or two, maybe more, I forget. You all pass through here on your way to Haiti. You and the journalists.'

'You've got to start someplace,' Max said. He could feel the priest's stare probing beyond his eyelids. The priest smelled faintly of sweat and an old-fashioned soap, like Camay. 'These other children –?'

'*Les enfants perdus*,' the priest said. 'The lost children.'

'Kidnapped too?'

'Those are the ones we know of. There are many many more. Most Haitians can't afford cameras.'

'How long's this been happening?'

'Children have always gone missing in Haiti. I started putting photographs on the board very soon after I started working here, in 1990. In our other religion a child's soul is highly sought after. It can open many doors.'

'So you think it's a voodoo thing?'

'Who knows?'

There was a sadness in the priest's voice, a weariness that suggested he'd gone through every possibility a million times over and come back empty.

Then Max realized that this was personal for the priest. He looked back at the board, and searched through the photographs that hung off it like sad scales, hoping to find a striking family resemblance so he could broach the subject. He found nothing so he went for it anyway.

'Which one of these is yours?'

The priest was initially shocked, but then he smiled broadly.

'You're a very perceptive man. God must have chosen *you*.'

'I played the right hunch, father,' Max said.

The priest stepped forward up to the board and pointed at a photograph of a girl right next to Charlie's.

'My niece, Claudette,' the priest said. 'I confess I put her there so some of the rich boy's aura would rub off.'

Max took Claudette's picture down: 'Claudette Thodore, 5 ans, 10/1994'.

'Went missing a month later. Thodore? Is that your surname?'

'Yes. I'm Alexandre Thodore. Claudette is my brother

Caspar's daughter,' the priest said. 'I'll give you his address and number. He lives in Port-au-Prince.'

The priest took a small notebook out of his pocket and scribbled his brother's details on a piece of paper, which he tore out and handed to Max.

'Did your brother tell you what happened?'

'One day he was with his daughter, the next day he was looking for her.'

'I'll do my best to find her.'

'I don't doubt that,' the priest said. 'By the way, the kids in Haiti? They have a nickname for the bogeyman who's stealing the children. *"Tonton Clarinette"*. Mr Clarinet.'

'Clarinet? Like the instrument? Why?'

'It's how he lures the children away.'

'Like the Pied Piper?'

'Tonton Clarinette is said to work for Baron Samedi – the *vodou* god of the dead,' Father Thodore said. 'He steals children's souls to entertain the dead with. Some say his appearance is part man, part bird. Others say he is a bird with one eye. And only children can see him. That's because he was a child himself, when he died.

'The myth goes that he was originally a French boy soldier, a mascot – very common in those days. He was in one of the regiments sent to rule Haiti, back in the eighteenth century. He entertained the troops by playing his clarinet for them. The slaves working in the fields used to hear his playing and it made them angry because they associated the sound and the music the boy made with captivity and oppression.

'When the slaves rose up, they overpowered the boy's regiment and took a lot of prisoners. They made the boy play his wretched instrument while they slaughtered his comrades one by one. Then they buried him alive, still playing his clarinet.' Thodore spoke gravely. It might have been folklore, but he was taking it very seriously. 'He's a relatively new spirit, not one I grew up fearing. I first heard people talking about him twenty or so years ago. They say he leaves his mark where he's been.'

'What kind of mark?'

'I haven't seen one, but it's supposed to look like a cross, with two legs and half a beam.'

'You said children have "always" gone missing in Haiti? You got any idea how many that is a year?'

'It's impossible to say.' Thodore opened his palms to indicate hopelessness. 'Things there are not like here. There's nowhere and no one to report the missing to. And there is no way of knowing who these children are or were, because the poor don't have birth or death certificates – that is only for the rich. Almost all of the children who go missing are poor. When they disappear it's as if they never existed. But now – with the Carver boy – this is different. This is a rich society child. Suddenly now *everyone* is paying attention. It's like here in Miami. If a black child goes missing, who cares? Maybe one or two local policemen go looking. But if it's a little white child you call the National Guard.'

'With all due respect, father, that last part, that's not quite true, no matter how it sometimes appears,' Max said, keeping his tone level. 'And it was *never* that way with me, when I was a cop here. *Never.*'

The priest looked at him hard for a moment. He himself had cop's eyes, the ones that can tell sincerity from bullshit at a thousand paces. He offered Max his hand. They shook firmly. Then Father Thodore blessed him and wished him well.

'Bring her back,' he whispered to Max.

PART TWO

7

The flight out to Haiti was held up for an hour while it waited on a homeward-bound con and his two US Marshal escorts.

Inside it was packed to near capacity. Haitians, mostly men, heading home with bags of food, soap and clothes, and boxes and boxes of cheap electrical goods – TVs, radios, video recorders, fans, microwaves, computers, boomboxes. They'd half- or quarter-jammed their purchases into overhead luggage compartments, or slipped them under seats, or left them out in the aisle when they wouldn't fit anywhere else, violating all safety and emergency rules.

The stewardesses weren't complaining. They appeared to be used to it. They picked their way past the brand-name obstacles with straight-backed poise and stuck-on professional smiles, always managing to squeeze through without creasing their bearing, no matter how tight the space.

Max could tell the visiting expats apart from the natives. The former were tricked out in standard ghetto garb – gold chains, earrings and bracelets; more on their backs and feet than they had in the bank – while the latter were dressed conservatively – cheap but smart slacks and short-sleeved shirts for the men, mid-week church dresses for the women.

The atmosphere was lively, seemingly unconcerned with the delay. The conversations rolled out loud and clear, Kreyol's duelling rhythms bouncing back and forth off each other and from all corners of the plane. Everyone seemed to know everyone else. The voices – deep and guttural –

collectively drowned out the in-cabin pre-flight muzak and all three pilot announcements.

'Most of those people live in houses with no electricity,' said the woman sitting next to Max, in the window seat. 'They're buying those things as ornaments, status symbols – like we'd buy a sculpture or a painting.'

Her name was Wendy Abbott. She had lived in Haiti for the past thirty-five years with her husband George. They ran an elementary school in the mountains overlooking Port-au-Prince. It catered for both rich and poor. The rich parents paid cash, the poor in kind. They always made a profit because very few of the poor believed in education let alone knew what it was for. Many of their pupils either went on to the Union School, where they were taught the American curriculum, or to the more expensive and prestigious Lycée Français, which prepared them for the French baccalaureate.

Max had introduced himself to her and left it at his name.

Fifty or so Canadian troops – part of the UN Peace Corps – sat together in the middle of the plane; a copse of pink and white sweaty faces, left side partings, Village People moustaches – silent, tense and altogether miserable in the midst of the boisterous people they'd helped subjugate. Seeing the looks on their faces you would have sworn it was the other way round.

The con came on board, led in by his two escorts in a loud clunk-chink clunk-chink of thick chains. Max read him: heavy-duty denim pants, no belt, loose white T-shirt, blue-and-white headscarf, no gold, no rocks – low-ranking gangbanger, probably caught selling rocks or coming back from his first kill, reeking of chronic and gunsmoke. Strictly smalltime, hadn't even left the second rung of the ghetto ladder. He was still in his prison clothes because he'd outgrown his court ones working out on the yard. He puffed his chest out and kept his cellblock face on, but Max could see his eyes running to panic once he'd taken in the crowd on the plane and absorbed his first big whiff of freedom without parole. He'd probably expected to die in prison.

The Haitians ignored the con but the Canadians all paid strict attention, watching the US Marshals, looking like they were expecting one of them to step up and explain what was going on.

They didn't. One of them, who had a goatee, talked to a stewardess instead. They wanted to sit in the three front row seats nearest the door, but they were taken. The stewardess was protesting. The Marshal pulled a piece of paper from inside his jacket and handed it to her. She took it, read it and disappeared through a set of curtains behind her.

'I wonder if he knows what an insult he is to his heritage? – returning to Haiti as his forefathers arrived – in *chains*,' Wendy said, looking at the con.

'I shouldn't think he gives a shit, mam,' Max replied.

Up until then the con had kept his gaze locked in some vague middle distance, not focussing on anyone or anything in particular, but he must have felt Max and Wendy's stare because he looked their way. Wendy dropped her gaze almost as soon as she touched looks with the prisoner, but Max went eyeball to eyeball with him. The con recognized his own kind, smiled very faintly and nodded to Max. Max acknowledged the greeting with an involuntary nod of his own.

None of that would have happened in prison, a black con bonding with a white one – unless he was buying or selling something, most usually dope or sex. Once you were locked up you stuck to your own kind and didn't mix and mingle. It was like that and no other way. The tribes were always at war. Whites were the first to get gang-raped, punked-out and shanked by blacks and Latinos who saw them as symbols of the judicial system that had ranked against them from the day they were born. If you were smart you unlearned any liberal views you had and got in touch with your pre-judice as soon as the cell door slammed behind you. That prejudice – the hatred and fear – kept you alert and alive.

The stewardess came back and told the three people sitting at the front of Max's section that they'd have to move. They started to protest. The stewardess said that they'd be sitting in first class, that they'd get free champagne and more leg room.

Hearing that the passengers promptly stood up and gathered their belongings. They were nuns.

The US Marshals sat the con down in the middle seat and took their places either side of him.

The plane left Miami International ten minutes later.

Shaped like a lobster's pincer with most of the top claw chewed off, Haiti from the air looked completely out of place after the dense luscious green of Cuba, and all the other smaller islands they'd passed. Arid and acidic, the country's rust on rust coloured landscape seemed utterly bereft of grass and foliage. When the plane circled over the edges of the bordering Dominican Republic you could clearly see where the two nations divided – the land split as definitely as on any map; a dry bone wasteland with an abun-dant oasis next door.

Max hadn't slept much the night before. He'd been in Joe's office, first photocopying the old files on Solomon Boukman and the SNBC, then looking up the former gang members on the database.

Although he'd founded the SNBC, Boukman was a delegator. He had had twelve deputies, all fiercely loyal to him and every bit as ruthless and cold-blooded. Of these, six were now dead – two executed by the State of Florida, one executed by the State of Texas, two shot and killed by police, one murdered in prison – one was serving twenty-five to life in maximum security, and the remaining five had been deported to Haiti between March 1995 and May 1996.

Rudy Crèvecoeur, Jean Desgrottes, Salazar Faustin and Don Moïse had been the most fearsome of Boukman's subordinates. They were the enforcers, the ones who watched over the gang, made sure no one was stealing or snitching or shooting off their mouths where they shouldn't. Moïse, Crèvecoeur and Desgrottes had also been directly responsible for kidnapping the children Boukman sacrificed in his ritual ceremonies.

Salazar Faustin was in charge of the SNBC's Florida drug operation. He was a former Tonton Macoute – one of the Duvaliers' private militia – who had used his connections in Haiti to set up a highly efficient cocaine smuggling network into Miami. The drugs were bought direct from the Bolivian manufacturers and then flown into Haiti on two-seater passenger planes, which landed on a secret airstrip in the north of the country. The pilot was changed and the plane was refuelled and flown on to Miami. US customs didn't bother to check the plane because they thought it was only coming from Haiti, a non-drug-growing zone. Once in Miami the cocaine was taken to the Sunset Marquee, a cheap hotel in South Beach which Faustin owned and ran with his mother, Marie-Félize. In the basement the cocaine was cut with glucose and distributed to the SNBC's street dealers who sold it all over Florida.

Both Salazar and Marie-Félize Faustin received life

sentences for drug trafficking. They were deported on the same day – 8 August 1995 – tearfully reuniting at the airport.

They landed at 2.45 in the afternoon. Airport staff in navy-blue overalls wheeled a white ladder up to the plane doors. They'd have to walk across the tarmac to the airport building, an unimposing and untidy rectangular structure with cracked and flaking whitewashed walls, a flight tower sticking out of it to the right, three empty flagpoles in the middle and *Welcome to Port-au-Prince International Airport* painted across the bottom front, above the entrances in crude black block capitals.

The pilot asked the passengers to wait for the prisoner to leave the plane first.

The door opened. The US Marshals, both now wearing sunglasses, stood up with the con and led him out of the aircraft.

When Max stepped off the plane he was surprised by the heat, which smothered him in a dense, airless blanket that not even the slight breeze that was blowing could dislodge or loosen. The hottest days in Florida seemed cool in comparison.

He followed Wendy down the steps, heavy holdall in hand, breathing in air that seemed like steam, popping sweat through every pore.

Walking side by side, they followed the passengers as they made their way to the terminal. Wendy noticed the red flush in Max's face and the damp film across his brow.

'You're lucky you didn't come in the summer,' she said. 'That's like going to hell in a fur coat.'

There were dozens of troops around the runway area – US Marines in short-sleeves, loading up trucks with crates and boxes, relaxed and unhurried, taking their time. The island was theirs for as long as they wanted it.

Ahead of them, Max could see the Marshals handing the con over to three shotgun-toting Haitians in civilian clothes. One of the Marshals was crouched down, unlocking the shackles around the prisoner's ankles. From where Max was standing it could have passed for something quite considerate, the Marshal tying his charge's shoelaces before handing him over.

Once the chains and cuffs were off, the Marshals boarded a waiting US Military jeep and were driven off towards the plane. The three Haitians, meanwhile, talked to the con, who was massaging his wrists and then his ankles. When he was finished they walked him off to a side door at the furthest end of the terminal.

Music came from the terminal. A five-piece band was performing near the entrance, playing a mid-tempo Kreyol song. Max didn't understand any of the words but he picked up on a sadness at the heart of what might otherwise have passed him by as a sweet, inconsequential tune.

They were old musicians, thin and stooped men in identical Miami dimestore beach shirts with palm trees in the sunset motifs; a bongo player, a bass guitarist, a keyboard player, a lead guitarist, and the singer, all plugged into a stack of amps set against the terminal wall. Max saw how some people were swaying in time as they walked, and he heard others in front of him and behind him, singing along.

'It's called "*Haïti, Ma Chérie*". It's an exile's lament,' Wendy explained, as they passed by the band and were at the entrance, which was split into two doorways – Haitian citizens and non-Haitians.

'This is where we part, Max,' Wendy said. 'I've got dual-nationality. Saves on queues and paperwork.'

They shook hands.

'Oh – watch out for the luggage carousel,' she said, as she got into line at passport control. 'It's the same one they've had ever since 1965.'

Max got his passport stamped red and moved into the Arrivals section, which he found was in the same cavernous room as Departures, customs, ticket collection and purchasing, car rentals, tourist information, the entrance and the exit. The place was heaving with people – old and young, male and female – toing and froing, pushing and shoving, all shouting at the tops of their voices. He saw a chicken darting through the crowd, slaloming past legs, clucking manically, flapping its wings and shitting on the floor. A man chased after it, bent over, arms outstretched, knocking down anyone who didn't move out of his way.

Max had called Carver before he'd boarded. He'd told him the flight number and its time of arrival. Carver said someone would be waiting for him in the airport. Max looked around in vain for a stranger holding up his name.

Then he heard a commotion coming from his left. A large crowd, four or five bodies deep, was gathered at the end of the Arrivals area, everyone jostling and pushing their way forward, everyone shouting, everyone volatile. Max spotted their focus of attention – the luggage carousel.

He had to pick up his suitcase.

He made his way over to the rabble, trying to gingerly sidestep people at first, but when he found he wasn't getting any closer to the carousel he did as the Haitians did and prodded, pushed, elbowed and shoulder-bashed his way through the crowd, stopping only once, so as not to step on the chicken and its owner.

He got to the front of the crowd and moved down until

he had a clear view of the carousel. It wasn't working and looked like it hadn't in years. Its chrome sides were held together by rivets, many burst or half bursting, leaving sharp, ragged corners twisting outwards dangerously. The conveyor belt, once black rubber, was mostly worn down to the steel plates, bar odd areas where scraps of its original rubber coating stubbornly clung to it like fossilized chewing gum.

The carousel was the highlight of an area with high grubby white walls, a dark marble floor and wide, rickety-looking fans which barely stirred the air or relieved the accumulated heat, as much as they threatened to come crashing down and decapitate the people below.

When Max looked closer he realized that the conveyor belt was in fact moving and luggage was coming round, although its progress was so intensely slow, the cases coming around at a surreptitious creep, inch by inch, a moment at a time.

There were many more people standing around the carousel than had been on his flight. The majority of them had come to steal the luggage. Max quickly began to sort the legitimate passengers out from the thieves. The thieves snatched at each and every case that came within reach. The real owners would then try to grab or wrestle their property back. The thieves would put up a struggle for a while, then give up and push their way back to the carousel to try their luck with more luggage. It was a free-for-all. There was no airport security around.

Max decided he wasn't going to start off his stay in Haiti by punching someone out – no matter how justified his actions. He pushed his way through the crowd until he was as close as possible to where the cases emerged.

His black Samsonite came out after an age. He got his hands to it and crudely pushed his way through the throng.

Once out and away from the mass, Max noticed the chicken again. Its master had fastened a noose-shaped lead around its neck and was tugging the bird away towards the exit.

'Mr Mingus?' a woman asked behind him.

Max turned around. He noticed her mouth first – wide, lips plump and pouting, white teeth.

'I'm Chantale Duplaix. Mr Carver sent me to collect you,' she said, holding out her hand.

'Hello, I'm Max,' he said, shaking her hand, which was small and delicate-looking, but her skin was hard and rough and she packed a tight grip.

Chantale was very beautiful and Max couldn't help smiling. Light-brown skin with a few freckles about her nose and cheeks, large honey-brown eyes and straight shoulder-length black hair. She was slightly shorter than him in her heels. She wore a dark-blue, knee-length skirt and a loose short-sleeved blouse, with the top button undone over a thin gold chain. She looked mid twenties.

'Sorry about the trouble you had with your bag. We were going to come help you, but you did OK,' she said.

'Don't you people have security here?' Max said.

'We did. But *you* people took our guns away,' she said, light eyes darkening, voice toughening. Max could imagine her losing her temper and flattening all before her.

'Your army disarmed us,' Chantale explained. 'What they failed to realize is that the only authority Haitians respect is an *armed* authority.'

Max didn't know what to say. He didn't know enough about the political situation to counter and comment, but he knew vast proportions of the outside world hated Americans for doing as they were in Haiti. He knew then how hard the job ahead would be, if Chantale was meant to be on *his* side.

'But never mind about that,' Chantale said, flashing him a bright white smile. There was, he noticed, a small oval beauty spot to the right of her mouth, right on the demarcation line between her face and her bottom lip. 'Welcome to Haiti.'

Max bowed his head, hoping the gesture didn't come over as sarcastic. He promoted Chantale to late twenties. There was maturity and self-control in her, a certain smooth diplomacy that only comes from experience.

She led him through customs – two tables where everyone was being made to open their bags for inspection. All along there had been two tall men standing in the background, watching. Moustaches, sunglasses and distinct gun-bulges on their sides, under their overhanging shirts. They followed Max.

Chantale smiled at the customs officials who smiled back and waved her through, stares following her until she was out of range. Max couldn't help himself. He checked her out from behind. He saw what they meant and let out a silent whistle. Broad shoulders, straight back, elegant neck. Slender ankles, very athletic curves to her calves; she looked after herself, running, no doubt, and working out with weights. Her ass was perfect – high, pert, round and firm.

They walked out of the airport and crossed the road to where two navy-blue Toyota Landcruisers were parked one behind the other. Chantale got into the first car and opened the boot for Max to put his bags in. The men got into the car behind.

Max got into the front seat next to her. She turned on the air-conditioning. He broke out into a heavy sweat as his body fought to acclimatize after the heat of the airport.

He looked at the airport entrance through his window and saw the con he'd been on the plane with, standing near the entrance, rubbing his wrists and taking in his surroundings, looking left and right. The man looked lost and vulnerable, sorely missing his cell, the safety of familiarity. A woman sitting crosslegged on the ground in front of a pair of battered, ruptured sneakers was talking to him. He shrugged his shoulders and held up his empty palms in a sign of help-lessness. There was worry in his face, a dawning fear. If only the punks and the hardmen could see him now, cornered by the free world, life calling his bluff. Max entertained the notion of playing good Samaritan and giving the con a lift into town, but he let it slide. Wrong association. He'd been to prison but he didn't consider himself a criminal.

Chantale seemed to read his mind.

'He'll get picked up,' she said. 'They'll send a car for him, like we did for you.'

'Who's "they"?'

'Depends which bit of porch-talk you eavesdrop. Some people say there's an expat criminal collective operating here, like a union. Whenever someone comes in from a US prison, they get picked up and assimilated into the gang. Other people say there's no such thing, that's it's all really Vincent Paul.'

'Vincent Paul?'

'*Le Roi de Cité Soleil* – the King of Cité Soleil. Cité Soleil is the biggest slum in the country. It's next to Port-au-Prince. They say he who rules Cité Soleil rules Haiti. All the changes of government have started there – including the fall of Jean-Claude Duvalier.'

'Was Paul behind that?'

'People say all sorts of things. They talk *a lot* here. Sometimes it's *all* they do. Talking's like a national pastime, what with the economy being the way it is. No jobs. Not enough to do. More time than purpose. You'll notice,' Chantale said, shaking her head.

'How do I get to meet Vincent Paul?'

'He'll come to you if it gets to that,' Chantale said.

'Do you think it will?' Max asked, thinking of Beeson. Had Chantale collected Beeson from the airport? Did she know what had happened to him?

'Who's to say? Maybe he's behind it, maybe he isn't. He isn't the only person who hates the Carver family. They have *a lot* of enemies.'

'Do *you* hate them?'

'No,' Chantale said, laughing and locking eyes with Max. She had beautiful doe-like eyes and a telling laugh – loud, raucous, vulgar, smoky, knowing and irresistibly filthy; the laugh of someone who got drunk, stoned and fucked complete strangers.

They drove off.

8

The road away from the airport was long, dusty and milky grey. Cracks, fissures, gaps, gouges and splits shattered the road surface into a crude latticework which frequently converged into random potholes and craters of differing sizes and depths. It was a miracle the road hadn't long fallen apart and regressed to dirt track.

Chantale drove deftly, swerving around or away from the biggest holes in the road and slowing down when she had to roll over the smaller ones. All of the cars in front of them, and on the opposite side of the road, were moving the same way, some negotiating the road like classic drunk drivers, steering more dramatically than others.

'First time in Haiti?' she asked.

'Yeah. I hope it's not all like the airport.'

'It's worse,' she said and laughed. 'But we get by.'

There were, seemingly, only two types of car in Haiti: luxury and fucked up. Max saw Benzes, Beemers, Lexes and plenty of jeeps. He saw a stretch limo. He saw a Bentley followed by a Rolls Royce. Yet for every one of these there were dozens of rusted-out, smoke-belching sand trucks, their holds full of people – so full, some were hanging off the sides, others clinging to the roof. Then there were the old station wagons brightly painted all over with slogans and pictures of saints or field workers. These were taxi cabs, Chantale told him, called *tap-taps*. They too were filled with people and loaded on top with their belongings – crammed baskets, cardboard boxes and cloth-wrapped bundles. To

Max it looked like everyone was fleeing the scene of a natural disaster.

'You'll be in one of the Carver houses in Pétionville. It's a suburb half an hour out of Port-au-Prince. The capital's too dangerous right now,' she said. 'The house has a maid called Rubie. She's very nice. She'll cook for you, wash your clothes. You'll never see her – unless you spend all day indoors. There's a phone, TV and a shower. All the essentials.'

'Thanks,' Max said. 'Is this what you do for the Carvers?'

'Chauffeur?' she said with a smirk. 'No. This is a one-off. I'm on Allain's team. He offered me the rest of the day off if I collected you.'

The road bisected an endless dry plain, a dustbowl peppered with thinning, yellowy grass. Scenery flew by. He noted the dark mountains to the left and the way the clouds hung so low, so close to the ground they seemed to have broken their moorings and drifted loose from the sky, threatening to land. There were occasional lollipop speed signs – black on white; 60, 70, 80, 90 – but no one was paying much attention to them, let alone staying to a particular side of the road, unless something bigger was coming the other way. Chantale kept to an even seventy.

Painted billboards, thirty feet high and sixty feet wide, stood on the roadside, advertising local and international brands. In between were smaller, narrower billboards for local banks, radio stations and competing lottery syndicates. Once in a while Charlie Carver's face appeared, those intense, haunted features blown up and planted high in black and white, eyes still staring straight into you. 'REWARD' was painted in tall red letters above the image, '$1,000,000' below it. To the left, in black, was a telephone number.

'How long has that been up?' Max asked, after they'd passed the first one.

'For the last two years,' Chantale said. 'They change them every month because they fade.'

'I take it there've been a lot of calls.'

'There used to be, but it's died down a lot since people worked out they don't get paid for making stuff up.'

'What was Charlie like?'

'I only met him once, at the Carver house, before the invasion. He was a baby.'

'I guess Mr Carver keeps his private and professional life separate.'

'That's impossible in Haiti. But he does his best,' Chantale replied, meeting his eyes. He picked up a hint of sourness in her tone. She had a French-American accent, a grudging collision, with the former tipping over the latter: born and raised on the island, educated somewhere in the States or Canada. Definitely late twenties, enough to have lost one voice and found another.

She was beautiful. He wanted to kiss her wide mouth and taste those plump, slightly parted lips. He looked out of the window before he stared too hard or gave anything away.

There were a few people about, men in ragged shirts and trousers and straw hats shepherding small flocks of pathetically thin, dirty, brown goats, others pulling donkeys saddled with overflowing straw baskets, or men and women, in pairs or on their own, walking with jerry cans filled with water on their shoulders, or balancing huge baskets on their heads. They all moved very slowly, at the same lazy, listing gait. Further on they came to their first village – a cluster of one-room square shacks painted orange or yellow or green, all with corrugated-iron roofs. Women sitting at the roadside in front of tables selling melting brown candy. Naked children played nearby. A man tended to a pot cooking on a fire, billowing plumes of white smoke. Stray dogs nosing at the ground. All of this roasting under intense bright sunlight.

Chantale flicked on the radio. Max was expecting more '*Haïti, Ma Chérie*', but instead heard the familiar bish-bosh-bullshit machine beat of every rap record ever made. A remake of 'Ain't Nobody', a song Sandra had loved, ruined by a rapper who sounded like half the inmates in Rikers.

'Do you like music?' Chantale asked him.

'I like *music*,' Max replied, looking at her.

She was pumping her head to the beat. 'Like what? Bruce Springsteen?' she said, nodding at his tattoo.

Max didn't know what to say. The truth would take too long and open up too many ways into him.

'I got that done when I didn't know better,' he said. 'I like quiet stuff now. Old man stuff. Ol' Blue Eyes.'

'Sinatra? That *is* old,' she said, glancing across at him, her eyes taking in his face and chest.

He caught her eyes straying down his shirt. It had been so long since he'd flirted. He'd known how to play situations like this in the past. He'd known what he wanted then. He wasn't so sure now.

'The most popular music here is called *kompas*. Compact. It's like one really long song that can go on for half an hour or more, but it's really lots of short songs put together. Different tempos,' Chantale said, eyes fixed on the road.

'Like a medley?'

'That's it, a medley – but not quite. You'd have to hear it to understand. The most popular local singer is Sweet Micky.'

'*Sweet Micky*? Sounds like a clown.'

'Michel Martelly. He's like a mixture of Bob Marley and gangsta rap.'

'Interesting, but I don't know him.'

'He plays Miami a lot. You're from Miami, right?'

'And other places,' Max said, checking her face to see how much she knew about him. She didn't react.

'And then there's the Fugees. You've heard of *them*, right?'

'No,' Max said. 'Do they play *kompas*?'

She burst out laughing – *that* laugh again.

Her dirty bellow echoed around his brain. He imagined himself fucking her. He couldn't help it. Eight years and nothing but his hand for relief.

Now he had a problem – a hard-on. He stole a quick glance at his crotch. It was a major one – a rock solid sundial he felt poking right past the fly of his shorts and pushing against his trousers, setting up a tepee over his groin.

'So . . . tell me about the Fugitives?' he said, almost gasping.

'*Fugees*,' she corrected with a giggle, and then she told him: two guys and a girl, the singer. The guys were Haitian–Americans and the girl was African–American. They played hip-hop soul, and their latest album, *The Score*, had sold millions worldwide. They'd had big hits with 'Ready Or Not', 'Fu-Gee-La' and 'Killing Me Softly'.

'The Roberta Flack song?' Max said.

'The same one.'

'With *rapping* over it?'

'No – Lauryn sings it straight, Wyclef says "One time . . . one time" all the way through – but it's set to that hip-hop beat.'

'Sounds terrible.'

'It works, trust me,' she said, defensively, and a little patronizingly, as if Max wouldn't get it anyway. 'Lauryn can really sing. I'll try and find it on here. They're live on the radio.'

She turned the radio dial and flipped through stations playing snatches of funk, reggae, calypso, Billboard Top 40, Kreyol language, hip hop, but she couldn't find the Fugees.

As she leant back Max stole a glance at her chest. His eyes passed through the gaps between the buttons of her blouse: white push-up bra with lace-trimmed cups, small teak-coloured breasts puffing over the edges. He noticed the traces of a smile on the edges of her lips, a slight flaring of her nostrils. She knew he was looking her over and liking what he saw.

'So what about you?' Max asked. 'Tell me about yourself. Where did you study?'

'I majored in economics at Miami University. Graduated in 1990. I worked for Citibank for a few years.'

'How long have you been back?'

'Three years. My mom got sick.'

'Otherwise you would've stayed in the US?'

'Yeah. I had a life there,' she said, a hint of regret waving behind her professional smile.

'So what do you do for Allain Carver?'

'PA stuff mostly. They're thinking of getting me into marketing because they want to launch a credit card, but that's on hold until the economy picks up. The US are supposed to be coming up with this aid package, but we haven't seen dollar one yet. Don't suppose we ever will.'

'You don't like us much, do you?'

'I don't know what you people think you're doing here, but it isn't making things any better.'

'Nothing like getting off to a positive start,' Max said, and looked out of his window.

Twenty minutes later they came to their first town, a dusty pit of peeling, battered buildings, and roads even more damaged than the ones they'd come down.

The Landcruiser slowed as it turned into the main street, which was choked with people; the dirt poor, wearing international charity clothes that slipped off their waists and shoulders, walking on shoeless feet calloused and deformed into human deep-sea-diver boots, all moving at a plod dictated more by habit than urgency or purpose. They looked like a defeated army, a conquered people, broken in two, shuffling off into a non-future. This was Haiti, barely a footprint out of slavery. Many were pushing crude carts cobbled together from planks, corrugated iron and old tyres stuffed with sand, while others carried big woven reed baskets and old suitcases on their heads and shoulders. Animals mingled freely among the people, at one with them, their equals: black pigs, sunstroked dogs, donkeys, skinny goats, cows with protruding ribs, chickens. Max had only seen this sort of poverty on TV, usually in news clips about a famine-hit African country or a South American slum. He'd seen misery in America, but it was nothing like this.

It killed his hard-on.

'This is Pétionville,' Chantale said. 'Home sweet home for as long as you're here.'

They drove up a steep hill, took a left and rolled slowly along a heavily potholed side-road flanked by tall white-washed houses. Two palm trees stood at the end of the road, where it curved off and led back down into the middle of the suburb. In between the trees was the entrance to a drive. 'Impasse Carver' was painted on both trunks in black lettering.

Chantale turned into the drive which was dark because it was lined on both sides with more palm trees, sprouting in front of high walls, whose leaves intertwined under the sky and filtered the light through in a murky, aqueous green haze occasionally broken up by sharp bolts of bright sunlight. The ground was perfectly smooth and even, a relief after the ruptured streets they'd driven down.

Max's house was at the far end of the drive. The gate was open and Chantale turned into a concrete courtyard overhung with more palm trees. He saw the house in the background, a single-storey orange building with a sharply sloping corrugated-iron roof, built three to four feet off the ground, with half a dozen wide stone steps leading on to a porch. Bougainvillea and oleander bushes grew close to the walls.

Chantale parked the car. The bodyguards rolled into the courtyard moments later.

'The Carvers have invited you to dinner tonight. You'll be picked up around eight,' she said.

'Will you be there?'

'No, I won't,' she said. 'Come. Let me show you around the house.'

She showed him around like an estate agent would a first-time buyer, telling him more than was strictly necessary and enthusing about fittings and appliances. It was a small house – two bedrooms, a living room, a kitchen and a bathroom. The place was spotless, the tiled floors polished and shiny, a smell of soap and mint hanging in the air.

When she was done, she told him to take a walk around the gardens out back and took her leave of him with a handshake and a smile, both still thoroughly professional, although he thought he detected a degree or two of warmth in there too. Or was he misreading signs? Or was it wishful thinking, the fantasies of a widower who hasn't had sex in eight years, getting turned on by a beautiful woman's touch, no matter how slight?

9

Night fell quickly in Haiti. One minute it was late afternoon, still broad daylight, then a second later it went dark, as sudden as someone flipping a switch.

Max had been inspecting the grounds behind the house. There was a Japanese-style rock garden, immaculately presented and tended to, with paving stones leading across green marble gravestone chips to a square granite slab set with a large round white metal mesh table and six matching chairs. The chair seats were slightly dusty, as was the top of the table, which had flecks of red candle wax in the centre. He imagined a couple might have sat there at night, sipping cocktails by candlelight and maybe holding hands and savouring the moment. He'd thought of Sandra, who'd liked doing things like that. Savouring the moment, cherishing it, holding his hand like she was holding on to time itself and pausing its hand mid-turn, claiming the moment as hers. He remembered their first anniversary, eating barbecued fish in the house they'd rented in the Keys. They'd watched sunsets and sunrises every day and danced on the beach to the sound of the waves. He wondered what she'd make of Haiti so far. It was one place she'd never mentioned.

The garden was bordered with young palm trees, maybe two or three years old at the most, still thin and breakable, only just finding their girth. A row of mango, orange and lime trees marked the end of the grounds. Between these ran a high fence capped with coils of razor wire. The fence was electric; it hummed constantly like the dying vibrations of a struck tuning fork. It had been disguised from both inside and out by deep green ivy. He walked to the far end of the fence until he reached a twenty-foot white wall, also capped with razor wire. The ground in front of the wall was strewn with broken glass, half buried in sand. He found a gap in the fake fence foliage and peered through. The house backed on to a ravine which ran the length of the estate. His half was marked out and separated by a retaining wall. The opposite end was a high ridge of dark earth. Tall trees grew out of the ground, but they were all bent precariously over the ravine, tilted at painfully acute angles, half their roots sprung from the soil and grasping at thin air, as if they'd been uprooted by an avalanche which had frozen in mid-cascade. A slick of stagnant, oily black water filled the bottom of the ravine. In front of him was a Texaco petrol station and a kind of diner.

He heard noises from the street. Every town had its particular traffic timpani. In New York it was car horns and sirens, gridlocks and emergencies. In Miami it was the smoother sound of moving traffic, brakes and skids, backfiring motorbikes and belching lowriders. In Pétionville the cars rattled like they were dragging busted fenders along their busted-up roads and the horns sounded like out of tune alto-saxophones.

He was standing there staring at the outside world when night had fallen and caught him by surprise.

He was grateful when he couldn't see anything any more. The air around him was chiming with crickets and cicadas, the inky darkness punctuated by fireflies, tiny lime-green flares burning for a meagre second before disappearing for ever.

The skies were clear and he could see thousands of stars

splashed out above him, closer than he'd ever seen them in America, a glittering white spray that looked almost within reach.

He headed back up to the house. As he did, a whole new sound made him stop in his tracks. It was a faint, faraway sound. He listened. He waded past the insects and the traffic and the sounds of breadline, shantytown humanity hunkering down for another night in the shitshack motel.

He found it. He turned a little to the right. There it was, coming from someplace above the town. A single drumbeat, repeated every ten or twelve seconds – *domm* . . . *domm* . . . *domm* . . . *domm*.

It was a bass drum, its sound carrying through the raucous chaos of the night, insistent and strong, like a giant's heart-beat.

Max felt the sound pass into his body, the rhythm of the lonesome drum seeping into his chest and then flowing into his heart, the two beats briefly becoming one.

10

The bodyguards from the airport collected Max for dinner. They drove out of the estate, down the street and then took a left at the end and headed up the steep road that would take them up the mountains. They passed a bar, its name framed in a proscenium of brightly coloured bulbs: La Coupole. Six or seven white men, beer bottles in hand, were hanging around outside, talking to some local women in tight short skirts and dresses. Max recognized his country-men straight away from their matching clothes – khakis, like his, and the same cut of shirt and T-shirt he'd packed for the trip. GIs on leave, the conquering army, getting wasted on US taxpayers' money. He made a mental note to stop by the bar when he was done meeting his clients. The search for Charlie Carver would start tonight.

The Carver estate doubled as a banana plantation, one of the highest yielding in Haiti. According to a footnote in the CIA report, the family ploughed the profit it made from the annual harvest into its philanthropic projects, notably Noah's Ark, a school for the island's poorest children.

The Carvers' home was a striking four-storey white and pastel-blue plantation house with a wide sweeping staircase leading up to the brightly lit main entrance. In front of the house was a well-tended lawn with a bubbling fountain and a fish-filled saltwater pool in the middle and park benches set around its edges. The area was floodlit like a football stadium from manned high towers set in the surrounding trees.

A security guard armed with an Uzi and a Dobermann on a button-release leash met them as they drove around the lawn to the staircase. Max hated dogs, always had, ever since he was chased by one as a child. The dumb ones tended to pick up on this and they'd growl and bark and bare their teeth at him. The trained ones bided their time and waited for the signal. This one reminded him of a police attack dog, standing obediently by its master's side, lining up homicidal thoughts, trained to go for the balls and throat in that order.

A maid showed Max into the living room where three of the Carvers were sat waiting for him: Allain, an old man Max guessed was Gustav and a blonde he supposed was Charlie's mother and Allain's wife.

Allain got up and walked over to Max, his leather heels clicking across the polished black-and-white tiled floor, hand already extended. He was flashing the same professional smile, but otherwise appeared markedly different to the cool creature Max had met in New York. He'd washed the pomade out of his hair and with it had gone a good five years off his age and most of his gravitas.

'Welcome, Max,' he said. They pumped hands. 'Good trip?'

'Yeah, thanks.'

'Is your house OK?'

'It's great, thanks.'

Carver looked like a preppy hotel manager in his brown brogues, khakis and short-sleeved light-blue Oxford shirt which complemented his passionless eyes. He had thin, freckled arms.

'Come on over,' Carver said, and led Max across the room.

The Carvers were sitting around a long solid-glass coffee

table with five neat cubes of magazines on the bottom shelf and a vase stuffed with yellow, pink and orange lilies on top. Gustav was sitting in a gold-trimmed black-leather armchair. The woman was sitting on a matching sofa.

The place smelled of furniture polish, window cleaner, floor wax and the same disinfectant they used in hospital corridors. Max also picked up a faint stench of stale cigarettes.

He had on the off-the-peg beige linen suit he'd bought at Saks Fifth Avenue at the Dadeland Mall, an open-necked white shirt, black leather shoes and his Beretta, clipped to the left side of his waist. They hadn't frisked him before he'd gone in. He made a note to tell the Carvers this if he finished the job with any affection for them.

'Francesca, my wife,' Allain said.

Francesca Carver smiled limply, as if offstage arms were desperately winding up her smile at great strain. She took Max's extended hand in a cold, clammy clasp, which briefly took him back to his and Joe's patrol car days, when they'd 'shit-sifted' – fingertip searched for drugs hidden at the bottom of backed-up toilets. Most of the time they'd had to use their bare hands because they hadn't brought gloves to the bust. He remembered how month-old sewage had the same texture as cold raw hamburger – the same feeling he was getting from Mrs Carver's hand.

Their eyes met and locked. Her irises were a light, washed-out shade of blue that registered faintly against the whites, like the ghost of a long-forgotten ink drop on laundered fabric. Her look was pure beat cop – wary, probing, doubtful, edgy.

Francesca was beautiful, but in a way that had never done it for him – a distinguished, distant beauty that spoke status not sexiness. Delicate, porcelain-pale skin; perfectly balanced features, with nothing bigger or smaller than it should be, everything symmetrical and in exactly the right place; high, sharp cheekbones, a pointed chin and a slightly turned up nose that was the perfect launchpad for a disdainful or withering look. Manhattan WASP, Florida belle, Palm Springs princess, Bel Air blue blood: Francesca Carver possessed the sort of face that launched a dozen country clubs and required annual membership or good connections to get close to. Her life as he saw it: four-hour lunches, crash diets, monthly colonic irrigations, manicures, pedicures, facials, massages, botox, twice-weekly trips to the hairdresser, a governess, a personal trainer, a daily/weekly/monthly allowance, limitless reserves of smalltalk. She was Allain Carver's perfect foil.

But all was not completely right about her. A few things let her down and fractured the image. She was drinking what must have been four straight shots of neat vodka out of a large tumbler; her dark-blonde hair was packed into a tight, severe bun which exposed her face and drew attention to its thinness and pallor, to the shadows under her eyes and the vein in her left temple, thumping away under her skin, her pulse accelerated, tense.

She said nothing and their exchange remained wordless. Max could tell she didn't approve of him, which was odd because parents who called him in to look for their missing children usually looked at him like he was the next best thing to a superhero.

'And, my father, Gustav Carver.'

'Pleased to meet you,' Gustav said to Max. His voice was gravelly and expansive, a smoking shouter's voice.

They shook hands. The elder Carver displayed a lot of strength for someone his age, who'd also suffered a stroke. His handshake, applied with minimum effort, was a bonecrusher. He had a forbidding set of paws, the size of catcher's mitts.

He took the heavy black and silver-topped cane he'd rested across the arms of his chair and rapped on the couch to his left, close to him.

'Sit with me, Mr Mingus,' he growled.

Max sat down close enough to the old man to smell mild menthol coming off him. Father looked nothing like son. Gustav Carver resembled a gargoyle at rest between demonic eruptions. He had a huge head topped with a swept back, brilliantined mane of thick silver. His nose was a broad beak, his mouth dense-lipped and bill-shaped, and his small dark-brown eyes, peering under the drapes of sagging eye sockets, glistened like two freshly roasted coffee beans.

'Would you care for a drink?' Gustav said, more order than invitation.

'Yes, please,' Max said and was about to ask for water, but Gustav interrupted him.

'You should try our rum. It's the best in the world. I'd join you, but I've had mutinies in the pumphouse.' He patted his chest, chuckling. 'I'll drink it through you.'

'Barbancourt rum?' Max asked. 'We get that in Miami.'

'Not the deluxe variety,' Gustav snapped. 'It's not for foreigners. It never leaves the island.'

'I don't drink, Mr Carver,' Max said.

'You don't look like a struggling alcoholic,' Gustav said, scrutinizing his face. His accent was closer to English than his son's.

'I quit before it reached that stage.'

'That's a shame. You might have liked our rum.'

'Rum wasn't my thing. I was a bourbon and beer kinda guy.'

'So what can I offer you?'

'Water, please.'

'That's another deluxe drink here,' Carver said.

Max laughed.

Gustav barked at a male servant who came quickly over from near the doorway, where Max hadn't noticed him standing when he'd walked in. Carver ordered Max's water in words that left his mouth like the blast from a starting pistol.

Looking at the servant practically fleeing the room, Max caught sight of Allain, sitting at the other end of the sofa, staring blankly into space, playing with his fingers. Max realized he hadn't been conscious of Allain's presence in the room after he'd been introduced to Gustav. He stole a look at Francesca on the opposite sofa and saw her sitting in the same way – back upright, hands folded on her lap – staring in the same way at a different nothing.

The dynamics of the family fell into place. Gustav Carver ruled the roost absolutely, without question or opposition. It was his show and everyone around him was an extra, a hired hand, even his family.

The old man sucked all the energy and personality out of the room and assimilated it into his. It was why Allain appeared so changed from when Max had last seen him, demoted from the regal to the regular; and it was why Francesca was reduced to a silent bit of arm candy, when her eyes blared that she was anything but. Gustav must have been a terrifying father to grow up under, thought Max, the sort who disowned what he couldn't break and bend.

The living room was vast. Three of the walls were lined with antique books, hundreds of them; collection after gold-embossed collection – their spines forming tasteful blocks of colour – maroons, greens, royal blues, chocolate browns – against which furniture was offset to highlight its subtleties.

He wondered how many of their books the Carvers had actually read.

It took a certain type of person to lose themselves in a book. Max wasn't one of them. He preferred physical activity to sitting down and he'd outgrown made-up stories as a kid. Until he'd gone to prison Max had only read the papers and anything related to a case he was working on.

Sandra had been the reader in the household – and a voracious one too.

The light in the room – coming from spotlights in the ceiling, and tall lamps placed in all four corners – was a warm, comforting, intimate golden ochre, the glow of fireplaces, candles and oil lanterns. Max could make out two armour breastplates and peaked helmets, mounted on pedestals, stood at either end of the bookcases to the right of the room. On the wall opposite him, between two arched windows, was a large portrait of a woman, while below it ran a long mantelpiece, massed with framed photographs of various shapes and sizes.

'Your name? Mingus? It's black American, no?' Gustav said.

'My dad was from New Orleans. A failed jazz musician. He changed his name before he met my mom.'

'After Charles Mingus?'

'Yeah.'

'One of his pieces is called –'

'"Haitian Fight Song", I know,' Max interrupted.

'It's about *La Gague* – our cockfights,' Carver informed him.

'We've got those in Miami too –'

'They're rougher here – primal.' Carver smiled broadly at him. The old man's teeth were sandy coloured and black at the roots.

Max's eyes fell on the lilies in the vase. There was something wrong with them, something that jarred with the room's nobility.

'Do you like jazz?' Carver asked him.

'Yes. You?'

'Some. We saw Mingus give a concert here once, in Port-au-Prince, at the Hotel Olffson. Long time ago.'

Gustav fell quiet and stared over at the portrait on the wall.

'Come,' he said, pushing himself up out of his chair with his cane. Max stood up to help him, but Gustav shooed him away. He was about Max's height, although slightly stooped and a lot narrower about the shoulders and neck.

Carver took Max over to the mantelpiece.

'Our Hall of Fame – or In-Fame-ey, depending on your politics,' Carver announced with a guffaw, spanning the breadth of the mantelpiece with a sweep of the arm.

The mantelpiece was made of granite, with a thin band of intertwined laurel leaves painted around the middle in gold. It was a lot wider than he had expected, more ledge than mantelpiece. Max looked across at all the photographs. There were well over a hundred massed there, five rows deep, each one turned at a different angle, so that its core figures were visible.

The photographs were in black frames, with the same gold-leaf pattern running around the inside of their borders. At first glance Max saw only unfamiliar faces staring back at him, in black and white, sepia and colour – Carver's fore-bears: men old and older, women, mostly young, everyone Caucasian – and then, flitting in between the aristocratic profiles and posed box camera shots of yesteryear, were shots of the younger Gustav – fishing, playing croquet in plus fours, with his wife on their wedding day, and, most of all, shaking hands with celebrities and icons. Among those Max recognized were JFK, Fidel Castro (those two photographs placed side by side), John Wayne, Marilyn Monroe, Norman Mailer, William Holden, Ann-Margret, Clark Gable, Mick Jagger, Jerry Hall, Truman Capote, John Gielgud, Graham Greene, Richard Burton, Elizabeth Taylor. Carver never seemed dwarfed or rendered irrelevant in the stars' auras; on the contrary, Max thought his seemed the more commanding presence, as if he was really posing in *their* snapshots.

There were two photographs of Sinatra – one of the Chairman meeting Carver, the other of him kissing an awestruck Judith Carver on the cheek.

'How did you find him? Sinatra?' Max asked.

'A tadpole who thought he was a shark – and a complete vulgarian too. No class,' Carver said. 'My wife adored him though, so I forgave him virtually everything. He still writes to me. Or his secretary does. He sent me his last compact disc.'

'*LA Is My Lady*?'

'No. *Duets*.'

'A *new* album?' Max said, too excitedly for his liking. He hadn't thought to check any record stores before he'd left. Before he'd gone to prison he'd habitually shopped for new music on Tuesdays and Fridays.

'You can have it if you want,' Carver said, with a smile. 'I haven't even opened it.'

'I couldn't.'

'*You* can,' Carver said, patting him affectionately on the shoulder and then looking up at the portrait.

Max studied it and recognized an older version of Judith Carver from the mantelpiece photographs and, from her near lipless face, the mother of Allain Carver. She was seated, legs crossed, hands folded one over the other and placed on her knee. In the background, on a stand behind her, were the same vase and lilies found on the coffee table. It was then that Max realized what had been bothering him about the flowers – they were fake.

'My wife, Judith,' Carver said, nodding up at the portrait.

'When did you lose her?'

'Five years ago. She died of cancer,' he said, and then he turned to Max. 'Husbands shouldn't bury their wives.'

Max nodded. From the side he saw Gustav's eyes welling up, his bottom lip trembling until he bit it still. Max wanted to do or say something comforting or distracting, but words failed him and he didn't trust his motives.

He noticed for the first time that he and the old man were both dressed the same: Gustav was wearing a beige linen suit, white shirt and well-polished black leather shoes.

'*Excusez-moi, Monsieur Gustav?*' the servant said behind them. He'd brought Max's water – a tall glass with ice and a slice of lemon, sitting alone in the middle of a wide round silver tray.

Max took the glass and thanked its bearer with a nod and a smile.

Carver had picked out a family photograph from the pile. Max could see it had been taken in the living room. Carver was sat in an armchair, cradling a baby in his arms, beaming. Max vaguely recognized the baby's face as Charlie's.

'This was after the little man's baptism,' Carver said. 'He farted all through the ceremony.'

Carver laughed to himself. Max saw he loved his grandson. He saw it in the way he held him in the photograph, and in the way he looked back at the pair of them together.

He handed Max the photograph and walked along the mantelpiece, stopping almost at the very end and retrieving a smaller picture from a back row. He stood where he was and studied it.

Max looked at the photograph – the Carver family gathered around the patriarch and his grandson. There were four daughters – three took after their mother and were beauties moulded from the same template as Francesca's, while the last one was short and fat and looked like a younger version of her father in drag. Francesca stood next to her, and Allain ended the row on the right. Another man was in the picture – about Allain's age, but much taller and with short dark hair. Max guessed he was an in-law.

Carver came back to where he'd been standing. Max noticed he walked with a slight limp on his left side.

He took the baptism photo back and he leant in close to Max.

'I'm very glad you're working on this,' he said, dropping his voice to a whisper. 'I'm honoured to have a man like you here. A man who understands values and principles.'

'As I told your son, this may not have a happy ending,' Max said, also whispering. He usually kept his feelings in check with clients, but he had to admit he liked the old man, despite everything he'd read about him.

'Mr Mingus –'

'Call me Max, Mr Carver.'

'Max, then – I'm old. I've had a stroke. I don't have much time left. A year, maybe a little more, but not much. I want our boy back. He's my only grandson. I want to see him again.'

Gustav's eyes were watering again.

'I'll do my best, Mr Carver,' Max said and he meant it, even though he was almost a hundred per cent sure Charlie Carver was dead and was already dreading having to tell the old man.

'I believe you will,' Carver said, looking at Max admiringly.

Max felt ten feet tall, ready to get to work. He'd find Charlie Carver – if not his body, then his ghost and the place he haunted. He'd find out what happened to him and who was responsible. Then he'd find out why. But he'd stop there. He wouldn't dispense justice. The Carvers would want that satisfaction to themselves.

His eyes fell on something he hadn't seen, something not immediately apparent unless the viewer was up close – words, stamped into the mantelpiece pillars and filled in with gold paint. They were from Psalm 23, the best-known one, which starts '*The Lord is my shepherd . . .*' – only these quoted the fifth verse:

Thou preparest a table before me in the presence of mine enemies: thou anointest my head with oil; my cup runneth over.

A maid walked up to them.

'*Le dîner est servi.*'

'*Merci*, Karine,' Carver said. 'Dinner. I hope you've come with an empty stomach.'

As Max and Carver began to walk towards the door, Allain and Francesca rose from their seats and followed them. For a while Max had completely forgotten they were all in the same room.

11

Dinner was served by two maids in black uniforms with white aprons. They were silent and unobtrusive, serving the first course – two crossed slices of Parma ham, with pieces of chilled cantaloupe, honeydew, galia and watermelon, moulded into individual snailshells, squares, stars and triangles and placed in the corners of the cross – with the minimum of fuss, their presence a brief shadow at the shoulder.

The dining room, black-and-white tiled like the living room, was brightly lit by two huge chandeliers and dominated by the banqueting table, which could sit twenty-four. Judith's portrait hung on the left-hand wall, her face and torso looming over the end of the table, her essence filling the place she had no doubt occupied in body. The table was decorated with three vases of artificial lilies. Max and the Carvers were sat close together at the opposite end. Gustav was at the head, Francesca faced Allain, and Max was placed next to her.

Max looked down at his place setting. He'd landed in alien territory. He didn't stand much on ceremony and etiquette. Other than the restaurants he'd taken his wife and girlfriends to, the only formal dinners he'd attended were cop banquets, and those had been like frat parties, disintegrating into roll fights and rude food sculpture contests.

Working away at the ham, Max looked at the Carvers. They were still on the melon. They ate in silence, not looking at each other. The percussive tap of metal on porcelain was the only sound filling the cavernous dining room. Gustav kept his eyes fixed on his food. Max noted the way the fork trembled in his fingers as he brought it up to his mouth. Allain stabbed at his food like he was trying and failing to crush a zigzagging ant with the point of a pencil. He brought pieces of fruit up to his lipless mouth and snatched them in like a lizard swallowing a fly. Francesca held her cutlery like knitting needles, dissecting her fruit into small morsels she then dabbed into her mouth without really opening it. Max saw how thin and pale and veinless her arms were. He noticed she was trembling too, a nervous tremor, worries rattling inside of her. He glanced back at Allain and then again at her. No chemistry. Nothing left. Separate rooms? Miserable couple. Did they still argue or was it all silence? It was more than just the kid. These were two people staying together like bugs on sap. Max was sure Carver had someone on the side. He looked after himself, kept up his appearance, cut a dash. Francesca had given up. Poor woman.

'How long've you been in Haiti, Mrs Carver?' Max asked, his voice filling the room. Father and son looked his way, then Francesca's.

'Too long,' she said, quickly, just above a whisper, as if implying that Max shouldn't be talking to her. She didn't turn her head to look at him, merely glanced his way out of the corner of her eye.

Max swallowed the ham with a loud hard gulp. It hurt his throat going down. There was another piece to go but he didn't touch it.

'So, tell me, Max – what was prison like?' Gustav barked across the table.

'*Father!*' Allain gasped at the old man's brusqueness and indiscretion.

'I don't mind talking about it,' Max said to Allain. He'd been expecting the old man to ask him about his past.

'I shouldn't have taken the Garcia case,' he started. 'It was too close, too personal. My wife and I knew the family. They were friends. Her friends first, then mine. We babysat their daughter, Manuela, sometimes.'

He saw her again, now, in front of him. Four years old, her grown-up features budding, crooked nose, brown eyes, curly brown hair, impudent smile, always talking, a little Inca. She'd loved Sandra, called her 'Auntie'. Sometimes she'd want to come and spend the night with them even when her parents were with her.

'Richard and Luisa had everything most people wish for. They were millionaires. They'd been trying for a baby for years. There'd always been complications. Luisa had had three miscarriages and the doctors told her she couldn't get pregnant again – so, when Manuela came along they thought it was a miracle. They loved that little girl.'

Manuela hadn't liked Max much, but she'd inherited her father's smooth diplomatic skills and, even at that age, she'd understood the importance of not offending people unless you were sure you could get away with it. She'd been polite to Max and called him 'Uncle Max' to his face, but when she thought he couldn't hear she referred to him as 'Max' or 'he'. It had always made him smile, hearing the future adult in the child.

'They contacted me as soon as they got the ransom demand. I told them to go to the cops, but they said the kidnappers had warned them not to or the girl would die. Usual TV movie shit,' Max said, talking to the room. 'Never trust a kidnapper, least of all one who tells you not to go to the cops. You'll find they don't know what they're doing, and nine times out of ten the victim gets hurt. I told Richard all this, but he still wanted to play it by their rules.

'He asked me to be the bag man. I was to drop the ransom

off and wait for the kidnappers to call and tell me where to find Manuela. I delivered the money near a callbox in Orlando. Some guy on a motorbike picked it up. He didn't see me. I was hiding across the street. I got his registration, make of the bike, basic physical description of the rider.

'The call never came. I ran the bike details with a friend of mine on the job. It belonged to one of Richard's employees. I got the information I needed out of him and turned him over to the cops.

'He told me Manuela was being held at a house in Orlando. I went there and she was gone,' Max said. He saw Francesca Carver twisting her napkin tight under the table, loosening it and then twisting it again with a hard wrench of her hands.

'The ransom guy had given me the names of his accomplices. Three of them, still teenagers. Seventeen. Two boys, a girl. Black. All three had records. The girl was a runaway, turned hooker. One of the boys was the ringleader's cousin.'

The maids came in and cleared away the plates and refilled the glasses with water and juice. Allain and Gustav were giving him their full, undivided attention. He felt them hanging on his every word. Francesca wasn't looking at him. The vein in her temple was throbbing again.

'There was a manhunt, first state, then national, the FBI got involved. They spent six months looking for Manuela and the kidnappers and they found nothing. I was out looking for her too. Richard offered me a million dollars. But I did it for free.'

Max remembered his search all too clearly, mile after black and white mile of endless highway and freeway, hours and days of nothing but road, sitting in rented cars, all of them with different defects – no air-conditioning, no heating, no left indicator, slow gear change, no radio, radio too loud, fastfood fumes of previous occupants; the motel rooms, the

TVs, the plane rides; the tiredness, the legal speed pills washed down with pots of coffee, the calls home, the calls to the Garcia family; despair growing ever longer in him like an afternoon to early evening shadow. He was feeling it all over again, distanced, diluted in time, but its trace still potent enough.

'I've seen some pretty fucking horrible things in my time. I've seen people do things to each other you couldn't imagine. But all that time it was kind of OK. It was part of my job. It came with the territory. It was something I could leave behind at the end of every shift, wash off and dive back into a few hours later.

'But when it's personal it hits you bad. Those few hours' downtime – that space between doing your job and not doing your job – that disappears. You're not a professional any more. You're right there with the next of kin – the moms and dads, the husbands and wives, the boyfriends and girlfriends, the roommates, the pets – catching some of all those tears.

'Do you know they train you as part of the detective's course in the art of breaking bad news? They train you in professional sympathy. Some out-of-work Hollywood acting coach trained me. I was top of my class. I *oozed* professional sympathy at the drop of a hat. I tried to *ooze* some of that sympathy on myself. Didn't work.

'I found Manuela Garcia almost a year after her kidnapping. In New York. She'd been dead six or seven months. They'd done things to her. Ugly things,' Max said. He stopped himself in time from giving the details.

The maids brought in the main course. All Haitian food: *grillot* – cubed pork fried in garlic, pepper and chilli, and served with a lemon dressing; slivers of plantain, fried golden brown; a choice of either corn meal and thick kidney bean sauce, or *riz dion-dion* – rice with local mushrooms. There was also a tomato salad.

Max couldn't be sure if the Carvers ever really ate native, or if the food hadn't been specially prepared for him, as an induction. They weren't putting much of it on their plates. He had the rice, plantain, *grillot* and a hefty tong's worth of tomato, which he dumped into his dinner plate, ignoring the salad side plate. He noticed his gaffe when Francesca put a few sliced tomatoes into the salad plate and a single *grillot* on her main plate. He didn't let it bother him.

Allain Carver had the same as him. Francesca cut her pork cube into tiny fragments which she fanned out in her plate and looked at intently, as if divining her fortune.

They ate in silence for a few minutes. Max tried to take his time over it, but he was hungry and the food was delicious, the best he'd eaten in over eight years.

His plate was almost empty by the time conversation resumed.

'So what happened next, Max?' Gustav asked.

'Well,' Max began, taking a long drink of water, 'you know there's a whole shrink industry devoted to looking into the sort of mind that'll think up the most repulsive torture it can inflict on another human being and then see it through? These are the same fancy mouthpieces defence attorneys wheel out in court to explain that some sick fuck ended up the way they did because they were abused as children, because their parents were fuck-ups themselves. I don't buy that shit. Never have. I believe most of us know right and wrong, and if you go through wrong as a child you look for right as an adult. But for most Americans, therapy is like confession and shrinks are the priests. Instead of saying their Hail Marys they blame their parents.'

Gustav Carver laughed and clapped his hands. Allain

smiled tightly. Francesca had gone back to strangling her napkin.

'I knew those kids would get off. There's no death penalty in New York. They'd play the mental illness card and they'd win. Two of them were crack addicts, so that's diminished responsibility right there. They'd put most of the blame on the ringleader, the oldest one, the one who'd organized it – Richard's employee. In between Manuela would be forgotten about and the trial would be more about the kids. The media would get hold of it and make it into this big indictment of African-American youth. They'd get fifteen to twenty. They'd get raped in prison, sure. The men would get AIDS. Maybe. But for all their wasted, rotted lives, Manuela's would go unlived.

'I found the girl first. It wasn't hard. She was out turning tricks for rock. She took me to the other two. They were holed up in Harlem. They thought I was a cop. They confessed everything, down to the last shitty detail. I heard them out, made absolutely sure it was them . . . And then I shot 'em.'

'Just like that?' asked Allain, looking horrified.

'Just like that,' Max said.

He'd never told anybody this much about the Garcia case, and yet it had felt right. He wasn't after absolution or even understanding or empathy. He'd just wanted to free himself of the truth.

Gustav was beaming at him. There was a twinkle in his eye, as if he'd been both moved and invigorated by the story.

'So, you pleaded guilty to manslaughter, yet you committed premeditated cold-blooded murder? You received a very light sentence. The same system you criticized looked after you,' Gustav said.

'I had a good lawyer' – Max said – '*and* a great shrink.'

Gustav laughed.

Allain joined in.

'*Bra*-voh!' Gustav barked joyfully, his approval echoing around the room, coming back in sets of two and three, giving Max a small yet highly appreciative spectral audience.

Allain stood up and joined in.

Max was part amused, part embarrassed, part wishing himself away. The two Carvers were no better than the redneck vigilante freaks who'd written to him in jail. He wished now he could have taken it all back, fed them the same line of crap he'd fed the cops and his lawyer, about self-defence with intent.

Francesca broke up the fun.

'I *knew* it,' she said venomously, eyes turned to slits, rounding on Max. 'This isn't about Charlie at all. It's about *them*.'

'Francesca, you *know* that's not true,' Allain said, patronizingly, as if he was telling a child off for telling a blatant lie. He gave her a cutting, get-back-in-line look which made her lower her head.

'Francesca's understandably upset,' Allain explained to Max, leaning over to him, cutting her off.

'*Upset*! I'm not *up-set*! I'm *beyond upset*!' Francesca screeched. Her face was crimson, her blue eyes bulged, more washed-out-looking than ever. The pulsing vein in her temple had turned purple, forming a bruise-coloured whorl. Like her husband she had an English accent, only hers was the real deal, no East Coast edges or lopsided-sounding vowels.

'You know why you're here, don't you?' she said to Max. 'They didn't bring you here to find *Charlie*. They think he's *dead*. They have all along. They brought you in to find the kidnappers – to find whoever it is who dared go up against the all-powerful, all-knowing, all-seeing, all-*owning* Carver clan! That story you just told confirms it all. You're no "private detective". You're nothing more than a glorified hitman.'

Max looked at her, feeling chastized and embarrassed. This wasn't what he'd expected.

In some ways she was right. He had a short fuse. He acted on his impulses. His temper got the better of him and, yes, it had sometimes clouded his judgement. But that was then, when he still cared, before he'd fallen foul of his own system.

'Francesca, please,' Allain said, appealing to her now.

'God *damn* you, Allain!' she yelled, throwing down her napkin and standing up with such force her chair flew back and fell over. 'I thought you *promised* to find Charlie.'

'We're *trying*,' Allain said, pleading.

'With *him*?' Francesca said, pointing at Max.

'Francesca, please sit down,' Allain said.

'Damn you, Allain – and damn *you* too, Gustav! – damn you and your damn family!'

She shot Max a tearful, hate-soaked look. The veins in the corners of her eyes pushed up against her skin like early-morning worms. Her lips were trembling with rage and fear. Her anger made her look younger, less damaged and vulnerable.

She turned and ran out of the room. Max noticed she was barefoot and had a small tattoo over her left ankle.

Silence followed the explosion, a big pall of nothing which settled over the scene. It was so complete, so still in the room, that Max could hear the Dobermann's paws scrabbling on the gravel path outside, the crickets chirping in the night.

Allain looked humiliated. He was blushing. His father sat back in his chair, watching his son's discomfort with an amused expression playing on his thick lips.

'I'm sorry about my wife,' Allain said to Max. 'She's taken this whole business very hard. We all have, obviously, but she's – it's hit her *particularly* hard.'

'I understand,' Max said.

And he did. There were two kinds of victim-parent: those who expected the worst and those who lived in hope. The former didn't crack; they lived through their loss, grew thicker skins, became mistrustful and intolerant. The latter never recovered. They broke up and they broke down. They lost everything they'd ever loved and lived for. They died young – cancers, addictions, intoxications. Max could tell casualties from survivors the moment he met them, on the threshold of their greatest grief, not yet stepped over. He'd never been wrong, until now. He'd thought the Carvers would be OK, that they'd pull through. Francesca's outburst had changed his mind.

He put another *grillot* in his mouth.

'She was with Charlie in the car when he was kidnapped,' Allain said.

'Tell me what happened,' Max said.

'It was just before the Americans invaded. Francesca took Charlie into Port-au-Prince to see the dentist. On their way there the car was surrounded by a hostile mob. They smashed the car up and took Charlie.'

'What happened to her?'

'She was knocked out. She came to in the middle of the road.'

'Didn't you have security?' Max asked.

'Yes, the chauffeur.'

'Just him?'

'He was very good.'

'What happened to him?'

'We think he died that day,' Allain said.

'Tell me,' Max said to Allain, 'was your wife on TV here a lot? Or in the papers?'

'No – maybe just once, at a function for the US ambassador a few years ago. Why?'

'What about your son? Was he in the press?'

'Never. What are you getting at, Max?'

'Your driver.'

'What about him?'

'What's his name, anyway?' Max asked.

'Eddie. Eddie Faustin,' Allain answered.

Faustin? Max's heart skipped a beat. Was this Faustin any relation to Salazar Faustin of the Saturday Night Barons Club? He didn't want to start down that path just yet.

'Could he have planned Charlie's kidnapping?'

'Eddie Faustin didn't have the brains to tie his laces, let alone plan a kidnapping,' Gustav said. 'But he was a good man. Very very *very* loyal. He'd break his back for you and wouldn't even ask you for an aspirin to take away the pain. He took a bullet for me once, you know? Didn't complain. He was back at work a week later. He and his brother used to be Macoutes – you know, the militia? Not a lot of people liked them – because of things they did under the Duvaliers – but *everyone* feared them.'

Yes: same guys. Max remembered. *Salazar was ex-Haitian secret police. They'd trained him in viciousness. Those stories he'd told them in interrogation – initiation ceremonies where they'd had to fight pitbulls and beat people to death with their bare hands. Same people. One big happy family. Keep it to yourself.*

'Maybe people were out to get him,' Max said.

'We thought of that, but they could have come for him any time. Everyone knew he worked for us. Everyone knows where to find us,' Allain said.

'Including the kidnappers, right? Are you sure he couldn't have been behind it – or maybe involved?' Max said to Gustav.

'No, Eddie wasn't involved and I'd stake my life on it,' the old man said. 'No matter how clear-cut it appears.'

Max trusted Gustav's judgement – to a point. There were many ingredients to a kidnapping – the safehouse, the abduction planning, victim stakeout, abduction, getaway. You needed a calm, calculating, orderly, fairly rational brain to put them all together and make them work. You needed to be ruthless and cold blooded too. Gustav Carver wouldn't have had someone that intelligent so close to him. Most bodyguards were dumb lunks with great reflexes and nine lives. And Eddie Faustin must have been every bit as dumb as his former boss said to have carried on working after taking a bullet.

If Eddie was involved in the kidnapping he was manipulated into it. The mob was possibly a distraction, deliberately organized to kill Eddie and get him out of the way, while the kidnappers quietly made off with the kid. Were they part of the mob, or did they drive up and take the kid?

Wait a minute –

'Where was Eddie's body in relation to Mrs Carver?'

'There was no body,' Allain said.

'No body?'

'Just a pool of blood near the car. We think it was his.'

'All blood looks the same. It could've been anyone's,' Max said.

'True.'

'For now I'll treat Eddie as a missing person too,' Max said. 'What about witnesses? Your wife?'

'She only remembers up to the mob attacking the car.'

'So if Eddie's alive, then he'd know who took Charlie.'

'That's a big *if*,' Gustav interrupted. 'Eddie's dead. The mob killed him, I'm sure.'

Maybe, thought Max, but maybes didn't solve cases.

'What was Eddie's brother called?'

'Salazar,' said Allain, glancing over at his father.

'The same one you arrested when you brought down Solomon Boukman,' said Gustav, as if on cue.

'You're very well informed,' Max said. 'I guess you also know they all got deported back here?'

'Yes,' said Gustav. 'Does that bother you?'

'Only if they see me first,' Max said.

There was a moment's silence. Gustav smiled at Max.

'You'll have a guide,' Allain said. 'Someone to show you around and act as your interpreter. In fact, you've met her. Chantale.'

'*Chantale*?' Max said.

'She's going to be your assistant.'

Gustav guffawed and winked at Max.

'I see,' Max said. 'She doesn't look like the sort who has a ghetto passkey.'

'She knows her way around,' Allain said.

'That she does!' laughed Gustav.

Max wondered which of the two she'd fucked. He guessed Allain because he was blushing to the roots. Max felt stupidly jealous. Carver's money and status was an aphrodisiac. Max tried to picture Chantale and Allain together and couldn't. Something didn't fit. He chased her from his mind, told himself to focus, to think of her as a colleague – a partner, a life support unit, same as when he was a cop. That was always a passion killer.

He ate another *grillot* but the meat had gone cold and rock solid. He was still hungry. He ate some tomatoes.

'My son hasn't had a lot of luck with assistants,' Gustav said.

'*Father!*' Allain started.

'I think you should tell Max what he's up against, don't you? It's hardly fair on him, is it?' Gustav said.

'I met Clyde Beeson, if that's what you mean?' Max said.

'I was thinking more about the unfortunate Mr Medd,' Gustav said.

Allain looked uncomfortable. He eyed his father angrily.

'When did he come into the picture?' Max asked.

'January, this year,' Allain said. 'Darwen Medd. Ex-Special Forces. He'd tracked drug cartel members in South America. He didn't get very far, before he –'

Allain trailed off and looked away from Max.

'Medd disappeared without trace,' Gustav said. 'The day before he vanished he told us he was going to Saut d'Eau – it's like a voodoo version of Lourdes – a waterfall you go to purify yourself in. Charlie had apparently been sighted there.'

'And you never heard from him again?'

Allain nodded.

'Do you know who gave him the information?'

'No.'

'Did you follow it up – the waterfall lead?'

'Yes. A false one.'

'Did you pay Medd a lot of money up front?'

'Less than you.'

'And you checked the airport –?'

'– and the ports, and the border – no sign of him.'

Max didn't say anything. There were more than just official exits out of any country and Haiti was no different. The boat people who washed up on the Florida coastline every day were proof of that. And then Medd could quite easily have slipped into the Dominican Republic over the mostly unpatrolled border.

But – assuming he was still alive – if he had left the country, why had he wanted to get out so quickly, without telling Carver?

'You're not telling him everything, Allain,' Gustav growled at his son.

'Father, I don't think *that's* relevant,' Allain said, avoiding looking at either of them.

'Oh, but it is,' Gustav said. 'You see, Max, Medd and Beeson had a predecessor –'

'Father – this is *not* important,' Allain said, all bared teeth and fierce eyes and clenched fists.

'Emmanuel Michelange,' Gustav said, raising his voice to a boom.

'Did he disappear too?' Max asked Allain, trying to draw him away from his father's orbit, hoping to divert another family explosion before it happened.

But the question caught Allain off-guard, and panic crept into his eyes.

Gustav stirred. He was going to speak, but Max quickly signalled for quiet with his index finger to his lip.

Allain didn't notice. He'd gone pale. His eyes were fixed but unfocussed, his mind gone from the present, digging back through time. He didn't get too far before he drew up bad memory. Sweat had pooled in the lines on his forehead.

'No, just – only Medd disappeared,' Allain said, his voice fluttering. 'Manno – Emmanuel – was found in Port-au-Prince.'

'Dead?' Max said.

Allain replied, but the effort was so slight the word got caught in his throat. 'Was he split in two?' Max offered.

Allain lowered his head and held it up between his thumb and forefinger.

'What happened, Mr Carver?' Max said, firmly, but staying on the right side of empathy.

Allain shook his head. Max thought he was going to cry. Emmanuel Michelange must have been a close friend.

'Mr Carver, please,' Max said in the same tone, only leaning over to create a sense of intimacy. 'I know this is hard for you, but I've really *got* to know what happened.'

Allain was silent.

Max heard something dragging across the floor near Gustav's seat.

'*Tell him!*' Gustav erupted from the end of the table.

Max and Allain looked up in time to see the old man standing up in his place and bringing his cane down through the air.

There was a huge crash as the cane met table and place setting. Glass and crockery smashed and flew across the room in shards and splinters.

Gustav stood over the table, angry, tottering and malevolent, his presence filling up the room like toxic gas.

'Do as I *say* and *tell him,*' Gustav said slowly and loudly, raising his cane and pointing it at Allain. Max saw squashed kidney beans and grains of rice stuck to the edges of the stick.

'No!' Allain shouted back at him, pushing himself out of his seat by the points of his fists, glaring at his father, rage hammering at the insides of his face. Max got ready to jump between them if the younger man attacked the older.

Gustav looked back at him, defiantly, an unflustered smirk cresting his jowls.

'Emmanuel Michelange,' Gustav said, wiping his stick clean on the table cloth and resting it by his chair. 'Was the one and only *local* we enlisted' – he growled the word out like it was a hairball he was hawking up – 'I was against using the natives – dumb and lazy is what they are – but junior here *insisted*. So we gave it a try. He was next to useless. Lasted two weeks. They found him in his jeep in Port-au-Prince. They'd taken the wheels and engine out – and much more. Emmanuel was sitting there, in the driving seat. His penis and testicles had been cut clean off – actually, not *clean* off – they'd used *scissors*.'

Max felt fear bundle up in his stomach and trickle towards his balls.

Gustav was staring at Allain the whole time he was talking. Allain was staring back at him, fists still clenched, but Max could tell he wasn't going to use them. His father had known it all along.

'Michelange was asphyxiated on his own genitalia,' Gustav said. 'His penis was blocking his throat. And each testicle was lodged in either cheek like so –'

Gustav demonstrated by putting his index fingers in his mouth and pushing out his cheeks. He looked grotesque but hilarious. Then he stuck his tongue out at his son and wiggled it from side to side. Now his resemblance to a gargoyle was uncanny.

'That's something Chantale won't have to worry about, I suppose,' Max said.

Gustav roared with laughter and slapped the table.

'*At last!*' he bellowed. '*Someone with ooomph!*'

'You bastard!' Allain shouted. Max thought it was at him, but the son was still looking at his father. He stormed out of the room.

A ghastly stillness descended on the big room again, a vacuum within a vacuum. Max looked down at his unfinished food and wished himself someplace else.

Gustav sat down and called to the maids. They came in and cleared up around him, then they cleared away the plates.

On her way back from the kitchen one of the maids brought him the silver cigarette box, lighter and an ashtray from the living room. He spoke to her again, mumbling so she had to bend over to hear him. The old man cupped her shoulder as he spoke to her.

The maid left the room and Carver took an untipped cigarette from the box and lit up.

'I used to smoke forty a day before my first stroke,' Gustav said. 'Now I'm down to just the one – keeps the memory alive. You?'

'I quit.'

Gustav smiled and nodded.

Some people are born smokers. Carver was one of them. He loved his habit. He inhaled the cigarette smoke and held it in his lungs, getting the most out of each puff before slowly exhaling.

'Sorry you had to witness that earlier. All families argue. It's rough but healthy. Do you have any family, Mr Mingus?'

'No. My mother's dead. I don't know where my dad is. Probably dead too now. I guess I got cousins and nephews and stuff, but I don't know them.'

'What about your late wife's family? Are you in touch with them?'

'On and off,' Max said.

Gustav nodded.

'Allain got upset about Emmanuel because they were childhood friends. I put Emmanuel through school, college. His mother was Allain's nanny. He loved her more than he loved his mother,' Carver said. 'In Haiti we have a servant culture. We call them *restavec*. It's Kreyol for "stay with", derived from the French *rester* – to stay – and *avec* – with.

You see, we don't pay our servants here. They live with us, "stay" "with" us. We clothe them, feed them, give them decent accommodation. And in return they cook, clean, do things around the house and garden. It's feudal, I know,' Carver smiled and showed his caramel-coloured teeth. 'But look at this country. Ninety-eight per cent of the population are still rubbing two sticks to light a fire. Have I offended you?'

'No,' Max said. 'Prison was kind of like that. Bitch culture. You'd see people getting bought and sold for a pack of smokes. A tape recorder'd buy you a blow job for life.'

Gustav chuckled.

'It's not as barbaric here. It's a way of life. Servitude is in the Haitian gene. No point in trying to reform nature,' Carver said. 'I treat my people as well as possible. I put all their children through school. Many have gone on to be modest middle-class achievers – in America, of course.'

'What about Emmanuel?'

'He was very bright, but he had a weakness for women. Stopped him concentrating.'

'His mother must have been proud.'

'She would have been. She died when he was fifteen.'

'That's way too bad,' Max said.

Gustav stubbed his cigarette out in the ashtray. The maid returned. She brought something over to Max and put it on his table. Frank Sinatra's *Duets* CD, personally autographed to Gustav in blue ink.

'Thank you very much,' Max said.

'I hope you enjoy it,' Carver said. 'There should be a CD player in your house.'

They looked at each other across the table. Despite witnessing the old man's undeniable cruelty, Max liked him. He couldn't help himself. There was a fundamental honesty to him that let you know where you stood.

'I'd offer you coffee but I feel like turning in,' Carver said.

'That's OK,' Max said. 'Just one more thing: what can you tell me about Vincent Paul?'

'I could talk about him all night – although most of it wouldn't interest you,' Carver said. 'But I'll tell you this one thing: I think he's behind Charlie's kidnapping. He's not only someone I think *could* have organized it, but the only one who *would*.'

'Why's that?'

'He hates me. Many do. It's an existential hazard.' Carver grinned.

'Has he been questioned?'

'This isn't America,' Carver guffawed. 'Besides, who'd *dare* go talk to him? The mere mention of that ape's name makes brave men shit their panties.'

'But Mr Carver,' Max said, 'surely you – a man in your position – you could've paid people to . . .'

'To *what*, Max? Kill him? Arrest him? On what "charge" – to put it in your terms? – *suspicion* of kidnapping my grandson? Doesn't hold water.

'Believe me, I looked at every way to bring Paul in – "for questioning", as you say. Can't be done. Vincent Paul's too big a deal here, too powerful. Take him down for no reason and you've got a civil war on your hands. But, with proof, I *can* move on him. So get it for me. And bring back the boy. *Please*. I *implore* you.'

12

Back in the car, heading down the mountain to Pétionville, Max heaved a big sigh of relief. He was glad to be out of that house. He hoped he never had to have dinner with the Carvers again.

He hadn't realized how much the pressure of the evening had gotten to him. His shirt was sweat-stuck to the lining of his jacket and he was picking up the beginnings of a stress headache behind his eyes. He needed to walk, unwind, be alone, breathe free air, think, put things together.

He got the men to drop him off at the bar he'd spotted on their way out. They weren't happy about it, told him 'it not safe' and insisted that they had orders to drive him all the way home. Max thought of showing them his gun to reassure them but he told them everything would be OK, that he wasn't far.

They drove away without so much as a wave. Max watched their tail lights disappear in the night faster than pennies down a well. He glanced down the road to get his bearings.

At the very bottom was the middle of Pétionville – the roundabout and marketplace – lit up in bright orange neon and totally deserted. In between was near complete darkness, broken, here and there, by stray bare bulbs over doorways and in windows, small fires on the roadside and random headlights. Max knew he had to turn down a side-street, walk to the end of it, find the Impasse Carver and follow it home. He now realized he should have let the men drive him back: not only would it be a bitch finding the gate to his compound in the dark, but, more immediately, he didn't know which street led to home. He could see there were at least four to choose from.

He'd have to walk down the hill and try each of the streets until he came to the right one. He remembered being in simple stupid situations like this when he was younger, always drunk and stoned when he hadn't scored. He'd always made it home. Safe and sound. He'd be OK.

But first he needed a drink. Just one – maybe a shot of that six-star deluxe Barbancourt old man Carver had offered him earlier. That would see him home, help him along his way, isolate him from the fear that was starting to whisper in his mind. He was seeing Clyde Beeson in his diaper again and asking himself what had happened to Darwen Medd. He was imagining Emmanuel Michelange with his dick scissored off and stuffed down his throat and wondering if he'd been alive when they'd done that to him. And he was thinking about Boukman, sitting there, somewhere on the street, maybe by one of those small fires, watching him, waiting.

From the outside La Coupole was a small bright-blue house with a rusted corrugated-iron roof, whose eaves were hung with a string of flickering multi-coloured bulbs, similar to the ones surrounding the sign – two wooden planks with the bar name painted in white in a crude jumbled script, part capital, part joined up, part straight, part bent. Small spotlights were trained on the walls and highlighted the chips and cracks in the concrete. The windows were boarded up. Someone had spray-painted 'La Coupole Welcome US' in black on one of the boards, and painted a list of drinks and prices on the other – Bud, Jack and Coke were on sale; nothing else.

Music was thudding from within, but it wasn't loud enough for him to make out more than the bass. It was the only noise in the street, although plenty of people – all of them locals – were hanging around outside the bar talking.

A bald teenager in a grubby white suit with no shirt or shoes was sitting on an old motorbike without mudguards. The seat was sprouting springs and foam from its four corners. The kid was surrounded by a semi-circle of little boys, also bald, all of them looking up at him with awe and respect. The picture belonged in a church – Jesus cast as a Haitian slum kid dressed in a soiled John Travolta disco suit.

Max walked inside. The light was dim and rust tinted, but he could make everything out. It was a lot bigger than he'd expected. He could see where they'd knocked down the back of the original house and built an extension because they either couldn't afford or hadn't bothered to paint the walls a uniform colour. A third of the interior was the same blue as the exterior, while the rest was rough, unadorned, unsanded grey brickwork. The floor was plain cement.

Wooden tables and chairs were stood around the edges of the room and clustered up in the corners. No two tables and chairs were the same. Some were tall and round, others squat and square, one was made up of four banged-together school desks, another was once part of a larger table that had been sawn in half and modified, while there was one table with brass- or copper-capped corners that looked suspiciously like an antique.

There were plenty of people inside, most of them white males. All off-duty American and – he supposed – UN troops. Max could spot his countrymen. Twice as big as their multinational counterparts; one part exercise, one part overeating, one part genes – hefty arms, broad shoulders, small heads and no necks; just like him. Even most of the few women who were around were put together the same way. They were all talking among themselves, telling stories and jokes, laughing, drinking only Bud or Coke out of bottles. They gave Max a blatant once-over when he passed them by. He stood out in his suit and shiny black shoes, overdressed in a room of jeans, shorts, T-shirts and sneakers.

He made his way to the bar. There were no stools, only standing and leaning room. There was exactly one bottle on display behind the counter – standard Barbancourt rum, unopened, yellow paper-cap seal still intact. The beer and Cokes were being served out of an icebox.

Max surprised the barman by asking for rum. The barman got the bottle down, opened it and poured out slightly more than a double measure in a clear plastic beaker. He was going to dump a handful of ice into it but Max remembered being warned not to drink the tap water and shook his head no. He paid in dollars. Two bucks. No change.

The music was coming from the courtyard to the left, through a doorway with no door. An amused-looking Haitian DJ was manning a CD player behind a table, pumping some God-awful HiNRG with an androgynous singer rhyming 'love' with 'dove' in a Germanic accent, while in front of him a few dozen off-duty peacekeepers were dancing like epileptics having fits on an ice rink.

Max felt eyes on him. He turned his head and followed the feeling back to a dark corner near the bar. Two Haitian women were smiling at him, catching his eye, beckoning him. Prostitutes. They had the same look the world over. He felt a tug in his groin, a pull on his balls. Black women and brown women were his favourites, the ones he always gravitated to, the ones who made him stop and double take.

One of the whores started coming over to him, walking awkwardly in a too tight black dress and tall silver heels. He realized he'd been staring at them without seeing them, all the while playing host to his memories and fantasies. They'd sensed his need in an instant, smelled the curdled lust on him. Max stared the woman in the eye and stopped her in her tracks, her smile giving way to a worried look. He shook his head and looked away, back at the DJ and his dancers.

He sipped his drink. The rum was surprisingly good: sweet and mellow on his tongue, easy on his throat. Instead of the bareknuckle hook to the gut he was expecting, it gave him a comforting feeling. First drink in over ten years. The embrace was warm and familiar.

You never really got over an addiction. You could stay clean for the rest of your life, but it was always there, the impulse to start again, shadowing you, walking parallel, ready to catch you if you slipped. It was best to quit a habit when the high was still greater than the low and the pleasure outweighed the pain. That way you kept good memories and had no regrets, like people you meet and leave behind on vacation.

Max hadn't been an alcoholic, but he'd been getting there. He'd had a drink at the end of every shift, no matter when they'd finished up. As early as seven or eight in the morning he and Joe would find the first open bar and sit with people knocking one back on their way to work, and others getting ready to find breakfast after an all-night binge. It was always only the one drink in the mornings – a shot of Irish whiskey, neat, no rocks.

He'd drunk a lot when he'd gone out, but never so much that he'd lost control. It had helped him forget he was a cop and lose the tell-tale aura of battered rectitude and all-seeing otherness cops have about them. It had eased him through difficult social situations. It had gone well with meals and lonely nights. And it had helped him get laid. A lot.

Max had never taken his pleasures by halves. He'd smoked a pack of red Marlboros a day, more when he was drinking and even more when he was on the verge of cracking a case. He'd smoked plenty of reefer with Joe too – good Jamaican shit that never failed to put you in a good place. Joe had stopped when he'd read that smoking too much weed made you psychotic and gave you tits. Max dismissed it as a scare story dreamt up by the FBI's PR department and carried on regardless.

Sandra had helped him quit it all – booze, weed, cigarettes and his job.

Then she'd said yes to marriage.

The night before his wedding he'd deliberately slipped off the wagon. He'd bought a bottle of whiskey and a pack of Marlboro. He'd been free of both for a year, but he wanted to say goodbye to his old ways in style, just the three of them – cigarettes, booze, solitude – together one last time.

He'd driven out to Ocean Drive, sat by the sea and got reacquainted. The cigarette had tasted horrible, the booze had scalded his throat and he felt like a freak looking for trouble out there on his own in the sand, with the cruisers, petty criminals, beach bums and dumb-ass tourists looking to get mugged. He'd doused his cigarette in the bottle, screwed it shut, lobbed it out into the sea and walked away, feeling more stupid than satisfied.

Now the bottle had washed back.

No one was smoking in the bar. Max finished his glass and ordered another.

The drink was loosening him up, helping him to relax and think.

The Carvers: Gustav was scary, but remarkable. Max admired him. The old man ran the show, despite his illness. They'd have to prise the strings from his cold dead hand.

Allain was probably a nicer guy. He'd had other ideas about their business, a more inclusive way of running things. Though he was crushed at home, he wasn't lacking in courage.

There wasn't a lot of love between father and son, maybe none whatsoever, but there was respect – at least from Allain's side – and there was Charlie. Charlie Carver was holding the family together, uniting them.

And the same went for Francesca Carver. She hated him but he saw where she was coming from and he empathized with her, even pitied her. She wanted out of her marriage and out of the Carvers and out of Haiti, but she wasn't leaving without her boy – either literally or figuratively; once she'd found out what had happened to him, once she'd got closure.

The Carvers were dysfunctional but they weren't the worst family he'd ever met. They were standing together in adversity, supporting each other in their own way.

In all likelihood Charlie had been stolen to get back at the old man rather than the son. Gustav was likely to have a phone book's worth of enemies. If they were rich they'd have enough money and clout to delegate a kidnapping to hired hands who wouldn't know who they were working for.

Or did they? Three private investigators had come and gone – one was dead, one was missing presumed dead, one was gruesomely fucked up. All three must have come real close to finding the kid – or led someone to believe they were.

Beeson must have been spooked to hell not to want to come back. He'd once taken a bullet in the gut on a job and he'd been back as soon as they'd let him out of hospital. Nothing stood between him and money.

But what had happened to Darwen Medd? Where was he?

He downed his third rum. People were staying well out of his way. A couple of Americans were talking to the prostitutes. They were all on first-name terms but they'd never done any business. The girls looked uninterested. The soldiers probably didn't want to get AIDS and there wasn't a condom thick enough to dispel the myth that the disease had started in Haiti.

A Haitian man was clinging to the fringes of a small group of Americans, listening intently to their conversation, hanging on to every word, parroting the ones he understood. If someone said 'fuck' or 'shit' or dropped a brand or celebrity name, the Haitian would echo it, slapping his thigh and laughing at an obscenity, or nodding his head and saying 'Yes, man!' or 'That's right yo!' in his impression of an American accent, which sounded like Chinese yodelling. Once in a while the group would look at the guy and laugh, some indulgently, some mockingly. A few would stay quiet; they'd taken a profound dislike to their hanger-on. Max could see it in their faces, the way they stood, the smallness of their eyes when they tried not to look at him, the way they winced when they heard him imitating them. They'd probably wanted nothing more than a quiet night out.

The Haitian was wearing a back-to-front baseball cap, a baggy T-shirt with the stars and stripes on the front and back, loose jeans and Nike sneakers. A real fan of his conquerors.

Then Max saw what was really happening.

The Haitian was actually talking to someone Max hadn't seen, standing in the middle of the group, hidden from view by his comrades. Max only noticed him when one of them went to the bar for more drinks.

He was a buzzcut blond with a tiny nose and a thick moustache. He was having fun with the Haitian, pretending to teach the guy English when all he was really doing was making him demean himself.

Max listened in.

'Repeat after me: – "I",' Buzzcut said, hands moving like an orchestra conductor's.

'Aye –'

'Live –'

'Leave –'

'In –'

'Eeen –'

'A –'

'Ayy –'

'Zoo –'

'Zoooo –'

'Called –'

'Kall –'

'No – Call-*dah* –'

'Kall – *durgh* –'

'Good – I live in a zoo called – Haiti.'

'– Ayiti?'

'What? Yeah, yeah – High tits – whatever the fuck you sambos call this fuck hole,' Buzzcut laughed and his crew harmonized – except for the dissenters, one of whom had caught Max's eye and looked at him in helpless apology, as if to say, it's them not me.

Max didn't give a fuck about him and his educated guilt. It was the Haitian he felt for. It was pitiful to watch and it made Max mad. He was reminded of Sammy Davis Jnr's Uncle Tom routine in those Rat Pack Vegas shows he had on videotape. Frank and Dean would be humiliating him on stage, calling him every polite racist epithet in front of the audience, who'd be whooping and laughing, while Sammy would slap his thigh and clap his hands and open his mouth

147

wide, looking like he thought it was all just a good joke, but his eyes would be cold and detached, his soul someplace else entirely, and that open mouth would suddenly seem to be howling in pain and – mostly – anger, drowned out by a drum roll and cymbals, and more audience guffawing. The Haitian was like Sammy had been, only he wasn't having it so hard because he, at least, didn't understand what Buzzcut was saying and doing to him.

Right then, for the first time in his life, Max felt very briefly ashamed to be an American.

He turned back to the bar and shook his glass at the barman for a refill. The barman poured him his fourth Barbancourt and asked him how he was liking it. Max told him it was just great.

A man walked up to the bar and ordered a drink, speaking in Kreyol. He talked a little with the barman and made him laugh.

He turned to Max, smiled politely and nodded to him. Max nodded back.

'Did you just get here?' the man asked.

Max didn't know if he meant the bar or the country. The rum was starting to kick in hard. He was looking over the edge of sobriety, contemplating the plunge.

'Max Mingus, right?' the man asked.

Max stared at him too long to feign mistaken identity. He said nothing and waited for the man's next move.

'Shawn Huxley.' The man smiled, holding out his hand. Max didn't take it. 'Relax – I'm a journalist.'

Ingratiating tone, ingratiating smile, ingratiating body language: all the mannered sincerity of a snake posing as a used-car salesman.

'Look, I get a list of daily arrivals from my man at the airport – Mingus, Max, AA147. It's not a common name.'

Franco–American accent. Not Haitian, not Cajun. Canadian?

Good-looking guy, close to pretty: smooth caramel skin, oriental eyes, a thin moustache crowning his upper lip and his hair cut in a fade, carefully shaped around the forehead and temples. He wore khakis, a short-sleeved white shirt and sturdy black shoes. He was Max's height and a third of his build.

'Not me,' Max grunted.

'Come on – it's no big thing. I'll buy you a drink and tell you about myself.'

'No,' Max said, turning away and facing the bar.

'I can imagine how you feel about the press, Max. What with those guys in the *Herald* digging all that stuff up about you before your trial – and all the trouble they gave your wife –'

Max glared at Huxley. He didn't like journalists, never had, not even when they'd technically been friends, on the same side. When his trial had gone nationwide the press had dug up every single piece of dirt they could find on him, enough to bury him twenty times over. It played so well – one of the most decorated and respected detectives in Florida, a hero cop, had really built his glittering career on brutalizing suspects into confessions and allegedly planting evidence. They'd camped outside his house, dozens of them. They couldn't get enough of the fact that he was in an interracial marriage. White journalists had asked Sandra if she was his cleaner; black journalists had called her a sell-out, an Aunt Jemima, and condemned him for having a plantation mentality.

'Listen: I wasn't bothering you, but *you* are bothering *me*,' Max barked, loud enough to make people leave their conversations and look over. 'And you mention my wife again and

I *will* tear your head off and shit in the stump. You got that?'

Huxley nodded, looking petrified. Right then Max could have played with Huxley's fear, toyed with it, stirred it into terror and offloaded a few grudges that way, but he let it go. The guy – and all those media guys – had just been doing their jobs and chasing promotions, same as everyone born with ambition and enough ruthlessness to trample over people to get there. If he'd been an upright cop, never cut any corners, done absolutely everything by the book, the press would have been on his side, championing his cause – and he *still* would have done prison time for manslaughter. Either way he'd have lost.

Max needed a piss. He hadn't been since he'd been driven to the Carvers. The tension of the evening had distracted him from his expanding bladder. He looked around the bar, but there didn't seem to be any obvious doorway people disappeared through, let alone anything marked out. He asked the barman, who tilted his head right to a spot behind where the prostitutes were standing.

Max walked over. The girls perked up and smoothed and straightened their dresses with lightning downstrokes and turned on their open, inviting stares. Their looks reminded him of Huxley's look – instant, one-spoon-and-stir friend-ship, trust and discretion, all available for the asking, as long as you paid the price – a salesman shedding his soul piece by piece with every successful deal. Journalists and whores slept in the same bed. Mind you, he thought, how much different was he? Working for the people he had? Looking the other way as he cleaned up their messes? We all did things we didn't want to do for money. It was the way of the world – sooner or later, everything and everyone was for sale.

There were two bathrooms, male and female gender symbols sloppily painted on in bright blue and pink on doors fitted at ankle height above the sloping, dusty floor. In between them was a room behind a wooden bead curtain. There was an open camp bed with a bare pillow on it and an overturned box of Bud with an oil lantern on it. Max guessed it was where the barman or caretaker slept.

Inside the cubicle a polished black cistern was fitted low, level with Max's face. The toilet didn't have a seat and there was no water in the bowl, just a black hole. He pissed a long stream and heard it gurgle where it hit something soft and wet and hollow a few feet under. It smelt faintly of ammonia and rotten flowers – the flavour of the industrial-strength lime and disinfectant they were throwing down after the day's sewage.

Max heard someone walk past the cubicle, light a cigarette and inhale deeply. He stepped out and saw Shawn Huxley in the corridor, close by, back to the wall, one foot up against it.

'Was that interesting? Listening to me piss? Did you get it on tape?' Max sneered. He was drunk, not badly, but enough to recalibrate his centre of balance.

'The Carver boy,' Huxley said. 'That's why you're here, right?'

'What if I am?' Max replied, getting up in Huxley's face, unintentionally spraying him with spit. Huxley blinked but didn't wipe it off. Max focussed on a small pearly drop, hanging off the edge of the journalist's moustache, close to his lip. He'd catch it if he stuck his tongue out.

Max was drunker than he thought. He'd mistaken the point of stopping and turning back with the point of no return. It had been a very long while. When he spat in people's faces he'd already lost control.

'I can help you out,' said Huxley, dragging on his cigarette.

'Don't need you,' Max replied, looking Huxley over. The

journalist was even slighter in bright light, as if he lived on a diet of celery, cigarettes and water.

'I've been here close to three years. Arrived a few months before the invasion. I know my way around. I know the people – how to work their combinations, make them open up.'

'I've got one better,' Max smiled, thinking of Chantale.

'That could be the case, but I think I'm on to something that could be tied in with the kidnapping.'

'Yeah? What's that? And how come you haven't followed it through, all the way to the reward money?' Max asked.

'It's not something you can do alone,' Huxley said, dropping the cigarette he'd smoked to the filter on the floor and grinding it out under his heel.

Max couldn't be sure Huxley was for real. That was the trouble with journalists. You couldn't trust them, not ever. Most of them were born backstabbers with more faces than diamonds.

What's more, why was Huxley offering to *help* him? Journalists never helped anyone but themselves. What was Huxley's angle? Probably financial, Max guessed. The Charlie Carver case wasn't exactly going to make the front pages in North America.

Max decided to go along with Huxley – albeit guardedly. He was in a foreign country that seemed to be losing its grip on the twentieth century and falling backwards through time. Huxley could be useful to him.

'You meet any of my predecessors?' Max asked.

'The short guy – sleazy-looking dude.'

'Clyde Beeson?'

'That's him. I saw him around my hotel a lot –'

'Hotel?'

'The Hotel Olffson – where I'm staying.'

'What was he doing there?'

'Hanging around the journalists, picking up scraps.'

'Sounds about right,' Max muttered. 'So how did you know where he was headed?'

'I heard him asking someone at the bar for directions to the waterfalls one night.'

'Waterfalls?' Max stopped him, remembering where Medd had gone. 'The voodoo place?'

'Yeah. Said he was following up a lead. Last time I ever saw him,' Huxley said. 'Did you know him?'

'Florida PI, what do you expect?' Max replied.

Beeson went to the waterfalls too. What kind of lead were they chasing?

'Were you friends?' Huxley asked.

'No, the opposite,' Max said. 'I went to see him before I came out here. He was pretty fucked up, to say the least.'

'What happened to him?'

'Don't ask.'

Huxley looked Max right in the eye and pulled an ambiguous smile – part knowing, part amused – the sort that people used when they wanted you to think they knew more than they did. Max wasn't going to fall for that shit. He'd used it himself.

'Did Beeson mention Vincent Paul to you?'

'Yeah, he did,' Max said.

'Vincent Paul, *Le Roi de Cité Soleil*. That's what they call him, the scared rich folk – after Louis XIV, the glamorous French king. It's meant as an insult.'

'How so?'

'Vincent lives in or around Cité Soleil – Shit City, as I call it. It's this gigantic slum outside of Port-au-Prince, by the coast. Makes your hoods back home look like Park Avenue. In fact, there's nothing like Cité Soleil anywhere in the *world*.

I've been to slums in Bombay, Rio, Mexico City – *paradise* in comparison. Here you're talking close to half a million people – that's near ten per cent of the population – living on six square miles of shit and disease. Literally. Place even has its own canal. "The Boston Canal", they call it. It's filled with old oil from the power plant.'

Max had taken everything in. Concentrating on the inflowing information had sobered him, helped clear his mind.

'And you say that's where I can find Vincent Paul?'

'Yeah. They say he who runs Cité Soleil runs Haiti. The people there are so poor, if you promise them food, clean water and clothes they'll throw bricks at whoever you point to. Some say Paul's paid by the CIA. Whenever they want a President ousted they get him to stir up Cité Soleil.'

'Do you think that's true?'

'The only way would be to ask the man himself, and you don't do that. He talks to *you*, not the other way round.'

'Has he talked to you?'

'Had an appointment a while back, but he changed his mind.'

'Why?'

'Didn't say,' Huxley chuckled.

'Do you know anything about this town he's meant to have built?' Max asked.

'Only that no one knows where it is. No one's ever been there.'

'Do you think it exists?'

'Maybe, maybe not. You never can tell very much about anything in Haiti. This country runs on myths, rumours, hearsay, gossip. The truth has a way of getting lost and disbelieved.'

'Do you think Vincent Paul's got anything to do with Charlie Carver's disappearance?' Max asked.

'Why don't we meet up tomorrow or the day after and have a long talk, see what we can see, maybe work out a way of helping each other,' Huxley said, smiling. He crushed his cigarette out.

Max guessed Huxley had been leading up to this moment, feeding him bigger and bigger scraps of information, getting him hungrier and hungrier before closing the kitchen and rewriting the rules his way. He'd been played.

'What's in it for you?' Max asked.

'My Pulitzer,' Huxley smiled. 'I'm writing a book about the invasion and its aftermath – you know, the bullshit you'll never read about in the papers. You wouldn't believe what's been going on here, what people have been getting away with.'

'Like what?'

Just then Buzzcut walked in. He looked over at Max and Huxley and smiled snidely, showing wolfish canine teeth.

'Hello, ladies,' he sneered.

He tossed Max a disgusted look. His grey-green eyes might have been attractive, were they not so small and cold, icy bright pinpricks in a face which breathed meanness.

He walked into the room between the cubicles. They heard him draining his bladder all over the bed and the box and the floor. They looked at each other. Max saw contempt in Huxley's eyes – but it ran deep, all through him, from the very bottom of his heart.

The soldier finished and came out of the room, doing up his zipper. He shot them another look and belched long and loud in their direction.

Max looked at him, gave him the right amount of attention, but was careful not to lock eyes with him. Most people you could stare down if you let them think you had nothing to lose; others you had to let stare you down, no matter how much you knew you could fuck them up. It was all about choosing your moment and reading your people. And this was all wrong.

Buzzcut walked out of the corridor and back to the bar.

Huxley took out another cigarette. He tried to light it but his hands were shaking worse than a detoxing wino's. Max took the lighter from him and worked the flame.

'It's shit like that – shit like *him* – I'm writing about,' Huxley spat through his first cloud of smoke, his voice quivering with anger. 'Fucking Americans should be ashamed of themselves having a scumbag like *that* fighting in their name.'

Max agreed with him, but didn't say so.

'So you *are* Haitian, Shawn?'

Huxley was taken aback.

'You see a lot, don't you, Max?'

'Only what's there,' Max said, but he'd only just guessed.

'You're right: I was born here. I was adopted by a Canadian couple when I was four, after my parents died. They told me about my heritage a few years back, before I went to college,' Huxley explained.

'So this is like a *Roots*-type thing for you?'

'More a fruit from the tree-type thing. I know where I came from,' said Huxley. 'Call this – what I'm doing – giving a little something back.'

Max warmed to him. It wasn't just the rum or their shared loathing of Buzzcut. There was a sincerity about Huxley you didn't find in the media: maybe he was new to the game and still had most of his cherry or maybe he hadn't wised up that it *was* a game at all, thought he was on a mission, chasing 'the truth'. Max had had ideals once, when he'd started out as a cop, young enough to believe in bullshit like people's inherent good and that things could improve and change for the better; he'd fancied himself some kind of superhero. It had taken him less than a week on the streets to turn into an extreme cynic.

'Where can I reach you?' Max asked.

'I'm at the Hotel Olffson. Most famous hotel in Haiti.'

'Is that saying anything?'

'Graham Greene stayed there.'

'Who?'

'Mick Jagger too. In fact I'm in the same room he stayed in when he wrote "Emotional Rescue". You don't look too impressed, Max. Not a Stones fan?'

'Anyone important been a guest of the place?' Max smirked.

'None you'd know,' Huxley laughed, and handed him his business card. It gave his name and profession, and the hotel's address and phone number.

Max palmed the card and slipped it in his jacket pocket, next to the signed Sinatra CD Carver had given him.

'I'll be in touch as soon as I've found my bearings,' Max promised.

'Please do that,' Huxley said.

13

Max left La Coupole at around 2.00 am. The Barbancourt rum was making his head reel, but not in an unpleasant way. Booze had always promised to take him up someplace good only to fuck with his controls and leave him stranded midway, tasting the inevitable crash. This was a different kind of drunk, closer to an opiate float. He had a smile on his face and that good feeling in his heart that everything would be all right and the world wasn't such a bad place really. The booze was *that* good.

Dark telegraph poles leaned out of the concrete, tilting slightly forward, towards Pétionville's brightly lit centre. The wires were slung so low and loose Max could have touched them if he'd wanted to. He was walking in the street, barely feeling his footsteps, bracing his body against the downward pull of gravity which threatened to send him sprawling flat on his face. Behind him people were coming out of the bar, spilling conversation and laughter that died to murmurs and splutters in the deep silence that confronted them. Some Americans tested the rigidity of the stillness with a one-off scream or shout or a bark or miaow, but the quietness sucked the noise into more silence.

Max didn't know exactly which street he had to turn down. He couldn't remember how many he'd passed on his way up before he'd noticed the bar. He was close to the centre of town, but not that close, somewhere in the middle. He passed one road, looked down it but it wasn't the right one. There was a supermarket on the left and a graffitied wall to the right. Maybe the next road. Or the next. Or the one before. He'd meant to ask Huxley for directions, in-between one of the four or five other drinks they'd had together. He'd forgotten. Then he'd stopped caring sometime after he'd lost count of the amount of drinks he'd had. The Barbancourt had told him he'd find his way home *no problem*. He carried on walking.

His shoes were starting to pinch the sides of his feet and scrape off the flesh on his ankles. He hated them, those nice new shiny leather slip-ons he'd bought at Saks Fifth Avenue at Dadeland Mall. He should have broken them in before he'd put them on. He didn't like the clack-clack the heels were making in the road. He sounded like a young horse in *its* first shoes.

And then there were the drums – not any closer than when he'd first heard them, but clearer, the sound raining down from the mountains like rusty cutlery; a full battery of snares, tom-toms, bass drums and cymbals. The rhythms had a jagged edge. They'd gone straight for the drunk part of his brain, the part he'd hit when he'd fallen off the wagon, the part that would hurt like a motherfucker in the morning.

Someone tugged at his left sleeve.

'Blan, blan.'

It was a child's voice, hoarse, almost broken, a boy's.

Max looked from side to side and saw no one. He turned around and looked back up the road. He saw the bar's lights and people in the distance, but nothing else.

'Blan, *blan*.'

Behind him, the other way, downhill. Max turned around, slowly.

His brain was on the graveyard shift, everything taking its time to fall into place, adjust, calculate. His vision had dancing ripples before it, as if he was at the bottom of a deep lake, watching pebbles falling through the surface.

He barely made the boy out in the darkness, just a hint of silhouette against the orange neon.

'Yes?' Max said.

'Ban moins dollah!' the boy shouted.

'What?'

'*Kob*, ban moins ti kob!'

'Are you – hurt?' Max inquired, stumbling in and then out of cop mode.

The boy came right up to him. He had his hands out.

'Dollah! Ban moins *dollaaarrrggh*!' he screamed.

Max blocked his ears. The little fucker could scream.

'*Dollah*'? Money. He wanted money.

'No dinero,' Max said, putting his hands up and showing him his empty palms. 'No money.'

'Ban moins dollah donc,' the boy whined, breathing hotly all over Max's still open palms.

'No dollar. No peso, no red fucking cent,' Max said and carried on walking down.

The boy followed him, from behind. Max stepped a little faster. The boy stayed on his heels, calling after him, louder.

'*Blan*! *Blan*!'

Max didn't turn around. He heard the sound of the child's feet scuttling after him, soft footfalls underscoring his cracking heels. The boy wasn't wearing any shoes.

He walked faster. The child stayed right on his tail.

He passed a road he thought looked familiar and stopped abruptly. The boy thudded against the back of his legs and pushed him. Max bounced two steps down, losing his balance and his bearings. He took a couple of wild desperate steps to steady himself but put his foot through a sudden empty space where there should have been road. His leg went down, down, down. And then his foot splashed into a puddle. By then he'd already tilted too far over. He fell straight down, landing hard on his front, bumping and grazing his chin. He heard something scrape away down the road.

He lay still for a few seconds and assessed the damage. His legs were OK. No real pain. His torso and chin didn't hurt, much. He was conscious of something nasty, the notion of pain, waving at him behind opaque glass, but it was a crooked shadow in a still beautiful, silky mist. In the days before general anaesthetic, they must have given future amputees Barbancourt communion.

The boy laughed, frog-like, over his head.

'Blan sa sou! Blan sa sou!'

Max didn't know what the fuck he meant. He got up, pulled his leg out of the crater and turned around, uphill, pissed off as hell, his chest now stinging with pain. The rum's spell was broken and all the nightmares had come rushing back. Half his trouser leg was soaked in a cocktail of piss, dead oil and matured sewage.

'Fuck off!' he shouted.

But he couldn't see the boy. He was gone. In his place, in front of him, stood about a dozen street urchins, all no taller than ten year olds. He picked out the edges of their heads and their teeth, those who had them or were baring them, and the whites of their eyes. They weren't tall, below his shoulder-height at the most. He could smell them – stale woodsmoke, boiled vegetables, earth, moonshine, sweat, decay. He could feel them peering at him through the darkness.

There were no lights on this stretch of road, no inbound or outbound cars. The bar lights were now pinpoints in the distance. How far down had he come? He stared quickly to the street on his left. Two rows of boys were standing across

161

it, blocking his way. He wasn't even sure it was the street he wanted. He had to retrace his steps, maybe go back to the bar, start again. Ask for directions this time.

He started forward but stopped. He'd lost his shoe in the crater. He looked down at the road, but he couldn't find the hole he'd gone down. He touched at the ground with the ball of his foot but felt solid asphalt.

The drumming had suddenly stopped, as if the players had seen what was happening and come over to look. Max felt like he'd gone deaf.

He took off his other shoe, slipped it in his jacket pocket and started to walk up the hill. He stopped again. There were more kids than he thought. They were stretched out all the way across the road. He was standing right in front of them, close enough to inhale nothing but their gutter-fresh stench. He was going to say something but he heard small whisperings behind him, words evaporating in the air like raindrops on a hot tin roof.

When he turned around there was another cordon of boys, roping off the way down. He noticed shapes now moving up from Pétionville town centre. More children, heading his way. They were carrying things – sticks, it seemed, big sticks, clubs.

They were coming for him. They were coming to kill him.

He heard a rock fall off a pile to his left and roll down into the street. The whispering around him increased to tones of rebuke, all coming now from the same direction. He followed the sound and traced it to the doorway of an empty building. He looked closer, pushed into the darkness for the lightest tones, and he saw that they were passing out rocks, to each other down the line. Half of them already had one in their hands, held down by their sides. When everyone was armed, he supposed, they'd rain them down on him. Then the others would beat the life out of him with their clubs.

His mouth went dry. He didn't know what to do. He couldn't think. He couldn't sober up.

The rum came rushing back to him. His body suddenly felt good, his throbbing chin dulled, his head was light again. He was brave and invincible.

It didn't seem so bad. He'd been through worse than this. He could push his way through. Why not give it a try? What the hell?

He took a couple of steps back and squared his shoulders for the bulldozer run. He could hear them behind him. He didn't look. Could they see what he was doing? Probably. These kids lived in the dark. Had they second-guessed him?

When he charged he'd knock three or four of them down. They'd pelt him with rocks, but if he kept his head covered and ran like a motherfucker he'd escape the worst of the barrage.

Uphill, drunk, not so young any more. Where was he going?

They'd chase him and he wouldn't know where to turn. He'd worry about that later.

And how many were there?

A hundred. Easily. He was dead.

The rum rush deserted him. Optimism split on him too.

The drum started again – just the one, the same deep slow beat he'd heard in the courtyard earlier in the evening. This time it sounded like bombs dropping on a distant town or a battering ram striking a city's gates. The beat didn't go into his heart but right behind his ears, every note a grenade exploding in his skull, sending shockwaves down his spine, making him wince and shudder.

Think again, he told himself. One more try. If that fails, run.

'You want money?' he pleaded, despite himself. No response. The rocks were passed on in silence, the kill hands filling up, the circle almost closed. It seemed hopeless.

Then he remembered his gun. He was armed, full clip.

Suddenly a motorbike roared into life at the top of the hill, the engine shocking the night like a chainsaw in a chapel. It was the kid in the white suit.

He came down the hill, the bike slowing to a growl and then a purr as it came up to the circle around Max.

The kid put his bike down and came over to Max.

'*Sa wap feh là, blan?*' he spoke in a deep ragged voice that belonged to someone five times his age.

'I don't understand,' Max slurred. 'You speak English?'

'Inglishhh?'

'Yeah, English. You speak?'

The kid stood his ground and looked at him.

Max heard it before he saw it, something slicing through the air, something heavy, aimed right at his head. He ducked and the kid in the suit swung into space.

Max dug a furious left-right combination into the kid's ribs and solar plexus. The kid gasped and cried out as he folded over like paper, sticking his chin straight out for a right hook, which Max slammed home and sent him sprawling to the floor.

Max grabbed the kid in a choke hold, pulled out his Beretta and jammed the barrel through his mouth.

'Back the fuck up or he dies!' he yelled, looking all around him. The kid was flailing at him with his hands, kicking at the ground, trying to tip Max over. Max stamped on one of the kid's hands with his bare heel. He heard bones give and a strangled cry boil in the middle of the kid's throat.

No one moved.

What now?

He couldn't exactly drag the kid around with him as he looked for his way home, checking every street until he found it. No way. Maybe he could use him as a shield, push him as far away from the crowd as possible, then cut him loose and go on his way.

No way would they let him.

He could try and shoot his way out.

But no, he wouldn't use it. Not on fucking *children*.

He'd fire in the air and run as they hit the deck or scattered or panicked.

'*Put your gun away!*'

Max jumped.

The booming voice had come from above, in the black sky, behind him, downhill. Still keeping his hold on the kid Max shuffled round towards Pétionville. The view ahead was completely blocked by the man's body, which Max couldn't see but sensed, massive and heavy, the thunder in dark roiling clouds.

'I *won't* ask you again,' the man insisted.

Max took his gun out of the kid's mouth and slipped it back in his holster.

'Now let him go.'

'He tried to fucken' kill me!' Max yelled.

'*Let him GO!*' the man boomed, making some children jump and drop their rocks.

Max freed his assailant.

The man barked something in Kreyol and blinding white overhead lights came on. Max looked away, hand up against the glare. He saw the kid on the floor, blood all down the front of his suit.

Suddenly Max could see every millimetre of the immediate street. The children were standing around him three rows deep. They were all skinny, dressed in filthy rags, many only in shorts, turned away from the light, hands shielding their eyes from the glare.

The same voice barked in Kreyol again.

The kids all dropped their rocks in a collective crash. The rocks rolled down the road, some thudding into Max's bare feet.

Max squinted into the lights. The voice was coming from above the row of swamplights.

The voice boomed again and the children scampered, a stampede of tiny, mostly bare feet ripping down the road, puttering away as fast as they could. Max saw them running through Pétionville's square, over a hundred of them. They would have torn him to pieces.

He heard the sound of a big engine turning over and saw twin sets of exhaust fumes rising up behind the lights in the shape of upended pine trees. It looked like a military jeep. He hadn't even heard it coming.

The man's accent was straight-up English – not a hint of French or American in it.

Max felt the man looking down on him, at least a good extra foot taller. And he felt his presence – powerful, magnetic and crushing – enough to fill a palace.

He came closer to Max.

Max looked but couldn't see his face.

The man reached down and grabbed the kid by the middle of his jacket and plucked him clean off the ground like he was picking up something he'd dropped and come back for. Max only saw his bare forearm – thickly veined and heavily muscled, bigger than one of Joe's biceps – and his fist – blunt and heavy and crude as a sledgehammer head. Max swore the man had six fingers. He'd counted five knuckles not four when he'd seen the hand bunch up the boy's suit jacket into a handle.

166

The man was a giant.

And the man, Max guessed, was Vincent Paul.

The overhead lights went out and the main ones flicked on, dazzling Max all over again. The engine kicked into action.

Max's vision regrouped in time to see the jeep reversing quickly down the hill. It reached the roundabout, turned left and headed off down the road. Max tried to see the people inside but he couldn't make anyone out. From where he stood it looked empty, driven by spirits.

14

When they were gone Max stumbled around the now empty streets, looking for the elusive road home. The drunkenness came and went in waves, dumb dizziness tripping over moments of lucidity.

Eventually, by a process of elimination which involved retracing his steps to the bar and then going down each of the four right-hand turn-offs between the bar and the centre of town, he found the Impasse Carver.

It was the road he'd been closest to when he'd been surrounded by the kids.

Back at the house, Max went to his room and took out his wallet, unclipped his holster and gun and dropped them on the bed. He peeled off his suit, turned beige to brown, sweat-soaked all the way through to his back and underarms and butt. It was ruined. The trousers stank. The left leg was black and stiff and sticky up to the knee.

It was hot and humid inside. He turned on the fan to stir up the dead air and blow up some cool breeze. His hands were shaking, currents of fear and rage passing back and forth through his veins and arteries, making his heart pound fast, pumping adrenalin into his bloodstream. He was thinking back to those kids. Part of him wanted to go back outside and kick their raggedy, Live Aid handout asses to voodoo heaven. Another part of him wanted out of this godforsaken country on the next boatpeople armada. And another part of him was curled up and made small and hiding its humbled head in shame.

He remembered Huxley's card and the Sinatra CD in his pocket. The card was still there but the CD was gone. He realized that it had been knocked out of his pocket when he'd fallen down the crater. He bundled the suit up and tossed it into a corner of the room. He undid his shirt and wiped himself down, then he took off his underwear, balled them all together and walked to the bathroom where he tossed them into the laundry basket before getting into the shower.

He turned on the water and a freezing cold white streak tore out of the showerhead and blasted his skin. He gasped in shock and went to turn down the jet, but he sensed all the pent-up rage and fear and frustration churning inside him, unspent and untapped, the kind of thing that would bug him every time he stepped out of the house if he didn't release it, vent it. He turned the faucet up full, making the pipes shake and rattle and threaten to pop the brackets that held them against the wall. He let the icy water bash and pound into his flesh until it started to hurt. He held on to the pain as he focussed on the humiliation he'd just had to crawl his way out of.

He'd been shamed, shamed by a bunch of little *kids*. They'd have killed him if it hadn't been for that guy in the jeep. What could you do when it was *kids* who were threatening to take your life? If you killed them you burnt in hell. If you didn't they burned you.

No solution, no release. His anger crawled away until it found a hole big enough to hide in and wait for the poor unsuspecting bastard who provoked it.

He dried off and went back to his room. He was too damn hopped up to sleep. He wanted more rum. He knew he shouldn't, that it was the wrong way to drink, that if he did he'd be taking familiar steps back to alcoholism, but right now, at this moment, he didn't give a good fuck about any of that.

He changed into khakis and a white T-shirt and padded to the kitchen.

He opened the door and switched on the light.

Francesca Carver was sat at the table.

'The fuck are you doing here?' Max snapped, taking a step back in shock.

'I've come to talk to you.'

'How did you get in?'

'We *own* this house, remember?' she answered with haughty impatience.

'What do you want to talk about?'

'It's about Charlie – things you need to know before you go any further.'

Max went off and got his notebook and tape recorder, while Francesca sat at the table, drinking a glass of bottled water she'd found in the fridge and smoking a French Gitane cigarette that came in a fancy-looking blue and white pack. They stank like hell but they suited her – the sort of thick all-white cigarettes classic movie heroines from the forties and fifties were always puffing on at the end of holders.

Max guessed he hadn't smelled her cigarettes when he'd walked into the house because the stench coming off him had been far worse.

'Before I start, you've got to promise me one thing,' she said, when Max returned.

'That depends,' Max said. She looked very different, much prettier, more relaxed, less ravaged. She'd changed into a pale-blue blouse and long denim skirt and sneakers. She wore her hair down and a little make-up, much of it concentrated around her eyes.

'You can't repeat *any* of this to Gustav.'

'Why not?'

'Because it'd break his heart if he knew — and with his heart already hanging on a thread. Can you promise me this?'

Bullshit, Max thought. She had no love for Gustav Carver. Besides, what kind of fool did she take him for, packaging it all in soft, plaintive tones, reaching for his nearest fattest heartstring? She must have been to acting school to do that with her voice, change pitch, wrap each word in a tear before uttering it.

'What's the real reason?' Max asked, looking her straight in the eyes, finding the pupils, holding them.

She didn't flinch. Her eyes met his and held them. Her stare was cold and hard and remorseless. It said: seen the very worst, seen it all, seen *too much* of it; *still* standing — *fuck you*.

'If Gustav knew what I'm about to tell you, he'd be absolutely livid.'

'You mean Charlie's not *his* grandson?'

'*No!* — and how *dare* you!' she snapped. She looked disgusted. Her face flushed light purple, stare-stabbing him. She took a short drag on her cigarette and dumped it in the cup half filled with water she'd taken to using as an ashtray. The butt hissed as it went out.

'Sorry,' Max smiled at her. 'Just checking.'

She'd walked right into it. Good — a weakness. He didn't know if he'd hit a raw nerve buried under a truth or upset an applecart of prudity. He was stabbing in the dark, testing the depth of her sincerity. So far she was holding up.

'Tell me what you want to tell me, Mrs Carver.'

'I want your word.'

'Are you sure?' Max asked.

'You haven't much else to offer me, have you?'

He laughed. Stuck-up bitch. She wanted his word? Sure, why not? What was the big deal? He could always break it. It wouldn't be the first time. Words, promises, handshakes and vows meant nothing to him outside friendship.

'I give you my word, Mrs Carver,' Max said, sounding sincere and reflecting it in the steady eyes he fixed on Francesca. She appraised him and seemed satisfied.

The cassette recorder was on and picking up everything she was saying. Max had done this from time, taped all conversations with clients and witnesses and suspects incognito.

'You were on the right track, back there in the house, about Eddie Faustin,' she began. 'He *was* involved in the kidnapping. He was the inside man.'

'You came *here* to tell me that?'

'I wanted to speak to you freely. I couldn't talk to you in front of Gustav. He won't hear a bad word about Faustin. The man took a bullet for him and that makes him a saint in Gustav's book,' Francesca said, pulling hard on another cigarette. 'He's so *stubborn*. No matter what I told him happened during the kidnapping, he just dismissed it completely – said I couldn't *possibly* remember anything because I'd been knocked out. And even afterwards, when we went through Faustin's quarters and found what he had in there –'

She broke off and held her forehead in her fingertips, rubbing circles around her skin. It looked more dramatic than therapeutic.

'What did you find?'

'Faustin used to live in the old stables, behind the main plantation house. They were converted into small apartments for the family's most trusted *restavecs*. After the kidnapping his apartment was emptied and they found a doll – a voodoo doll – in a box under his bed. The doll was of me.'

'Did he hate you?'

'No. This was a love – or lust – charm. It was made with my real hair, and the wax was embedded with my fingernail and toenail clippings. He'd collected them, or paid one of the maids to collect them.'

'Did you ever suspect he was doing that?'

'Not at all. Faustin was a trusted employee. Always polite, very professional.'

'You didn't feel that he had any desires for you – ever catch him looking at you . . . inappropriately?'

'No. Servants know their place here.'

'Sure they do, Mrs Carver. That's why Faustin helped kidnap your son,' Max slipped in sarcastically.

Francesca flushed angrily.

Max didn't want to piss her off too much in case she clammed up. He moved it along:

'What happened on the day of the kidnapping?'

She stubbed out her cigarette and lit another almost immediately.

'It was on the morning of Charlie's third birthday. You could see the American warships that were bringing the invading troops, right there on the horizon, opposite Port-au-Prince harbour. Everyone was saying the Americans were going to bomb the National Palace. There was rioting and looting going on in Port-au-Prince. People would leave their homes in the mountains and walk down to the city with carts and wheelbarrows to carry the stuff they were looting from shops and houses in the capital. It was anarchy.

'You'd know how bad it was by smelling the air. If you picked up the smell of burning rubber, it meant looting and rioting was going on. Protesters closed off roads with barricades of burning tyres. Sometimes you could look out and see these two or three columns of thick black smoke stretching all the way from Port-au-Prince up to the sky. That would mean it was *really* bad.

'And it was *really* bad when we drove into town in the bulletproof SUV that morning. Rose – his nanny – was sitting in the back with Charlie and me. He was happy. He let me play with his hair: I was running it in and out of my fingers. We were going to the Rue du Champs de Mars, not too far from the National Palace.

'It was very *very* dangerous in town that day. Constant gunfire. I lost count of the bodies we passed in the streets. Faustin said we needed to stop somewhere secluded and wait for the shooting to stop, so we parked in the Boulevard des Veuves. It's usually packed, but that day it was deserted. I knew something was very wrong with Faustin. He was sweating a lot and he'd been looking at me in the rearview mirror the whole drive down.

'All our cars are meant to have loaded guns under the seats. I checked under mine. Nothing. Faustin saw me looking and when I caught his eye again he smiled as if to say "they're not there, are they?" He'd locked the doors. I tried not to show how scared I was getting.

'The gunfire died down. Rose asked Faustin why we weren't moving. Faustin told her to mind her own business – really rudely. I shouted at him to watch his mouth. He told me to shut up. That's when I knew something was really *really* wrong. I got hysterical. I screamed at him to let us out of the car. He didn't reply. Then some kids turned up outside. Just street kids. They saw our car and came over. They looked inside. One of them said Faustin's name and started shouting and pointing at us.

'More people started coming over – adults now, with machetes and clubs and tyres and cans of gasoline. They were chanting "Faustin-*Assassin*, Faustin-*Assassin*" over and over. Faustin used to be a feared Tonton Macoute. He'd made a lot of enemies, a lot of people wanted him dead.

'The crowd massed up around the car. Someone threw a rock at the back window. It bounced off without damaging the car, but it was some kind of signal because they stormed us. Faustin drove out of there, but he didn't get far because people had put up a barricade at the end of the road. He started reversing but the mob had caught up with us. We were trapped.'

Francesca stopped there and took a deep breath. She'd turned pale, her stare cowering.

'Take your time,' Max said.

'People came out from behind the barricades and rushed at the car,' she continued. 'Pretty soon it was surrounded. People were chanting "Faustin-*Assassin*" and then they were hitting the car with clubs and rocks, kicking it and rocking it. They smashed the windows. And then they started stabbing at the corners of the roof with something. Faustin got a machine gun out from under his seat. Rose was screaming. So was I, I suppose. Charlie was calm through it all, just looking out at everything like it was so much scenery. The last thing I remember is running my hand through his hair, hugging him, telling him everything would be OK. After that ... The next thing I remember was coming to in the road.

'I was lying in the same street, but hundreds of yards away from the car. I don't know how I got that far. There was this old woman in a pink dress, sitting on the other side of the road, in front of a cobbler's, looking straight at me.'

'*Where* was she sat?'

'In front of a cobbler's – a shoemaker's,' she explained.

'What did you do next?'

'I went back to the car. It was overturned. The street was empty. There was blood everywhere.'

'How badly were you hurt?'

'Just concussed. A few bruises, a couple of cuts. Rose was dead. Faustin was gone. And so was my little boy,' she said, lowering her head.

She started crying. Silent rolling tears first, then sniffles, and finally the deluge.

Max paused the tape and went to the bathroom and fetched some toilet tissue. He gave it to her and sat and watched as she cried herself dry. He held her and it helped her get through the worst. He didn't mind her so much now, and he was sure she wouldn't mind him much now either. She had no choice.

'Let me fix us some coffee,' Francesca offered, standing up.

He sat back and watched as she took a steel percolator and a round metal tin from one of the row of fixed glass-fronted cupboards running along the wall over the sink. The kitchen was painted a glossy cream-yellow, easy to wipe clean.

Francesca added bottled water and coffee to the pot and put it on the stove. She went to another cupboard and pulled down two cups and saucers. She wiped the insides of the cups with a dishcloth she found on top of the fridge. She seemed to be enjoying herself, as a tiny smile made its way to her lips and lit up parts of her eyes as she busied herself. Max supposed she missed a life without servants.

He looked at his watch. It had gone 4.15. It was still dark outside but he could hear the first birds of morning chirruping in the garden, competing with the insects. Chantale was due at the house at 8.00. Too late to go to bed. He'd have to skip a day.

The coffee brewed with a low whistle. Francesca decanted the coffee into a Thermos pot and brought it over to the table with the cups, saucers, spoons, a jug of cream and a bowl of sugar all on a tray. Max tasted the coffee. It was the same stuff he'd had at Carver's club. Probably the family's homegrown brand.

They sat in near silence. Max complimented her on the coffee. She smoked first one then another cigarette.

'Mrs Carver —?'

'Why don't you call me Francesca?'

'Francesca — what were you and your son doing going to Port-au-Prince that day?'

Max lifted the pause button on his tape recorder.

'We had an appointment.'

'Who with?'

'A man called Filius Dufour. Well, no ordinary man, a *houngan* — a voodoo priest.'

'You were taking Charlie to see a *voodoo priest* on his *birthday*?' Max said, sounding more surprised than he actually was. The local religion was well entrenched in the Carver household. He remembered how defensive of it Allain had been.

'I'd been taking him to see Filius once a week every week for six months.'

'Why?'

'Filius was helping us — Charlie and me.'

'How?'

'How long have you got?'

'As long as you need,' Max said.

Francesca checked Max's watch. Max inspected the amount of tape in his machine. It was a two-hour cassette, almost through on the first side. He fast forwarded it and turned it over. He hit record as soon as she started speaking.

'Charlie was born in Miami on 4 September 1991. One of the nurses screamed when she saw his face. It looked like he'd been born with a pitch black caul, but it was only his hair. He was born with it all, you see. It sometimes happens.

'We came back to Haiti three weeks later. The country was then being run by Aristide – a kind of mob rule masquerading as a government. A lot of people were leaving. Not just the boat people, but the rich, all the business brains. Gustav insisted on staying put, even though Aristide had twice singled us out in public speeches as white people who'd "stolen" everything from the poor black Haitians. Gustav knew Aristide was going to get overthrown. He was friendly with some of the military and he was just as friendly with some of Aristide's key people.'

'He gets around,' Max said.

'Gustav subscribes to the "Keep your friends close, your enemies closer" maxim.'

'Does he have any friends?' Max asked.

Francesca laughed hard and then met his eyes and held them for a moment. Max sensed her probing him, looking for where his comment had come from. She found nothing she could be sure of.

'Aristide was overthrown on 30 September. Gustav threw a party that night. Aristide was meant to have been assassinated, but there was a change of plan. It was a happy party, nonetheless.

'Charlie was christened a month later. I knew something wasn't right with him from the very beginning. When I was a teenager I baby-sat my nephews and niece when they were babies and they were very different to Charlie. They were responsive. They recognized me. Charlie wasn't like that. He never looked at me directly. He never seemed particularly interested. He never reached out to me, he never smiled. Nothing. And – here's the odd thing – he didn't cry.'

'Not at all?'

'Not ever. He made *sounds* – baby sounds – but I never heard him cry. Babies cry all the time. They cry if they wet themselves or poo themselves. They cry when they're hungry. They cry when they want your attention. Not Charlie. He was very *very* quiet. Sometimes it was like he wasn't there.

'We had a doctor checking up on him every week or so. I mentioned it to him, the boy's silence. He joked and told me to make the most of it, that it wouldn't last.

'But, of course, it did. Allain told me not to worry, that Gustav himself didn't start talking until he was almost four.'

Francesca stopped and lit another cigarette. Max was getting used to the smell.

'Actually, I say Charlie wasn't responsive, but he *always* smiled at Gustav. And I heard him laugh too whenever the old man pulled faces at him or tickled him. They had a real bond. Gustav was really really proud of Charlie. He always made time for him. Took him with him to the bank a few times. Sat with him at night, fed him, changed him. It was very touching, seeing them together. I'd never seen Gustav happier. He isn't too good with his other grandchildren. Not as attentive. Charlie's his only grandson. I think he wants to die safe in the knowledge that the family name will be preserved, live on. He's old-fashioned, but this whole country isn't much more advanced than him.'

Max poured himself another cup of coffee. The first had chased the tiredness out of his bones and out from behind his eyes.

'So, this – Charlie's condition – was playing on your mind

when you went to see the voodoo priest? It wasn't about you at all, was it? It was about your son. You thought something was wrong with him so you took him to the priest for an opinion?'

'Yes and no. It's not quite like that. Charlie had a thing about his hair . . .'

'I saw the picture,' Max said shortly. 'Him in that dress.'

'He wouldn't let anybody cut it . . .'

'So your husband explained,' Max said distastefully.

'We really had no choice. People were making Charlie's life a misery.'

'Was this before or after you put him in a dress?' Max said sarcastically.

'That was for his own *good*,' Francesca insisted, testily. 'You know that Charlie screamed anytime someone went near him with a pair of scissors?'

'Yes, Allain told me.'

'Did he tell you *how* he screamed? It wasn't a baby's scream, or even a little boy's scream. It was pure *pain* – this blood-curdling, ear-splitting screech. Imagine a cave of screeching bats. People said they could hear it two miles away.'

Max paused the tape. Francesca had upset herself with the recollection. She was biting her lip and trying hard not to cry. He wanted to hold her and let her loose the grief on his shoulder, but it didn't feel appropriate. He was interviewing her, gathering evidence, not acting as her counsellor or confessor.

'Explain the dress,' he said, after she'd seen off the tears. He already knew the answer but was easing her back into the Q & A.

'Charlie's hair was never cut. It got unwieldy. We tied it in bunches and bows, and finally we plaited it. It was easier to put him in a dress and present him to the outside world as a girl than to explain why his hair was that way. It worked, you know. He wore a dress the whole time,' Francesca said.

'How did you find out about the voodoo priest?'

'One day, out of the blue, Rose brought me a handwritten message from him. It mentioned things about me and Charlie that no one – and I mean *no one* – could have known.'

'Care to elaborate?'

'No,' she said bluntly. 'But if you're as good as Allain says you are, you'll surely find out.'

Max continued with his questions.

'How did Rose know the priest?'

'Her friend, Eliane, works for him.'

'I see,' Max said, already lining up potential suspects. 'Could Rose have known about these "things" you won't tell me about?'

'No.'

'Not even in a place as small as this?'

'No.'

'OK. So you and Charlie went along to see the priest? What happened there?'

'He talked to me, and then he talked to Charlie, separately, in private.'

'How old was Charlie then, two?'

'Two and a half.'

'Had he started talking by then?'

'No. Not a word.'

'Then how did they communicate?'

'I don't know because I wasn't there, but whatever it was, it worked because Charlie changed towards me. He opened up. He looked at me. He even started smiling – and he had such a lovely smile, the sort that really made your day when you saw it.'

Francesca's voice had gone down to a whisper, all her words dwarfed by a mounting grief.

She blew her nose loudly, honking like a seal, and then she lit another cigarette, the last one she had. She crushed the packet in her fist.

'How often did you and Charlie see the priest?'

'Once a week.'

'Same day and time?'

'No, it always varied. Rose would tell me when.'

'I'll have to see this guy.'

Francesca took a folded piece of paper out of her breast pocket and slid it across to him.

'Filius's address and directions. He's expecting you at around two this afternoon.'

'He's *expecting* me?'

'He saw you coming. He told me two months ago.'

'What do you mean he "saw me coming" two months ago? *I* didn't know I was coming two months ago.'

'He sees things.'

'Like a fortune teller?'

'Something like that, but what he does isn't the same.'

'How come you acted that way at dinner?'

'I didn't realize it was you.'

'So you've talked to Doofoor since?'

'Yes.'

'Which is why you came down here?'

She nodded.

'He must have some hold on you.'

'It's not like that.'

'Did you tell my predecessors any of this?'

'No. I only told them about the kidnapping.'

'Why?'

'Emmanuel was a nice guy, but he was indiscreet, a gossip.

182

I *hated* Clyde Beeson and I didn't care too much for Medd either. They were only here for the money.'

'It's what they do for a living, Mrs Carver,' Max said. 'Same as anybody else doing a job. Could be in an office, could be pumping gas, could be a cop, could be a fireman – most people do what they do for money. Those that don't are either lucky or stupid.'

'Then you must be stupid, Max,' she smiled, looking him straight in the eye. 'Because you're not lucky.'

She had little else to tell him after that.

Max walked her to the gate. She shook his hand and apologized for her outburst at dinner. She begged him to find Charlie. He said he would do his best and watched her head up the path at the end of which she'd told him a car was waiting for her.

Dawn had broken and a greyish blue light hung about the courtyard and garden, which was noisy with birds no doubt breakfasting on sluggish insects. Beyond him the street was starting to come alive.

As he went back to the house he heard a car start up in the driveway. A door opened and closed and the car drove away.

15

Max washed his face and shaved and made more coffee.

He sat out on the porch with his cup. The sun rose and in seconds his surroundings were flooded in brightness, as if a searchlight beam had been pointed down on the country.

He sipped his coffee. He wasn't tired any more, not even hung over.

Max checked his watch. 6.30 am. Same time in Miami. Joe would be up, setting the breakfast table for his wife and kids.

Max went to the bedroom and called Joe's home number. The phone was an old ring dialler model.

'Joe? It's Max.'

'Hey, wasshappenin', man?!!? I was jus' thinkin' about you.'

'That ole time voodoo's starting to work,' Max said, thinking of Charlie's priest.

Joe laughed.

'You in the kitchen, Big Man?'

'No, my home office. Soundproof. That way my wife says she don't have to listen to Bruce. She hates him as much as you.'

'Amen to that,' said Max. 'Listen, I need some information on someone. Is that going to be a problem?'

'Nope. I can do it right here, right now. Got the database right in front of me.'

'How so?' asked Max, incredulous.

'Whole thing's online now,' Joe said. 'I do my brain work at home these days. The workplace is just for keepin' tabs on the little juniors, hobnobbin' with the brass and gettin' away from the family every now and again. Things've moved on a lot since you went away, Max. Technology's like rust – never sleeps, always movin' forward, slowly takin' over what we're too lazy to do . . . Anyway, this search you want done could take time, dependin' on how many eyes are on the system right now.'

'I've got time if you have, Joe. You may need to cross-reference with the Interpol database.'

'Shoot.'

'First name: Vincent, last name: Paul. Both spelled the way they sound.'

'He Haitian?'

'Yes.'

Max heard Joe's fingers typing in the information, music in the background, turned low. Bruce Springsteen's voice over spare acoustic guitar. He wondered if Gustav's Sinatra CD was still in the street.

'Max? *Nada* on the nationwide database, but there's a Vincent Paul on Interpol. Low priority. Listed as an MP – Missing Person. Brits want him. Scotland Yard.'

Joe tapped some more.

'Picture here too. Mean-looking bastard – like Isaac Hayes on a *really bad* day. *Big* motherfucker too. They've got his height down here as six nine and change. Probably straight seven in shoes. *Go-Liath* baby! There's a lot of cross-referencing I've got to do here . . . There's a Known Associate come up. No ID yet. Machine's slow . . . Listen, this could take another hour, and I've got to see to the kids. I'll put this thing on auto search and select. The minute I got it I'll call you. What's your number?'

Max gave it to him.

'I'd better call you, Joe. I don't know when I'll be back here.'

'OK.'

'If I need it, can you run some forensics tests?'

'Depends what it is you're looking for.'

'DNA, blood typing, fingerprint cross-referencing?'

'That's OK. Small stuff. Just don't be sending no whole body over – or a chicken.'

'I'll try not to,' Max laughed.

'How's it goin' out there?' Joe asked.

'Early days,' Max said.

'If you walk away now the only thing you lose is money. Remember that, brother,' Joe said.

Max had forgotten how well Joe knew him. He'd heard the doubt in his voice. Max thought of telling him about the kids outside La Coupole, but he thought it best not to mention it, let it go, sink through his memories. If he kept it uppermost in his mind it would cloud his vision, mess with his perceptions. Keep the channel clear.

'I'll remember that, Joe, don't worry.'

Max heard the music – Bruce flailing away on acoustic guitar, piping notes through a harmonica like Bob Dylan on steroids. He guessed Joe was at his happiest now, at moments like these, listening to his music, right in the bosom of his beloved family. Joe would always have someone around who cared about him and would care for him. Max wanted to stay there a little longer, listening to Joe's life, listening to the sounds of warmth and tenderness, his home, its parts as fragile as a new-born baby's.

PART THREE

16

'Max, you *stink*,' Chantale told him, and laughed her dirty laugh.

She was right. Although he'd washed and brushed his teeth, the scent of a night of neat booze was a hard one to shake off in a hot climate. The rum he'd been drinking fairly steadily up until a few hours ago was evaporating back out through his pores and reeking up the inside of the Landcruiser, sweet and stale and acrid, candy boiling in vinegar.

'Sorry,' he said and looked through the window at the landscape passing them by in a brown, yellow and sometimes green blur as they headed down the winding road to Port-au-Prince.

'No offence meant,' she smiled.

'None taken. I like people who speak their minds. It usually means they mean what they say — saves trying to figure them out.'

Chantale smelled great — a fresh, sharp yet delicate citrus fragrance hummed about her and insulated her from his odour. She was dressed for the day, in a short-sleeved turquoise blouse, faded blue jeans and desert boots. Her hair was scraped back in a short pony-tail. Sunglasses, a pen and small notebook poked out of her blouse pocket. She hadn't just come to drive around. She'd come to work with him, whether he liked it or not.

She'd arrived at the house early at seven thirty, rolling into the courtyard in a dusty Honda Civic whose windscreen looked like it hadn't been cleaned in a year. Max was eating the breakfast Rubie, the maid, had cooked for him. He'd wanted eggs over easy, sunny-side down, but when he'd tried explaining it to her she'd misinterpreted his hybrid of slowed down English, sound effects and sign language because he'd ended up with an omelette served up on cassava tortillas. Still it was delicious and filling. He'd washed it down with extra strong black coffee and a tall glass of a juice she'd called *chadec* – grapefruit without the tartness.

'Heavy night?' Chantale asked.

'You could say that.'

'You go to La Coupole?'

'How would you know?'

'Not exactly spoilt for bars round your way.'

'Have you been there?'

'No,' she laughed. 'They'd mistake me for a hooker.'

'I don't know about that,' Max said. 'You're way too classy.'

There: he'd made his first move on her – no deep breath, no summoning dormant strength, no scrabbling around for the right words; he'd just opened his mouth and exactly the right thing to say had come out, smooth and simple; the sort of ambiguous compliment that didn't stray beyond platonic flattery. He'd slotted straight back into velvet predator mode like he'd never given it up. Things went either way from here – either she'd pick up on his words and bat them back to him with a spin of her own, or she'd let him know no way was it going any further.

Chantale gripped the wheel a little too tight with both hands and looked straight ahead.

'I don't think your countrymen know the difference out here,' she said bitterly.

She wasn't going for it. It wasn't a direct rebuff, but she wasn't yielding. Max tried to guess at the amount of men she'd been with. He heard a corrosive bitterness in her words, the sort of defence mechanism you build after heartbreak. Maybe she'd recognized his play because she'd fallen for it before – and been burnt.

'He must've hurt you pretty bad, Chantale,' Max said.

'He did,' she replied curtly, speaking to the windscreen, cutting off the conversation's circulation by clicking on the radio and turning it up loud.

They took a sharp left turn around the side of the mountain they were driving down and, as they cleared it, Max saw Port-au-Prince spread out before him, a few miles down below, spilling out from the coastline like a splurge of dried vomit waiting for the sea to wash away.

There was a heavy US military presence in central Port-au-Prince, a cordon of humvees, machine-gun-mounted jeeps and footsoldiers in body armour massed opposite and all around the National Palace where the current President – Aristide's successor and close associate, a former baker and rumoured alcoholic called Préval – lived and ran his country as far as his puppet strings would stretch.

According to Huxley, who'd filled Max in, the current Haitian constitution forbade a President from serving consecutive terms, but did allow him or her to serve alternate ones. Préval was considered by many to be little more than Aristide's gofer, keeping the seat warm and ready for his master's inevitable return. Democracy was still a fluid thing.

'Damn Americans!' Chantale said as they passed a jeep full of Marines. 'No offence.'

'None taken. Don't you agree with what's happening?'

'I did at first, until I realized invading this place was nothing but a pre-election publicity stunt on Clinton's part. He'd messed up in Somalia, the US was humiliated, his credibility hurt. What do you do? Pick on a near-defenceless black country and invade that in the name of "democracy" and "freedom",' Chantale said bitterly, and then she laughed. 'You know how they sent Jimmy Carter in to negotiate peace with the junta, after they'd refused to stand down?'

'Yeah, I saw that . . .' Max said. *In prison*, he thought. 'Mr Human Rights himself. I hated that asshole. He ruined Miami.'

'In 1980. The boatlift?'

'Yeah. It used to be an OK place, full of retired Jewish folk and right-wing Cubans plotting to kill Castro. It was real quiet, real conservative, low crime, peaceful. Then Castro sent his criminals and psychos over in the boats, mixed in with all the decent, law-abiding refugees who just wanted to start a new life and, thanks to El Jimbo, we were fucked without a guidebook. It was hell bein' a cop back then, let me tell ya. We didn't know what hit us. One minute Miami's a nice place to bring up your kids, the next it's Murder Capital, USA.'

'Guess you voted for Reagan?'

'Every single Miami cop did in 1980. Those that didn't were sick or weren't registered,' Max smiled.

'I used to be a Democrat. I voted for Clinton in '92, Dukakis before. Never again,' Chantale said. 'Did you hear what happened in the so-called peace talks between Carter and General Cedras – the head of the junta?'

'No. Tell me.'

'Carter came over, TV cameras rolling. He meets with General Cedras and his wife. And it's Mrs Cedras who does the negotiating. She gets Carter to agree to pay each member of the junta ten million dollars, guarantee them safe passage out of the country and immunity from prosecution. Done Deal.

'Then she wants the US to protect their houses. And she negotiates with Carter for the US government to rent out their houses to embassy staff. Done Deal. And finally – and this is where it almost fell apart – Mrs Cedras wanted her black leather sofa freighted out to Venezuela, where they were all moving to. Carter said No Deal. Why? Because Carter wasn't authorized to pay for a removals company. Everything else was fine, but not that.

'They argued and bickered and it went back and forth. Finally, when it looked like it was going to be a deal breaker, Carter rang Clinton and got him out of bed to explain the situation. Clinton was pissed off. He really chewed Carter out, screamed at him so loudly people said they could hear what he was saying in the other room. Anyway, Clinton okayed it and the sofa went into exile with the junta.'

Max burst out laughing. 'Bullshit!'

'True rumour,' Chantale said.

They laughed.

The Presidential Palace itself was a gleaming, expansive, two-floored, brilliant white edifice which soaked up and part reflected the sunlight so that it appeared luminous when viewed against its dark backdrop of surrounding mountains. The red and blue Haitian flag hung from a mast above the main entrance.

They drove around a pedestal mounted with a statue of General Henri Christophe, one of Haiti's first leaders, on his horse, facing the Palace and the US troops. Groups of young Haitian men sat or stood around the bottom of the pedestal, clothes fluttering off skinny limbs eyeing their occupiers, watching the traffic or staring vacantly into space.

The rest of the city, what he saw of it, was a dump – a rancid, rusted, busted-up, busted-out ruin of a place. Port-au-Prince wasn't just in bad shape, it was in no shape at all.

Reeling, tilting, tottering, on the verge of collapse, virtually everything about the place needed a million dollar facelift or, better still, a complete demolition and rebuilding job. A row of gingerbread houses – doors long gone, shutters hanging off hinges – in what must once have been a wealthy part of town, stood filthy and derelict, squatted in by God knows how many people, some of whom Max saw hanging off the balconies.

There were no traffic lights anywhere. Max had seen exactly one set since they'd left Pétionville, and those weren't working. The streets, like almost every street he'd been down in Haiti, were cracked and potholed. The cars that rolled down them were belching, farting, patched-together, wrecking-yard salvage, bursting with people. A few colour-fully painted tap-taps went by, hooting, overloaded with people and their possessions, bundled up in tied-off sheets and clothes and heaped on the roof, along with as many passengers as could fit on. And then there were the occa-sional luxury cars, tens of thousands of dollars of imported high-maintenance automobile daintily threading their way across the wrecked roads with their sudden craters and bumpy surfaces.

The city made Max sad in a way he'd never been before. Through the detritus, the near rubble, Max saw a few proud and fine grand old buildings that must have looked glorious in their prime and would have been impressive again if restored. Yet he couldn't see this ever happening. If capital cities are meant to be shop windows for the rest of the country, then Port-au-Prince was a car showroom that had been looted and set on fire and left to burn, nearly unno-ticed, until rain had finally come and doused the flames.

'I remember when the Pope came here,' Chantale said, turning down the radio. 'It was in 1983, a year before I went to the States. Jean-Claude Duvalier – Baby Doc – was still in power. Well, it was really his wife Michele. She was running the country by then.

'She cleaned the streets up, all the ones you see here. They were full of beggars and merchants who sold their stuff off big wooden tables. She made them pack up and move elsewhere, where the Pope couldn't see. There were handicapped people here too – physical and mental – they used to camp out here and beg at the roadside. She got rid of them too. The streets were resurfaced and whitewashed. A few hours before the Pope drove down in his motorcade, Michele had the road hosed down with Chanel perfume. I was standing right there when it happened. The smell was so strong it gave me a headache and stayed in my clothes for months and months, no matter how many times my mother washed them. I've had a Chanel allergy ever since. If someone's wearing it I get headaches.'

'What did they do with the handicapped people?'

'Same thing that happened to them in the mid-seventies, when they decided to make the country more attractive to tourists: they rounded them all up – the sick, the lame, the needy – and they shipped them off to La Gonâve. It's a small island off the coast.'

'I see,' Max said, patting himself down for a notebook. He couldn't find one. 'What happened to them? Are they still there?'

'I don't know. Some of them, I suppose, stayed on. These were dirt poor people living as close to the ground as rats. No one cared about them,' Chantale replied as Max picked up the small army knapsack lying at his feet, where he'd put his camera and tape recorder. He'd packed a pen but no paper.

Chantale opened her breast pocket and handed him her small notebook.

'Never forget the fundamentals,' she laughed.

Max scribbled down the details.

'Have you heard of Ton Ton Clarinet?'

'You say *Tonton*, Max, not "tonnn-tonnn". You sound like you're imitating an elephant walking.' She laughed again. 'Tonton Clarinette's an urban legend, a spook story parents tell their kids: be good or Tonton Clarinette will come for you. He's like the pied piper, hypnotizing children with his music and stealing them away for ever.'

'Do they say Tonton Clarinet took Charlie?'

'Yes, of course. When we were putting up the posters the street people would come up and say: "You'll never find that child – Tonton Clarinette's got him – just like he's been taking our children."'

Max nodded as he thought of Claudette Thodore.

'See that over there?' Chantale said, pointing to a shabby-looking street of stunted buildings with fading signs painted on their roofs and walls. People were jumping out of a dump truck that had just parked itself in the middle of the road. 'That was once the red light district. Lots of gay bars and brothels and clubs. Really wild carefree place. Every night was party night here. People may not have had much but they knew how to have fun. Now you can't even drive through here at night, unless you're in a military vehicle.'

'What happened to the bars?'

'Jean-Claude closed them all down during when AIDS hit in 1983. Most of the rich American gays who used to come here for dirty weekends stayed away because your media said Haiti was the birthplace of the disease. Jean-Claude rounded up all the gays too.'

'Did he send them to La Gonâve?'

'No. No one knows what happened to them.'

'In other words they were killed?'

'Probably. No one's sure. No one followed it up – not publicly anyway. Didn't want to start any whispering. Homosexuality's a big no-no here. They call gays "massissi" and lesbians "madivine" in Kreyol. There's a saying now: "There are no gays in Haiti: they're all married with children." It's a secret society,' Chantale said. 'But Jean-Claude was known to be bisexual for a time. I think it was all the coke he was doing, and the fact that he'd screwed every woman he wanted in Haiti. He was supposed to have had this high-society boyfriend, René Sylvestre. Big fat guy, drove around in a gold-plated Rolls Royce and wore dresses.'

'Sounds like Liberace.'

'They called him "Le Mighty Real" – after that gay disco singer.'

'As in "You Make Me Feel Mighty Real"?'

'You know it?'

'Sure do. I have the twelve inch in my loft.'

'*You*?!' Chantale laughed.

'Yeah.'

'For real?'

'Yeah. What's the big deal? I'm the original Tony Manero. "You Make Me Feel Mighty Real?" – that's my song!'

'I can't see it.' She laughed her laugh again.

'Look a little closer,' Max said.

'We'll see.'

17

They drove down Boulevard Harry Truman, a wide, palm tree-lined and surprisingly smooth stretch of road that ran alongside the coast. To the left Max could see a tanker and a warship on the horizon, while ahead of him, some distance away, he could make out the port, with its rusted and half-sunk ships clogging up the waters. A procession of blue-helmeted UN troops passed them by, heading along on the other side of the road.

The Banque Populaire d'Haïti, the Carver family's business nucleus, was an imposing cream-coloured cube which might have been better suited for a library or a courthouse. It vaguely reminded Max of pictures he'd seen of the Arc de Triomphe in Paris.

The bank was set back from the road, built on top of a gentle slope and surrounded by an expanse of lush green grass. A sandstone wall ran around the building, topped with bright pink and white flowers half hiding stiletto spikes and razor wire. A high metal gate stood between the bank and the street. Two armed guards were sat either side of it. One of them spoke into a radio when Chantale drew up, and the gate opened back from the inside.

'This is the special person's entrance,' Chantale said, as they drove in and started up a short path which split the surrounding grass into two squares. 'Only the family, certain staff and special customers are allowed to use it.'

'Which are you?' Max asked, noticing a silver Mercedes jeep with blacked-out windows following them in.

They followed the path around to a half-empty parking lot. A steady stream of people were entering and exiting the bank through a revolving door.

As they got out, Max saw the Merc parked a few spaces behind them. Max glanced over, long enough to take in the scene and break it down, but not long enough for someone to notice him staring. Four men got out – heavy Hispanic types. They walked around to the open boot.

Max had seen all he needed to. He knew what would come next, even before they overtook him and Chantale on the way to the bank, run-walking two very heavy suitcases apiece towards the entrance.

'Special customers?' Max asked.

'Money doesn't know where it came from. And neither do my employers,' she said, without a hint of embarrassment or surprise or worry, like she'd had to deal with this sort of remark before – or been trained to deal with it.

Max said nothing. He expected plenty of drug money had gone through the Banque Populaire. Since the early eighties, at least ten to fifteen per cent of the world's cocaine was being distributed via Haiti and most of the major players in the South American cartels had built up strong links with the country, many using it as a place to lie low for a year or two. He was sure the Carvers never actively solicited for drug business – Gustav was way too shrewd an operator for that – but they didn't refuse the custom when it came knocking either.

Max had wanted to start his investigation at the bank, on the Carvers' home turf. It was the way he'd always worked, from the client out: the more he knew about the people who were paying him, the more he knew how their enemies thought; he saw what they hated and coveted and wanted to take away and destroy. He'd first establish motive, then he'd throw a net around the likely suspects and haul it in. He'd eliminate them one by one until he found the culprit.

They followed the case carriers through the doors. The inside was predictably magnificent, a cross between an aircraft hangar and a corporate mausoleum where dead CEOs might be laid to rest under brass plaques embedded in the ground for future generations to ignore and tread on. The frescoed ceiling was almost a hundred foot high, suspended by huge dark granite Delphic pillars. The fresco depicted a light-blue sky with fluffy clouds, and God's hands opening up and showering down all of the world's major paper currencies, from dollars to roubles, francs to yen, pounds to pesetas. The Haitian gourde was conspicuous by its absence.

The counters were at the far end of the bank. There were at least thirty of them, separated into numbered cubicles, built of granite and bulletproof glass. Max noticed how well dressed the customers were, as if they'd all made a special trip to the clothes store and hairdresser before they'd come to do their business. He guessed that having a bank account in Haiti gave you a certain social status, made you part of an exclusive circle, and the whole ritual of withdrawing and investing money was the social equivalent of taking communion and giving to the collection on a Sunday.

The men with the cases were ushered through a door to the right of the counters. Two security guards stood by the door, pump-action shotguns draped casually across their arms.

The centre of the highly polished dark granite floor was inlaid with the national flag, which took up half the total space. Max walked around it, studying it: two horizontal bands, dark blue on top of red, with a crest depicting a palm tree flanked either side by cannon, flagpoles and bayonet-fitted muskets. A blue and red cap dressed the top of the tree, while '*L'Union Fait La Force*' was written on a scroll at the bottom.

'It used to look a lot better when it was the Duvalier flag, black and red instead of blue. It meant business. The flag was changed back to its original colours ten years ago, so the floor had to be redone too,' Chantale said, as she watched Max walking around it, taking in its detail. 'It's a very French flag. The colours – the blue and the red – were basically the French tricolore with the white symbolizing the white man torn out. The slogan and the weapons all symbolize the country's struggle for freedom through unity and violent revolution.'

'A warrior nation,' Max said.

'Once,' Chantale replied sourly. 'We don't fight any more. We just roll over and take it.'

'*Max*!' Allain Carver called out as he crossed the floor towards them. A few heads – all female well-to-doers queuing for service – turned and stayed turned, eyes hanging on him as he crossed the floor briskly, heels clicking, hands extended a little in front of him, as if anticipating a catch.

They shook hands.

'Welcome!' Carver said. Warmish smile, suit crisp and well fitting, hair plastered back; he was back in control, lord and master.

Max looked around the bank again, wondering how much of it had been built from drug money.

'I'd love to give you a guided tour,' Carver apologized, 'but I'm going to be tied up with customers all day. Our head of security – Mr Codada – will show you around.'

He took them back the way he'd come, Carver ushering them through a guarded door and into a cool and long, blue-carpeted corridor that stopped, some way down, at an elevator.

They stopped outside the only office in the corridor. Carver rapped twice on the door before opening it brusquely, as if hoping to catch the inhabitant off-guard, in the middle of something embarrassing or forbidden.

Mr Codada was on the phone, one foot on his desk, laughing loudly and making the tassels on his patent leather loafers rattle in time with his outbursts of mirth. He looked over his shoulder at the three of them, waved vaguely and carried on his conversation without changing his posture.

The office was spacious, with a framed painting of a modern white building overlooking a waterfall dominating one wall, and another traditional painting – also framed – of a street party outside a church. His desk was bare apart from the telephone, a blotter and some small black wooden figurines.

Codada said '*A bientôt ma chérie*', blew a couple of kisses into the receiver and rang off. He spun his chair around to face his new guests.

Without moving from his spot near the door, Carver talked to him brusquely in Kreyol, motioning to Max with his head as he spoke his name. Codada nodded without saying a word, his face a mixture of professional serious-ness and leftover jollity. Max understood the dynamic right away. Codada was Gustav's man and didn't take the son at all seriously.

Next Carver addressed Chantale, far more gently, smiling, before turning on the surface charm a little more as he took his leave of Max.

'Enjoy your tour,' he said. 'We'll talk later.'

Maurice Codada stood up and walked around his desk.

Codada air-kissed Chantale on both cheeks and pumped her arms warmly. She introduced him to Max.

'*Bienvenu à la Banque Populaire d'Haïti, Monsieur Mainguss*,'

Codada gushed, bowing his head and showing Max an odd-looking freckled pink bald spot on his crown, before taking Max's hands and also shaking them vigorously. Although he was a slender little man, shorter and narrower than Max, his grip was strong. Chantale explained that she would have to translate as Codada couldn't speak English.

Codada took them back outside to the main entrance and immediately started showing them around the bank, running a quickfire commentary in Kreyol that seemed to rattle out of his mouth like telex script as he walked them across the floor.

Chantale packaged up his verbal geysers into one liners: 'The pillars come from Italy' / 'The floors too' / 'The Haitian flag' / 'The counters come from Italy' / 'The staff do not – ha, ha, ha.'

Codada moved about the line of customers, shaking hands, slapping shoulders, air-kissing the ladies, working the crowd with the gusto of a politician campaigning for office. He even picked up a baby and kissed it.

Codada favoured a lion made up as a circus clown – a cartoon character looking for a comic strip. He had a flat broad nose, round ginger afro and a redhead's naturally pale complexion, pocked with a heavy spray of freckles. His lips were red – the lower one rimmed purple – and permanently moist from where he darted the pink tip of his tongue all around them like a praying mantis chasing and missing a fleet-footed bug. His stare was hooded, roasted coffee bean irises peering out from under eyelids criss-crossed with a spaghetti junction of fine veins and arteries.

A lot about Codada didn't fit. The jewellery was all wrong for a start. He wore a lot of gold – two chunky bracelets on either wrist and two fat ingots as pinkie rings. When he smiled he showed his gold front tooth, and as he bounced up and down across the bank floor Max heard clinking under his shirt and guessed three or more gold chains were roped around his neck.

Max thought Codada lacked virtually every personality trait for working in security. People who worked those jobs were inward, secretive and above all discreet; they said little, saw everything, thought and moved quick. Codada was the opposite. He liked people or liked their attention. Security personnel blended into the crowd but saw everyone in it as a potential threat. Even his clothes were wrong – white duck pants, a navy-blue blazer and a maroon and white cravat. Security staff went for dull tones or sombre uniforms, while Codada could have passed himself off as a maître d' on some gay cruise liner.

They took a mirrored elevator up to the next floor, the business division. Codada stood to the left of the door so he could get the full three-dimensional view of Chantale his position allowed. Max had thought he was gay, but Codada spent all of the few seconds the ride lasted tracing the outline of Chantale's bust, his gaze slurping up the detail. Just before they reached the floor he must have felt the intensity of Max's stare because he looked straight at him, then flicked the briefest look at Chantale's bosom and then went back to Max and nodded to him very slightly, letting him know they'd broached common ground. Chantale didn't notice.

The business division was tile-carpeted, air-conditioned and reeked faintly of Plasticine. The corridors were lined with framed black-and-white dated photographs of all the major constructions and projects the bank had financed, from a church to a supermarket. Codada led them past various offices, where three or four smartly dressed men and women were sat behind desks furnished with computers and phones, but none of them were actually doing anything. In fact, nothing seemed to be happening on the entire floor. Many of the computer screens were blank, no phones were ringing, and some people weren't even bothering to disguise their inactivity. They were sitting on desks and chatting, reading papers or talking. Max looked at Chantale for an explanation but she offered none. Codada's tones cut straight through the silence. Many looked up and followed the guided tour, some laughing out loud at some of the things he said, but whatever it was was either left out of the translation or didn't make it through the interpretation.

Max was beginning to understand Gustav's mentality, his attitude towards people. There was something to hate about it, but then again there was much more to admire.

It was slightly livelier on the next floor – mortgages and personal loans. The set-up of the area was the same, but Max heard a few telephones ringing and saw that some computers were on and being worked at. Codada explained through Chantale that Haitians tended to build their homes from scratch rather than buy them from previous owners, so they often needed assistance to buy the land and hire an architect and a building crew.

The Carvers had their offices on the upper floor. Codada used the elevator's walls to straighten himself up and pat down his hair. Chantale caught Max's eye and smiled him a what-a-jerk-this-guy-is look. Max patted down his bald head.

The lift doors opened on to a reception area manned by a woman behind a tall mahogany desk, and a waiting area of low black leather couches, a coffee table and a water cooler. Two Uzi-toting security guards in bulletproof vests hovered about at opposite ends of the area. Codada led them out of the elevator to a set of heavy double doors on the left. He typed in an access code on a keypad in the frame. A camera eyed them from the right. The doors opened on to a corridor which led to another set of double doors at the end.

They walked down to Gustav Carver's office. Codada spoke their names through an intercom and they were buzzed in.

Gustav's secretary, an imposing light-skinned woman in her late forties, greeted Codada with perfunctory warmth.

Codada introduced Max to her but not the other way round, so Max never caught her name. She didn't have it on her desk either. She shook Max's hand with a curt nod.

Codada asked her something and she said '*Non*'. He thanked her and led Max and Chantale out of the office and back down the corridor.

'He asked if we could see Gustav Carver's offices, but Jeanne said no,' Chantale whispered.

'What about Allain?'

'He's VP. His office is on the first floor. We passed it.'

Codada took them back downstairs to the ground floor. Max handed him two hundred bucks to change for him into Haitian currency. Codada glided off towards the tills, glad-handing and air-kissing a few more customers on his way there.

He came back a few fast minutes later holding a small brown brick's worth of gourdes between his thumb and index. The currency had been so hopelessly devalued by the invasion and Haiti's parlous economic state that a dollar was worth anything between fifty and a hundred gourdes, depending on which bank you went to. The Banque Populaire had the most generous exchange rate in Haiti.

Max took the pile of money from Codada and flicked through it. The notes were humid and greasy and – despite their varying blue, green, purple and red colours – all were varying shades of greyed brown. The smaller the denomination (five gourdes) the more obscured the value and design by dirt and grime, while the highest denomination (500 gourdes) were mildly smudged, the bill's details completely discernible. The money reeked strongly of toe cheese.

Codada walked them through the revolving doors and they said their goodbyes. As they were speaking the men with the cases – now empty – came out through the doors. Codada broke off his farewell to greet them, embracing one of the men warmly.

Max and Chantale walked back to the car.

'So what do you think?' Chantale asked.

'Gustav's a generous man,' Max said.

'How so?'

'He's keeping a lot of people on the payroll with nothing to do,' he said. He wanted to throw Codada into the mix too, but he didn't. It was never good to judge on appearances and instinct alone, even if they'd yet to let him down.

'Gustav understands the Haitian mentality: do something for someone today and you've got a friend for life,' Chantale said.

'I guess that cuts both ways.'

'Yes it does. We go an extra mile to help a friend and an extra twenty to bury a foe.'

18

They drove to the Boulevard des Veuves, where Charlie had been kidnapped.

They parked the car and got out. The heat fell over Max in a fine net of molten lava, baking his skin, boiling him inside. He broke out into an immediate rush of sweat which flooded down his back and seeped through his shirt. Outside the bank the heat had been tempered by the breeze blowing straight off the sea, but here the air was flat, airless and bone dry; and the heat was so intense he could see it rippling in front of him in solid currents, blurring his view.

The sidewalks were raised high above the ground, their hazardous surfaces worn ice smooth and mirror bright by billions of footsteps and decades of neglect. They moved very slowly down the street, which was jammed with people – some selling, some bartering, some buying, many hanging around and talking. Max heard his rubber soles squelching as he walked across the baked concrete. Everyone was looking at them, following them – especially Max, who sensed mass bemusement and incredulity coming at him, instead of the suspicion and hostility he'd been used to when going through the ghettos at home. Bearing in mind what had happened to him a few hours before, he avoided making eye contact. They stepped off the sidewalk and down into the road, which was only slightly less congested.

If the whole city wasn't already dragging itself around on what was left of its last legs, Max would have said that they were in a bad neighbourhood. The Boulevard des Veuves had once been paved with small hexagonal stones. All but the ones still hugging the edges of the sidewalk were gone, ripped out, sometimes professionally, in geometric strips, or haphazardly, in clumps of one or two dozen. Every two metres there were drains – gaping square holes cut out of the kerbs – and every four or five metres parts of the road had collapsed and left huge, stinking, fly-infested black craters, which doubled up as rubbish dumps and public toilets where men, women and children would piss and shit in full view of everyone, not remotely disturbed by the passing traffic. The place stank of shit, rank water, putrefying fruit, vegetables and carcasses.

There was dust everywhere, on and in everything, blowing down from the mountains that ringed the capital. The mountains had once been heavily forested but successive generations had cut down all the trees for homes, carts and firewood. Left bare and exposed, the sun had dried up the once rich and fertile soil and the wind had blown it back into Haitian faces. He tasted it on his tongue, and he knew if he closed his eyes just once and tried to plug into the place he'd know exactly what it would be like to get buried alive in this God forsaken fucked-over place.

Charlie's face was plastered all over the street, the stark black-and-white posters offering a cash reward for information about his kidnapping, competing with larger, colourful ones advertising concerts by Haitian singers in Miami, Martinique, Guadeloupe and New York.

He pulled down one of Charlie's posters to start showing around. He noticed a small hand-drawn symbol in black in the left-hand margin – a cross, slightly curved in the middle, with a round head, a split base and two-thirds of its right beam missing. He looked at the other posters and saw that they were all scored with the same mark.

He pointed the mark out to Chantale.

'Tonton Clarinette,' she said.

They started canvassing the street for witnesses to Charlie's kidnapping. First they went to the shops – small food stores with no air-conditioning and threadbare shelves; stores selling pots and pans and wooden spoons and ladles; hooch shacks; a bakery; a butcher's with one dead, half-skinned chicken hanging up; a used-auto-parts place; another place selling only bright-white chicken eggs – all producing a variant on the same answer: *Mpas weh en rien* – I saw nothing.

Then they quizzed people on the street. Both times Chantale showed them the poster and did the talking.

Nobody knew anything. They shook their heads, shrugged their shoulders, replying in one or two phrases or long throaty outbursts. Max stood and watched, filtering the people they approached through interrogator's eyes as they answered, looking out for the tell-tale signs of lying and concealing but all he saw were exhausted, half-asleep men and women of indeterminable ages, confused by the attention they were getting from the white man and the light-skinned lady.

After more than an hour of this Max thought of seeking out the shoemaker's store Francesca had mentioned. He'd been looking out for it the whole while they'd been on the street, but he hadn't seen anything even close. Maybe they'd passed it, or the store had closed down. At least half of the people he saw were barefoot, with feet so thick and crooked, so built up with waxy keratin about the sole and heel, he doubted they'd ever worn shoes.

They headed back to the car. An old man selling snow-cones out of a wooden trolley equipped with an icebox and bottles of brightly coloured syrup was standing nearby with his wooden cart, shovelling ice into a paper cup.

Max could tell he'd been waiting for them. He'd spotted him out of the corner of his eye, while searching the crowd, always on the periphery wherever they moved, pushing his cart, shaving the ice block in his box, watching them.

He started talking to Max as he approached. Thinking he was trying to sell them some of his polluted refreshments, Max waved him off.

'You want to listen to this, Max,' Chantale said. 'He's talking about the kidnapping.'

The man said he'd seen it happen, close to where they were parked, but on the opposite side of the road. His version of events followed Francesca's very closely. Faustin had parked the car in the road and waited a long time. The snowcone seller said he heard Faustin yelling at both women.

By then a crowd had gathered around the car. Faustin lowered the window and told them to mind their own business and get out of the way. When they didn't move he pulled a gun out and fired a couple of shots in the air. As Faustin was firing, Rose grabbed at his face from behind and tried to tear his eyes out. That was when he shot her.

Many in the crowd had by then recognized Faustin and they stormed the car, armed with machetes, knives, bats, metal pikes and rocks. They smashed the windows, turned the car over twice, jumped on the roof and began hacking into it. The man said close to three hundred people swarmed all over the vehicle.

The crowd dragged Faustin out through the roof. Although covered in blood, he was still alive, screaming for his life. They threw him into the mob. The man said they must have hacked the bodyguard into mincemeat, because all that was left of his body when the crowd moved on was a big puddle of blood and guts, with some cracked-off pieces of bone and bloody scraps of his clothes. He remembered, laughing, how they'd cut off his head, stuck it on a broom-stick and run off down towards La Saline with it. Faustin, he said, had an abnormally big tongue – easily as big as a cow's or a donkey's. They tried to pull it out of his head, as they'd done his eyes, but it was stuck so fast they left it dangling down his mouth to his chin, where it bounced and flopped around in the air as the crowd ran towards the slums with their trophy, singing and dancing all the way.

The snowcone seller wasn't too clear about what happened next. The people who'd stayed behind started stripping the car for parts. Then Vincent Paul and his men arrived in three jeeps and people scattered. Then Paul started shouting, running up and down the road, asking where the boy and the woman were. Someone pointed to where the mob had gone with Faustin's head. They put Rose's body in the back of the jeep and took off after at high speed.

The man said he never found out what happened next. The incident had taken place a few days before the American troops invaded the island, the man said, when the Haitian army and militia were going around, randomly spraying poor neighbourhoods with bullets and setting others on fire. So many wires had gotten crossed and much had been forgotten or ignored in that climate of dread and fear.

Max thanked him and gave him five hundred gourdes. The snowcone seller looked at the money and pumped Max's hand, promising to sacrifice a little something in his honour the next time he went to a temple.

19

The old woman was as Francesca had described her, wearing a faded pink dress and sitting outside on the porch of a shoemaker's shop at the far end of the Boulevard des Veuves. The shop was in a house whose front was covered in a mural depicting a black man in dungarees and rolled-up white sleeves, hammering the soles of a boot while a shoeless child looked on and an angel watched above them both in the middle. It was the only indication of the shop's trade. The doorway, although open, revealed a deep impenetrable darkness impervious to sunlight. Someone had put up a poster of Charlie on the wall directly opposite her.

Chantale introduced them and told her what their business was. The woman told Chantale to stand closer and talk into her ear. Max didn't blame her. He could barely hear her himself above the street din of people shouting over the traffic, growling and beeping its way through the clogged road.

The woman listened and spoke loudly, the way the hard of hearing do, her voice still managing to sound muffled and trapped in her cheeks.

'She says she saw what happened. She was right here,' Chantale said.

'What did she see?' Max asked and Chantale translated, almost as soon as the words left the woman's mouth.

'She says she's heard you're paying people for their memories.'

The woman smiled and showed Max all that was left of her teeth – two curved brown-stained canines that looked like they belonged in the jaws of a vicious dog. She looked over her shoulder into the open doorway behind her for a moment, nodded and then, looking from Max to Chantale, addressed her interpreter in a lower voice. Chantale screwed her face up into a wry smirk and shook her head before relaying back to Max what she'd just been told.

'She wants more than you paid the last guy.'

'Only if what she says is true and any good.'

The woman laughed when she was told what Max had just said. She pointed a finger, crooked and spindly like a twig, at the opposite side of the road, where someone had plastered a poster of Charlie.

'That's where he was,' she said through Chantale.

'Who?' Max asked.

'Big man . . .' she said, 'the biggest man.'

Vincent Paul?

'Have you seen him before?'

'No.'

'Have you seen him since?'

'No.'

'Do you know Vincent Paul?'

'No.'

'What's that you people call him?' Max said.

'*Le Roi Soleil?*' Chantale asked her and got a bewildered stare back. She didn't know what Chantale was talking about.

'OK. The man? What was he doing?'

'Running,' was the reply, then, nodding to the poster on the opposite wall, 'running with that boy.'

'*That* boy?' Max said, pointing to the image of Charlie's face. 'You sure?'

'Yes,' she said. 'The man was carrying him over his shoulder, like an empty sack of coal. The boy was kicking and waving his arms.'

214

'What happened next?'

The woman showed Max her stained fangs again. Max reached into his pocket and showed her his roll of greasy gourdes. She held her hand out to him and beckoned with her fingers: *pay me*.

Max shook his head with a smile. He pointed to her and made a gabbing motion with his fingers: *you talk*.

The woman smiled at him again and then she laughed and made a remark about him to Chantale, which Chantale left untranslated, although it made her smile.

The woman was well within her last quarter century. Her hair, the little he saw of it escaping under the green scarf she'd tied around it, was pure white, matching her eyebrows, which were falling out in small lumps. Her nose was boxer flat and the eyes she looked at Max with were a shade darker than her skin, their whites beige.

'A car came out of the Cité Soleil road,' the woman told Chantale, pointing it out to them both. 'The big man got in the car with the boy and they left.'

'Did you see the driver?'

'No. It had black windows.'

'What kind of car was it?'

'A nice car – a rich person's car,' Chantale translated the woman's words.

'Can she be more specific? Was it a big car? What colour was it?'

'A dark car with dark windows,' Chantale said. The woman carried on speaking. 'She says she'd seen it around here – a few times before the incident – always turning up that road.'

'Has she seen it since?'

Chantale asked her. The woman said no she hadn't and then said she was tired, that remembering things too far back made her sleepy.

Max paid out eight hundred gourdes. The woman quickly counted the money and gave Max a sly, conspiratorial wink, as if they shared a deeply personal secret. Then, quickly stealing another glance over her shoulder, she divided the money up into each hand, dropping the five hundred gourde note down her dress and deftly slipping the balance in her shoe, her motions fast, her hands and fingers phantoms barely glimpsed. Max looked at the front of the woman's dress – faded and threadbare, patched and stitched up – and then down at her feet. She wore unmatched shoes, of different sizes and colours; one black, scuffing back to grey and held together by fraying twine, the other originally a reddish brown with a busted clasp and bent buckle. They were so small they might have fitted a child. He didn't see how she could have stashed money in either shoe.

Max looked over into the shop doorway, to see what it was she'd been checking on. It was too dark to see inside and there was no sound coming from within, although he sensed someone was in there, watching them.

'The shop is closed,' the old woman said, as if reading Max's mind. 'Everything closes in time.'

20

'So what do you think? Did Vincent Paul kidnap Charlie?'

'I don't know,' Max said. 'No proof either way.'

They were sitting in the car, parked on the Rue du Dr Aubry, sharing one of the bottles of water Max had packed in a portable icebox for the trip.

Chantale took a sip of the water. She was chewing a cinnamon Chiclet. A UN jeep went by, trailing a tap-tap.

'They blame Vincent Paul for everything here – everything *bad* that happens,' Chantale said. 'All the crime. A bank gets robbed? – it's Vincent Paul. A car gets jacked? – it's Vincent Paul. A petrol station gets held up? – it's Vincent Paul. A house gets broken into? – it's Vincent Paul. *Bullshit* is what it is. It isn't him. But people here, they're so *dumb*, so apathetic, so scared, so – so damn *backward* – they believe what they want to believe, no matter how stupid and nonsensical. And these aren't the illiterate masses who are saying this, but *educated people* who should know better – the same people who run our businesses, the same people who are running the country.'

'Well, judging by the state of this place, that's no surprise,' Max chuckled. 'What do you think about him, Vincent Paul?'

'I believe he's mixed up in something very big, something very heavy.'

'Drugs?'

'What else?' she said. 'You know about the criminals Clinton's sending back to us? Well, Vincent Paul always sends someone over to the airport to pick up whoever's coming home.'

'Where do they go?'

'Cité Soleil – you know, the slum I told you about yesterday.'

'*He who runs Sitay So-lay runs the country.* Ain't that the way it goes?' Max said, remembering what Huxley had told him.

'Impressive,' Chantale smiled as she passed him the water. 'But what do you know about the *place*?'

'Some,' Max nodded, and repeated much of what Huxley had told him.

'Don't *ever* go in there without a guide – and an oxygen mask. You go there on your own and get lost? If the people don't kill you the air will.'

'Will you take me?'

'*No way*! I don't know the place and I don't *want* to know it,' she responded, almost angrily.

'That's too bad because I wanna go there tomorrow. Check it out,' Max said.

'You won't find anything – not just by looking. You need to know where you're going.'

'Ain't that the truth,' Max laughed. 'OK. I'll go there on my own. Just tell me how to get there. I'll be all right.' Chantale looked at him worried. 'Don't worry, I won't tell your boss.'

She smiled. He took a pull on the water and tasted her cinnamon on the spout where her lips had been.

'What else can you tell me about Vincent Paul? What is it with him and the Carvers?' Max asked.

'Gustav bankrupted his father. Perry Paul was a big wholesaler. He had a lot of exclusive deals going with the Venezuelans and the Cubans, and he was selling things very cheaply. Gustav used his influence in the government to put him out of business. Perry lost everything and shot himself. Vincent was in England when it happened. He was quite young, but hatred's a genetic thing here. Whole families will hate each other forever because of their great-grandparents falling out.'

'That's fucked up.'

'That's Haiti.'

'What was he doin' in England?'

'Getting an education – school, college.'

Max remembered the man's English accent the previous night.

'Have you ever met him?' Max asked.

'No,' she laughed. 'What I'm telling you's what I've been told, what I've heard. Not hard fact.'

He scribbled a few notes in his book.

'Where to, Detective?'

'The Roo Doo Chumps Da Mars.'

'*Rue du Champs de Mars*. What's there?'

'Felius Doofoor,' Max read off the notebook.

Chantale said nothing. When he looked up at her he saw she'd gone pale and looked scared.

'What's the matter?'

'Filius *Dufour*? *Le grand voyant*?'

'What was that last thing in English?'

'Out here it isn't the politicians or the Carvers who have the *real* power, it isn't even your President. It's people like the man you're going to meet. Filius Dufour was Papa Doc's personal fortune teller. Duvalier never did *anything* important without consulting him first.' Chantale lowered her voice as if she didn't really want to be heard. 'You know Papa Doc died at least two months before it was announced to the public. He was so scared of his enemies discovering his body and trapping his spirit that he ordered his body be buried in a secret location. To this day no one knows where it is – except for Filius Dufour. He was said to have conducted the burial ceremony. Just like he was said to have married Baby Doc to his mother on the day of Papa Doc's death out by the sacred waterfalls – some sort of rare voodoo ritual that very few people in the world know how to perform; it ensures the smooth transfer of power from father to son. After the Duvaliers fell from power everyone who was associated with them either went into exile or went to jail or got killed – everyone except Filius Dufour. Nothing happened to *him*. Everyone was too scared of him, what he could do.'

'I thought he was just a voodoo priest.'

'A *houngan*? *Him*? No. A *voyant* is like a fortune teller, but they go much deeper than that. For example, if you really want a woman you can't have – say she's happily married or not interested in you – you can go to your *houngan*, who'll try and fix it for you.'

'How?'

'Spells, prayers, chants, offerings. It's very personal and informal and it depends on the *houngan*. A lot of it involves some really disgusting things, like boiling the woman's used tampons and drinking the fluids.'

'Does it work?'

'I've never known anyone who tried it,' Chantale laughed. 'But I've seen plenty of ugly men walking around here with beautiful women, so draw your own conclusions.'

'What would the voyeur –?'

'*Voyant*. Now they're very different. Absolutely nothing to do with voodoo – but go telling that to a non-Haitian and they won't believe you.' Chantale scrutinized Max as she spoke to see if he was taking her seriously. She was pleased to see he had his notebook open and was scribbling furiously.

'All over the world you've got fortune tellers – tarot card readers, palm readers, gypsies, psychics, mediums. *Voyants* are like that, but they go a lot further. They don't use any gimmicks. They don't need them. You go to them with a specific question in mind – say, you're getting married in a month and you're having doubts. The *voyant* looks at you and tells you, in broad strokes, what will happen. Just like you're having a conversation. He or she can't ever tell you what to do, merely show you what the future has in store and let you make your mind up.'

'So far so Psychic Hotline,' Max said.

'Sure, but the *grands voyants* – and there are maybe two in the whole of Haiti, and Filius Dufour is as powerful as any man can be – they can *change* your future. If you don't like what they tell you, the *grands voyants* can talk directly to spirits. To get back to the woman you can't have – imagine you've got spirits watching over you.'

'Like guardian angels?'

'Yeah. The *grands voyants* can talk directly to these spirits and cut deals with them.'

'*Deals?*'

'If the woman's been letting them down, not following her destiny, being cruel to people around her, then they will agree to let the *voyant* in to push her towards the man.'

'Is that right?' Max said. 'And of course, the success of all this depends on believing what you've just told me?'

'It works on non-believers too. It's worse for them because they don't know what's hit them – the run of bad luck they're suddenly getting, their wife of fifteen years leaving them for their sworn enemy, their teenage daughter falling pregnant – that kind of thing.'

'How come you know so much about all this?'

'My mother is a *mambo* – a priestess. Filius Dufour initiated her when she was thirteen. He initiated me too.'

'How?'

'At a ceremony.'

Max looked at her but he couldn't read her face.

'What did he do?'

'My mother gave me a potion to drink. It made me leave my body, see everything from above. Not very high up, more like a couple of feet. Do you know what your skin looks like when you step out of it?'

Max shook his head no – not even when he was stoned on the best Colombian or Jamaican grass.

'Like grapes going off – all wrinkled and hollow and sagging, even when you're as young as I was.'

'What did he do?' Max asked again.

'Not what you think,' she replied, reading his mind through his tone. 'Ours may be a primitive religion, but it's not a savage one.'

Max nodded. 'When did you last see Dufour?'

'Not since that day. What do you want with him?'

'Part of the investigation.'

'And . . . ?'

'Client confidentiality,' Max said sharply.

'I see,' Chantale snapped. 'I've just told you something very personal, something I don't exactly spread around, but you won't tell me –'

'You *volunteered* that information,' Max said, and immediately wanted to take it back. It was an asshole thing to say.

'I didn't *volunteer* anything,' Chantale sneered and then softened. 'I felt like telling you.'

'Why?'

'I just did. You've got that confessional quality about you. The kind that listens without judging.'

'Probably cop conditioning,' Max said. She was wrong about him: he *always* judged. But she was flirting with him – nothing overt, everything tentative and ambiguous, nothing she couldn't deny and dismiss as wishful thinking on his part. Sandra had started out the same way, fed him enough to suspect she was interested in him, but kept him guessing until she was sure of him. He wondered what she would have made of Chantale, if they would have gotten along. He wondered if she would have approved of her as a successor. Then he dismissed the thought.

'OK, Chantale. I'll tell you this much. Charlie Carver was visiting Filius Dufour every week for six months before he vanished. He was due there the day he was snatched.'

'Well, let's go talk to him,' Chantale said, starting up the engine.

21

The Rue Boyer had once been a gated community of exclusive gingerbread houses set behind coconut palms and
hibiscus plants. Papa Doc had moved his cronies there
during his reign, while Baby Doc had converted two of the
houses into exclusive brothels he'd filled with $500 an hour
blonde hookers from LA to entertain the Colombian cartel
heads who were in and out of the country to oversee their
drug distribution and wash the profits in the national banks.
The cronies and whores had fled with the Doc regime and
the masses had claimed the road as theirs, first looting the
houses down to the floorboards, then squatting in the shells,
where they remained to this day.

Max couldn't understand why Dufour had chosen to stay
behind. The street was a tip, as bad as he'd seen in any ghetto
or bottom-of-the-ladder trailer park.

They drove through the remains of the gate – an iron
frame, tilting back away from the road, one corner bent all
the way down, pointing at the ground, ruptured hinges bent
and twisted into the shape of malign butterflies, needles for
antennae and razors for wings. The road was the usual
obstacle course of potholes, craters, bumps and gulleys,
while the houses – once glorious and elegant three-storey
structures – hung back from view, dark and shadowy
symmetrical blurs, stripped of all features, corroded by their
sudden influx of poverty, fit only for the wrecking ball. They
were now home to small villages of people – old and very
young, dressed almost identically in rags which barely

preserved their dignity and sometimes differentiated their gender. They all followed the passing car as one, a flock of blank and hollowed stares clustering around the windows.

Dufour lived in the very last house on the road, which turned out to be a cul-de-sac. His house was completely different from the rest. It was a dull pink, with a blue frill running along the tops and bottoms of its balconies, and the shutters – all closed – were a bright white. Green grass covered the front yard, and a rock- and plant-lined path led up to the porch steps.

A group of maybe a dozen children were playing in the road. They all stopped what they were doing, and watched Max and Chantale get out of the car.

Max heard a whistle behind him. He saw a young boy sprint across the grass and disappear around the side of the house.

As they started walking towards the path the children in the road came together in a tight group and barred their way. They all had rocks in their hands.

Unlike all the other kids he'd seen in the streets, these were dressed in proper clothes and shoes, and they looked healthy and clean. They couldn't have been more than eight, but their faces were hard with experience and wisdom beyond their years. Max tried to smile disarmingly at a girl with bows in her hair, but she gave him a ferocious stare.

Chantale tried talking to them, but no one answered or moved. Grips tightened on the rocks and young bodies tensed and shook with aggression. Max looked at the ground and saw they had plenty of ammunition if they needed. The road was a quarry.

He took Chantale's arm and moved her back a few steps.

Suddenly they heard a whistle from the house. The boy ran back shouting. Chantale let out a sigh of relief. The children dropped the rocks and went back to their game.

22

A teenage girl with a warm smile and braces on her teeth opened the door and let them in. She motioned for them to wait in the yellow-and-green tiled foyer while she ran up an imposing flight of wide carpeted stairs that led up to the first-floor landing.

The house was initially pleasantly cool after the baking heat of the outdoors, but once they were acclimatized the cool turned out to have a chilly edge. Chantale rubbed her arms to warm herself up.

Although there was a skylight which illuminated the foyer, Max noticed an absence of any lights – electrical or otherwise – and there were no switches of any kind on the walls. He could barely make out anything further than five feet in front of him. The darkness teemed all about them, almost solid, practically alive, waiting at the edges of the light, ready to pounce on their spot as soon as they left it.

Max noticed a large oil painting on the wall – two Hispanic-looking men with thin, near-ossified faces stood behind a pretty dark-skinned woman. They were all dressed in Civil War-era clothes, the men resembling Mississippi gamblers in black frock coats and grey pinstriped trousers, the woman in an orange dress with a white ruffled collar and an umbrella in her hand.

'Are any of those guys Doofoor?' Max asked Chantale, who was studying the portrait quite intently.

'Both,' she whispered.

'Has he got a twin brother?'

'Not that I've heard.'

The girl reappeared at the top of the stairs and beckoned them up.

As they climbed the stairs, Max noticed that the walls were hung with framed black-and-white photographs, some dated, some sepia toned, all of them hard to properly discern in the light, which seemed to get dimmer the further away they got from the floor, despite their relative nearness to the skylight. One photograph in particular caught Max's eye – a bespectacled black man in a white coat talking to a group of children sat outdoors.

'Papa Doc – when he was good,' Chantale said when she noticed what Max was looking at.

The girl led them to a room whose door was wide open. Inside it was pitch black. Still smiling she took Chantale's hand and told her to take Max's. They shuffled in, seeing absolutely nothing.

They were taken to a couch. They sat down. The girl struck a match and briefly lit up the room. Max caught a short glimpse of Dufour sitting right in front of them in an armchair, a blanket over his legs, looking right at him, smiling; and then it went dark as the match subsided to a small flame which was transferred to the wick of an oil lamp. He couldn't see Dufour any more, which wasn't a bad thing because the little he'd seen of him hadn't been pleasant. The man reminded him of a monstrous turkey, with a long and sharp nose that seemed to start from right in between his eyes, and a loose and floppy pouch of flesh dangling under his lower jaw. If he wasn't a hundred years old, he couldn't have been far off.

The lamp gave off a feeble bronze glow. Max could see Chantale, the mahogany table in front of them, and the silver tray bearing a pitcher full of chilled lime juice and two glasses with blue patterns around the middle. They couldn't see Dufour or anything else of the room.

Dufour spoke first, in French not Kreyol. He explained, in a voice so soft it was barely audible, that he knew only three words of English – 'Hello', 'Thank You' and 'Goodbye'. Chantale translated this to Max and asked Dufour if he objected to her being there as an interpreter. He said he didn't and addressed her as 'Mademoiselle'. For an instant Max got a glimpse back into another era, when men touched their hats, stood up, pulled chairs and opened doors for women, but the vision was quickly overtaken by present concerns.

'I'm sorry for the darkness but my eyes no longer see like they did. Too much light gives me terrible headaches,' Dufour said in French and Chantale translated. 'Welcome to my house, Mr Mingus.'

'We'll try not to take up too much of your time,' Max said, as he set his tape recorder and notebook and pen down on the table.

Dufour joked that the older he got the smaller things became, remembering an era when tape recorders meant cumbersome reel to reel players. He told them to try the lemonade, that he'd had it made for them.

Chantale poured them both a glass. Max was amused to see that the designs on the glasses were oriental ones showing men and women in various sexual positions, some commonplace, some exotic, and a few requiring the suppleness of professional contortionists to pull off. He wondered how long it had been since Dufour had had any pussy.

They made smalltalk as they sipped their drinks. The lemonade was bittersweet but very refreshing. Max tasted both lemon and lime juice mixed together with water and sugar. Dufour asked Max how long he'd been in the country and what he thought of it. Max said he hadn't been in Haiti long enough to form an opinion. Dufour laughed loudly at this but didn't define his laughter with a quip or a retort.

'*Bien, bien*,' Dufour said. 'Let's begin.'

23

Max opened his notebook and pressed record.

'When did you first meet Charlie Carver?'

'His mother brought him to me a few months before his disappearance. I don't remember the exact date,' Dufour said.

'How did you meet her?'

'She found me. She was *very* troubled.'

'How so?'

'If she hasn't told you, neither can I.'

His response to the latter had been polite but firm. There wasn't much life left in Dufour but Max could detect an iron will propping up his crumbling body. Max was playing the interview like a conversation, keeping his tone neutral and his body language relaxed and friendly – no arms on the table, no leaning forward, sitting back in the couch; tell me everything, send it my way.

Chantale was the opposite, virtually coming off her seat, as she strained to listen to the old man because the little that remained of his voice faded in and out, rising, when it did, to no louder than the hoarse hiss of hot grit hitting a snowbound road.

'What did you make of Charlie?'

'A very clever and happy boy.'

'How often did you see him?'

'Once a week.'

'The same day and time every week?'

'No, they changed from week to week.'

'Every week?'

'*Every* week.'

A sound of a lid being unscrewed came from Dufour's direction, then a smell of kerosene and rotting vegetables overtook and flattened the pleasant scent of fresh lime that had been the room's only perfume. Chantale screwed up her face and moved her head out of the way of the worst of the stench. Max paused the tape recorder.

Dufour said nothing by way of explanation. He rubbed his palms, then his wrists and forearms, and then he did his fingers one by one, popping their respective knuckles when he was finished. The smell went from bad to nasty to nearly unbearable, forming an acrid, rubbery taste in the back of Max's throat.

He looked away from the old man's direction and glanced around the room. His eyes had acclimatized to the quarter light and he could see more now. All about him surfaces gave off the tiniest reflections of lamplight, reminding Max of photographs of crowds holding their lighters aloft during rock concerts, a butane milky way. To his left were the shuttered windows, the fierce sun penetrating through the smallest fissures in the wood, beaming in from the outside in phosphorescent dots and dashes, a blinding morse code.

Dufour closed the container and said something to Chantale.

'He says he's ready to continue,' she said to Max.

'OK.' Max switched the recorder back on and stared straight ahead of him, where he could vaguely make out his host's head and a pallid blur where his face was. 'Who made the appointments? You or Mrs Carver?'

'Me.'

'How did you notify them?'

'By telephone. Eliane – my maid, who you met when you came in – she called Rose, Charlie's nanny.'

'How much notice did you give them?'

'Four, five hours.'

Max scribbled this down in his notebook.

'Was there anyone else with you at the time?'

'Only Eliane.'

'No one came to the house while you were with him? No visits?'

'No.'

'Did you tell anyone Charlie was coming to see you?'

'No.'

'Did anyone see Charlie coming here?'

'Everyone in the street.'

Dufour laughed as soon as Chantale had finished translating, to confirm that he was joking.

'Did they know who he was?' Max asked.

'No. I don't think so.'

'Did you notice anyone suspicious watching your house? Anyone you hadn't seen before?'

'No.'

'No one hanging around?'

'I would have seen.'

'I thought you didn't like daylight?'

'There is more than one way to see,' Chantale translated.

Fasten your seatbelts, hold on tight – mystic mumbo-jumbo Disneyland here we come, Max felt like saying, but didn't. He'd been here before, in a similar situation, talking to a voodoo priest who was rumoured to have supernatural powers. That was back when he was looking for Boukman. The most powerful thing about that guy had been his smell – bathtubs of rum and months of skipped showers. He'd humoured the priest, cut him some slack, and come away from their encounter with a working understanding of Haiti's national religion. Sometimes – but not often – it paid to tolerate and indulge.

'You're not asking me the right questions,' Dufour said through Chantale.

'Yeah? What should I be asking?'

'I'm not the detective.'

'Do you know who kidnapped Charlie?'

'No.'

'I thought you could see into the future?'

'Not everything.'

How convenient. I guess that's what you tell people when their relatives suddenly die.

'For example,' Dufour continued, 'I can't tell people when their loved ones are going to die.'

Max's heart skipped a beat. He swallowed dry.

Coincidence: no such thing as mind-reading.

Something – or someone – stirred behind him. He heard a floorboard subtly creak like it was being stepped on firmly but slowly. He glanced over his shoulder but he couldn't see anything. He looked at Chantale who looked like she hadn't heard anything.

Max turned back to Dufour.

'Tell me about Charlie. About when he came to see you. What did you do when he came?'

'We talked.'

'You talked?'

'Yes. We talked without speaking.'

'I see,' Max said. 'So you – what? Used telepathy – ESP, *ET* – what?'

'Our spirits talked.'

'Your *spirits* talked?' he asked, as neutrally as possible. He desperately wanted to laugh.

233

They had officially entered the realm of bullshit, where everything happened and the far-fetched was never far enough. He'd play along, he told himself, until the rules got too fucked up and the situation threatened to change owners. Then he'd weigh in and turn the tables.

'Our spirits. Who we are inside. You have one too. Don't confuse your body with your soul. Your body is simply the house you live in while you're here on earth.'

– And don't confuse me with a dickhead.

'So, how did you do that – talk to his spirit?'

'It's what I do, although . . . it's not something I've ever done with a living person before. Charlie was unique.'

'What did you talk about?'

'Him.'

'What did he tell you?'

'You were told why he came to see me?'

'Because he wasn't talking, yeah – *and* . . . ?'

'He told me the reason why that was.'

Max saw something cross his peripheral vision to his right and quickly turned to catch it, but there was nothing to see.

'So, let me get this right – Charlie *told* you – or his "spirit" told you – what was wrong with him? Why he wasn't talking?'

'Yes.'

'And . . . ?'

'And what?'

'What *is* wrong with him?'

'I told his mother. As she hasn't told you, neither will I.'

'It could help my investigation,' Max said.

'It won't.'

'I'll be the judge of that.'

'It *won't*,' Dufour repeated firmly.

'And his mother took your word for it? Whatever it was you claim Charlie told you?'

'No, like you she was sceptical. Actually she didn't believe me,' Chantale said hesitantly now, her tone questioning and confused. What she was hearing made no sense to her.

'What changed her mind?'

'If she wants to tell you, she will. I'm saying nothing.'

And Max knew he'd get nothing out of him, not this way. Whatever it was, Francesca or Allain Carver would have to tell him. He moved on.

'You said your "spirits talked"? Yours and Charlie's? Do you still talk? Are you in touch with Charlie now?'

Chantale translated. Dufour didn't answer.

Max realized that he hadn't seen the maid leave the room. Was she in there with them? He scanned the area in the direction of the door, but the surrounding darkness was too finite, too determined to yield no more than it had to.

'*Oui*,' Dufour said, finally, shifting in his seat.

'Yes? Have you talked recently?'

'Yes.'

'When?'

'This morning.'

'Is he alive?'

'Yes.'

Max's mouth went dry. His excitement briefly dispelled all his doubts and disbelief.

'Where is he?'

'He doesn't know.'

'Can he describe anything to you?'

'No – only that a man and a woman are caring for him. They're like his parents.'

Max scribbled this down, even though he was recording their exchange.

'Does he say anything about where he's at?'

'No.'

'Is he hurt?'

'He says he is being well looked after.'

'Has he told you who took him?'

'You have to find out yourself. That's why you're here. That is your purpose,' Dufour said, raising his voice, a hint of anger there.

'My *purpose*?' Max put down his notebook. He didn't like what he'd just heard, the arrogance of it, the presumption.

'Everyone is put on earth for a *purpose*, Max. Every life has a reason,' Dufour continued calmly.

'And . . . *so*?'

'This – here and now – is *your purpose*. How things take their course is up to you, not me.'

'Are you saying I was "*born*" to find Charlie?'

'I never said you were going to find him. That hasn't been decided yet.'

'*Oh*? And who decides *that*?'

'We don't yet know why *you're* here.'

'Who's "we"?'

'We don't know what's keeping you here. With the others it was easy to see. They were here for money. Mercenaries. Not right. But that's not what brought you here.'

'Well, I ain't here for the climate,' Max quipped, and then almost immediately remembered the dream he'd had in his hotel room in New York, where Sandra had told him to take the case because he had 'no choice'. He remembered how he'd weighed up what remained of his options, how he'd glimpsed his future, how bleak it had all seemed. The old man was right – he was here to rescue his life as well as Charlie's.

How much had Dufour already known about him? Before he could ask him, the old man started talking.

'God gives us free will and insight. To a few He gives a

lot of both, to many He gives more of one than the other, and to most He limits what He gives. Those with both are aware of where their futures lie. Politicians see themselves as presidents, employees as managers, soldiers as generals, actors as superstars, and so forth. You can usually tell these people at the starting gate. They know what they want to do with their lives before they turn twenty. Now, how and when we fulfil our purpose – our "destiny" – is a lot up to us and also a little out of our hands. If God has a higher purpose in mind for us and sees us wasting time with a lowly one, He will intervene and set us back on the right path. Sometimes it's a painful intervention, sometimes a seemingly "accidental" or "coincidental" one. The more insightful recognize His hand shaping their lives and follow the path they were meant to. Max, you were *meant* to come here.'

Max breathed in deeply. The stench had gone and the sweet tang of lime was back. He didn't know what to think.

Stick to what you know, not what you'd like to know. You're investigating a missing person, a young boy. That's all that matters – what you're going after. As Eldon Burns used to say: do what you do and fuck the rest.

Max took Charlie's poster out of his pocket and unfolded it on the table. He pointed out the cross scored in the poster's borders.

'Can you see this?' he asked Dufour, pointing to the marks.

'Yes. Tonton Clarinette. That's his mark,' Dufour replied.

'I thought Ton Ton Clarinet was a myth.'

'In Haiti all facts are based on myths.'

'So you're saying that he's for real?'

'It is all for you to discover.' Dufour smiled. 'Go to the source of the myth. Find out how it started and why, and who started it.'

Max thought of Beeson and Medd and where Huxley had

told him they'd gone: the waterfalls. He made a note to talk to Huxley again.

'Back to Charlie,' Max said. 'Did he see Ton Ton Clarinet?'

'Yes.'

Max glanced at Chantale. She caught his stare. Max saw fear in her eyes.

'When?'

'The last time he came here, he told me he'd seen Tonton Clarinette.'

'Where?' Max leant in closer.

'He didn't say. He just told me he'd seen him.'

Max scribbled '*interview Carver servants*' in his notebook.

'People steal children here, don't they?' Max asked.

'It happens a lot, yes.'

'Why do they steal them?'

'Why do they steal them in your country?'

'Sex – mostly. Ninety-nine per cent of the time. Then it's for money, or it's childless couples who want to cut out adoption agencies, lonely women with a mothering fetish, that kind of thing.'

'Here we have other uses for children.'

Max thought back for a second and quickly got to Boukman.

'Voodoo?'

Dufour chuckled mockingly.

'No, not vodou. Vodou is not evil. It's like Hinduism, with different gods for different things, and one great big God for all things. No children are ever sacrificed in vodou. Try again.'

'Devil worship? Black magic?'

'Black magic. Correct.'

'Why do they sacrifice children in black magic?'

'Various reasons, most of them insane. Most black magic

is the preserve of deluded idiots, people who think if they do something shocking enough the devil will ride out of hell to shake their hands and grant them three wishes. But here it's different. Here people know *exactly* what they're doing. You see you, me – all of us – we are all watched over, guarded by spirits –'

'Guardian angels?'

'Yes – whatever you want to call it. Now, almost the strongest protection anyone can have is a child's protection. Children are innocent. Pure. Very little lasting harm comes to you when one is watching over you – and that which does is the sort of harm you learn and grow from.'

Max thought things through for a moment. This was the Boukman case all over. Boukman had sacrificed children to feed some demon he'd supposedly conjured up.

'You say children make the most powerful guardian angels, because they're innocent and pure?' Max asked. 'What about Charlie? What would they want with him – apart from his being a child?'

'Charlie is *very* special,' Dufour said. 'The protection he offers is greater, because he is among the purer spirits – those sometimes known as the Perpetually Pure, those who will never know evil. Other spirits trust them. They can open many doors. Not many people have them as guardians. Those who do are usually people like me, those who can see beyond the present.'

'So is it possible to . . . "steal a spirit"?'

'Yes, of course. But it's not a simple procedure and not everyone can do it. It's very specialized.'

'Can you do it?'

'Yes.'

'*Have* you done it?'

'To do good you have to know bad – you, Max, more

than most, know what I mean. There *is* a bad side to what I do – a reversal of my process, a sort of black magic, which involves enslaving souls, forcing them to become the protectors of evil. Children are a major element of that. They're a premium here in Haiti, a currency.'

Just as Chantale finished translating the maid came into the room and walked over to them.

'It's time,' Dufour said.

They said their goodbyes. The maid took Chantale's hand and Chantale took Max's and they filed out of the room. In the doorway, Max looked back at where they'd been sitting. He swore he saw the faint outline of not one, but two people standing where Dufour had been. He couldn't be sure.

24

They headed back to the bank, Max at the wheel now, getting used to Port-au-Prince's ruined streets. Once he'd dropped Chantale off he'd return to the house. His head was heavy, pounding. He was done for the day. He couldn't think clearly. He hadn't had time to release the information he'd been steadily accumulating throughout the day and his brain was fit to burst. He needed to process all the data, break it down into useful and useless, chuck out the trash and keep the good stuff, then work it, break it down again, look for common threads and connections, promising leads, things that didn't quite seem to fit.

Chantale had barely said a word since they'd left Dufour's house.

'Thanks for your help today, Chantale,' Max said, and looked over at her. She was pale. Her face shone with a dull dew of perspiration, which pooled and crested into small droplets on her upper lip. Her neck and jaw muscles were tensed.

'Are you OK?'

'No,' she croaked. 'Stop the car.'

Max pulled over on a bustling road. Chantale jumped out, took a few steps and threw up in the gutter, prompting an exclamation of shocked disgust from a man who was pissing up against a nearby wall.

Max steadied her as she heaved a second time.

When she'd finished he stood her up against the car and made her take deep breaths. He got the water bottle out, poured some on to his handkerchief and wiped it around her brow, wafting his notebook to cool her off.

'That's better,' she said, after she'd recovered and the colour had returned to her face.

'Was that too much for you? Back there?'

'I was real nervous.'

'Didn't show.'

'Trust me, I was.'

'You did great,' Max said. 'So much so I'll give you tomorrow off.'

'You're going to Cité Soleil, right?'

'You got me!'

They got back in the car and she drew him a map. She told him to get some surgical masks and gloves – which he'd find in one of the two main supermarkets – and to throw his shoes away if he planned on leaving his car and walking around. The ground was quite literally made of shit – animal and, most of it, human. Everything that breathed in the slum had a textbook of diseases on it and in it and all around it.

'Be real careful out there. Take your gun. Don't stop your car unless it's absolutely necessary.'

'Sounds like what they used to tell folk about Liberty City.'

'Cité Soleil is no joke, Max. It's a bad bad place.'

He drove her to the Banque Populaire and watched her and her ass until she'd gone through the entrance. She didn't turn around. Max wasn't sure if that still meant something now.

25

He called Allain Carver from the house and gave him a rundown of what he'd done, who he'd talked to and what he was planning to do next. He could tell from the way Carver listened – grunting affirmatively to let Max know he was still on the line, but asking no questions – that Chantale had briefed him thoroughly.

Next he called Francesca. No answer.

Sitting out on the porch, notebook in hand, he played his interview tapes.

The questions came to him:

First up: Why had Charlie been kidnapped?

Money?

Absence of a ransom demand ruled that out as a motive.

Revenge?

A strong possibility. Rich people always had their fair share of mortal enemies. It came with the territory. The Carvers, with their history, must have had a phone book's worth.

What *was* wrong with Charlie?

He hadn't started talking yet. Some people start slow.

What about that thing with his hair?

He was a little kid. One of the few things Max remembered his dad telling him was how, when he was a baby, he used to cry every time someone laughed. Shit happens, then you grow up.

Sure, but Dufour had found *something*.

Did the kidnappers know what it was?

Maybe. In which case the motive became blackmail. The Carvers hadn't mentioned anything about that, but that didn't necessarily mean it wasn't going on. If there was something really wrong with the kid Allain and Francesca were probably keeping it from Gustav because of his fragile health.

Why hadn't Francesca told him about Charlie's condition herself?

Too painful? Or she didn't think it was relevant.

Had the kid been kidnapped for black magic purposes?

Possibly.

He'd have to start checking up on Carver's enemies and then cross-reference against involvement in black magic. But how was he going to do *that*? The country was upside down, running on a faint pulse. There was no police force to speak of, and he doubted there were any criminal records or files he could go through.

He'd be doing it the hard way, looking under every rock, chasing every shadow.

What about Eddie Faustin?

Eddie Faustin *had* been involved. He was a major player. He'd known who was behind the kidnapping. *Find out who he knew.*

Who was the big guy the shoemaker woman had seen?

Faustin? He was supposed to have been killed and beheaded near the car, so it may not have been him. But if he shared the same genes as his mother and brother he wasn't a big man. Both Faustins were medium build, soft going on flab.

Of course Vincent Paul had been on the scene.

Was Charlie alive?

He only had Dufour's word on that, and unless Dufour was the kidnapper or was holding him captive he dismissed the claim and continued to presume him dead.

Did Dufour really know who'd kidnapped Charlie?

As before.

How serious was his hold on Francesca?

She was rich and vulnerable, ripe for exploitation. It happened all the time, phoney psychics and mystics taking advantage of the lonely, the bereaved, the chronically self-obsessed, the naïve, the plain fucking dumb – all promised a glorious future for just $99.99 plus tax.

What if Dufour was the real deal?

Stick to what you know.

Was Dufour a suspect?

Still unresolved. Yes and no. A man that close to Papa and Baby Doc must have had the juice to pull off a simple kidnapping. He was bound to know a few unemployed Tonton Macoutes, starving for cash and pining for their glory days, who would have done it at the drop of a hat. They used to abduct people all the time. But what would be his motive? At his age, with very few more years of life left? Had Gustav Carver fucked him or his family over in the past? He doubted it. Gustav would not have messed with one of Papa Doc's favourites. Still, for now, he couldn't rule anything out.

Later he tried to sleep but couldn't. He went to the kitchen and found an unopened bottle of Barbancourt rum in one of the cupboards. As he took it out he spotted something tucked away in the corner. It was a four-inch-tall wire figurine of a man in a straw hat, standing with his legs apart and his arms behind his back.

Max stood it up on the table and inspected it as he drank. The figure's head was painted black, its clothes – shirt and trousers – dark blue. It wore a red handkerchief and carried a small bag, like a school satchel, slung across its shoulder.

The pose was militaristic and the look that of a colour-coordinated scarecrow.

The rum went down well, filling his belly with a soothing warmth which soon seeped into the rest of him and translated into a pleasant feeling of utterly groundless hope. He could see himself getting used to the stuff.

26

No matter what Huxley and Chantale had told him about Cité Soleil, nothing could have prepared him for the horrors that paraded past his windshield as he waded into the slum. A small part of him, once hard and rigid in its ways, broke off and drifted towards the place where he hid away his compassion.

At first, going in, driving down the narrow soot-covered track that served as a main thoroughfare, it seemed like a shanty-town maze, thousands of densely packed one-room shacks stretching out as far as the eye could see, east and west, horizon to horizon, no clear way in or out, just trial, error and lucky guesses. The more he saw of the shacks and the closer he looked at them, the more he realized that there was a sort of pecking order in the slum, a class system for lowlifes. About a quarter of the homes were adobe huts with corrugated-iron roofs. They looked fairly sturdy and habitable. Next down were huts which had thin planks of wood for walls and light-blue plastic sheeting for roofs. A medium wind would probably carry them and their inhabitants out to sea, but at least they were better off than the bottom layer of the slum's housing pyramid – homes made out of patched-together cardboard, a few of which collapsed as soon as Max looked at them. He supposed the adobe huts belonged to veteran slum dwellers, those who'd survived and crawled to the top of this shit heap. The cardboard shacks belonged to the new arrivals and the weak, the vulnerable and the almost dead, while the wooden ones were for those in-between gutters.

Thick plumes of black charcoal smoke came out of crude holes in the middle of the roofs and dispersed into the sky, forming a Zeppelin-shaped pall of grey smog which hung over the area, churning but not breaking up in the breeze. As Max passed he felt the stares coming his way from the huts, hundreds and hundreds of pairs of eyes falling on the car, cutting through the windshield, peeling him down to his basic core – friend or foe, rich or poor. He saw people – thin, wasted, bone shrink-wrapped in skin, clinging to the edges of extinction – leaning against their hovels.

Randomly spaced, between blocks of shacks, were areas that hadn't yet been claimed and built on, where the ground was a cross between a mammoth garbage dump and a snapshot of World War I killing fields, post-conflict – broken, muddy, blasted to fuck, strewn with death and despair. In some areas the muck was piled into imposing great mounds where children with insect-thin legs, distended bellies and heads too big for their necks played and scavenged.

He passed two horses, hooves buried in muck, barely moving, so emaciated he could clearly see their rib cages and count off the bones.

There were open sewers everywhere, gutted cars and buses and trucks serving as homes. All the windows in the car were shut and the air-conditioning was on, but the sharp stench of the outside still crept in – every bad, evil smell mixed into one and multiplied by two: month-old dead bodies, fermenting trash, human shit, animal shit, stagnant water, stale oil, stale smoke, crushed humanity. Max started feeling sick. He pulled on one of the masks he'd bought in the supermarket before he'd set out that morning.

He crossed over the 'Boston Canal' on a makeshift bridge made of lashed together metal girders. The thick sludge river of used oil split Cité Soleil down the middle, a permanent wound on the slum's poisoned soul, bleeding its black venom into the sea. It was simply the worst place he'd ever seen – a circle of hell served up to earth as a warning. He couldn't believe that the UN and US had occupied the country for two whole years and done nothing about Cité Soleil.

He was looking for signs of Vincent Paul – cars, jeeps, things that worked, things that didn't belong here. All he could see was misery living in misery, sickness sucking on sickness, people trailing their shadows.

He reached an elevated stretch of ground and got out of the car to look around. Mindful of what Chantale had told him about walking in the slum, Max had bought some throw-away footwear – a pair of scuffed army boots with ground-down heels – from a woman selling a basket of the things on the sidewalk near the Impasse Carver. He was glad he had because with every step he took, his feet were sucked a little into the ground, which, in spite of the raw, blistering sunlight, was soft and gooey instead of baked rock solid.

He looked over the chaotic mess all around him, at the multitude of hovels erupting from the ground like metallic pustules, giving the landscape the texture of a battered and corroded cheesegrater. The place was home to over half a million people, yet it was eerily quiet, with barely a noise heard above the sound of the sea, a quarter of a mile away. It was the same cowed stillness he recognized from the worst parts of Liberty City, where death struck by the hour. Here he supposed it came by the second.

Could Vincent Paul really have a base here? Could he live in a place so defiled?

His feet suddenly plunged deep into the ground with a thick slurping sound and he was instantly up to his ankles in muck, feeling it pulling at his soles. He yanked his feet out and got back on solid ground. The deep footprints he'd

left where he'd gone down immediately began to disinte-
grate as the ground corrected the break in its smooth sticky
surface, and oozed thick, poisonous treacle over the blemish.

Max heard the sound of approaching cars.

In the distance, off to his left, he saw a small convoy of
military vehicles – three army trucks topped and tailed by
jeeps – heading off towards the sea.

He ran back to the Landcruiser and started the engine.

27

Max followed the convoy to a clearing near the sea where a semi-circle of large olive-green tents had been erected. Two of them flew Red Cross flags.

Hundreds of Cité Soleil inhabitants were queuing for food which soldiers were dishing out to them from behind long foldaway tables. The people took their paper plates and ate where they stood, many walking to the back of the line to eat and go back for more.

Elsewhere others waited their turn in front of a water truck, empty buckets, cans and gallon tanks in their hands. Further on there were three more trails of people, ready to receive rations of rice, cornmeal or coal. The queues were surprisingly orderly and quiet. There was no pushing or shoving, no fighting, or panic. Everyone would receive what they were waiting for, as in communion.

Max started thinking he'd been wrong, that the UN was actually doing something to relieve the suffering of these desperate people it had freed in the name of democracy, but when he looked a little more closely at the vehicles, he noticed they were all unmarked. None of the soldiers were wearing the sky-blue headgear of the occupying forces, and neither were any of them carrying matching ordnance. Instead they had a miscellany of gangbanger hardware – Uzis, pumps and AKs.

Max realized he was looking at Vincent Paul's band of brothers moments before he got his first clear view of the man himself, emerging from a medical tent. Like his men he didn't wear a mask, surgical gloves or temporary shoes. He was dressed top to toe in black – T-shirt, combat trousers and paratrooper boots. He was tall, hulking, dark and bald. Max wasn't too sure if he was Joe's size or slightly bigger. He certainly cast a longer shadow and had a lot more presence than his friend, who wasn't exactly lacking in it.

The big man moved to one of the food tables and helped out, serving people, talking to them and laughing with them. It was the laughter – deep, booming rolls of joviality, the sound of a formation of incoming jets heard from afar – that confirmed Vincent Paul's identity. Max recognized the voice from two nights before, when he'd been saved from the street robbers.

After he'd dished out a few platefuls to the food queue, Paul went among the people. He talked to children, squatting down so he could be at eye level with them, he talked to men and women, stooping down to listen to them. He shook hands and accepted hugs and kisses. When an old woman kissed his hand, he kissed hers right back and made her laugh. People stopped moving forward in their lines and stood where they were to watch him. Some started leaving their places and walking towards him.

And then Max heard it – a hissing murmur at first, the scraps of a song – '*ssssan-ssssan /sssssan-ssssan /sssssan-ssssan*', and then it grew louder as more people picked it up and gave the chant body and definition – 'Vinnn-*ssssan*/ Vinnn-*ssssan*/ Vinnn-*ssssan*'. He had become the focus of all attention, the place all eyes had turned to. The inhabitants of Cité Soleil had forgotten all about their hunger and misery and were crowding around Vincent Paul, surrounding him completely, yet leaving a broad respectful halo of space around him so he could move with ease, shake hands and accept embraces. Max noticed two striking women in military fatigues flanking him, watching the crowd, hands close to the pistols at their hips.

Paul raised his hands and the crowd fell quiet. He stood a good few inches above the tallest person there, so most had a good view of his huge dome-like head. He addressed them in a deep baritone which reached Max, although he couldn't understand a word he was saying. The crowd lapped it up, breaking out into cheers, applause, whistles, foot stamping and hollering. Even Paul's own men, who must have heard it all a million times over, were clapping with unforced enthusiasm.

Max had seen this kind of shit before, on the streets of Miami. Every few years the biggest homegrown dealers – the ones who'd managed to stay alive and out of jail through luck, ruthlessness, money and good connections – would decide to 'give something back' to the community they'd helped decimate with their drugs and turf wars. They and their crews would roll into the hoods on Christmas Day and hand out roast turkeys, presents and even money. It was what happened towards the end of their street lifespans, the last grand gesture before they got taken down by rivals or cops. They'd got everything their limited minds had ever dreamed of – wealth, pussy, petty power, fear, cars and clothes. Now they wanted love and respect too.

Here Max admired Paul's philanthropy, irrespective of his long-term ulterior motives. He'd begun to understand that this was a part of the world where everything he knew and took for granted had either long broken down or never existed. The only way people could help themselves was by leaving the country altogether, like thousands did every year when they took to the seas and risked their lives heading for Florida. Those who remained were doomed to a life lived on their knees, slaves to the kindness and mercy of strangers. *Someone* had to help them – and as it looked for sure that that someone wasn't going to be the US and the UN, why not the man people claimed to be the biggest druglord in the Caribbean?

Watching Paul lapping up the adulation, pressing more flesh, Max was sure he was looking at Charlie Carver's kidnapper. He could quite easily have snatched the kid and hidden him in Cité Soleil. He had the power to pull it off and get away with it. He had the power to do almost anything he wanted.

28

In the late afternoon, Vincent Paul got into a jeep and left the slum. A truck and two more vehicles followed him out.

Max tailed them out of town, through dusty arid flatlands and clumps of buildings which were either half built or half ruined. Then, as night fell, they headed up into the mountains, clinging to a steep thin crust of dirt road, which was all that separated them from hundreds of feet of thin air.

The last stretch of the journey took them across a plateau. They made for a small bonfire, near where the convoy came to a halt. The vehicles then positioned themselves so that they were facing each other, and their headlights intersected and lit up a square of rough, rocky earth.

Max killed his lights, rolled a little closer to the place where they'd stopped and got out of the car. He established his bearings so he could find his way back, then he approached the convoy.

The back of the truck was opened. There was fierce shouting both inside and out, and then a man was thrown out. He hit the ground with a thud, a scream and the thick jingle of chains. One of Vincent's men picked him up and slammed him up against the truck.

Then more men were pushed out of the truck, all landing on top of each other. Max counted eight of them. They were marched into the lit-up space between the vehicles.

Max got a little closer. A group of a dozen or more civilians were watching what was happening.

Max walked off to the left, staying in the darkness. He had a clear view of the captives, who were lined up in a row. They were dressed in UN military uniform and looked Indian.

Arms behind his back, Paul inspected them, glaring down at each and every one of them as he passed. He resembled a father angry with his unruly brood; the men, compared to him, were small and snappable.

'Do any of you speak and understand English?' Paul asked.

'Yes,' they answered as one.

'Who's the commanding officer here?'

A man stepped forward and stood to attention. He tried to meet Paul's eyes but his head travelled so far back he seemed to be staring up at the sky, seeking out some distant star.

'And you are?'

'Captain Ramesh Saggar.'

'Are these your men?'

'Yes.'

'Do you know why you've been brought here?'

'No. Who are you?' he asked in a heavy accent.

Paul glanced briefly over at the civilians, then back at the Captain.

'Do you know why you're in this country?'

'I'm sorry?'

'What is the purpose of your presence here, in Haiti? What are you *doing* here? You, your men, the Bangladeshi division of the United Nations army?'

'I-I-I don't understand.'

'You don't understand *what*? The question? Or what you're *doing* here?'

'Vye are you asking me dis?'

'Because I'm the one asking the questions and you're the one answering them. They're simple questions, Captain. I'm not exactly asking you to divulge military secrets.'

Paul was all business, his tone pointed but even, without emotion. If he was following the sort of interrogation procedure Max thought he was, his calm, no-nonsense manner was the prelude to an explosion. Joe had been brilliant at that – used his bulk to intimidate and terrify the suspect, and then confused them by coming over all reasonable and quiet and to the point – 'Look, just tell me what I want to know and I'll see what kind of deal I can cut you with the DA' – and then, if it wasn't working or the scumbag was a particularly sick fuck, or Joe was just having a bad day – KA-FUCKING-BOOM! – he'd backhand them to the floor.

'Answer my question. Please.'

'Ve are here to keep de peace.'

Max heard the first tremor in the Captain's voice.

'To "keep the peace"?' Paul repeated. 'Are you doing that?'

'Vat is dis about?'

'Answer my *question*. Are you doing your *job*? Are you "*keeping the peace*"?'

'Yes, I – I dink so.'

'Why?'

'Dere is no civil var here. The people are not fighting.'

'True. For now.' Paul looked at the other seven soldiers, all standing at ease. 'Would you say your job – this "*keeping the peace*" you think you're doing so well – would you say an aspect of it would involve protecting the Haitian people?'

'Pro-protecting?'

'Yes, protecting. You know, preventing harm from coming to them. Do you understand?'

Now there was a hint of venom in Paul's voice.

'Yes.'

'Well, then? Are you doing your job here?'

'I – I – I dink so.'

'You think so? *You* think so?'

The Captain nodded. Paul glared at him. The Captain averted his eyes. His composure was cracking.

'So then, tell me, Captain. Do you think "protecting the Haitian people" does or does *not* include raping women – actually, *no* – let me be more *specific*. Do you think, Captain Saggar, that "protecting the Haitian people" involves raping and beating up *teenage girls*?'

Saggar said nothing. His lips were trembling, his whole face quaking.

'Well?' Paul asked, leaning in close.

No reply.

'ANSWER MY DAMN QUESTION!' Paul roared and everyone, including Paul's own troops, jumped. Max felt the voice in his gut like deep speaker bass.

'I – I – I –'

'Aie – Aie – Aie,' Paul mimicked in a faggot voice. 'Are your feet on fire, Captain? *No?* Well, answer me.'

'N-N-N no it does not, but – but – but –'

Paul held his hand up for silence and Saggar flinched.

'*Now* you know what this is about –'

'Sorry!' the Captain blurted.

'What?'

'Ve said ve vere sorry. Ve wrote *letter*.'

'What – *this*?' Paul took a folded piece of paper out of his pocket and read it out. '"*Dear Mr Le Fen*" – that's that man over there by the jeep, red shirt, that's him – "*I am writing to apologize on behalf of both my men and the United Nations Peace Keeping Force for the regrettable incident involving your daughter and some men under my command. We will endeavour to make sure this kind of incident is not repeated. Yours sincerely, Captain Ramesh Saggar.*"'

Paul slowly folded the letter and slipped it back into his pocket.

'Do you know that ninety per cent of the Haitian population is illiterate? Did you *know* that, Captain?'

'N-n-no.'

'No? Do you also know that English isn't the first language here?'

'Yes.'

'It's actually the *third* language, if you like. But ninety-nine per cent of the people *don't speak English*. And Mr Le Fen is one of the majority. So what good's a LETTER WRITTEN IN ENGLISH going to do? HEH? More to the point – what good's a LOUSY LETTER going to do to Verité Le Fen? Do you know who that is, Captain?'

Saggar didn't answer.

Paul called to the group and held his arm out. A girl came over, limping badly. She faced Saggar. They were the same height, although the girl was in an unnatural slouch. Max couldn't see her face, but judging from the Captain's expression, she must have been in real bad shape.

Max looked over to the soldiers. One – a skinny bald man with a thick moustache – was shaking.

'Do you recognize her, Captain?'

'I'm *velly* sorry,' Saggar said to her. 'Vat ve did to you vas bad.'

'As I explained, Captain, she *can't understand* you.'

'P-p-please translate.'

Paul told the girl. She whispered into Paul's ear. Paul looked at Saggar.

'Vat did she say?'

'*Get maman ou* – literally, your mother's clit. Figuratively, "Fuck you".'

'Vat – vat are you going to do to us?'

Paul reached into his breast pocket again. He pulled out something small, and handed it to Saggar, who looked at it, his expression stunned, then disbelieving, then confused. It was a photograph.

'Vere – vere did you get this?'

'In your office.'

'But – but –'

'Nice-looking girls. What are their names?'

Saggar looked at the picture and started to sob.

'Their *names*, Captain?'

'If – if you – if you hurt any of us dere vill be *velly* much trouble for you.'

Paul beckoned the last man on the row over. He positioned him opposite Saggar, took a few steps back, drew his pistol and shot the man through the temple. The soldier's body crumpled into a heap on the ground, blood geysering out of the hole in his head. Saggar cried out.

Paul holstered his pistol, walked over and kicked the body to one side.

'What are your *daughters' names*, Captain?'

'M-M-M-Meena and Ssss-Su-Su-Sunita.'

'Meena?' Paul pointing to the picture. 'The eldest? The one with the hairband?'

He nodded.

'How old is she?'

'Th-thir-thirteen.'

'Do you love her?'

'Yes.'

'What would you do to me if I raped her?'

Saggar said nothing. He looked down at the ground.

'Don't look at your *feet*, Captain – look at your *daughter*.

'Good. Now, imagine I *raped* your daughter. Can you?' Paul looked at the officer. 'Picture the scene: me and my buddies are driving down the street one day. There are eight of us. We see Meena, walking, on her own. We stop and talk to her. We ask her to come for a ride with us. She refuses, but we take her anyway. Right there, in broad daylight, plenty of witnesses to identify us, but no one to stop us because we're in military uniform and we have guns.

'Oh, I *forgot* to mention this minor point – in our spare time we're UN "*peace-keeping*" troops. We're here to "*protect*" you. Only, the people we're protecting are actually *terrified* of us. You know why? Because we're always snatching young girls like Meena off the street.'

Saggar was looking back at the ground, head hung, shoulders slumped, stance crumbling: fear and guilt, but not yet resignation to his fate. He couldn't believe Paul was going to kill him and his men. That hadn't registered. Max knew he was. He'd given the leader of the gang that had kidnapped Manuela a similar speech. He'd used the guy's kid sister as an example, trying to throw the crime back in his face, personalize it, make him feel it, the damage, the pain. It hadn't gone to plan. The gangleader told Max he'd got so wasted on crack and PCP one time he'd fucked his kid sister in the arse. Five months later he'd started pimping her out to the local paedophile. Max had blown the motherfucker's brains out without regret or remorse.

'We drive your daughter to an isolated place. She's a brave girl – a *gutsy* girl – your daughter, Meena. She's a fighter. She bites one of my buddies, almost takes his finger off. So he caves her teeth in with his rifle butt. And then he grabs her by her ears and forces his cock down her throat while another of my guys holds his gun to her head. Everyone has their turn. Everyone except me and the driver. I'm above all that. You know, if *I* want pussy I put on two condoms and go to one of those Dominican whores near my barracks. As for the driver? He *refuses* to join in.

'When my guys are done in her mouth, they rape little Meena. Twice. *Each*. We take her virginity – we really *rip* the little bitch open, tear her apart inside. Literally. She's haemorrhaging. We notice – obviously. So what do we do? Stop and take her to a doctor? *No*. We turn her over and fuck her in the arse. Twice. *Each*. Then, you know what we do? We piss on her and drive off, looking for the next girl.

'Meena's found, two days later. Nearly dead. Do you know how many stitches it takes, just to sew up her vagina? One hundred and eighty-three! And she's thirteen years old.'

Saggar started crying.

'I-I-I . . . I didn't do anything,' he whimpered.

'You stood by and let it happen. They're *your* men, under *your* command. One word from you and they would've stopped. You have to accept full responsibility.'

'Look – report me to my superior. I sign confession. They vill –'

'– "Discipline you in accordance with UN military regulations"? ABSOLUTELY NO FUCKING WAY!' Paul shouted. 'The Le Fen family went to your superiors *before* they came to me. Did you know that? And what did your superiors do? They made you send a *written apology* to the family. So what'll they do this time? *Sentence you to washing my car?*'

'Please,' Saggar said, falling to his knees, 'please don't kill me.'

'If that had been your daughter you'd want to kill *me*, wouldn't you?'

'Please,' he blubbered.

'Answer my *question*.'

'I vood turn you over to *justice*,' Saggar bawled.

'Do you know we have no laws here in Haiti? No laws

for *absolutely anything*? Bill Clinton's torn up our Constitution so he can pay his Arkansas lawyer clique to write us a new one? So, while we're waiting for Bill to play Moses, why don't we give you some *Bangladeshi justice*? Tell me, Captain. What is the penalty for rape in your country?'

Saggar didn't reply.

'Come on. You know.'

Saggar sobbed but didn't answer.

'You know I know. I looked it up,' Paul said. 'I just want to hear you say it.'

'D-D-D-Death.'

'Sorry?'

'Death penalty.'

'So rape is judged so *extreme* a crime in your country it's punishable by death, but you think it's OK here? Is that it?'

'You said dere is no justice here.'

'Only among Haitians. You see, this is *our* country. *Not* yours. You can't come over here and treat us like this. Not without consequences. And *I* am those *consequences.*'

'My men just vanted to have zome fun. Dey not mean do hurt de girl.'

'Try *explaining* that to her, will you? Do you know you bastards didn't just ruin her face for ever, you ruptured her spine, so she'll never be able to walk properly again? She won't be able to carry anything on her back. Women *carry everything* in this country. So she's as good as dead when she grows up. You ruined her *life*. You might as well have killed her,' Paul said.

Saggar's face was shiny with tears.

Paul pointed to the right. 'Go and stand over there.' Saggar stumbled forward. 'Stop. Stay.' One of Paul's men trained a rifle on the Captain's head.

Paul went up to the Bangladeshis and grabbed one of

them by the arm. He inspected his hand and then jerked him out of the line. The soldier didn't have time to move his feet. His legs went limp and Paul dragged him along the ground by his shirtfront and stood him up where Saggar had been.

'Are you Sanjay Veja?'

'Yes!' he shouted. He was bald and clean shaven. There was steel in his voice.

'She bit your finger so you broke her face with your rifle. You were the first one in. The one who hurt her the most. Do you have anything to say to that?'

'No,' Veja said, utterly impassive.

'Take off your trousers.'

'V-*vat*?'

'Your trousers.' Paul pointed and repeated slowly, 'Take-them-off.'

Veja looked back at his fellow soldiers. None of them looked at him. He complied. Paul stepped away from him and began rummaging on the ground, picking up, weighing and rejecting rocks until he found what he wanted – two large flat smooth ones that he just about got his huge hands around.

'And your underwear. That too,' Paul said, without turning around.

After another look back at his comrades-in-arms, Veja timidly stepped out of his white boxers.

Paul went up to him, arms behind his back.

'Hold up your dick.' Paul looked to make sure he'd complied. 'Now stand at ease.'

Max watched Paul lower himself into a tensed-up catcher's crouch, eye to eye with the soldier. He took a deep breath through his nose, and then, at the speed of a blink, he whipped his rock-holding hands around from behind his back and slammed them together on Veja's dangling

264

scrotum. Max heard two sounds – the loud crack of the rocks impacting and, right behind it, a strained wet pop.

The soldier's mouth dropped wide open, as if all his jaw muscles had dissolved. His eyes pushed up out to the rims of his sockets and every vein and artery in his skull bulged up in a network of thick, gorged knots.

Veja first screamed in an unnaturally low register. Then, as the realization of what had happened to him caught up with the pain, the scream cracked into a rush of terrible, terrifying howls, delivered in searing bursts from the pit of his soul. Max felt Veja's cries all the way down deep inside of him and wanted to puke. Some of the soldier's comrades did just that, while two fainted and the rest – including Captain Saggar – wept, whimpered and pissed themselves.

Paul wasn't finished. He jerked his arms sharply to the left, until his elbows were in line with his neck and his whole body shook with the strain and effort. Max saw the soldier's naked right leg lifted up off the ground, his foot shaking. Paul repeated the whole motion with his right side, before bringing his arms back down and then twisting them rapidly back and forth, as if he was wringing out wet clothes.

He stopped. He gulped down air, filling and clearing his airways with great big breaths before he uttered a heavy, exhausted grunt and tore Veja's mangled scrotum from his body with a massive backward lurch. The sound of it going reminded Max of stitches popping and tight fistfuls of feathers being simultaneously ripped out of chickens.

Veja staggered backwards, two steps, three, one, mouth working soundlessly, throat spasming up and down, all screamed out, unable to expel any more of his immense pain. He lurched forward and then went back again.

Max saw the bloody gash in the middle of his legs, the crimson rivulets pouring down his thighs.

Veja reached for his violated crotch and touched the mush below his dick.

Paul tossed the blood-soaked rocks and flesh into a corner.

Veja brought his bloody fingers up to his eyes, studied them closely and then, just as his face began to crumple into tears, he keeled back and slammed into the ground, cracking his skull.

He was dead.

Paul took out his gun and put a round in Veja's head. Then he dragged another soldier screaming and pleading and crying out of the shattered group. Paul slapped the man's face with a huge bloody paw.

'You stay here and watch your friends. Just like you did when they raped the girl,' he said, and turned him around to face his comrades. He then shouted over at the two guards who were watching Saggar. They shoved him over to his men.

'You are animal – *monster*!' Saggar yelled out at Paul. 'You vill be *punished* for this.'

Paul stepped away to a corner and whistled. The rocks began to fly.

The first volley came from the girl's family, who'd moved into position, opposite the rapists. They threw large rocks at them, over- and underarm, and fired smaller ones by catapult. All found their target – heads were opened, brows were split, eyes were put out.

The rapists tried to run backwards but they met an immediate hail of rocks flying out of the darkness, hurled and shot at them by unseen hands. One soldier was knocked out, another dropped to the floor and pulled his legs up in foetal position.

The rocks flew into heads and faces and knees and chests. Max saw a man killed when one catapulted rock struck his cheek and spun him right into the path of another high-velocity stone which caved his temple in and rammed skull bone into his brain.

Saggar was on all fours, scrambling around, feeling his way along the ground, blood covering his face from a gash in his forehead, one eye buried under a mound of swollen skin.

None of the rapists were left standing when the Le Fen family moved in, sticks and machetes in hand, Verité leading the way, helped along by her father. The other rock throwers came out of the darkness and together they formed a circle around the fallen men.

Moments later the sounds of beating and pounding and stabbing and slashing came from the circle. Max heard a few cries of pain, but it all seemed so minor after Veja's screams, which were still clearly echoing around his head.

The crowd worked on the bodies, letting out their hatred, sucking up as much raw vengeance as they could before their muscles gave out and tiredness got the better of them.

When they staggered away they left behind a pulped vermilion mass, a gleaming viscous lake of retribution.

A guard went around and put nominal bullets in the skulls that were still intact.

Paul looked at the driver.

'Now – you – I want you to go back to your barracks in Port-au-Prince and tell everyone what happened. Start with your friends and colleagues, then tell your commanding officer. Tell them I was responsible. Vincent Paul. You understand?'

The man nodded, his teeth shaking.

'And when you tell them what happened, tell them this from me – if *any* of you *ever* rape or harm any of our women and children in any way, we *will* kill you – like *that*,' he said, pointing at the tangle of body parts. 'And if any of you come looking for revenge, rounding up our people, we will all rise up and massacre each and every one of you. And that isn't a threat, it's a *promise*. Now go.'

The driver started walking away, very slowly, head down, slouching, steps uncertain, as though they were the first he'd taken in a long while and he half expected his legs to give way. He put a good few metres between himself and the scene, and then he broke into a run and disappeared into the night like a man on fire who's spotted water.

Paul went to be with the family.

Max couldn't move. He was numb with shock and disgust, his mind paralysed by conflict. He hated all rapists and, in theory, up to the moment it had happened, he had had nothing against what Paul had done.

True, what the soldiers had done was evil, and their official 'punishment' had been a joke, an insult to the victim, but justice hadn't been served by Paul's act. The girl hadn't got her life and innocence back, just the satisfaction of knowing that the rapists had been punished, that they'd suffered before dying. But what good would that do her next year, and the year after? What good was it doing her now?

Sure, the punishment Paul had meted out would be a deterrent – *in Haiti* – but once the UN troops moved on they'd do it somewhere else, in another land they'd been dispatched to 'to keep the peace' in.

A better, more responsible, way would have been for Paul to have talked to the press, stirred up a major stink about the rape and forced the UN to prosecute its troops and make it plain that such conduct was unacceptable.

But then, Max thought of Sandra and asked himself, what would he have done in Paul's place. Taken them in and waited a year for some judge to maybe sentence them to fifteen to life if the evidence stood up? No, of *course* not. He would have castrated the motherfuckers with his bare hands too.

What was he thinking, *exactly*? Paul *was* right. What did Paul give a fuck what the UN did elsewhere? This was *his* homeland and these were *his* people. That's as far as he saw.

Fair play. Fuck 'em.

Max sneaked away back to his car and drove off.

29

What passed for nightlife in Pétionville was in full swing when Max drove down the main road leading to the market square. A few bars and restaurants had opened their doors wide out on to the sidewalk and lit up their painted signs to show they were ready for business. There was barely anyone there.

Max needed a drink and a little company around him to redress the balance, a little brightness and banality to chase away the shadowy aftershocks he was feeling in his gut and running up and down his veins. It had been years since he'd seen someone die, not since he'd shot those kids. They'd deserved it too, but that didn't make it any easier to absorb and move on from. A little dying always stayed with you. He was glad it wasn't as hard to deal with now as it was then, when he'd had more to live and care for. He'd seen people get the chair a few times, their heads had caught fire under their hoods and the skin had melted right off their bones like so much candlewax. He'd watched cops gun down criminals and criminals murder cops. And then there were all those people he'd killed himself – in the line of duty, and a step or two over it. He didn't know how many – he couldn't bring himself to count – but he remembered all their faces, their expressions, those who'd begged for their lives, those who'd told him to go fuck himself, those who prayed, the one who'd forgiven him, the one who'd wanted his hand held, the one who'd blown his last breath in his face and the way it had smelled of fried gunpowder and bubblegum. His boss, Eldon Burns, had kept a tally of all the people he'd taken down, but then he was morbid that way, and he liked numbers. He kept his service revolver in a glass case on his desk. There was a notch on the butt for every kill. Max had counted sixteen.

He passed La Coupole and spotted Huxley standing in the doorway talking to three street kids. He parked the car and went over to the bar.

'Good to see you again, Max,' Huxley said warmly as they pumped hands. The boys he'd been talking to shied away a little, the smallest hiding behind the tallest of the trio.

Huxley said something to them. The tallest boy babbled something back, talking fast and excitedly, a hoarse catch in his throat, making the sound of a flock of singing sparrows hitting a tin roof. He pointed to Max with his fingers and eyes, stabbing in his direction with both.

'What's he saying?' Max asked, guessing he'd been among his prospective attackers.

'He says to tell you he's sorry for the other night,' Huxley said, frowning with incomprehension. Max looked at the kid. He had a small head where very little hair grew, and tiny eyes that shone like onyx buttons. The child seemed more fearful than apologetic. 'He says he didn't know who you were.'

'Who does he think I am?'

Huxley asked him. Max heard Vincent Paul's name in the ensuing babble.

'He says you're Paul's friend.'

'His *friend*? I ain't –'

The boy interrupted him with another rush of words.

'He says Paul warned them to look out for you around here,' Huxley translated, looking impressed. 'You meet him?'

Max didn't answer.

'Ask the boy when he last saw him.'

'Yesterday,' Huxley said. 'Wanna grab a drink and fill me in?'

Huxley laughed when Max told him about what had happened after they'd last met.

'All you had to do was treat the kid with a little respect, just said no, firmly. He would've left you alone. They don't persist,' Huxley explained. 'Being rude to someone who's born with nothing to lose isn't wise – and being rude to them in their own country, on their own streets is pretty fucken' stupid, Max. You're lucky Vincent Paul came along when he did.'

The bar was nearly empty and no music was playing. In the courtyard outside, however, was a large group of Americans. They sounded like Midwesterners, straw-sucking cowpokes out on the weekend. Max heard the rifles being dry fired and magazines being slapped into place.

Max was on his third straight Barbancourt. The measures were more than generous. The booze was starting to work its charms again, loosen him up.

'So, how was Shitty City? You went there today, right?' Huxley asked, lighting a cigarette. Max shot him a suspicious look.

'"Cmon, Max. You smell like a skunk hit *you*,"' Huxley laughed. 'You know how everyone here can tell a riot's coming? 'Cause the air smells like you – the smell of the Shitty City. When all the people come out of Cité Soleil and head for Port-au-Prince to bring down the government, the clouds turn their noses up, the wind blows in the opposite direction and birds fall out of the sky. I *know* that smell. You can't fool me, Mingus. I'm Haitian.'

Max realized he was still wearing his throwaway boots, caked to the toecaps in Cité Soleil muck.

'Sorry 'bout that.'

'Don't worry. You find anything out there?' Huxley asked.

'Not much,' Max said. He wasn't going to tell him what he'd witnessed. 'Just some kind of relief operation – Vincent Paul's charity work.'

'The green tents? Yeah, he's famous for that. That's why they love him in the slums. He looks after them. Rumour is – this mythical town he's supposed to have built? – it's got hospitals and schools for the poor. All free, paid for out of the proceeds of his drug trade. Guy's like a cocaine Castro.'

Max laughed.

'Know where this place is?'

'No. It's like Eldorado. Nobody knows where it is or how to get there, but *everyone* swears it exists. You know how things go around here,' Huxley said. 'How's the investigation?'

'Early days,' Max replied, sinking his drink.

The Americans came in. Marines, about thirty of them, walking heavily through the bar and out into the street, all armed, blacked up and dressed head to toe for combat.

'What's goin' on? A raid?' Max asked quietly.

'No,' Huxley smiled and shook his head as he watched the troops filing out. 'You know how this whole "invasion" went down? Not a single shot fired. No opposition. Well, a lot of the soldiers are pissed they didn't see any combat, so every couple of weeks they go downtown and play wargames with the UN troops. The UN guys defend this old barracks in the Carrefour district of Port-au-Prince. The Marines have got to go and try and take it.'

'Sounds like fun,' Max said sarcastically.

'There's a catch.'

'Yeah?'

'They use live rounds.'

'*Bullshit*!'

'No word of a lie.'

'*No*!'

'On my mother.'

'She alive?'

'Sure,' Huxley laughed.

'What about casualties?'

'Not as high as you'd expect. There've been a couple of fatalities on both sides, but high command have covered it up – said it was an enemy attack or a blue on blue.'

'I still don't believe you,' Max chortled.

'Same as me 'til I saw it for myself,' Huxley said, standing up.

'Where you goin'?'

'I've got a video camera in the car. I'm just waiting for one of the guys to take a direct hit so I can sell the tape to CNN.'

'I thought you were here for a noble cause?' Max laughed.

'I am. But a man's gotta eat,' Huxley laughed. 'Feel like coming?'

'Not tonight. I've had a full day. Maybe some other time. Don't get shot.'

'You too. Take care.'

They shook hands. Huxley took off after the troops. Max ordered another drink and stared at the still smouldering cigarette butt the journalist had left behind, following the smoke up to the ceiling. He didn't care if what he'd just heard wasn't true. It was a good story and it was making him laugh. Right now that was all that mattered.

30

Max called Allain Carver the next morning and told him he wanted to interview all the servants who'd been working for them at the time of Charlie's kidnapping.

Allain said he'd fix it up for the following day.

Max interviewed the servants in a small room on the first floor of the main house, overlooking the lawn and the thick perimeter of trees surrounding it. Other than the table and chairs he and Chantale were sat at, there was no other furniture in the room. It quickly dawned on Max that the set-up was a deliberate way of reinforcing the household's social code – servants always stood when spoken to. Max made a point of offering his seat to everyone he spoke to. He was politely turned down and thanked for his kindness at every occasion by both the very old and the very young, all of them casting a quick, fearful look up at the only painting in the room – a large oil canvas of the present-day Gustav, dressed in his beige suit and black tie, glowering down on them above their interrogators. At his side, on a thick leather leash, sat a bulldog the same colour as Gustav's suit, its head and expression bearing more than a passing resemblance to its master's gargoylic mien.

The Carver domestic staff were broadly divided into culinary, cleaning, mechanical, gardening and security. The bulk worked directly for Gustav. Allain and Francesca employed their own retinue.

The interviews followed the same pattern. Max started

with the old man's staff. He asked them their names, what they did, who they worked with, how long they'd been there, where they were on the day of the kidnapping, and if they'd seen or heard anything suspicious in the weeks leading up to it. Other than their names, responsibilities and times of service, their answers were very similar. On 4 September 1994, they'd been working in or around the house either with or in plain sight of several other people.

When he asked them about Eddie Faustin, he found that the bodyguard had seemingly passed through their lives like a perfect stranger. They all remembered him well enough but none had much else to say about him. They'd only known him by sight. Gustav Carver forbade the household staff from having any personal contact with his security and vice versa. Even if they'd wanted to get acquainted with Faustin, it would have been next to impossible because he'd spent all day out of the house. They didn't see him when he finished his shifts either, because he didn't live in the servants' quarters with the rest of them, but in the main house, in one of the basement rooms reserved for key personnel.

The servants themselves were personally so alike – in their smiling, benign, deferential manner – Max had a lot of trouble remembering any of them after they'd left the room and the next one had come in.

They took a break for lunch, which was brought up to them – grilled fish so fresh they could still taste the sea in the meat, and a salad of tomatoes, kidney beans and red and green peppers.

When they'd finished, Chantale rang the bell that had come with their food. The servants came into the room and cleared the plates.

'I meant to ask you about Noah's Ark,' Max said to

Chantale, spotting the words as he rifled through his note-book for a clean page.

'Ask the next person who walks in,' she said curtly. 'They'll know more about it than me. They all come from there.'

He did just that. The next interviews were with Allain and Francesca's retinue. Noah's Ark, he learnt, was an orphanage-school in Port-au-Prince owned and run by the Carvers. The family recruited not just their domestic staff from there, but virtually everyone who worked for them.

The new interviewees were different to Gustav's servants: they had clearly discernible personalities.

They opened up about Faustin. They described how they used to see him going through Francesca's rubbish, stealing things from the bins and taking them back into his room. When they'd cleaned out his room after his disappearance, they'd found a voodoo doll he'd made out of her hair, fingernail clippings, tissues, old lipstick tubes and tampax. Some told Max they'd heard rumours that the bodyguard picked up light-skinned Dominican whores in Pétionville and paid them extra to wear long blonde wigs while he fucked them. Many said they'd often seen Faustin regularly entering or leaving a bar called *Nwoi et Rouge*, run by ex-Macoute friends. One or two muttered that they'd seen him taking Charlie's soiled nappies out of the rubbish, while the last person they interviewed claimed he'd overheard Faustin talking about a house he owned in Port-au-Prince.

They finished the interviews in the late afternoon. As they drove down the mountain towards Pétionville, Max opened the windows and let the air in. Chantale looked exhausted.

'Thanks for your help – again,' he said, and then added, awkwardly, 'I don't know what I'd do without you.'

'Feel like getting a drink?' she offered, with a hint of a smile.

'Sure. Where do you suggest?'

'I'm sure you've got *just* the place in mind,' she smiled.

'How about Eddie Faustin's old hangout?'

'You take me to the classiest joints,' she said, and laughed her dirty laugh.

31

Nwoi et Rouge was named after the colours of the Haitian flag under the Duvaliers. Black and red. Papa Doc had changed the flag's original blue to black to cement the country's complete break with its colonial past, better reflect the country's largest ethnic majority and to underline his beliefs in *noirisme* – black supremacy; beliefs which didn't extend to the woman he married – Simone, a light-skinned *mulâtresse* – nor to the pre-Civil Rights Act USA, whose military and financial aid he happily accepted to keep his regime in place. For many people the revised flag's colours came to symbolize the darkest, bloodiest period in the country's already turbulent and violent history.

To Max, the flag recalled that of the Nazis – whose colours it shared. The coat of arms – cannon, muskets and flagpoles dominated by a palm tree crowned with a ski hat – could have been the work of a stoned surfer with a yen for eighteenth-century military history. Who the fuck would ever take a place like that seriously?

The flag was proudly displayed behind the bar, between framed photographs of Papa and Baby Doc. Papa was dark and white-haired, his thick black-rimmed specs slightly humanizing a pinched face whose features suggested an unlimited capacity for cruelty. His son, Jean-Claude, was a doughy lump with soft, Arabic features, bronze skin and dopey eyes.

The bar was in a stand-alone one-room house on a stretch of road between the end of the mountain and the start of

Pétionville. It was easy to miss, yet easy to find if you were looking for it.

When Max had stepped in with Chantale the first thing he'd noticed hadn't been the flags or the portraits, but the heavy-set old man sweeping the floor around a wide pool of light cast by a single lightbulb, burning so brightly at the end of its flex, it seemed almost liquid, a drop of molten steel gathering volume before dropping to the ground and burning a hole all the way through the cement floor.

'Bond-joor,' Max nodded.

'Bon-*soir*,' the man corrected him. He was wearing a short-sleeved white shirt, loose, faded blue jeans held up by red suspenders, and a pair of worn open-toe sandals. He'd swept the dirt into a small brownish pile to his left.

There was a water-cooler behind the bar, a long row of clear bottles lined up next to it, and, at the very end, right before a tall fan, Max read the word 'TAFFIA' written in crude block capitals on a blackboard. Below were two equations – a drawn glass = a hand with five fingers raised, a drawn bottle = two hands with all fingers raised.

Max searched the bar for seats and saw none at all. There were small towers of crates stacked against the walls. He guessed the patrons arranged those as stools and tables. This was drinking at its most rudimentary, frontier-style.

The man looked at Chantale and started talking to her, his voice making the sounds of a train going off the rails and rolling down a long steep hill, dumping its cargo of logs with every turn and bounce and crash. Max heard the name 'Carver' crop up twice in the spill.

'He says if you're looking for the Carver boy too, you're wasting your time with him,' Chantale translated. 'He'll tell you what he told the others.'

'What's that?' Max asked the man, trying to meet his eye,

but failing to, because the way he stood under the bulb drowned them in shadows. The man replied, laughed and waved.

'He hasn't got him. Goodbye.'

'Very funny,' Max said. His head was beginning to sweat. He felt it sprouting all over his scalp, neighbouring droplets fusing, seeking out others, finding them, fusing, building up, getting set to run. The bar stank of stale smoke, sweat and, above all, ether.

'Why did they think you had the boy?' Max asked.

'Because of my great friend, Eddie Faustin,' the man answered and pointed off to his right.

Max went over to where the lightbulb's reflection marked out a single photograph in a frame. He recognized Faustin straightaway – he'd inherited the family resemblance to a furious donkey: big head, bulbous nose, protruding chin, eyes and ears, and a genetically transferred scowl where nostrils were flared and the upper teeth fully exposed. Faustin wasn't a big guy. His body was slight, too small for his head. Max was surprised he'd survived the bullet he'd taken for Carver.

In the picture he was standing between two people – his brother, Salazar, and the barman, who had a revolver in his hand and one booted foot parked on a dead body. Jagged exclamation marks of blood splashed the ground near the corpse's head and back. The hands and feet had been tied. The trio were smiling proudly for the camera.

'Those were good times,' the barman said.

Max turned and saw him smiling through a few jagged teeth with plenty of empty space in between them.

'Who took the picture?'

'I can't remember,' he replied, leering at Chantale as she translated, the space around his eyes twitching as his head moved gently up and down her curves, his grip fastening on his broomstick.

Just then there was a quiet *fff-fut*, as something struck the lightbulb and fell to the ground with a faint trail of smoke. It was a moth, wings instantly burnt useless by the bulb. It lay on its back, struggling furiously in the air for a moment before it ceased all motion.

The man chuckled and swept the moth into the pile he was building up. When Max looked at it he saw it was made up of nothing but dead moths. The broom was crude and homemade – a long stick with a bunch of dried reeds wrapped around the end for a brush.

'What's your name?'

'Bedouin,' the man said, straightening up a little.

'Bedouin . . . *Désyr*?' Chantale asked, her tone dropping to a hush.

'*Oui. Le même.*'

'*Dieu . . .*' Chantale whispered, stepping back.

'What is it?' Max asked her, moving in.

'I'll tell you later,' she said. 'When we're out of here.'

Another moth self-destructed on the bulb. It fell on Max's head, bounced off and landed burning and kicking on his shoulder. He flicked it off. Désyr tutted and said something under his breath as he walked over with his broom and swiped the dead insect deftly across the floor into the pile like it was a puck.

'Taffia?' he said to Max, making a drinking motion with his hand.

Max nodded and followed Désyr to the bar. Désyr got a paper cup from under the counter and held it under the water cooler. The liquid came out, releasing an air bubble inside the plastic bottle and a sharp, chemical smell that was close to gasoline.

Désyr handed the paper cup to Max. Max took it. The fumes stung his eyes.

'People *drink* this?' Max asked Chantale.

Désyr chuckled.

'Yeah. They also clean and run their engines on it when they can't get gas. Runs almost as well. It's a hundred and eighty per cent proof rum. Be *very* careful with that. It can make you go blind.'

Max took a very small sip of taffia. It was so strong it was tasteless and burnt his tongue all the way down to his throat.

'Jesus!' Max said, wanting to spit it out.

Désyr laughed and motioned to Max to throw it down his throat in one go. Max sensed that this might win him a little credibility with the bar owner, and he might tell him something more about Faustin and the kidnapping. There was only about a finger of booze in the cup.

He took a deep breath and tossed back the taffia. It hit the ends of his mouth like a firebomb and proceeded to burn its trail all the way down into his stomach.

The alcohol rush was almost instantaneous – the equivalent of five double bourbons on an empty stomach smashing into him all at once, filling his head with a dizzy euphoria. His vision blurred and swayed as his eyes tried to regain focus. Tears ran down his face and blood rushed to his head. His temples pounded. His nose dripped. The hit was like coke and amyl nitrate and smelling salts all rolled into one. Only he didn't feel remotely good. He gripped the bar but his palms were sweaty and his hands slid back. He felt a turbulence in his stomach. He breathed deep, smelling nothing but the taffia. *What the fuck was he thinking drinking that shit?*

'*Bravo blan!*' Désyr shouted and clapped his hands in front of him.

'Are you OK, Max?' Chantale said in his ear as she placed a steadying hand against his back.

Fuck's it look like? he heard himself think but not speak. He took another deep breath and let it out slowly, then another, and another after that. The air coming out of his mouth was hot. He repeated his breathing, keeping his eyes locked on Désyr, who was watching him with high amusement, no doubt waiting for him to keel over.

The nausea passed, as did the spinning in his head.

'I'm OK,' he said to Chantale. 'Thanks.'

Désyr shook another cup at him. Max shook his hand no. Désyr laughed and spilled more capsized train talk Chantale's way.

'He says you're not only the only white man who's ever drunk taffia without passing out – you're also among the very few Haitians who've managed it too.'

'That's great,' Max said. 'Tell him I'll buy him a drink.'

'Thank you,' Chantale said. 'But he doesn't touch the stuff.'

Max and Désyr both laughed at once.

'Eddie Faustin drank here, didn't he?'

'*Oui. Bien sûr,*' Désyr said, taking a bottle of Barbancourt from under the counter and pouring some out into a paper cup. 'Before he died he drank more than usual.'

'Did he say why?'

'He was coming to the end of his future and this made him nervous.'

'He knew he was gonna die?'

'No. Not at all. He told me his *houngan* had predicted things for him – good things, women things,' Désyr said, leering at Chantale and sipping his rum. He took a tobacco pouch out of his trouser pocket and rolled himself a cigarette. 'He was in love with the blonde Carver woman. I told him it was madness, impossible – him and her?' He struck

284

a match on the countertop and lit it. 'That's when he went to Leballec.'

'This his hoone-gun?'

'He only deals in black magic,' Chantale explained. 'They say you go to him if you're ready to sell your soul. He doesn't accept cash like the other black magicians do – he takes . . . I don't know. Nobody knows for sure, except those who've gone to him.'

'Did Faustin tell you what happened when he went to see Le – the hoone-gun?' Max asked Désyr.

'No. But he changed. Before he used to talk and laugh about old times. He used to play dominoes and cards with us, but not after he'd been to see Leballec. He'd stand where you are now and just drink. Sometimes he'd drink a whole bottle.'

'Of *that* shit?'

'Yes. But it didn't affect him.'

Max started to think that maybe the hoone-gun had asked Faustin to kidnap Charlie.

'Did he ever talk to you about the boy? Charlie?'

'Yes,' laughed Désyr. 'He said the boy hated him. He said the boy could read his mind. He said he couldn't wait to get rid of him.'

'He said *that*?'

'Yes. But he didn't steal the boy.'

'Who did?'

'Nobody took him. The boy's dead.'

'How do you know?'

'I've heard that he was killed by the people who attacked the car. They trampled him to death.'

'No one found the body.'

'*Cela se mange*,' Désyr said, and extinguished his cigarette by pinching the coal.

'What did he just say, Chantale?'

'He said . . .'

'Le peuple avait faim. Tout le monde avait faim. Quand on a faim on oublie nos obligations.'

'He said . . .' Chantale began. 'He said they ate him.'

'Bull-*shit*!'

'That's what he said.'

The taffia had filled Max's stomach and chest with a strong heat. He could hear the low murmur of digestive gases as they worked their way up his gut.

'This Le –'

'– *Ballec*,' Chantale finished.

'This Le-Ballack? Where does he live? Where can I find him?'

'Far from here.'

'Where?'

Another train accident, this one prolonged because Chantale kept on either interrupting him or asking more questions. Max listened out for familiar words. Désyr said 'Oh' a few times, Chantale said something like 'zur'. Then he heard something he recognized.

'Clarinette.'

'What did he say about clarinet?' Max interrupted them.

'He says you'll find Leballec in Saut d'Eau.'

'The voodoo waterfalls?' Max asked. *Where Beeson and Medd both went before they disappeared.* 'What about the clarinet?'

'It's a town – a small town – closest to the waterfall. It's called *Clarinette*. It's where Leballec lives. Faustin used to go there to see him.'

'Have you heard of this place, Chantale?'

'Not of the town, but that doesn't mean anything. Someone sets up a home on a piece of land here, gives it a name, it becomes a village.'

Max looked at Désyr.

'You told the others about this place, didn't you? The other blanks who came here?'

Désyr shook his head.

'*Non, monsieur.*' Then he chuckled. 'I couldn't. They failed the taffia test.'

'They pass out?'

'No. They refused to drink my drink. So I told them nothing.'

'So, how come they went to So – to the waterfalls?'

'I don't know. *I* didn't tell them. Maybe somebody else did. I wasn't Eddie's only friend. Were they looking for Leballec?'

'I don't know.'

'Then maybe they went there for another reason.'

'Maybe,' Max said.

Another moth flew into the bulb and dropped to the floor. Very soon after Max heard another go the same way, and then almost simultaneously two moths smacked into the light and made it shudder and shake.

Désyr clapped a friendly paw on his shoulder.

'I like you, *blanc*, so I'll tell you this: if you go to Saut d'Eau, make sure you leave before midnight passes.'

Max laughed out loud.

'Or what? The zombies are gonna come and get me?'

Désyr scowled at him.

'White magic – good magic – honest magic is done before midnight,' he said, addressing Chantale directly. 'Black magic is done after midnight. Don't forget it.'

'Why are you helping me?' Max asked.

'Why not?' Désyr laughed.

32

Chantale drove Max to a café where she ordered a pot of strong coffee and a bottle of water. Over the next hour he got himself sobered up and cleared the taffia from his head.

'You always so reckless? It could have been battery acid for all you knew.'

'I'm the try-most-things-once kinda guy,' Max said. 'Anyway, why would he have wanted to poison me?'

'Bedouin Désyr? I wouldn't put anything past him. They used to call him "Bisou-Bisou". It literally means "Bedouin Le Baiseur". Bedouin the Stud. Only it wasn't meant the way you'd think. Back when he was a Macoute, Bedouin Désyr was a serial rapist. His thing was raping wives in front of their husbands, mothers in front of their children, daughters in front of their fathers – the age didn't matter.'

'How come he's still alive? And out in the open like that?'

'Myths are stronger than death, Max. A lot of people are still terrified of the Macoutes,' Chantale explained. 'Very few of them were ever brought to trial for all the things they did. Even then they went to prison for a week and got let out. Some got killed by the mobs. But most of them just disappeared, went to another part of the country, went abroad, went to the Dominican Republic. The cleverer ones joined the army or hooked up with Aristide.'

'*Aristide*?' Max said. 'I thought he was supposed to be against all that.'

It was now night-time. They were the only ones in the café. The overhead fan was on and the radio was playing *kompas*, loud enough to distract from the sounds spilling in from the street outside and the creaking blades beating at the dead hot air inside. Right in between the music and the sidewalk hubbub, Max heard the familiar exploratory rhythms of the drums starting up in the mountains.

'That's how he started out,' Chantale said. 'I believed in him. A lot of people did. Not just the poor.'

'Don't tell me,' Max smiled. 'Us evil racist white Americans decided we didn't want another Commie on our doorstep – especially not a black one – so we had him overthrown.'

'Not quite,' Chantale retorted. 'Aristide turned into Papa Doc quicker than it took Papa Doc to turn into Papa Doc. He started sending the mobs round to beat up or kill his opponents. When the Papal Nuncio criticized what was going on he had him beaten up and stripped naked in the street. That's when people decided enough was enough, and the army took over – with the blessing of President Bush and the CIA.'

'So what's Aristide doing back here?'

'Bill Clinton had a re-election this year. In 1993, barely a year into his first term, he'd messed up big time in Somalia. His approval ratings took a dive. America suddenly looked weak, vulnerable. He had to do something to get his credibility back. Restoring a president deposed by a coup seemed like a good idea. America as a champion of democracy – even if it *was* Aristide – the third Duvalier in waiting,' Chantale explained. 'They've got him on a leash now, so he'll have to behave himself until Clinton's gone. Then who knows? Hopefully I'll be far away from here,' she said, looking out on the street where a UN car had stopped and the driver was handing out cartons of cigarettes to someone on the street.

'Where are you planning on going?'

'Back to America, I suppose. Maybe I'll move to LA. Nothing left for me in Florida,' Chantale said. 'What about you? What'll you do when you've finished here?'

'I don't have the faintest idea,' Max laughed.

'Thought of moving on yourself?'

'What? Like to LA?' Max looked at her and met her eyes. She looked down. 'LA ain't my scene, Chantale.'

'I thought you said you were the try-most-things-once kind.'

'I *know* LA,' he laughed. 'Did a few cases out there. Hated it every time. Too sprawled out, disconnected. Worked twice as fast so I could get out fast. Movies, résumés, headshots, tit jobs and bullshit. Everyone tryin' to crawl through the same hole. Lots of people gettin' left out. Victims and broken dreams. I've got that kind of shit at home – only there I actually feel sorry for some of them. Their hard-luck stories change a bit every time. In LA they're all reading off the same page. You're better off staying here if you're gonna move there.'

'I'm not staying here a second longer than I have to.' She shook her head.

'That bad?'

'No, but not much better,' she sighed. 'I had happy memories of growing up here, but when I came back what-ever I'd known was all gone. I guess I had a happy childhood. Made coming back here as an adult that much harder, dis-appointing.'

A couple walked in and greeted the waiter with a hand-shake. First to third episode daters, Max decided, still checking each other out, circling, everything formal and polite, timing the move. They were in their late twenties, well-dressed. The guy ironed his jeans and the woman had just bought hers or only wore them on special occasions.

They both sported polo shirts, hers turquoise, his bottle green. The waiter showed them to a corner seat. Chantale watched them with a wistful smile.

'Tell me about Faustin's hoone-gan.'

'Leballec?' she said, lowering her voice. 'First up, he's not a houngan. Houngans are good. Leballec is a *bokor* – a black magician. He's meant to be as powerful as Dufour, but a hundred times worse.

'You know, in life, certain things aren't meant to happen to you. Say you're in love with someone who just doesn't want to know, or you really want a job you can't have – disappointments, things that don't go your way. Most people shrug their shoulders and move on to the next thing. Here people go to their houngan or their mambo. They look into the future and see whether or not the person's desires are going to be there for them. If they're not, the houngan or mambo might try to fix it – as long as it's not going to alter the direction of the person's life. But a lot of things you want but can't have are just not meant to be.'

'So they go to Leballec?'

'His kind, yes. They call them "Les Ombres de Dieu". *God's shadows.* Those who walk behind God, in the dark, where He doesn't look. They give you what you're not supposed to have,' Chantale whispered, looking fearful.

'How?'

'Remember what Dufour told you about black magic? How they use children to fool your guardian angels.'

'Le Balek kills kids?'

'I don't want to say,' Chantale said, sitting back. 'No one knows for sure what they do. That's between the people he's working for and him. But it's guaranteed to be extreme.'

'What kind of people would go to him? Generally?'

291

'People who've lost all hope. Desperate people. People at death's door.'

'That's everybody sometime,' Max said.

'Faustin went.'

'To make Francesca Carver fall in love with him – or whatever. Maybe that's why he stole Charlie,' Max said, thinking things through. 'Dufour said Charlie was *very* special. Le Balek thought so too.'

'Maybe,' Chantale said. 'Maybe not. Maybe Charlie was payment.'

'Payment?'

'"Les Ombres" never ask you for money. They ask you to do something for them in return.'

'Like a kidnapping?'

'Or a murder.'

'What happens if the spell doesn't work?'

'They don't ask you to do anything for them upfront, not until you've got what you want. *Then* you start paying. That's how it starts.'

'What?'

'Well, whatever you ask to happen to someone you get three times back,' Chantale said. 'It's how things maintain their balance. No bad deed goes unpunished. In the early eighties, before AIDS hit the headlines, Jean-Claude Duvalier had a mistress and a mister. He was bisexual. The mistress was called Veronique, the boyfriend was called Robert. Veronique got jealous of Robert, who was getting more attention from Jean-Claude. She was scared of losing favour and scared of getting dumped for a man. So she went to Leballec. I don't know what she asked for but Robert died quite unexpectedly in the middle of Port-au-Prince. Like *that*' – she snapped her fingers – 'at the wheel. When they opened him up they found water in his lungs, like he'd drowned.'

'Couldn't someone have drowned him and dumped him in the car?'

'Lots of people saw him driving the car. He even stopped to buy cigarettes a few minutes before he died,' said Chantale. 'Word got back to Jean-Claude that Veronique had been seen at Saut d'Eau with Leballec. He knew what that meant. He was terrified of Leballec. Even Papa Doc was said to be scared of him. He cut Veronique off. A month later they found her, her mother and two of her brothers drowned in the family swimming pool.'

'Doesn't sound demonic to me,' Max said. He'd recovered from the taffia, although he felt tired. 'Any idea what this Le Balek looks like?'

'No. No one I know's ever seen him. When are we going to look for him?'

'How about tomorrow?'

'How about the day after? It's a long trip over bad roads. We'll have to leave here early – three or four in the morning,' she said, looking at her watch. 'You can get some rest, sleep off the taffia, go at it fresh.'

She was talking sense. He'd need a clear head if he was going to the place where one of his predecessors had disappeared and the other had returned from the place with his torso opened up from neck to navel.

33

'It's not that we don't care. We do – only we appear not to. And appearance is *everything*,' Allain Carver said with a grin. He'd woken Max up three hours earlier with a phone call telling him to meet up at Noah's Ark.

Max was badly hungover, feeling much worse than he had the night before, with a sack of greasy cannonballs for a stomach and a headache that felt like someone was using his skull for a mixing bowl. He couldn't understand it. He was pretty much OK when he'd got out of bed, but the sickness and the pain had kicked in the minute he'd finished his first cup of coffee. He'd taken four super-strength migraine pills, but they hadn't done a thing.

Noah's Ark was situated on a side road off the Boulevard Harry Truman. Carver led Max and Chantale through a small wrought-iron-bar gate and up a white footpath bordered with dark-blue bricks. They crossed a lush lawn, part-shaded by leaning coconut palms and dotted with sprinklers whose mist made miniature rainbows above the ground. To the right was a small playground with swings, seesaws, a round-about, a slide and a climbing frame.

The path ended at the steps of an impressive two-storey house with bright whitewashed walls and a navy-blue tiled roof. The window frames and the front door were also navy blue. The institution's emblem – a dark-blue boat with a house in the middle of it instead of a sail – appeared as a relief on the wall above the door.

Once inside they came face to face with a mural of a

white man in a safari suit. He held two semi-naked Haitian children – a boy and a girl, dressed in rags – by the hand. He was leading them away from a dark village whose inhabitants were all either dead or hideously deformed. The man was looking straight at the viewer, his jaw set in grim determination, his face assuming a heroic cast. The sky behind them was stormy with blades of lightning splitting the horizon and spears of rain attacking the diseased township. The man and his charges were dry and bathed in the golden hue of a rising sun.

'That's my father,' Allain said.

When Max looked a little harder he indeed recognized Gustav in his younger days, albeit in a very flattering light, making him look a lot more like his son than his true self.

As he led them down a corridor into the heart of the institution, Carver explained that Gustav had played a big part in helping his friend François Duvalier cure the population of yaws – a highly contagious tropical disease which, untreated, resulted in its victims being covered in painful runny sores before losing their noses, lips and eventually limbs, which withered up into the colour and shape of unattended cigarette ash before dropping off. He'd bought all the medicines and supplies from America and helped them reach Duvalier. On a visit to the village depicted in the mural Gustav had come across two orphans, a boy and a girl. He decided to rescue them and look after them. This later led to the establishment of a Carver-funded school-orphanage.

The corridor they walked down was lined with annual school photographs going back to 1962. Further on there were wide corkboards covered with children's drawings, grouped into age ranges, starting at four and ending at twelve. There were so few sketches in the teenage category that they had all been grouped on to a board they didn't even half fill, and even those had been done by only two people, both of whom were exceptionally gifted.

Carver went on to explain that Noah's Ark cared for children from birth right through to their teens or college graduation. They were fed, clothed, housed and educated according to either the French or American curriculum. French was the primary language in Noah's Ark, but pupils who showed an aptitude for English – as many unsurprisingly did, with the prevalence of American television and music in their lives – were steered towards the American system. French-spoken lessons taught downstairs, English upstairs. Once they had finished their formal education, those who wanted to were sent to college, fully funded by the Carvers.

There were classrooms on either side of the corridor. Max looked through the windows in the doors and saw small even-numbered groups of pupils, boys and girls, all dressed in smart uniforms of blue skirts or shorts and white shirts or blouses. They were all immaculately turned out and paid complete attention to their teachers, even in the back rows. Max couldn't imagine any classroom in America being so orderly, so disciplined and so interested in their lessons.

'So what's the catch?' Max asked, as they headed to the next floor.

'Catch?'

'The Carvers are businessmen. You don't give money away. What do you get out of it? It can't be publicity because you're too rich to care what people think about you.'

'Simple,' Carver said with a smile, 'they finish their studies, they come and work for us.'

'*All* of them?'

'Yes, we have many businesses – worldwide, not just here. They can work in the US, the UK, France, Japan, Germany.'

'What if they get a better offer elsewhere?'

'Ah – there's what you'd call a "catch",' Carver laughed. 'From the age of sixteen all pupils at Noah's Ark sign a contract, stating that upon completion of their studies, they will either work for us until they have repaid our investment in them –'

'*Investment*?' Max said. 'Since when's charity been about investing?'

'Did I ever say this was a charity?' Carver said.

Max heard English being spoken in a mixture of American and Franco-Haitian accents as they toured the next floor, looking into the classrooms, seeing the same model pupils.

'It usually takes a period of six to seven years to repay our investment – more for girls, eight or nine years,' Carver said. 'Of course they can simply repay us the full amount in one go and they're free.'

'But that don't ever happen because where are they gonna get that kind of cash from?' Max said, anger in his tone and eyes. 'I mean, it's not like they're like *you*, say, Mr Carver? Born breathing in silver and gold.'

'I can't help being born rich any more than they can help being born into poverty, Max,' Carver replied, his thin lips smiling uneasily. 'I understand your misgivings, but they're perfectly happy with the arrangement. We have a ninety-five per cent retention rate. Take – for example – the person teaching here.' He pointed to a petite light-skinned woman in a roomy olive-green dress that seemed to have been designed with a monk in mind, so close was it to a habit. 'Eloise Krolak. One of ours. She's the headmistress here.'

'Krolak? Is that Polish?' Max asked, studying the headmistress a little closer. Her hair, pulled back in a severe bun, was black save a halo of grey at the roots. She had a small protruding mouth and a slight overbite. When she spoke she resembled a rodent gnawing at a piece of soft food.

'We originally found Eloise outside the town of Jérémie. A lot of the people are very light skinned. Many have blue eyes like Eloise. They descend directly from a garrison of Polish soldiers who deserted Napoleon's army to fight for Toussaint L'Ouverture. Once they'd helped overthrow the French, Toussaint gave the soldiers Jérémie as a reward. They intermarried and produced some quite beautiful people.'

With exceptions, Max thought, looking at the headmistress.

They moved on to the next floor. Carver showed them the refectory and the staff areas – a common room and a variety of offices.

'Where do the kids sleep?' Max asked.

'In Pétionville. They're driven in every morning and taken home at the end of the day,' Carver said. 'This is the junior house. Up until twelve. There's another Noah's Ark on the next road.'

'You only told me about the successful ones, right? The smart ones?' Max said.

'I don't follow.'

'Your servants came from here too, right?'

'We can't all be high flyers, Max. Airspace is limited. Some of us have to walk.'

'So, how do you separate them? High and low? Do the low walkers show an aptitude for shining shoes?' Max said, trying and failing to keep the indignation out of his voice. Here was a people whose ancestors had gone to war to free themselves from slavery, and here were the Carvers as good as putting them right back where they'd started.

'You're not from here so you don't understand, Max,' Allain replied, an impatient edge to his voice. 'We make a commitment to each and every one of these kids here *for life*. We look after them. We find something for them to do

– something that suits them, something that earns them money, something that gives them dignity. The jobs we provide allow them to build or buy a house and some clothes, allow them to eat and have a better standard of living than ninety per cent of the poor bastards you see in the streets. And if we could help all of *them*, believe me we *would*. But we're not *that* rich.

'You're judging us – this place, what we're doing – by your American standards. This *empty rhetoric* of yours – liberty, human rights, democracy. They're just empty words to you people. You talk of these things, yet blacks in your country only got the same rights as you less than forty years ago,' Carver said, lowering his voice but driving his point home with well-aimed fury. He took a handkerchief out of his pocket and dabbed at the sweat which had accumulated on his upper lip.

There were things Max could have said right then in defence of his homeland, about how America at least offered people free choice, about how anyone with enough will, determination, discipline and drive could make a success of themselves there, and how it was *still* the land of opportunity. But he didn't go there. This wasn't the time and place for a debate.

'Ever make a mistake?' Max asked instead. 'Have an Einstein cleaning your toilet all his life?'

'No. Never,' Carver replied defiantly. 'Anybody can be an idiot but not everybody can be intelligent.'

'I see,' Max said.

'You don't "approve", do you? You don't think it's "fair"?'

'As you said, Mr Carver. This ain't my country. I'm just a dumb-ass American with a head full of rhetoric and no right to talk about right and wrong,' Max replied sarcastically.

'The average life expectancy is around forty-eight. That

means you're middle aged at twenty-four.' Carver's tone got back on an even keel. 'People who work for us, who go through our system, they live *beyond* that. They get old. They see their children grow up. Just like people are *meant* to.

'We are *saving* lives and we are giving lives. You might not understand but the whole of Europe used to run that way before the French Revolution. The rich looked after the poor.

'Do you know that when they see us coming, people abandon their children so we might pick them up and give them a better life? It happens all the time. What you see here may look bad from a distance, Max, but close up it's really quite the opposite.'

34

They left for Saut d'Eau at 4.00 am the following day, Chantale at the wheel. The waterfalls were only forty miles north of Port-au-Prince, but thirty of those constituted the worst roads in Haiti. On a good day a round trip by car took an average of ten hours; double that on a bad day.

Chantale had brought a small hamper of food for the trip. Although there were plenty of places to stop off along the way and the waterfalls had a little tourist town nearby called Ville Bonheur, you could never be sure what you were eating. Household pets and pests alike were often passed off as pork, chicken and beef.

'Why are you going to Saut d'Eau – *exactly*?' Chantale asked.

'First up: I want to talk to this Le-Ball-eck guy. Faustin knew who kidnapped Charlie. He might've shared the information, or left a clue with him. Plus Clarinet was the last place my predecessors went to before they disappeared. I want to find out why, what it was they saw or heard. They must've been on to *something*.'

'Don't you think whoever's behind this would've taken care of any loose bits of evidence by now?'

'Yeah,' Max nodded. 'But you never know. Maybe they overlooked something. There's always that chance.'

'Slim,' Chantale said.

'Way it always is. You always hope your perp's dumber and sloppier than you are. Sometimes you get lucky,' Max chuckled.

'You didn't mention Filius Dufour.'

'What, that "go to the source of the myth" crap? Last thing I'm gonna do is act on a fortune teller's advice. I deal in fact, not fantasy. You know an investigation's running on fumes when you bring the occult in as a partner,' Max said.

'I don't think you believe that,' Chantale said.

'If he cared about the kid and really knew anything he'd have said.'

'Maybe he wasn't *allowed* to say anything.'

'Oh? Who by? The ghosts he talks to – or whatever the fuck he does. *Come on*, Chantale! The guy knows as much as me – nothing, *nada*, bupkis.'

For the first hour they drove in complete darkness, leaving Pétionville and crossing a billboard-and-telegraph-pole studded plain on their way to the mountains. The ride was surprisingly smooth until they took a long hairpin bend around the first hills, and the terrain turned first to gravel then to rubble. Chantale killed the speed and turned on the radio. American Forces Radio was playing 'I Wish I Could Fly' by R Kelly. Chantale quickly changed the dial and got the Wu Tang Clan rapping 'America Is Dying Slowly'; then she turned to another station and got Haitian talk radio, the next was broadcasting a church service, the ones after that were from the Dominican Republic and blasted out a mixture of salsa, talk, a sports match – probably soccer, judging from the pace – and another church service – all in Spanish. It made Max smile because it reminded him of Miami radio – only far more shambolic than they would ever have allowed back home.

Chantale dug a cassette tape out of her bag and pushed it into the player. She pressed play.

'Sweet Micky,' she explained.

It was a recording of a concert. Sweet Micky had a voice

like sandpaper cleaning a cheesegrater, his singing was a repertoire of shouts, barks, screams, laughter and – for the higher notes – the whining yelps of fighting cats; the music behind him was madcap funk, played at a frenetic pace that didn't let up. It was like nothing Max had ever heard before. Chantale was getting into the song, dancing with her whole body, tapping her hands on the wheel and her feet on the pedals, moving her head, torso and hips. She whispered the chorus – '*Tirez sur la gâchette – baff!-baff!-baff!*' – making her hand into a gun shape and stabbing at the air, smiling away to herself, her eyes alive with joy and aggression, as she dipped below the surface and connected with the song's furious groove.

'I guess that wasn't "imagine all the people, livin' life in peace"?' Max said when the song finished and she ejected the tape.

'No,' she said. 'It's about the *raras*. It's a kind of travelling dance people do at carnival time – moving through the streets, village to village. It lasts for days. Pretty wild too. Plenty of orgies and murders.'

'Sounds fun,' Max quipped.

'You might see it.'

'When is it?'

'Before Easter.'

'Not if I can help it,' Max laughed.

'Are you going to stay here until you find Charlie?'

'I hope it doesn't take me that long, but yeah, I'll be here until the job's done.'

By the green and red lights of the dashboard Max saw her smile.

'What'll you do if the trail runs cold?' she asked.

'It ain't exactly hot now. We're checking out rumours, myths, hearsay. Nothin' solid.'

'What about when those run out? What then?'

'We'll see.'

'What if he's dead?'

'He probably is, if I gotta level with you. We're just gonna have to find the body and the person or persons who took his life – and why. Motive's always important,' Max said.

'You're not the kind that gives up, are you?'

'I don't believe in unfinished business.'

'Did you get that from childhood?' she asked, looking across at him.

'Yeah, I guess. Not from my parents. I didn't know my dad. He took off when I was six and never came back. Closest I had to a dad was this guy called Eldon Burns. He was a cop who ran this boxing gym in Liberty City. Trained local kids. I went there aged twelve. He taught me to fight – and much more. I learned some of my life's lessons in the ring. Eldon had these rules taped to the changing-room walls, so's you wouldn't miss 'em. One of 'em was "Always finish what you start". If it's a race and you're comin' in last, don't pussy out and walk the rest of the way – run to the finish line anyway. If it's a fight and you're gettin' beat – don't say "*no más*" and quit on your stool, fight to the last bell.' Max smiled at the memory. '"Go out standing," he'd say, "and one day you *will* be *out-standing*." It's a good rule.'

'Was he why you became a cop?'

'Yeah,' Max said. 'He was my boss back in them days too.'

'Are you still in touch?'

'Not directly,' Max said. He and Eldon had fallen out before he'd gone to prison and they hadn't spoken in over eight years. Eldon had come through for him at his trial and he'd been there at Sandra's funeral, but he'd done both out of duty, to square favours. They were quits now.

Chantale sensed Max's animosity and turned the radio

back on, rolling the dial until she came to some unobtrusive piano picking out the notes of 'I Wanna Be Around'.

The sun was starting to rise and the mountains were
appearing ahead of them, peaks silhouetted black against a
sky painted shades of black, indigo and mauve by the dawn.

'What about you?' Max asked. 'How's your mother?'

'Dying,' she said. 'Slowly. Sometimes painfully. She's saying
she'll be glad when it's over.'

'What's your dad doin'?'

'Never knew him,' Chantale said. 'My mother got pregnant during a ceremony. She was possessed by a spirit at the
time, so was my father. It's called "*Chevalier*". It means
"knight" in French, or "ridden by the gods" in our language.'

'So you're a god's child?' Max quipped.

'Aren't we all, Max?' she countered with a smile.

'That ever happen to you — Chevrolet?'

'*Chevalier* not "Chevrolet",' she corrected him with mock
indignation. 'And no. It hasn't. I haven't been to a ceremony
since I was a teenager.'

'There's always time,' Max said.

She turned and gave him a look he felt in his crotch —
bedroom eyes coupled with a searching gaze. He couldn't
stop his eyes from slipping down to her mouth and the small
dark brown mole under her bottom lip. It wasn't perfectly
oval, more like a comma which had been knocked on its
back. Not for the first time he wondered what she was like
in bed and guessed she was spectacular.

It was now light. The road they were taking was a dirt track
cut into a dry, barren plain of white rocks, boulders and —
once in a while — the carcasses of dead animals, picked
clean and bleached pale. There were no trees or bushes in
sight, only cacti. It reminded him of postcards he'd received

from friends who'd taken a trip to the great southwestern states.

They drove up into the mountains. They were nothing like the ones he had back home. He'd been to the Rockies and the Appalachians, but these were completely different. They were brown mounds of dead earth slowly but systematically being eroded by every breath of wind, every drop of rain. It was hard to imagine that the whole island had once been rainforest; that this environmental catastrophe of a place had had life, that it had been the commercial cornerstone of a foreign empire. He tried to imagine what the people who lived in the mountains would look like, and he came up with a cross between concentration camp survivor and an Ethiopian famine victim.

But he was wrong.

They might have been every bit as poor, but the country people lived somewhat better than the miserable souls in town. The children, although thin, didn't have the bloated bodies and starved, haunted looks of their Port-au-Prince counterparts. The villages they passed weren't anything like the desperate hovels of Cité Soleil. They were collections of small huts with thatched roofs and thick walls painted in bright colours – reds, greens, blues, yellow, red and white. Even the animals looked better off, the pigs less like goats, the goats less like dogs, the dogs less like foxes, the chickens less like anorexic pigeons.

The road got bad and they slowed to a crawl. They had to drive around potholes five feet deep, drive in and out of craters, creep around hairpin bends in case someone was coming their way. They saw no cars at all, but there were a few wrecks, stripped right down to pencil outlines. He wondered what had become of the drivers.

Despite the air-conditioning keeping the car cool, Max

could feel the heat outside, pouring down out of the light-blue, cloudless sky.

'Allain didn't tell you everything about Noah's Ark,' Chantale said. 'Not surprisingly – given your attitude.'

'You think I was out of line, sayin' what I did?'

'You were both right,' she answered. 'Yeah, it's wrong, but look at this place. More people than crops.'

'What didn't he tell me?'

'Background stuff, about the contracts. All the time those children are growing up, they're constantly reminded where they came from and who it was who took them away from that. They're taken to Cité Soleil, to Carrefour, to other nasty places. They get to see people dying of starvation and disease – not to teach them charity or compassion, but to teach them gratitude and respect, to teach them that the Carvers are their saviours, that they owe their lives to the family.'

'So they're brainwashed?'

'No, not really. They're *educated*, taught the Carver creed along with their verbs and their times tables,' Chantale said. 'Anyway, they're basically convinced that the minute they leave the Ark they'll end up in the slums with poor folk.'

'So, when they turn seventeen or eighteen and the contracts come out they happily sign their lives away?' Max concluded. 'So they trade Noah's Ark for the Carver empire?'

'That's right.'

'How come they hired you?'

'Allain likes to hire outsiders,' she said. 'Apart from his servants.'

'But this contract – it's not enforceable if you go overseas, right? Say you're studyin' in America and decide you wanna go work for JP Morgan instead of Gustav Carver, they can't stop you.'

'No, they can't, but they do,' she said, lowering her voice, as if someone was listening.

'How?'

'They have contacts everywhere. They're very rich, powerful people. People with influence. Try and break a deal and they break *you*.'

'Have you known it to happen?'

'It's not something they exactly brag about or anybody finds out about, but I'm sure it's happened,' Chantale said.

'What happens to the kids who don't conform? The problem kids? The ones who rebel in the back row of class?'

'Again it's not something they openly talk about, but Allain told me the kids who don't get with the programme are taken back to where they were found.'

'Oh, that's real civilized,' Max said bitterly.

'That's *life*. Life isn't easy anywhere, but here it's worse. It's hell. It's not like those kids don't know how lucky they are.'

'You need to change job. You sound like your boss.'

'Fuck you,' she said under her breath. She turned up the volume on the radio.

Max thought about what he'd heard for a while, then he switched off the radio.

'Thanks,' he said to her.

'What for?'

'Opening up a whole new dimension to this investigation: Noah's Ark.'

'You're thinking the person who kidnapped Charlie might have been expelled from there?'

'Or had his or her future destroyed by the Carvers, yeah. A life for a life. Third oldest motive in the book.'

'You should know,' she said.

35

To most Haitians, Saut d'Eau is a place where the waters run with the stuff of miracles. The story goes that on 16 July 1884 the Virgin Mary appeared before a woman who was standing in the stream, washing her clothes. The vision then transmogrified into a white dove which flew off into the waterfall, forever imbuing the cascade with the powers of the Holy Spirit. Since then Saut d'Eau has attracted thousands of visitors every year, pilgrims who come to stand under the blessed waters and pray out loud for cures for illnesses, relief from debts, good crops, a new car and quick solutions to US visa entry problems. The anniversary of the Virgin's appearance is also celebrated with a famous festival around the waterfall, which lasts all day and all night.

When he first set eyes on the place, Max almost fell for the legend himself. The last thing he expected to find after hours driving through the arid wilderness was a small piece of tropical paradise, but that's exactly what it was – a proverbial oasis, a mirage made real, or a sanctuary – a reminder of the way the island had once been, and all it had lost.

To reach the waterfall Max and Chantale had to walk along the banks of a wide stream which cut through a forest of densely packed trees, overflowing plant life, thick dangling vines and riots of sweet-scented, brightly coloured flora. They weren't alone. As they'd drawn closer to their destination, more and more people had joined them on the road – most on foot, but some riding donkeys and tired-looking horses – all of them pilgrims heading for a cure. Once they'd reached the stream they'd waded into the water and walked solemnly and humbly towards the hundred foot tall cascade. Despite the great roar of the crashing torrent up ahead, there was a deep quiet within the forest, as if the essence of silence itself was locked into the soil and the myriad vegetation. The people seemed to sense this because none of them spoke, nor made much noise in the water.

Max saw that some of the trees along the way were studded with candles and covered with photographs of people, Christian saints, cars, houses; postcards – most of them of Miami and New York – as well as pictures cut or torn out of magazines and newspapers. These trees, with their enormous thick trunks and thin spindly branches, some hanging with cucumber-shaped fruit, Chantale explained were called *mapou* in Haiti. They were sacred in voodoo, trees whose roots were said to be a conduit for the *loas* – the gods – from this world into the next, and whose presence was meant to signify the nearness of flowing water. The tree was inextricably linked to Haiti's history: the slave rebellion which resulted in Haiti's independence was rumoured to have started under a *mapou* tree in the town of Gonaïves, when a stolen white child was sacrificed to the devil in exchange for his help in defeating the French armies: Haitian independence was declared under the very same tree in 1804.

When they reached the waterfalls they stopped at the bank, near a *mapou*. Max put down the hamper he'd been carrying. Chantale opened it and took out a small drawstring bag of purple velvet. She removed four metal candle holders which she stuck into the tree at four equidistant points, like those of the compass. Moving anti-clockwise she spiked four candles into the holders – one white, one grey, one red and one lavender. Then she took a picture out of her wallet, kissed it with her eyes closed and tacked it in the middle of the candle arrangement. She sprinkled water on her hands from a small clear-glass bottle, and then rubbed what smelled like sandalwood lotion into her hands and arms. Whispering quietly, she lit each candle with a match and then, tilting her head back, she looked up into the sky and stretched out her arms, palms up.

Max moved a little away, out of her immediate range, to give her some privacy. He looked at the waterfall. Off to the left there was a break in the trees where the sun streamed through and made a gigantic rainbow in the mist rolling off the torrent. People were standing on the rocks directly under the falls, water pounding on their bodies. Others stood apart, off to the sides, where the cascade was not as forceful. They chanted and held their hands up to the sky, in much the same way Chantale was doing; some shook instruments like maracas, others clapped their hands and danced. They were all naked. Once they got close to the rocks near the falls they shed their clothes in the stream and let them float off with the current. In the stream itself the pilgrims stood waist deep, washing themselves with herbs and bars of yellow soap they bought off boys selling baskets of them on the banks. Max noticed several of the pilgrims were in trances, standing stock still in crucifixion poses; others were possessed, bodies shaking, heads snapping back and forth, eyes wide and rolling, tongues darting in and out of perpetually moving mouths.

Chantale walked over to him and rested her hand on his shoulder.

'That was for my mother,' she explained. 'It's a thing we do for the sick.'

'How come they get rid of their clothes?' Max asked, nodding at the worshippers.

'It's part of the ritual. First they shed the burden of their past bad luck – symbolized by the clothes – then they wash themselves clean in the waterfall. Like a kind of baptism. Only they're making a great sacrifice getting rid of their clothes, because all of these people you see here have very little.'

Chantale started walking down the bank towards the water, an empty bottle in her hand.

'You going in?' Max asked, incredulously.

'Aren't you?' she replied, smiling, her eyes full of suggestion.

Max was tempted as hell, but he held back.

'Maybe next time,' he said.

She bought a bar of soap and a handful of leaves from the boys with the baskets and then she waded in and began to cross the stream towards the dark rocks and the brilliant white deluge pummelling them.

Before she reached the falls, she took off her shirt and dropped it in the water. She soaped her face and her bare torso and then pulled herself up on the rocks. She stripped down to a black thong and tossed away her jeans after her shoes.

Max couldn't take his eyes off her. She was even better looking without her clothes on than he'd imagined. Her legs were strong, her belly flat, her shoulders toned, her breasts small and firm. Hers was a dancer's body – supple and graceful instead of athletic. He tried to work out how much of her was down to genes over exercise, but then he realized he was staring too hard and snapped out of it.

She saw him looking at her and she smiled and waved. He waved back, automatically, inanely, suddenly back down to earth, embarrassed that she'd caught him looking at her.

Chantale stepped back and forced herself into the middle

of the torrent, right under the innermost edge of the rainbow, where the water fell hardest and heaviest. Max lost sight of her completely, confusing her again and again with a variety of other bathers and their shadows, outlines blurred or invented by mist and motion. At times there seemed to be many people there with her, cleansing themselves, and then suddenly the waterfalls would appear completely empty, as if the pilgrims had been dissolved like so much dirt and washed into the stream with the banks of discarded clothes.

As he was looking for Chantale he felt his attention being pulled away from his search and off to his left, where he sensed someone observing him. He wasn't being watched out of curiosity or wonder, the way some of the people on their way to the stream had looked at him; he was being assessed and evaluated by a trained eye. He knew the feeling because he'd been taught to recognize it as a cop. Most criminals were paranoid as hell and had a naturally heightened sense of suspicion, same as the blind with their better developed senses of smell and sound. They'd know if they were being watched; they'd actually feel the person's presence, dogging their every breath, tracking their every thought. This was why cops were taught the 'Sun Rule of Observation': never look directly at a target, but focus on the space five degrees to its left or right, keeping the main attraction well within sight.

The person who was watching him hadn't learned this. He also hadn't learned the other important rule – always stay out of sight; if you're going to see, don't be seen.

He was standing on the rocks, away from the crashing water, part obscured in the mist; a tall thin man in ragged blue trousers and a long-sleeved Rolling Stones T-shirt that was torn and frayed around the hem. He was looking right at Max without the trace of an expression on the little that could be seen of his face under the thick mop of shoulder-length dreadlocks hanging from his scalp like the legs of a dead mutant tarantula.

Chantale reappeared on the rocks, shaking the loose water out of her head and slicking her hair back with her fingers. She stepped down into the stream and started walking back towards Max.

At the same time Dreadlocks stepped into the water and also began to head his way. There was something in his hands, something he didn't want to get wet because he was holding it high up above the stream. The worshippers who weren't in some other mental space got out of his way, exchanging worried looks, some hurrying for the bank. A possessed woman made a wild grab at what he was holding. He smashed his elbow into her face, sending her flying back into the water. The spirits fled her body as she splashed back to land, blood running down her face.

As Dreadlocks drew closer, Max motioned to Chantale to go back to the rocks. He was near the bank now. Max thought of pulling his gun on him and getting him to stop, but if the guy was a nutcase that wouldn't do anything. Some people just wanted you to shoot them because they didn't have the guts to put themselves out of their misery.

Dreadlocks slowed down and stopped right opposite Max, up to his ankles in water. He held out what he had in his hands – a battered, rusted tin box with some of its original design – a large blue rose – clinging to it.

Max was about to walk towards him when a large rock flew out and hit Dreadlocks on the side of the head.

'*Iwa! Iwa!*'

Children's frightened yells, right behind Max.

Suddenly Dreadlocks was hit from all sides by a crossfire

of rocks and large stones, thrown with surprising accuracy, all striking some part of his body.

Max ducked and moved back up the bank, where the stone throwers were gathered – a small group of children, the eldest being maybe twelve.

'*Iwa*! *Iwa*!'

This emboldened the worshippers who, up until that moment, had stood stock still, watching. They began pelting Dreadlocks with stones, but they didn't have the children's accuracy and their shots went wide, hitting the frozen human crosses and sending them toppling into the water, or striking the possessed, and either completely exorcizing them or driving them into even more demonic spasms.

Then Dreadlocks' hands took a direct hit. He dropped the box which fell in the stream, disappeared below the surface and then bobbed back up a few feet away.

Dreadlocks went after it, running as fast as he could, pushing through the water, pursued by volleys of stones and a few of the bolder pilgrims who, thinking he was fleeing them, made after him with sticks, but were in no hurry to catch up with him.

Dreadlocks vanished down the stream.

When it was clear he wasn't coming back, things went back to normal. The spirits repossessed the bodies they'd abandoned, worshippers returned to the stream water to soap themselves and climbed up the rocks to the falls, and the children on the bank tended to their baskets.

Chantale came back. Max handed her a towel and a new set of clothes from the hamper.

'What's *E-wah* mean?' Max asked as he watched her dry her hair.

'*Iwa*? Means devil's helper. People who work with *bokors*,' she said. 'Although I don't think that guy was one. He's probably just a local freak. Plenty of them around. Especially here. They come here normal, they get possessed, they never leave.'

'What did he want with me?'

'Maybe he thought you were a *loa* – a god,' she said, pulling on a sports bra.

'That would make a change,' Max laughed, but as he replayed the incident he didn't find it so easy to dismiss. He was sure Dreadlocks had known who he was, or what he was doing there, who he was looking for. It was in the way he'd first stared at him, deliberately, making sure he got his attention. Only then had he made his move. And what was in the box?

36

Clarinette was a village on its way to becoming a small town. The bulk of it was situated on top of a hill overlooking the waterfalls, but the slopes of the hill were littered with a tumble of one-room houses, huts and clapboard shacks; so randomly ordered that, from a distance, they made Max think of a forgotten cargo of cardboard boxes, spilled out of a long gone truck.

People stopped to stare at them as they got out of the car. The adults scoped them out from head to toe, checked out the Landcruiser and went on about their business like they'd seen it all before but were still interested in the upgrades. The children all ran away. They were especially scared of Max. Some went and got their parents to point him out to them, others went and got their friends who all came in cowering three-foot gangs and then ran off screaming as soon as he looked at them. Max wondered if their fear of him was only down to their never having seen his kind before, or if suspicion of the white man wasn't something that had been passed down in the genes, mixed into the DNA.

Clarinette's tallest building was its imposing church – a mustard-yellow ring of reinforced concrete, topped with a thatched roof and a plain black cross. Four times the size of the next biggest structure – a blue bungalow – it dwarfed the other amateurishly constructed clay and tin hovels clumped untidily around it. Max guessed from the way the church was positioned, right in the centre of the village, that it had been built first, and then the community had evolved around it. The church didn't look much more than fifty years old.

The top of the cross scraped the clouds, which hung incredibly low here, sealing the village in an impenetrable veneer of dusk, which the sun, although at its fullest, couldn't overcome. The gradual erosion of the nearby mountain ranges had brought the sky that little bit closer to the touch.

There was a freshness to the air, healthy nuances of oranges and wild herbs undercutting the smells of woodfires and cooking. In the background, over the hubbub of people going about their business, was the constant sound of the waterfall a few miles below, its great roar rendered as a persistent gurgle, water running down a drain.

They walked through the village, talking to people along the way. No one knew anything about Charlie, Beeson, Medd, Faustin or Leballec. They weren't lying as far as Max could see. Questions about Tonton Clarinette produced only laughter. Max wondered if Beeson and Medd had really come here, if Désyr hadn't deliberately misled them.

As they got closer to the church they heard drumbeats coming from inside. Max sensed the rhythms go straight into his wrists, mid tempo bass notes catching in his bones and creeping into his veins, getting in sync with his pulse beats before they eked down into his hands and fingers and moved up and down them, making him clench and unfurl his fists like he had pins and needles.

The door to the church was padlocked. There was a noticeboard fixed to the wall, with a prominent picture of the Virgin Mary on it. Chantale read it and smiled.

'This place isn't what you think it is. It isn't a church, Max,' she said. 'It's a *hounfor* – a voodoo temple. And that isn't the Virgin Mary, it's Erzilie Freda, our goddess of love – our

Aphrodite, one of the highest and most exalted goddesses.'

'Looks like the Virgin Mary to me,' Max said.

'It's camouflage. Back when Haiti was a French slave colony, the masters tried to control the slaves by eradicating the voodoo religion they'd brought over from Africa and converting them to Catholicism. The slaves knew there was no point in resisting the masters, who were heavily armed, so they apparently went along with the conversions – only they were very cunning. They adopted the Catholic saints as their own gods. They went to church just like they were supposed to, but instead of worshipping the icons of Rome, they worshipped them as their own *loas*. Saint Peter became Papa Legba, *loa* of the lost, Saint Patrick was prayed to as Damballah, the snake *loa*, Saint James became Ogu Ferraille, the *loa* of war.'

'Smart people,' Max said.

'That's how we got free,' Chantale smiled. She looked back at the noticeboard for a moment and then returned to Max. 'There's a ceremony today at six. Can we stay for it? I want to make an offering for my mother.'

'Sure,' Max nodded. He didn't mind, even if it meant making the trip back to Pétionville in pitch darkness. He wanted to see the ceremony, just to satisfy his curiosity. He'd never attended a real one. At least he'd come away with something from this place.

They left the main village and walked east where two *mapou* trees grew, Max marvelling at how tranquil and quiet the countryside was after the capital.

They came to a low, long sandstone wall that had been abandoned before completion. The structure's south-facing end, had it been finished, would have given people on its upper floors a clear and spectacular view of the waterfalls a mile down.

'Who'd want to build here? It's out in the middle of nowhere,' said Chantale.

'Maybe that was the whole point.'

'It's too big for a house,' Chantale said, following the wall with her eyes all the way back towards the mountains behind the village.

Both *mapou* trees were adorned with burnt-out candle stubs, ribbons, locks of hair, pictures and small scraps of paper with handwriting on them. A little further on a shallow stream trickled quietly down to the chasm of Saut d'Eau. It would have been an idyllic scene were it not for the two Rottweilers playing right in the middle of the water.

Their owner – a short, thickset man in jeans and a crisp white shirt – was standing on the other side of the stream, watching both his dogs and Max and Chantale, seemingly at the same time. He was holding a Mossberg pump shotgun in his left hand.

'*Bonjour*,' he called out. 'American?'

'That's right,' Max said.

'You with the military?' he asked, his accent putting him longer in New Jersey than Haiti.

'No,' Max replied.

'You visit the falls?' the man asked, walking along his side of the bank so he could face them. The dogs followed him up.

'Yeah we did.'

'You like 'em?'

'Sure,' Max said.

'Got nuttin' on Niagara?'

'I don't know,' Max said. 'Never been.'

'There's some flat stones up ahead'll get you over this side without you needing to step in the water.' He pointed to some vague spot in the water. 'That is, if you're meaning to come this way?'

'What's over there?' Max asked, not moving from under the shade of the trees.

'Just the French Cemetery.'

'Why "French"?'

'Where the bodies of French soldiers are buried. Napoleon's men. See all this land? Used to be a tobacco plantation. There was a small garrison stationed back where the town is. One night the slaves rose up and took control of the garrison. They brought the soldiers here, right where you stand, between those two *mapoux*.

'One by one they made 'em kneel down on a *vévé* dedicated to Baron Samedi – that's the god of the dead and graveyards – and they slit their throats,' he said, drawing his finger across his throat and clucking his tongue as he completed the motion. 'They drained their blood and made it into a potion which they all drank. Then they put on the soldiers' uniforms, painted their faces and hands white – so's they'd fool anyone watching them from a distance – and they went on the rampage, killin', rapin' and torturin' every white man, woman and child they found. Not one of them got so much as a scratch on him. When they was done and free, they all come back here and settled down.'

Max looked at the trees and the ground where he stood, as if something about them could betray their history, then, finding nothing remarkable there, he and Chantale followed the bank until they found the raised stepping stones which led across the stream.

The man and his dogs came to meet them. Max put him at about his age, mid-forties, maybe a few years older. He had a dark moon face and small sparkling eyes that were full of mirth, as if he'd just regained his composure after

321

hearing the funniest joke ever told. His forehead was heavily lined and there were deep brackets around his ears, light furrows continuing the ends of his mouth, and a spray of silver stubble around his jaw. He looked strong and healthy, with thick arms and a barrel chest. He could have been a professional body builder in his youth and, Max imagined, he still worked out now, pumping serious iron a few times a week to keep his flame alive and the flab at bay. They'd never met before but Max already knew him – his posture, the accent, the build and his stare gave him away: ex-con.

Max held out his hand and introduced himself and Chantale.

'The name's Philippe,' he said and laughed, flashing the best set of teeth Max had seen on a local. His voice was hoarse, not through shouting or any infection, Max reckoned, but through lack of use, no one to talk to, or not much worth saying to the one he was with. 'Come!' he said enthusiastically. 'Let's go see the cemetery.'

They crossed a field and another stream until they came to a wild orange grove whose powerful, heady smell had left its trace around the village. Philippe navigated his way through the trees, sidestepping piles of sweetly rotting fruit, naturally grouped into loose shapes, part square, part circle, where they'd dropped off the branches and bounced and rolled to a stop. The oranges were the biggest Max had ever seen, the same size as grapefruit or small honeydew melons, their skin thick and dull with a slight blush creeping out from the stem. Their insides, where they'd burst, were flecked with red. The orchard was buzzing too with flies, all feasting on the abundance of putrefying sugar.

The large cemetery was some way in, a large rectangle of tall thick grass and headstones large and modest, straight and crooked, enclosed by a waist-high metal bar fence and entered through one of four gates at the side.

The soldiers were all buried side by side, sixty bodies in five rows of twelve, their resting places marked out by large grey rocks of roughly the same size with smoothed down surfaces and the surnames chiselled out in deep crude capitals.

'I didn't tell you everythin',' Philippe said, as he led them past the makeshift tombstones. 'The slaves didn't *just* drink their blood and steal their uniforms, they took their names too. See?' He pointed out a rock with the name 'VALENTIN' gouged into it. 'Ask around town and every name you hear'll come right back to this place.'

'Wasn't that a contradiction in terms?' Max asked. 'If they wanted to be truly free, what would they want with the slave master's names?'

'Contradiction?' Philippe smiled. 'It was all about *eradication*.'

'So why leave this behind? Why bury the bodies?' Max asked.

'Haitians are big on respect for the dead. Even *white* dead. Didn't want to get haunted by no French-speakin' ghosts,' he smiled and looked at Max. On the walk over Max had undone the trigger guard on his holster.

'Somethin' went wrong somewhere though, with the spell,' Philippe said, as he led them to a wide clearing which separated the soldiers' graves from the other tombstones in the cemetery. A single rock stood up in the middle, marking out a plot of dry bare reddish-brown earth where no grass grew. No name was carved into it.

'Napoleon's army had a lot of boys in it – some as young as eight, orphans who got conscripted. The garrison here was real young. The commanding officer was twenty,'

Philippe said, looking down at the grave. 'That there is where they buried the garrison's mascot – don't know how old he was, but he wasn't more'n a boy. Don't know his name neither. He used to play the clarinet to the slaves working these fields. They took care of him last.

'They made him play his clarinet while they strung his buddies up by the legs and opened their throats into a bucket. They didn't do that to him. They put him in a box and buried him alive right here.' Philippe touched the ground with his foot. 'They say they heard him playin' his clarinet long after they'd put the last fistful of dirt down over his head. Went on for days, this thin music of death. Some people say when there's a strong wind blowin' through here, they hear the sound of the clarinet mixed in with the stench of these oranges here no one wants 'cause they feed off the dead.'

'What went wrong with the spell?' Max asked.

'If you believe in that kind of stuff, Baron Samedi turns up to claim the bodies the slaves have offered him and he finds the kid still alive. He adopts him as a sidekick, puts him in charge of his children's division.'

'So he becomes the children's god of death?'

'Yeah – only he ain't a *god* as such, 'cause no one worships him like they do the Baron. He's more a bogeyman. And he don't wait for the kids to die neither. He just takes 'em alive.'

Max remembered what Dufour had told him about going to the source of the Mr Clarinet myth to find out what had happened to Charlie. He was here, at the source, where the myth had sprung. So, where was the answer?

'How do you know all this? About the soldiers and stuff?'

'I grew up with our history. My mother told me when I was a kid. Her mother before that, and so forth, all the way back. Word of mouth keeps things alive better than books. Paper burns,' he replied. 'Fact, unless my radar's all wrong, my mother's the one you come here looking for, right?'

'Your *mother?*' Max stopped, confused. 'What's your surname?'

'Leballec,' Philippe smiled.

'Why didn't you say so sooner?'

'You didn't ask,' Philippe chuckled. 'You come 'bout the boy, right? – Charlie Carver? Same as them other white guys did.'

Just then Max heard heavy footfalls and twigs snapping in the orchard right behind him. He and Chantale turned around and saw three large oranges rolling across the ground towards the fence. One dribbled through and stopped at Chantale's feet. She pushed it away from them.

'So your *mother's* the –?'

'– *bokor*, yeah, that's right. Bet you wasn't 'spectin' *that*, right? *Woman* be up in here, runnin' shit? Women do *everythin'* in this country 'cept run the damn place. They *did*, Haiti wouldn't be on the A Train to Shitsville like it is now.' Philippe nodded.

'Where is she?' Max asked.

'A short way away.' Philippe flicked his head eastwards and started walking, then he stopped and turned around and looked Max right in the eye. 'When you get out?'

'When did *you?*' Max asked back. He could always tell an ex-con from the tension in their neck and shoulders, the way their bodies were in a permanent state of alert, ready to fend off an attack. Philippe had it in spades; and so did Max.

'Two years back.' Philippe grinned.

'They repatriate you?'

'Sure did. Only way I was ever gettin' out this side of a

body bag. I was one of the first they sent over, the guinea pig.'

'You ever meet someone called Vincent Paul?'

'Nope.'

'Know who he is?'

'Yup. Sure do.'

Philippe motioned with his thumb for them to get going, took a few steps forward then stopped again.

'Case you wonderin' what it was I did – it was a murder,' he said. '*Pre*-meditated. Got into some shit with a guy. Escalated into a no-way-out situation. One day I just rolled up to him and blew him away. Only part I regret's gettin' caught. You?'

'Same ballpark,' Max said.

37

The Leballecs lived half an hour away from the cemetery, at the end of a dirt road which crossed another field and was broken up by a stream, before leading down a sharp slope to a grassy plain overlooking the waterfalls. They hadn't had to look far for the building material: their house was a sturdy one-floor rectangle whose walls were made of the same sandstone as the abandoned building shell near Clarinette.

Philippe made them wait outside with the dogs while he went to talk to his mother.

Max heard the waterfall's distant crash and thought back to his first few months at Rikers Island, how all he'd heard was the sound of the water surrounding the prison. The sounds should have been soothing and imbued him with a sense of inner peace, but they'd had the opposite effect. They'd driven him close to crazy. He'd sworn the currents were whispering to him, calling to him from deep below. All the while it was happening, he'd known what it was; he'd heard about it happening to first-time cons on long-term stretches, paranoia, fear, anxiety and stress working together, playing tricks on the mind, offering up insanity as easy relief. He'd held on to his sanity real tight and stood firm. He'd gotten through it. He'd learnt not to listen to the water.

A dark shape appeared at the bottom of the window nearest the front door, hovered in the glass for a moment and then vanished.

A while later the door opened and Philippe beckoned them in. The dogs stayed put.

Indoors it was cool and dark. The air smelled pleasantly sweet, like a well-stocked candy shop, with hints of chocolate and vanilla, cinnamon, aniseed, mint and orange, all threading in and out of range, never quite settling into a definite fragrance.

Philippe showed them into a room where his mother sat waiting at a long table draped in black silk cloth, trimmed with purple, gold and silver thread. She was in a wheelchair.

The room was windowless, but brightly lit by thick purple candles positioned in tight rhomboid formations on the floor, or placed in multiple brass candelabra, stood on objects of varying height and length, themselves also shrouded in black cloth. The candles on the ground were three-quarter crosses, the heads substituted by the flame.

The room should have been boiling hot, but the temperature was the bearable side of chilly, thanks to the air-conditioning running on full power and an overhead fan they could hear clicking and grinding above them. The artificial breeze caused the flames to undulate gently on their wicks, making the walls appear to be turning slowly about them, like a great shapeless beast stalking its prey and biding its time, waiting for its moment, savouring the dread.

Philippe did the introductions. His voice was tender and his body language respectful when he addressed his mother, telling Max she was someone he both loved and feared in equal measure.

'Max Mingus, may I introduce you to Madame Mercedes Leballec,' he said and stepped off to one side.

'Bond-joor,' Max said, automatically and unconsciously bowing his head. There was an innate authority about her, a power that thrived off the humility and intimidation of others.

'Mr Mingus. Welcome to my house.' She spoke in French-accented English, slowly and graciously, enunciating each word in a smooth voice which came across as studied and mannered, one she specifically laid on for strangers.

Max put her in her late sixties or early seventies. She was wearing a long-sleeved blue denim dress with pale wooden buttons down the front. She was completely bald, her cranium so smooth and shiny it seemed as if she'd never had hair. Her forehead was high and sheer, while her facial features were cramped close together, squashed down, smaller and less defined than they should have been. Her eyes were so minute Max could barely find their whites, their movements those of shadows behind spyholes. She had neither eyelashes nor eyebrows, but wore an abstract version of the latter in the shape of two bold arcing black strokes beginning at the edges of her temples and tapering down to points that almost met in the gap between her forehead and the start of her flat, funnel-shaped nose. Her mouth was small and made a fish-like pout, she had a firm jaw and a chin so deeply clefted it resembled a hoof. She made Max think of an eccentric and slightly scary reclusive old movie queen, post-chemotherapy. He shot a quick comparative look at Philippe, now slouching on a stool behind her, his hands on his lap. He couldn't see one iota of a resemblance.

She bade them to be seated with a regal sweep of the hand.

'You're looking for the boy? Charlie?' She spoke as soon as they'd taken their places.

'That's right,' Max replied. 'Do you have him?'

'No,' Mercedes answered emphatically.

'But you know Eddie Faustin?'

'*Knew*. Eddie is dead.'

'How d'you know he's dead? They never recovered his body.'

'Eddie is dead,' she repeated, wheeling her chair up closer to the table.

Max noticed the big stainless-steel whistle she was wearing on a string around her neck. He wondered who it was for – the dogs, Philippe or both.

'Eddie ever tell you who he was working for – or with?'

'We wouldn't be sitting here right now if he had.'

'Why's that?' Max asked.

'Because I'd be rich and you wouldn't be here.'

Something behind her left shoulder caught Max's eye. It was a lifesize brass sculpture of a pair of praying hands, stood upright in the middle of a draped table. The table was flanked by two long candles on Delphic column-styled sticks. A chalice and an empty clear-glass bottle were placed either side of the hands. A dog skull, dagger, a pair of dice, a metallic sacred heart and a rag doll were arranged behind them in a semi-circle. But the display's focal point were the objects he noticed last of all, placed directly below the hands on a brass dish that may have been a communion wafer plate – a pair of porcelain eyes, the size of ping pong balls, with bright blue irises staring right into his.

It was an altar used in black magic ceremonies. He remembered finding a lot of them in Miami back in the early eighties, when the Cuban crime wave hit and broke all over the city; bad guys prayed to bad spirits for protection before they went off and did bad things. Most cops had loudly dismissed the altars as superstitious bullshit, but inside they'd been more than a little creeped out by them. It was something they didn't understand, an influence they couldn't curtail.

'So, Eddie said nothing at all about the people he was working for?' Max continued.

'No.'

'Not one *single* detail? Didn't he even tell you if he was working for a man or a woman? If they were black or white? Foreign?'

'Nothing.'

'Didn't you ask?'

'No.'

'Why not?'

'I wasn't interested,' she answered in a flat, matter of fact way.

'But you *knew* what was going down?' Max leant a little over the table, just like he used to do when he was shaking down a stubborn witness in the interrogation room. 'You *knew* he was gonna kidnap that kid.'

'It was none of my business,' she replied very calmly, completely unruffled.

'But surely you thought it was wrong, what he was doing?' Max insisted.

'I'm no one's judge,' she answered.

'OK,' Max nodded and sat back. He glanced across at Chantale, who was following the proceedings intently, and then at Philippe, who was yawning.

He glanced back at the altar, connected with the staring eyeballs and then took in the background. The wall behind Mercedes was painted turquoise. A headless wooden cross hung in the middle of it diagonally, its beam bristling with long nails, crudely hammered, some bent, most sticking out at crooked angles. The cross looked like it was meant to be falling from heaven.

'How long had you known Eddie?'

'I helped him get his job with the Carver family,' Mercedes

answered, smiling slightly as she saw Max looking at the things behind her.

'How did you help him?'

'It's what I do.'

'And *what* is that?'

'You know,' she said, and her mouth stretched into a smile that showed a row of tiny teeth.

'Black magic?' Max asked.

'Call it what you will,' she said with a dismissive wave.

'What did you do for him?'

'Mr Carver had a choice between Eddie and three others. Eddie brought me something from each of his competitors – something they'd touched or worn – and I went to work.'

'Then what?'

'Good fortune is not for ever. It has to be repaid – with interest.' Mercedes pushed her chair back a little.

'They say Eddie died bad. Is *that* how he paid?'

'Eddie owed *a lot.*'

'Want to tell me about it?' Max prompted.

'He came to me with all his problems after he got the job with Carver. I helped him out.'

'What kind of problems?'

'The usual – women, enemies.'

'Who were his enemies?'

'Eddie was a Macoute. Almost everyone he'd ever beaten and extorted wanted him dead. And then there were families of people he'd killed, women he raped, they were out to get him too. It's what happens when you lose power.'

'What did you get out of him in return?'

'You wouldn't understand – and it's also none of your business,' she said firmly and waited to see Max's reaction.

'OK,' Max said. 'Tell me about Eddie and Francesca Carver.'

'Some things in life you just can't ever have. I tried to warn him against pursuing that madness. I didn't see a good end for it. Eddie wouldn't listen. He *had* to have her, the same way he'd *had* to have everything else in his life. He thought he was in love with her.'

'Wasn't he?' Max asked.

'Not Eddie,' she chuckled. 'He knew nothing about that. He'd raped all the women he hadn't paid for.'

'And you *worked* for him?'

'And *you* haven't worked for bad people?' She laughed deeply, in the middle of her throat, without opening her mouth. 'We're not that different, we're both for hire.'

As far as Max could tell she had nothing to hide, but she was keeping things from him just the same; he sensed it, some vital piece of information slipping through the cracks of everything she was saying.

'How did you try and bring Eddie and Mrs Carver together?'

'What *didn't* I try? I tried everything I knew. Nothing worked.'

'Had that ever happened to you before?'

'No.'

'Did you tell Eddie?'

'No.'

'Why not?'

'He wasn't paying me to fail,' she said.

'So you lied to him?'

'No. I tried something else – a rare ceremony, something that's only done in desperation. Very risky.'

'What was it?'

'I can't tell you,' she said. 'And I *won't* tell you.'

'Why not?'

'I'm not allowed to discuss it.'

She looked a little afraid. Max didn't push her.

'Did this thing work?'

'Yes, at first.'

'How?'

'Eddie told me he had the chance to take off with the Carver woman.'

'"Take off"? Like elope?'

'Yes.'

'Was he more specific?'

'No.'

'And you didn't ask because it didn't interest you?' Max said.

She nodded.

'So how did it go wrong?'

'Eddie's dead. It can't go more wrong than that.'

'Who told you he was dead?'

'He did,' Mercedes said.

'Who? *Eddie?*'

'Yes,' she answered.

'How d'he do that?'

She pulled herself back closer to the table.

'Do you really want to know?'

Close up she smelled of menthol cigarettes.

'Yes,' Max said. 'I do.'

'Are you of a nervous disposition?'

'No.'

'Very well.' Mercedes rolled her chair back and talked to Philippe quietly in Kreyol.

'Could you two get up and step away from the table so's we can set up,' said Philippe, getting up from his stool and pointing vaguely to his right.

Max and Chantale went and stood close to the door. The wallspace was entirely taken up by wooden display shelves, screwed to the wall, starting close to the ceiling and ending just above the floor. There were twenty individual compartments, each displaying a thick glass cylindrical jar filled with clear yellowy liquid, which held its contents in perfect suspension. Max scanned them randomly, noting a huge egg, a black mamba, a small foot, a bat, a human heart, a fat toad, a chicken's claw, a gold brooch, a lizard, a man's hand . . .

'What are these for?' Max whispered to Chantale.

'Spells. Good *and* bad. My mother's got a few of these. The egg can be used to make a woman fertile or barren,' she said, then pointed to the foot, which Max noticed was professionally sawn off above the ankle. 'The foot can be used to cure broken bones or to cripple someone.' Then she directed Max's attention to the hand, shrivelled and greyish-green in colour. 'That's a married man's hand. See the wedding ring?' He saw the faded gold band hanging loose at the bottom of the second from last finger. 'It can either make or break up a marriage. Everything you see here has two possible uses. It all depends on who's asking and who's casting. The good spells are done before midnight, the bad after. But I don't think a lot of good gets done around here.'

'How did they get these?' Max asked.

'They bought them.'

'Where from?'

'Everything's for sale here, Max,' she said. 'Even the future.'

He looked back at what the Leballecs were doing.

Philippe had removed the cloth from where they'd been sitting, revealing the varnished wooden table it had been covering. There were markings of various sizes on the surface, indentations painted black. First and most prominent, set in two arches in the middle, facing Mercedes, were the letters of the alphabet; capitals running A to M, and then N to Z. Below, in a straight line, ran numbers 1 to 10. In either upper corner were the words *Oui* and *Non*, and on the opposite side were carved the words *Au revoir*.

'Is that what I think it is?' Max asked Philippe.

'It ain't Monopoly. You said you wanted to know,' Philippe smiled. 'This is knowledge. You two wanna come over here.'

Max hesitated. What if this was bullshit?

So what if it was, he told himself – bullshit only hurts the believer.

'I thought you charged for this kind of thing?' Max said, not moving.

'So you're going to do it?'

'Yeah.'

'Good,' Mercedes smiled. 'Then consider it a gift from me to you. You're much more of a man than your predecessors – Mr Beeson and Mr Medd.'

'You met 'em?'

'Beeson was very rude and arrogant. He called me a "hocus pocus bitch" and walked out as soon as he saw what we were doing. Medd was more polite. He thanked me for my time before he left.'

'They never came back?'

'No.'

Meaning they didn't believe in this shit either, thought Max. Which either made him more open-minded or a born again fool.

'Shall we begin now, Max?'

The table was a huge Ouija board. A notebook, pencil and a solid clear-glass oval pointer were placed at Mercedes's side.

They were about to have a séance.

*

They sat around the table, Max in front of Mercedes, Chantale opposite Philippe, heads bowed, holding hands in a circle, like they were saying grace. Everyone apart from Max had their eyes closed. He wasn't going to take it seriously. He didn't believe in it.

'Eddie? Eddie Faustin? *Où là?*' Mercedes called out loudly, filling the room with her voice.

If she was faking, Max thought, she was putting her heart and soul into it. Her face, under the strain of concentration, was even more bizarre than it was when relaxed. She'd screwed it up so much that her features almost disappeared entirely in whorls and bunches of pinched-together, scrunched-up flesh. She was squeezing Chantale's and Philippe's hands so hard her fists were shaking with the effort. They were both wincing in pain.

The room had gone a shade darker. Max thought he saw something move by the shelves and looked over. The exhibits seemed a fraction brighter and alive, vivid and empty like lit up clothes-store mannequins on an empty dark street. He swore he could detect movement in some of them – a pulse beat in the hand, the toes moving at the end of the foot, the snake darting out its tongue, cracks forming in the egg shell. Yet when he focussed on them individually they were utterly lifeless.

Philippe and Chantale tightened their respective grips on Max's hands, their lips moving soundlessly.

The atmosphere in the room had changed. He'd never felt oppressed in there, despite all the black magic paraphernalia, the knowledge that his predecessors had passed through here on their way to mutilation and, quite possibly, death. Now he felt a tightness creeping into his chest and back, a feeling of someone heavy standing on it.

When he first heard the sound, he didn't register it

337

as anything special. He mistook it for the fan.

When he heard it again it was closer and louder, coming from right under his nose: a single light tap, followed by the sound of something small scraping over a smooth surface, a sound not unlike that of a zipper being done up, top to bottom, low notes ending on high.

He looked down at the board. Things had changed. The pointer had moved – or been moved – from Mercedes' side up to the letters. It was indicating the letter 'E'.

Chantale and Philippe let go of his hands.

'Qui là?' asked Mercedes.

He saw the pointer turn, independently, to point at 'D'.

Max wanted to ask Mercedes how she was doing it, but his mouth was too dry and his balls ice.

Chantale's face was impassive.

Mercedes had written the first two letters down.

The pointer turned to the right and moved across the board slightly to stop at 'T', its motions jerky yet steady, as if really guided by an unseen hand. It looked impressive – even if it was fake, which he kept telling himself it was, so he wouldn't freak out.

He thought of looking under the table to see if there was a machine underneath, controlling the spook show, but he wanted to see where it was all going.

Both Mercedes' hands were on the table.

The pointer moved back to 'E' and stayed put. It looked like a big congealed teardrop.

'He's here,' Mercedes said. 'Ask what you want to know.'

'*What?*'

'Ask-him-your-question,' Mercedes said slowly.

Max felt suddenly stupid, like he was being taken in and massively conned, all the while being loudly laughed at by an invisible audience.

'All right,' he said, deciding to play along for the time being. 'Who kidnapped Charlie?'

The pointer didn't move.

They waited.

'Ask him again.'

'Sure he understands English?' Max quipped.

Mercedes gave him an angry look.

Max was about to say something about the batteries dying when the pointer jerked into motion and zipped around the two arches of letters, stopping there just long enough for Mercedes to write down what they were before moving on to the next.

When the pointer stopped moving she held up her pad: H-O-U-N-F-O-R.

'It means temple,' she said.

'As in voodoo temple?' Max asked.

'That's right.'

'Which one? Where? Here?'

Mercedes asked but the pointer didn't move.

And it never moved again for them. They repeated the ceremony. Max even tried to empty his mind of all doubting thoughts and cynicism and pretend he really believed in what they were doing, but even so the pointer didn't budge.

'Eddie has left,' Mercedes concluded, when she'd tried for the final time. 'He usually says goodbye. Something must have scared him. Maybe you did, Mr Mingus.'

'Was that for real?' Max asked Chantale as they walked back towards the orange grove.

'Did you see any trickery?' Chantale said.

'No, but that doesn't mean it wasn't going on,' Max said.

'You need to believe in the impossible once in a while,' Chantale retorted.

'I do,' Max grunted. 'I'm here, ain't I?'

He was sure there was a perfectly rational, humdrum explanation for everything they'd witnessed at the Leballec house. Accepting what he'd just seen at face value was just too much of a mind-fuck.

Max believed in life and death. He didn't believe life crossed over into death, although he did believe that some people could be dead inside and appear to be living on the outside. Most lifers and long-timers he'd seen in prison were like that. He was pretty much that way too, a corpse wrapped in living tissue, fooling everyone but himself.

38

When they returned to Clarinette they asked anyone who looked old enough to remember, or give them a sensible answer, who had been in charge of the construction site they'd crossed over on their way to the stream.

The replies were the same from person to person:

'Monsieur Paul,' they all said. 'Good man. Very generous. Built us our town and *hounfor*.'

Not *Vincent* Paul, Chantale explained, but his late father, Perry.

How long ago had they been working there?

No one was quite sure. They didn't measure time in terms of years, but in what they'd once been able to do – how much they could carry, how fast they could run, how long they could fuck and dance and drink. Some said fifty years when they didn't look much past forty, others said twenty years, a few claimed they'd been working on the building a hundred years ago. None of them had known what they were building. They'd followed orders.

Chantale estimated it would have been between the mid-sixties and the early seventies, before the Pauls had gone bankrupt.

What was Monsieur Paul like?

'He was a good man. Generous and kind. He built us houses and a *hounfor*. He brought us food and medicine.'

Like father, like son, Max thought.

Did any children go missing during that time?

'Yes. Two: the children of mad Merveille Gaspésie. The

brother and sister both disappeared the same day,' they said, shaking their heads.

Then they all told the same story: the Gaspésie children used to play near the building works. They were youngsters, about seven and eight years old. One day they both vanished. People searched high and low, but they were never found. Some said they'd fallen into the waterfalls, others that they'd met Tonton Clarinette out by the graveyard.

Then one day their mother, Merveille, by now an old woman, went to all her friends' houses, telling them her son had returned, and that they should all come and see him. She got together a large group of people and brought them back to her house, but when they arrived, there was no one there. She insisted the boy had returned, that he was well-dressed and very rich. She showed them the thick roll of money he'd given her, all crisp new bills. When she asked him what had happened, where he'd disappeared to, he said a man with a deformed face had taken him and his sister away.

The people didn't really believe her, but they went along with her because she was suddenly the richest woman in town. Privately, they said she was mad.

Merveille waited for her boy to return. He never did. She waited and waited and wouldn't leave her house in case he turned up. She called his name out over and over again. 'Boris.'

In the end she went crazy. She started hallucinating and turned violent whenever people tried to help her. She had no other family and lost all her friends.

And then one day all the noises in her house stopped. When a group of people finally plucked up the courage to enter the house, she was gone and she hadn't been seen since. No one knew what had happened to her. It was a mystery.

*

'So what do you think, detective?' Chantale asked, wiping her mouth with a paper napkin.

'About the missing kids? Maybe they were abducted, and maybe that woman's son did come back – how else would she have gotten all that money?' Max said. 'But you know, this whole story could just be another myth.'

They were sat in the car eating the lunch Chantale had made – pork loin, avocado and gherkin sandwiches on thickly sliced homemade bread, potato and red pepper salad, bananas and Prestige beer. The radio was on low, an American station playing AOR power anthems back to back – the Eagles, Boston, Blue Oyster Cult, Reo Speedwagon. Max flipped the dial to Haitian babble and left it there.

It was late afternoon. The light was starting to fade and the clouds were thickening above them, slowly sealing off the sky from view.

'What about Vincent Paul?'

'He's still my main suspect. He's the only constant, the one who keeps popping up everywhere. Perhaps he kidnapped Charlie to get back at the Carvers for an actual or perceived hurt to his family. Of course, I've got absolutely no proof of this.' Max finished off his beer. 'I need to talk to Paul, but I've got a better chance having a one to one with Bill Clinton. Besides, I'm assuming Beeson, Medd and that Emmanuel Michaelangelo guy tried to do exactly the same thing, which could be why they ended up the way they did.'

'What if it's not him?' Chantale said. 'What if it's someone you don't know about yet?'

'I'll have to wait and see. That's what most detective work comes down to, you know, waiting and watching.'

Chantale laughed out loud and shook her head with a weary sigh.

'You really remind me of my ex-husband, Max. This is

the kind of thing he used to say when he knew he was getting nowhere on something. He was a cop. Still is. Miami PD, in fact.'

'Yeah? What's his name?' Max was surprised but almost immediately realized he shouldn't have been. The voodoo aside, she was a straight arrow, conservative, a safe pair of hands – exactly the kind of woman most cops married.

'Ray Hernandez.'

'Don't think I know him.'

'You don't. He was still in uniform when you quit,' she said. 'He knew all about you. Followed your trial every day. Used to make me tape the news when he was out on duty, case he missed something.'

'So you knew who I was? Why didn't you say anything?'

'What was the point? Anyway, I thought you'd guess Allain had told me the basics about you.'

'You got that right,' Max said.

'Ray despised you. Said you were a thug with a badge. You, Joe Liston, Eldon Burns, the whole MTF division. He hated the lot of you, hated the way you brought down the good name of the police.'

'What did he do, your Raymond? What Division?'

'When he made plainclothes? First Vice, then Narcotics. He wanted Homicide but to get it he had to play ball with the kind of people who held you in high esteem.'

'That's the way of the world. It's all about politics, mutual dependencies, credit in the favours bank,' Max said. 'You don't get to where you want to be without breaking hearts and stepping on people.' He could imagine what type of guy her husband was – the kind of self-righteous, ambitious prick who'd end up working in Internal Affairs because they promoted faster and rewarded backstabbing and betrayal. 'How come you and him broke up?'

'He was cheating on me.'

'What an asshole!' Max laughed and she joined him.

'That he was. Were you faithful to your wife?'

'Yeah,' Max nodded.

'I can imagine.'

'Oh yeah?'

'You're about as broken-hearted as I've seen anyone be,' she said.

'That obvious?' Max replied.

'Yes it is, Max,' she said, looking him right in the eye. 'You didn't come here to find Charlie. You didn't even come here for the money. That's what other people do. *You* came here to get away from your ghosts and all that guilt and regret you've been carrying around with you ever since your Sandra died.'

Max looked away from her and said nothing. He had no comeback to that, no ready denial. Her words had bitten into him and they'd bitten deep; their truth noxious like venom.

Outside, the doors of the temple had been opened and people were starting to make their way into it, casually drifting in, as if compelled by curiosity and a need for a fresh experience.

The drums had started up too, a slow beat which Max felt passing into his ankles, reverberating in the bone, filling his feet with the urge to move, to dance, to walk, to run.

Inside, the temple was far larger than he'd anticipated – big enough to accommodate two separate ceremonies, their hundred or more participants and observers; and, seated on four-tiered benches almost covering the entire circumference of the wall, an orchestra of drummers.

From the sight of them he was expecting to hear pure

chaos – the rhythms of downtown Port-au-Prince tran-
scribed in tribal beats. Their instruments were all homemade
– crudely fashioned hollow wood or modified oil drums,
stretched animal hide fixed with nails, tacks, string and
rubberbands – but he recognized suggestions of tom-toms,
snares, bongos, bass and kettle drums there. The musicians
were randomly placed – wherever there was room – and
there was no one conducting or directing or shouting out
cues; they watched the proceedings, listened in and played
along with their hands, keeping to the same beat, steady as
a metronome, and making a sound no louder or quieter than
distant thunder.

Max sensed this was just the prelude.

It was steam-room hot thanks to the many bodies, the
lack of ventilation and the burning torches shedding an
amber light from their brackets on the wall. The air was so
still and thick it was virtually painted on. Clouds of incense
were wafting up towards the roof and then coming back
down as light smog.

When Max breathed in deep to get more oxygen into his
blood, he experienced a heady, near narcotic rush, both seda-
tive and amphetamine, a cool soothing sensation in his back
followed by a rush of blood to his eyes and a quickening
of the heartbeat. He picked up a cocktail of natural smells
– camphor, rosemary, lavender, gardenias, mint, cinnamon,
fresh sweat and old blood.

In the middle of the temple people were dancing and
chanting around a thick twisted column of black rock,
sculpted in the shape of an enormous *mapou* trunk, rising
up from the ground and passing through a large round hole
in the roof where it was topped by the cross they'd seen
from the street. As with the real tree, there were dozens of
lit candles stuck to the sculpture. Worshippers were walking

over it, sticking their pictures, scraps of paper, ribbons and candles on the rock, and then stepping into the mobile encirclement of bodies, falling into step, joining in the dance of swaying hips and nodding heads, adding their voices to the chants. Max tried to pick out what they were saying, find part of a word or phrase he could hold on to, but there was nothing discernible coming out of those mouths, only deep notes, held, extended, played with and transformed.

The floor was bare earth, trampled flat by motion and baked hard by the heat. There were three large *vévés*, drawn in maize, two of snakes – one with its body wrapped around a pole and its tongue pointing out towards the temple entrance, the second swallowing its tail – and, in between them, a horizontal coffin, split into four sections, each containing a crucifix and an eye, both drawn in sand.

'Loa Guede,' Chantale said over the drums and the chanting, pointing to the *vévé* of the coffin. 'God of Death.'

'I thought that was the good Baron,' Max said.

'He's god of the *Dead*,' she said, meeting his eyes, almost leering at him. She was a little giddy, unsteady, like she was on her third drink of the night and starting to feel the booze kicking away her restraints. 'You know what goes with death, Max? *Sex*.'

'He the god of that too?'

'Oh yeah.' She smiled and laughed her dirty laugh. 'There's going to be a *banda*.'

'A *what?*'

She didn't answer. She didn't explain. She'd started to dance, shimmying from the calves up, her body undulating in smooth, slow waves, feet to head, head back to legs. He felt the drums in his thighs and hips now, inspiring him to dance with her.

Chantale took his hand and they started moving towards

the *mapou* sculpture. He was dancing, despite himself, imitating those before him, the drums helping his legs and feet keep time, practically transforming him into a natural.

He sensed someone watching them but it was too dark and there were too many people looking their way to pick out the individual.

To the far right of the column Max saw a group of people standing around a pond of bubbling grey water. Two half-naked boys were standing in it waist-deep, beckoning to the bystanders, some of whom were tossing coins into the pool. Then a woman in a light-blue robe walked in. The boys grabbed her by the arms and plunged her under the water, holding her down hard, like they were trying to drown her, then letting go and staggering back out. The woman slowly re-emerged, naked now, except for her underwear and the thick grey muck she was completely caked in. She got back on to solid ground, took a few steps forward and then threw herself on the earth, writhing on her front and back, slapping the ground hard with her open hands, then throwing dirt all over her body and stuffing it into her mouth. Then she ran at the crowd of people gathered watching the worshippers dancing around the column, grabbed one of them – a man – by his shirt and spat a jet of purple fluid at his face. The man staggered backwards, crying, furiously rubbing at his face and eyes. The woman took hold of his wrist, pulled him over to the pond and pushed him in. The two boys dunked him and kept him under until he'd stopped thrashing around. When they let go the man slowly rose from the water. He too was the colour of ash and milk – and stark naked. He crouched down on the ground and watched the dancers.

Chantale stepped up to the sculpture and stuck a picture of a woman sitting up in a bed to it. Then she lit a candle and fixed it to a groove in the rock. She mumbled a few words in Kreyol and then began to chant as those around her were doing. They joined in the circle of people moving around them.

The drums beat a little faster, the bass dominated, vibrating in Max's thighs.

They danced. Max followed Chantale and all the others, shuffling, dipping his hips from side to side, touching the ground with his left hand, then his right, bringing them both together and separating them as if miming an explosion. He could barely feel himself doing it. The stuff they were burning in the air had first loosened him up and now he was beginning to feel himself being separated from his body, his being floating around his cage of bone and sinew. His brain had powered down to all but its basic functions. His senses had been wrapped in cotton wool, stuffed in a tube and dumped in a deep warm river, where they were floating slowly away from him, getting beyond reach. He was watching them go and he didn't care. This was bliss.

He heard the drums picking up the beat; he moved his feet a little faster. He heard himself joining in with the chanting, somehow finding a common note and sending it out from the bottom of his stomach. He wasn't a singer. He'd never sung in church when he was a kid. Too embarrassed. First he'd sounded like a girl, then when his balls dropped he sounded like he was belching. His dad had tried to teach him music, just the two of them at the upright piano one night, when he was five. No use. His dad had told him he was tone deaf. Not any more he wasn't, not in here.

His eyes fell on Chantale. She looked so beautiful, so sexy.

They were moving faster now. Worshippers were starting to fall away from the circle. Women were standing quaking, eyes rolling, tongues out, foaming at the mouth, in the full grip of spiritual possession. Meanwhile the muck-caked born-agains were running out of the pond, spitting purple jets at people in the crowd watching the dancers, and dragging them off to the grey waters.

Max felt simply wonderful now. He was smiling and heard laughter in his head, coming from deep within.

He was facing Chantale now, the two of them standing on their own, away from the circle. The drum beats had leapt into his loins, putting heat in his crotch. Chantale was looking right at him, grabbing and squeezing at her breasts, gyrating and thrusting her crotch in and out. She pressed herself up against him and rubbed her hand all over the front of his trousers. He closed his eyes for a moment and let the pleasure of her touch fill him completely.

But when he opened them she was gone.

In her place he saw a man coming towards him. He was naked, his skin covered in dry grey mud, cracked and flaking, the whites of his eyes turned brake-light red. He was sucking his cheeks rapidly in and out, purple juice dribbling out of gaps in his lips.

Max suddenly came to his senses, feeling like he'd been slapped out of a deep sleep.

Groggy and swaying on his legs, he tried to look for Chantale while keeping his eyes on the man. All around him the scene was beginning to change and change fast. He saw grey-caked men grabbing women from out of the dancing circle and throwing them to the ground, ripping their clothes off, raping them. The women weren't putting up any resistance. Most seemed to be welcoming the assaults.

The drumming was now fast and loud, an arrhythmic attack, devoid of form and order, coming from everywhere, the noise falling on the middle of the temple like hail after hail of bullets and flaming arrows. The drums were now serrated wheels tearing into Max's head.

He pressed his hands over his ears to kill the sound. Just then the mudman ran at him and spat a spear of purple fluid straight at his face. Max ducked in time, missing most of the projectile, but he still caught a few stray drops on his knuckles. They burnt like wet lava.

The mudman grabbed hold of his arm and tried to pull him forward. Max bent back and snapped three of the fingers gripping him and then he kicked the mudman hard in the chest. He flew back, smashed on the ground and slid a little way until he came to a stop. But he was up on his feet almost instantly, charging at Max again, red eyes ablaze with insane rage.

Max threw a combination of jabs and hooks at his assailant's head, stopping his run and forcing him back. Then he hit him with two huge fast uppercuts which connected in the same spot – right under the mudman's chin – one after the other, a split second apart, lifting him off the ground and scrambling his senses. The guy was as good as done. Instead of landing more punches to his head, Max simply pushed him over, letting him fall, knocked out cold.

He looked for Chantale. She wasn't by the column. She wasn't by the pond. He headed towards the crowd. They'd linked arms and weren't letting him through.

Max backed off. The drums were killing his head, a million pummelling jackhammers running relay around his brain.

He turned and went back towards the sculpture. She couldn't be far. All around him men and women were down on the ground, naked, fucking, multiple positions, both wild. The air reeked of sex and sweat.

He headed for the pond.

Then he saw Chantale standing near the water. A mudman

had ripped off her shirt and was tearing off her bra. She was offering no resistance, watching the man's titanic struggle with her underwear with a glazed look and a dumb detached smile.

Max sprinted over and pushed the mudman headfirst into the pond.

He grabbed Chantale's hand, but she pulled out of his grasp, slapped his face and started ranting at him in Kreyol. He stood there bemused, at a loss as to what to do. Then she gripped his head and crushed her lips against his, snaking her tongue into his mouth, running it up and down his tongue, licking it, tasting it. And then she grabbed his crotch, drew him towards her, and started dry humping him.

The pain left Max's skull and the drum migrated back to his loins. He felt himself slipping again, surrendering, wanting nothing more than to fuck Chantale in the dirt.

He was watching her pulling down her jeans when a mudman smashed into him. They went down together, Max taking the brunt of the fall and their combined weight on his shoulder. The mudman tried to punch him, but it was a wild bullshit strike and he missed completely. Max kneed him hard in the solar plexus, so hard he caught the blast of stinking air the blow forced out of him full in the face.

The mudman withered away, puking bile on the ground. Max took hold of his neck and what he could hold of his skinny buttock, picked him up like light luggage and tossed him towards the pool.

Chantale was still where he'd left her, only with another man – normal, but naked and glinting with sweat – standing in front of her, jerking off, getting himself hard, ready to rush her.

Max snatched Chantale by the arm and fast walked her away, heading for the exit. At first she snarled and kicked and tried to get away, but then, as they got closer to the crowd and further from the ceremony, she stopped fighting, grew limp and then heavy, her legs dragging. Max asked her if she was OK. She didn't reply. She tried to look at him through rolling eyes.

He hoisted her over his shoulder. He pulled out his gun and thumbed off the safety. The crowd didn't budge.

Then right in front of him stood Dreadlocks. People were moving out of his way, opening up space.

Max didn't slow down.

Dreadlocks came out of the crowd and headed towards them, carrying his blue rose box before him in his hands.

Max raised his gun and sighted Dreadlocks' head.

'Stop!'

Dreadlocks didn't pay any heed. He pushed the box into Max's chest and rushed past him. Max took the box in his free hand.

He glanced back.

Dreadlocks was gone, but five mudmen were running towards them, brandishing machetes and knives.

With Chantale on his back, Max pushed, nudged, kicked and stamped the rest of his way out of the temple.

Chantale slept most of the way back, dressed in Max's shirt, her snores accurate facsimiles of a busy farmyard.

He drove with the window cranked open and the radio playing an all-night Haitian talk show. He couldn't understand a word they were saying, but it was better than the wall-to-wall Bon Jovi all the other stations were blasting.

After five hours he was back on the airport road, heading up to Pétionville. Chantale woke up and stared at Max like she'd expected to find herself in bed at home.

'What happened?' she asked.

'What's the last thing you remember?' Max switched off the radio.

'We were dancing in the temple – together.'

'Nothing after?'

Chantale thought about it for a while but drew a blank. Max told her what she'd missed, starting backwards with the box, editing out what had gone on between them, but sparing no detail in describing how he'd saved her from a potential rapist.

'I was never going to get *raped*, Max,' she said angrily. 'It was a *banda*, a ritual orgy. People get possessed and they fuck each other's brains out. No one knows what they're doing.'

'Looked like rape to me – voodoo date rape, conscious or unconscious, whatever you wanna call it. The guy was tearin' your clothes off,' Max said.

'People do that when they're having consensual sex, Max. It's called *passion*.'

'Yeah? Well, I don't know how you can just go fuck a stranger like that. He could've had *AIDS. Jesus!*'

'You mean you've never fucked strangers before, Max?'

'*What*? Yeah, but that ain't the same thing.'

'Why? You meet a woman – where? In a bar, a nightclub? Music's loud, you're both loaded. You go some place, you fuck, and in the morning you leave and never see each other again. Same thing – only with us, it has more meaning.'

'*Right*,' Max sneered sarcastically. 'We decadent, soulless Americans just go around having empty one-night stands, but over here when you do it in a voodoo temple it's a *religious experience*. You know what I think, Chantale? I think it's a crock of shit. Fucking's fucking. Rape is rape. And that guy was gonna *rape* you. End of story. *No way* would you've made it with some guy covered in mud, if you'd been in your right mind.'

354

'How would you know?' Chantale snorted. 'You don't know that much as it is.'

Max didn't respond. He gripped the wheel tight and gritted his teeth, wishing for a good long while that he'd left the ungrateful bitch to get gang-raped in the dirt.

He'd intended to let her stay at the house, but he drove fast through Pétionville and took the road down to the capital. At night every big American city was lit up like a mini-galaxy. Port-au-Prince had a few grudging scraps of light floating in the black, like stray white butterflies caught in an oil slick; otherwise nothing. He'd never known a place so dark.

39

It was still dark when he got back, but the insects had gone to ground and the birds had started singing in the court-yard. Daylight was on its way.

There was a message on the answering machine from Joe. It was too early to call him back.

Inside the box Dreadlocks had given him, Max found a croc hide billfold containing numerous cards – ATM, AMEX, VISA, Mastercards, library, blood donor, Gold's Gym. They all belonged to Darwen Medd.

Max also found half a dozen black-on-white business cards held together by a paperclip. If he was still alive, Medd worked out of Tallahassee, where he specialized in missing persons and corporate affairs. The latter was prob-ably a recent diversification, something he was gradually setting himself up in so that he'd still be working when he got too old and too slow to look for runaways and abductees. Working in the business sector was safer and paid a lot better. You sat at a desk and followed paper trails by phone, fax and computer. The only field work involved was meeting your client for lunch, dinner or drinks. If you were good you never stopped working. Some companies kept you on a retainer. The better you were the more you were retained. It was a nice life. Boring as hell, but something Max had once been planning to move into himself.

There was no money in the wallet but, tucked in a corner

of the change pocket, he found a single folded piece of paper.

It was a page torn from a Haitian phone book dated 1990. Letters I to F, one section ringed in blue ballpoint: all the Faustins in Port-au-Prince – thirteen of them.

Medd had been on the same track.

Who was Dreadlocks? Why did he give him the box?

Was he Medd? No. Dreadlocks was a black man. He was crazy, and quite possibly mute. He hadn't made a sound near the falls, nor in the temple.

Perhaps Dreadlocks had seen Medd at the waterfalls when he'd visited Mercedes Leballec. Maybe Medd had befriended him. Or maybe he'd just found Medd's body and taken his wallet. Or maybe he'd just found the wallet. He'd sealed it in a box and given it to the first white man he'd seen at Saut d'Eau.

It occurred to Max that the best way of finding out was to go back to Saut d'Eau and ask him, but he wasn't going to go back there again, not if he could help it.

At 6.30 he called Joe. His friend answered on the second ring. Joe was in the kitchen with the TV news on low. Max could hear two of his girls in the background.

They talked and joked, Joe doing most of it. He had a three-dimensional life. Max only had what he was looking for.

'That guy you asked me to check out – Vincent Paul?'

'Yeah?'

'You know, I told you the Brit police wanted to question him.'

'Yeah?'

'It was in connection with a missing persons case.'

Max's grip tightened on the receiver.

'Who?'

'A woman,' Joe explained. 'Back in the early 70s, Vincent Paul was a student at Cambridge University in England. He was datin' this local girl called –' Max heard him thumbing through a notebook. 'Josephine . . . Josephine Latimer. The girl was an artist. She also liked to drink. A lot. One night she ran over this kid in her car and drove off. A witness made the car and her licence plate. She gets arrested and stuck in prison until the bail hearin'.

'Now, her parents are big shots in this small town. Everyone knows who they are, so their daughter bein' involved in a hit and run is big local news. The police want to make an example of her, show the people that everyone is equal before the law. They delay the bail hearin' for two weeks. The girl stays in jail and gets beaten up and raped. When she gets out she's a mess, tries to kill herself.

'The trial happens a year later – 1973. She's found guilty of manslaughter. She's due to be sentenced in two days. They're sayin' five years' jail time *minimum*. She knows she can't do no time. She knows she ain't gonna make it in there.

'The day she's due in court she disappears. There's this manhunt – local at first, then it goes nationwide. Her boyfriend – Vincent – he's gone too. Now Vincent is this giant – six-eight, six-nine – so he's not exactly gonna be *difficult* to spot, knowwhumsayin'? *But*, somehow, it takes a whole two months after her disappearance before someone comes forward and says they saw them on a boat goin' to the – the – the Hook of Holland.'

'So that time on the boat – was that the last sighting?' asked Max.

'Yeah. Him *and* his girl. She's still wanted in England for manslaughter *and* skippin' the country. But this is all kinda low priority now. Bonnie and Clyde they ain't.'

'Not over there, maybe.'

'You see this Vincent Paul in Haiti?'

'Yeah.'

'You talk to him?'

'Not yet – you don't talk to him, he talks to you,' Max quipped.

'What? Like God in the burnin' bush?'

'Somethin' like that,' laughed Max.

'What about the woman? Josephine? You see her?'

'Not that I know of. What she look like?'

'I ain't got a picture for her. But you see this Vincent Paul you ask him where she's at or where she went to.'

'I'll do that, if I get the chance.'

'You know the Brits sent two police officers out to Haiti to look for 'em. Scotland Yard guys.'

'Don't tell me – they found nothin'?' Max said.

'Exactly. You think Vincent or his family might've paid 'em off?'

'Maybe, but his family went bankrupt when he was in England. Besides, from what I know so far, payin' people off ain't Vincent Paul's style. He'd sooner kill 'em.'

They both laughed.

'You know a cop called Ray Hernandez – one of yours?' Max asked.

'Yeah, sure, I know him.' Joe lowered his voice so his kids wouldn't hear. 'If it's the same guy, we call him Ray Headuphisassez.'

'Sounds right.'

'How you know him?'

'His name came up in the joint,' Max lied.

'Used to be a narc,' Joe murmured. 'Was bangin' his partner's wife. Then he found out his partner was dirty so he snitched him out to IAD. They rewarded him with a desk and made him lieutenant. He's a full-on asshole. Time I met him he talked to me like I was a piece of ess-aitch-eye-tut, knowwhumsayin'? Thing I didn't get 'bout him? His wife was a hottie. Man must be blind and dumb to cheat on that.'

Max guessed Joe's wife wasn't within earshot. He'd never known a woman so jealous. If she caught Joe so much as looking at a woman on a billboard she'd throw a fit.

'I need you to do a couple of other things for me, Joe, please.'

'Name it.'

'I need you to look up the following people, see what you can get: first up – Darwen Medd. He's a PI out of Tallahassee.'

'No problem, but no guarantees on when neither,' Joe said. 'Say, Max?'

'Yeah?'

'Know what I'm hearin'?'

'What?'

'The sound of you enjoyin' yo'self.'

'I wouldn't quite put it that way, Joe.'

'I don't mean "enjoyin'" yourself like you *I' off* – enjoyin' yo'self, but you *enjoyin'* the *idea* of *maybe* nailin' these sonso-bitches. There's this spring in your voice. The old Mingus, no-bullshit steel.'

'You think so?'

'I *know* so. I know *you*, Mingus. You're *back*, Max.'

'If you say so, Joe,' Max chuckled. He didn't feel back at all. He didn't want to be anywhere near this.

Afterwards he went to bed and fell asleep as the sun started streaming through his window.

He dreamt he was back in the voodoo temple, caked in grey mud, fucking Chantale on the ground with the drums going crazy. Joe, Allain, Velasquez and Eldon were dancing all around them. Then he saw Charlie sitting on Dufour's lap, staring at him. They were by the pond. He couldn't see Dufour's face, only his seated silhouette. He tried to stand but Chantale was holding him down, her arms and legs wrapped around him tight. He finally managed to get up and began walking towards Charlie, but he and Dufour were gone. In their place were the three kids he'd killed. They all had his gun in their hands. They aimed and fired at him. He went down. He was still alive, looking up at the cross through the hole in the roof. Sandra came and stood over him, smiling. She was holding a little girl by the hand. The girl was pretty but looked immensely sad. Max recognized Claudette Thodore – the priest from Little Haiti's missing niece – and remembered that he'd forgotten to visit her parents.

He told the girl he'd go see them first thing in the morning, before he went looking for Faustin's house.

Sandra bent down to kiss him.

He reached up to touch her face and woke up with his hand in the air, fingers caressing nothing.

It was night again. He checked the clock. 7.00 pm. He'd slept for a full twelve hours. His mouth was dry, his throat tight, the sides of his eyes wet. He guessed he'd cried in his sleep. Outside the crickets were chirruping and the mountain drums were telegraphing their beats straight to his stomach, dancing with his hunger, telling him he should eat.

40

Before she'd disappeared in October 1994, Claudette Thodore had lived with her parents, Caspar and Mathilde, on the Rue des Ecuries in Port-au-Prince, close to an old military barracks.

The Rue des Ecuries linked two busy main roads, but was practically shielded from view at either end by gigantic palm trees. It was one of those tiny, blink-and-it's-gone places only ever known to locals, or outsiders looking for a short cut, who forget it as soon as they've passed through it.

Max had got directions from Mathilde. She spoke perfect English, her accent dotted with Midwest inflections, possibly Illinois, not a hint of Franco-Caribbean.

As Max and Chantale got out of the car Max caught a smell of fresh flowers mixed in with mint. Up ahead stood a man with a bucket and mop, washing the road. As they drew closer the smell doubled up and made Max's nostrils smart. The houses either side of them were hidden behind solid metal gates and walls topped with stiletto spikes and razor wire. Only the tops of trees and telegraph poles, the rims of satellite dishes and filaments of TV aerials poked over, but there was nothing else to see. Max guessed the houses were bungalows or single-storey buildings. He heard the furious sniffing of dog snouts under the gates, sucking up their smell through the gaps, breaking them down into familiar and unfamiliar. None of the dogs barked to alert their masters of strangers in their midst. That's because,

Max knew, they were attack dogs. They never made a sound. They let you come all the way into their terrain, too far in to get back out, and then they went for you.

The one part of busts he'd hated was when they brought in the dog squad. They were nasty twisted fucks who only respected the trainer who'd beaten them to a level of viciousness where, if they'd been people, they would have committed a whole string of murders with plenty of sick torture thrown in. You couldn't reason with attack dogs. You couldn't placate them or hypnotize them or toss them a stick to go after while you shimmied up the nearest tree. If an attack dog went for you the only thing to do was shoot it on the spot. Police attack dogs were trained to go for different parts of the anatomy depending on the state. In Florida they went for the balls, in New York City the forearms, in New York State, the calves. In some southern states they went for the face, in others the throat; in California they bit a chunk out of your ass, and in Texas they were partial to the thighs. Max didn't know what it was in Haiti, and he didn't care to find out. He hoped the Thodores didn't have one.

The mop-man eyed them as they approached, not once stopping what he was doing. Chantale nodded and greeted him. The man didn't reply, just looked them up and down through slitted eyes and a scowl, his body language oozing tension.

'I bet he's got Syrian roots,' Chantale whispered. 'He's washing the street with mint and rosewater. It's a back home custom, meant to ward off evil spirits and attract good ones. There was an influx of Syrian merchants here about forty or fifty years ago. They opened these little boutiques that sold everything to the poor. Every morning they'd sweep the street around the shop and douse it in herbal potions to bring them luck, prosperity and protection. A few of them obviously got it right because they made a lot of money.'

The Rue des Ecuries was the cleanest street Max had seen in Haiti so far. There wasn't a scrap of garbage anywhere, no stray animals and vagrants at the sides, no graffiti on the walls, and not a single crater or pothole in the road, which was immaculately paved with grey stone. It could have been any quiet prosperous middle-class sidestreet in Miami or LA or New Orleans.

Max banged on the Thodores' gate four times as Mathilde had asked him to. Soon after he heard footsteps coming from behind the wall.

'Qui là?'

'My name's –'

'– Mingus?' a woman asked.

A dead bolt snapped back and the gate was opened from the inside, groaning horribly on its hinges.

'I'm Mathilde Thodore. Thanks for coming.' She beckoned them in and pushed the gate shut. She was wearing sweatpants, sneakers and a loose Bulls T-shirt.

Max introduced himself and shook her hand. She had a firm grip that went with her direct, almost challenging stare. Had she smiled more she might have been an attractive, even beautiful woman, but her face was hard and unyielding, the sort of mien you develop after seeing the downside of life too much.

They were in a small courtyard, standing a few feet away from a modest orange and white bungalow with a sloping tin roof, half-hidden by untended bushes. A thick palm tree grew tall behind it, draping the structure in a blanket of yellow-dappled shade; while off to the right stood a swing, its chains rusted solid. Max guessed Claudette had been an only child.

Then his eyes fell on two bright-green dog bowls set out near the swing, one holding food, the other water. He looked back towards the wall and found a big house-shaped kennel.

'Don't worry about him. He won't bite,' Mathilde said, noticing Max staring at the kennel.

'That's what they all say.'

'He's dead,' Mathilde answered quickly.

'I'm sorry,' Max offered, but he wasn't.

'The food and water's for his spirit. You know how this country runs on superstition? We feed the dead better than we feed ourselves here. The dead rule this land.'

Inside, the house was small and cluttered, the furniture was too big for the available space.

The walls were covered in photographs. Claudette was in every one – bright-eyed, open-mouthed baby pictures framed and hung on walls, pictures of her in her school uniform, snaps of her with her parents, grandparents and relatives, all of their faces orbiting hers like planets in a solar system. She was a happy five-year-old, smiling or mugging in every pic, the centre of attention in group shots – physically and photogenically, the eye of the camera drawn to her. There was a photo of her standing outside the Miami church with her uncle, Alexandre, which looked like it might have been taken after a service, because he was in his robes and there were smartly dressed people in the background. There was another of her standing next to a black Dobermann. At least a dozen showed the girl with her father, who she seemed to resemble in looks and favour with the lion's share of her affections, because she didn't smile so broadly or laugh at all in the few snaps of her and her mother.

The couples sat on opposite sides of a dining table. Caspar had given his guests a nod and a quick grip of the hand when they'd walked in, but he hadn't so much as said a welcoming word.

He didn't take after his brother. He was short and stocky, thick arms, bulky shoulders, neckbreaker hands lashed with veins, flat wide fingers. His manner was gruffness skirting rudeness and aggression. His hair, thinning on top and cut low, was more salt than pepper. His face – far more forbidding than his wife's, starting to droop at the jowls and pool under the eyes – coupled with the way he was grinding his teeth, gave him a passing resemblance to a pissed-off mastiff. Max put him in his mid forties. He wore the same clothes as his wife, who sat next to him, drinking a glass of juice.

'You Bulls fans?' Max asked them both, but looked at Caspar, hoping to break the ice.

Silence. Mathilde prodded her husband with her elbow.

'Lived in Chicago sometime,' he answered, not making eye contact.

'How long ago?'

No answer.

'Seven years. We came back when Baby Doc was over-thrown,' Mathilde said.

'Should've stayed put,' her husband added. 'Come back here, want to do some good, bad's all that happens to us.'

He said a little more but Max didn't catch it. He had a gravelly voice that buried more than it carried.

Mathilde looked at Max and lifted her eyes up, as if to say he was like that the whole time. Max guessed then that Claudette's disappearance had hit him the hardest.

He found a picture of father and daughter, both laughing. Caspar looked younger there, his hair darker and fuller. The picture wasn't that old because Claudette looked like she did in the shot her uncle had given him.

'What else happened to you?'

'*Apart* from our daughter?' Caspar asked bitterly, finally looking Max straight in the face, his eyes small and bloodshot, silver points mired in sad, angry crimson. 'What *hasn't?* This place is *cursed*. Simple as that. Ever notice how *nothin'* grows here. No plants, no trees?'

'It hasn't been good for us here,' Mathilde quickly picked up. 'We used to be in the fire service in Chicago, then Caspar had an accident and got an insurance pay-out. We'd been talking about giving it up in the States and coming back here, so when we got the chance we thought let's go for it.'

'Why did you leave Haiti?'

'*We* didn't – I mean, our parents did, in the early sixties, because of Papa Doc. My dad had some friends with links to dissident groups in Miami and New York. They tried to mount a coup which failed. Papa Doc didn't just round up the culprits, but all their families and friends and *their* friends and family. Just to make sure. That was his way. Our parents guessed it was only a matter of time before the Macoutes came for all of us so we got out.'

'Why did you want to come back?' Max asked. 'Chicago's not a bad place.'

'What I been tellin' myself every time I *kick* myself,' Caspar grumbled.

Max laughed, more out of encouragement than mirth. Caspar looked at him like he'd read his angle and was having none of it. Nothing was shaking him out of his grief.

'I think we both grew up in America with this sense of loss for what we'd left behind,' Mathilde explained. 'We always called this place "home" . We had all these really fond memories of old Haiti, which, despite the tyranny, was a wonderful place. Especially the people. There was a lot of love here. Before we got married we swore we'd come back to live here one day – we swore we'd come "home".

'We used some of the insurance money to buy into a store opposite a gas station, selling cut price food and basic essentials to the poor. People didn't like us coming over here and just opening up a business and making money. They've got a word for us here. They call us "*diaspora*". It used to be an insult, like we'd chickened out, turned our backs on the country and only came back when things were good. Nowadays it's just another word, but back then —'

'Then it was all we heard,' Caspar interjected. 'Not among the everyday people – they were always cool to us, kind folk, mostly. We had a good relationship with them. Way we operated wasn't too different from the way Koreans operate in the black neighbourhoods in Chicago – employ a few locals, treat 'em well, be respectful to everyone. We had no problem there at all. But the ones like us – with the businesses, our peers and neighbours – we lived up in Pétionville then – they made it clear they didn't like us around. Called us all kinds of trash. See, the only way they woulda respected us was if they'd known us all their lives.'

'Envy's universal,' Chantale said. 'Not just here.'

'I know, I know – sticks and stones and all that, blah-blah-blah. Been there, thanks!' Caspar retorted, angrily.

Chantale held her hands up in embarrassed apology.

'So we ignored it and kept ourselves to ourselves to ourselves, worked hard, treated people as best we could. After a while we moved down here. It was better. Our neighbours are people like us – immigrants, outsiders,' Mathilde said, patting Caspar on the arm for him to calm down. 'It's nice here. Real clean too.'

'We're a tight community,' Caspar said. 'We operate a "zero tolerance policy" here.'

'Against who?'

'Everyone we don't know. They're discouraged from, you

know, settling down here. It's OK for them to pass through, as long as they do it *quick*. Animals and *especially* people. Plus we all take turns in sweeping the street, morning and evening, before sundown. We all look out for each other.'

Caspar allowed himself a small, knowing smirk that told Max that he enjoyed busting the heads of those luckless home-less folk who bedded down in his street for the night. It was probably the only thing that made him feel good any more. A lot of ex-cops Max had known were like that. They missed the juice of being out on the street and took the kind of jobs where they could still just about get away with roughing people up – club security, corporate muscle, bodyguards. Caspar was probably reverting to the person he'd been before happiness had intruded into his life and blown him off course.

'We've been happy here,' Mathilde picked up. 'Claudette made it complete. I had her a few months after we moved in. We hadn't been planning on starting a family, and I even thought I was too old, but she came into our lives and lit up all sorts of places in ourselves we didn't know were there.'

She stopped and looked at her husband. Max couldn't see her face but he knew from the way Caspar's look softened that she was about to cave in to tears. He put his arm tenderly around his wife's shoulders and pulled her into him.

Max glanced away towards the pictures on the wall above them. They were good people. Mathilde, especially. She was the guts and brains of the pair, the one who kept her husband in check, the one who kept their show on the road. She'd been the disciplinarian in the family, which was why her daughter had preferred her father, who no doubt gave in at her first demand. He thought of Allain and Francesca. They were a million miles apart, heading in opposite direc-tions, no warmth or closeness between them, despite their grief. He'd known the loss of a child to wreck the strongest of marriages as easily as it pushed the most dysfunctional ones over the finish line. Claudette's disappearance however had united the Thodores, reaffirmed, in the darkest way, the thing that had brought them together.

He focussed on a medium-sized photograph of Claudette on a swing, being pushed by her father, while the Dobermann watched from a corner.

Mathilde blew her nose and sniffed.

'Business was good, even though the political climate wasn't,' she continued, her composure regained. 'One month we had two Presidents and three coups. You could always tell whenever something was going down because our business wasn't too far from the Palace. Whoever was in power at the time would send his guys out to buy a load of extra gas for his getaway.

'The thing about this country is that all the gas comes from the US, so any time they want to bring down a President they threaten to stop the petrol from coming in. Whenever there was a *real* danger of that happening you'd see one of the oil company's management roll up to the gas station – always these big fat sweaty white Americans looking like Bible salesmen. They'd tell the station manager to expect extra shipments because they'd had "drought warnings" (their code for another changeover in leadership).

'The petrol never stopped coming in because they were *quiet* coups. Not a shot fired. You'd be watching some TV programme and then there'd be an intermission and a general would make an announcement on TV: this month's President had been arrested or exiled for treachery/corruption/speeding/whatever and the army had taken temporary control of the Palace, and that would be that. Everyone carried on as usual. No one thought an embargo would ever happen. And then it did.'

'We went out of business. A lot of our stuff came from the US or Venezuela. Ships couldn't get through,' Caspar said. 'Claudette used to ask me why I wasn't going to work. I told her it was so I could watch her grow.'

'They burned our business down – just before the Marines landed,' Mathilde said.

'Who?' Max asked.

'The military. They just wanted to make life as difficult for the invaders as possible. They set fire to a lot of amenities. I don't think it was personal – at least, not against us.'

'*Oh no?*' seethed Caspar. 'That was our *life*. It don't get more *personal* than that.'

Mathilde didn't know what to say. She looked away, found one of the pictures and fixed on it, as if willing herself there, back in time to happiness.

Max stood up and walked away from the table. Behind them were a sofa, two armchairs and a medium-sized television on a stand. The television had a layer of dust on it, as if it hadn't been watched in a while or simply didn't work. He noticed a shotgun parked near the window. He looked at the courtyard, taking in the swing and the kennel and the gate. Something wasn't right about it.

'What happened to your dog?' he asked, turning back to the table.

'He was killed,' Mathilde said, getting up and coming over to him. 'The people who took our daughter poisoned him.'

'You mean they came in *here?*'

'Yes. Come with me.'

She led Max out of the open-plan area and into a short dark corridor. She opened a door.

'Claudette's room,' she said.

The Thodores had resigned themselves to the fact that they weren't going to see their little girl again. The room was a shrine, preserved, probably, more or less the way they had last remembered it tidy. Pictures Claudette had drawn were on the walls – mostly family sketches – Dad (tall), Mom (not as tall), Claudette (minute), the dog (in between her and Mathilde), standing outside their house – drawn in crayon, as jerky stickpeople. Dad was always blue, Mom red, Claudette green and the dog was black. As he'd thought, the Pétionville house was a lot bigger because it dwarfed the family in scale. Her drawings of the Impasse Beaufort home showed the human figures twice the size of the house. Other pictures were simply squares of painted single colours with Claudette's full name at the bottom, written in an adult hand.

Max looked briefly out of the window and back to the room. He took in the bed – low, blue spread and a white pillow, rag doll peeking out from over the throw. He noticed the throw was smooth everywhere but in the middle, where it had been sat on and crumpled. He imagined either parent coming in and playing with the doll, soaking up their daughter's memory and crying their eyes out. He'd put money on Caspar being the more frequent visitor.

'The day she disappeared . . . I went to wake her up. I came in the room and saw her bed was empty and her window was wide open. Then I looked out and saw Toto – our dog – lying on the ground, near the swing,' Mathilde said quietly.

'Was anything broken in the house? Glass?'

'No.'

'What about the front door? Had it been forced?'

'No.'

'Did you notice anything about the lock? The keys don't often turn all the way after they've been picked.'

'It worked OK. Still does.'

'And it was just the three of you in here?'

'Yes.'

'Anyone else have the keys to this place?'

'No.'

'What about the previous owner?'

'We changed all the locks.'

'Who changed them?'

'Caspar did.'

'And you're sure you locked the front door that day?'

'Yes. Certain.'

'Is there a back way in?'

'No.'

'What about the windows?'

'Everything was closed. Nothing was broken.'

'What about a basement?'

'Not here.'

'What's behind the house?'

'Empty lot. There was an art gallery, but it's closed down. The wall's fifteen feet high and covered with barbed wire.'

'Barbed wire?' Max mumbled to himself. He looked out of Claudette's window at the wall. There were spikes running along it but none of the coils of razor wire he'd seen around the neighbouring houses.

'I refused to have it,' Mathilde said. 'I didn't want it to be the first thing my daughter saw when she woke up.'

'It wouldn't have made much difference,' Max said.

It never does, he thought. *They want to take your child, they'll take your child no matter what.*

He went back outside and walked over to the gate. There were bushes to the right. They would have made a noise if the kidnappers had landed in them. The kidnappers therefore came over the left-hand side of the wall where the drop was ten feet into clear ground. They probably used a ladder to get up from the street.

They had to have scoped the place out before they came in. That's how they knew where the dog kennel was and which side to go over.

Typical predator behaviour.

Max turned around and looked back at the house. *Something in that bedroom wasn't right. Something didn't fit.*

He started walking towards the house, putting himself in the mind of the kidnapper who had just poisoned the dog. Claudette's room was to the left of the front door. How many of them had come for her? One or two?

Then he caught sight of Mathilde through her daughter's window, standing with her arms crossed, watching him advance.

No windows broken. No locks picked. No doors forced. No way in around the back. How had they entered the house?

Mathilde opened the window and started talking to him. He didn't hear her. As she was speaking she accidentally knocked something off the sill, something small.

Max walked over and looked down at the ground. It was a painted wire figurine of a man with a bird-like face. Its body was orange, its head black. The figure didn't have a left arm, and, when he studied it closer, it didn't have a full face.

He'd just begun to understand what had happened.

He picked up the figurine.

'Who gave her this?' Max showed it to Mathilde.

Mathilde looked lost. She took the figurine and closed her hand around it, sweeping the windowsill with her eyes.

Max went back into the house.

There were half a dozen more wire birdmen lined up on the windowsill, by the bed, hidden by the glare of the sun coming through the glass. They were the same shape and colour, except for the last one, which was broader because it was two figurines – the birdman and a little girl in a blue and white uniform.

'Where did she get these?'

'At school,' said Mathilde.

'Who gave them to her?'

'She never gave me a name.'

'Man, woman?'

'I thought it was a boy, or one of her friends. She also knew a couple of children from Noah's Ark.'

'Noah's Ark? The Carver place?'

'Yes. It's a few roads down from the Lycée Sainte Anne – that's Claudette's school,' Mathilde said, and gave Max the name of the street.

'Did your daughter ever mention anyone talking to her near the school? A stranger?'

'No.'

'*Never?*'

'No.'

'Did she mention Ton-ton Clarinette?'

Mathilde sat down heavily on the bed. Her bottom lip was trembling, her mind churning. She opened her hand and stared at the figurine.

'Is there something you're not telling me, Mrs Thodore?'

'I didn't think it mattered – then,' she said.

'What?'

'The Orange Man,' she said.

Max searched the drawings on the walls anew, in case he'd missed one of someone with half a face, but he'd seen everything there was to see there.

He thought back to the story of the kids who'd disappeared in Clarinette. The mother said her son had told her that 'a man with a deformed face' had abducted him.

'Max?' Chantale called out from the doorway. 'You need to see these.'

Caspar was standing next to her with a tube of rolled-up papers in his hands.

From the way Claudette had told it, her friend the Orange Man was half man, half machine. At least his face was. He had, she said, a big grey eye with a red dot in the middle. It came out so far from his head he had to hold it with one hand. It made a strange sound too.

Caspar said he'd laughed when she'd told him. He had a thing for sci-fi films – *Robocop*, *Star Wars* and the two *Terminator* films were his favourites, and he often used to watch them on video with his daughter, despite Mathilde's protests that Claudette was too young. To him the Orange Man was a hybrid of R2D2 and the Terminator when his face comes off and reveals the machine beneath. Caspar didn't take it seriously because he didn't believe his daughter's friend was any more real than those movie robots.

Mathilde was even less inclined to believe in her daughter's stories about the Orange Man. When she'd been her daughter's age, she had had an imaginary friend too. She was an only child whose parents often left her alone, and even when they were with her they didn't give her the kind of attention she needed.

Neither of her parents worried unduly when, in the last six months before her disappearance, Claudette began drawing more and more pictures of her friend.

'You never saw him? The Orange Man?' Max asked the Thodores, all of them back at the dining table, the drawings spread out before them. There were over thirty of them – from tiny crayon sketches to big paintings.

The basic design was of an orange stick person with a huge head. The head was D-shaped and made up of two joined-up vertical halves – a rectangle on the left and a circle on the right. The circle resembled a face, albeit an indistinct one – a slit for an eye, another for the mouth, no nose, a lopsided triangle passing as an ear. The other half was more detailed and scary looking. It was dominated by a large swirling circle where the eye should have been, and a mouth of sharp upward pointing fangs, closer to daggers than teeth. The figure's body was missing its left arm.

'No.'

'Did you ever talk to her about him? Ask who he was?'

'I used to ask her if she'd seen him sometimes,' Caspar said. 'Usually she'd say yeah, she had.'

'Nothing else? She mention him being with anyone else?'

They both shook their heads.

'How 'bout a car? She say if he drove?'

Again a shake of the heads.

Max looked back at the drawings. They weren't in any kind of order but he could see what had happened, how the Orange Man had first gained Claudette's trust before moving in on her. The initial drawings showed the man from a distance, in profile, standing tall among three or four children, all in orange, head flat in front and round at the back; a protuberant beak where a nose should have been. The children became fewer – down to two, then, most frequently one – Claudette herself, standing before him, just like the figurine on her windowsill showed. In all the group pictures the children stood apart from the man, but in the ones where it was just the Orange Man and Claudette, they were holding hands. The paintings showing Claudette's family life chilled Max to the core. She depicted the Orange Man standing right in front of the house, next to the dog, or with the family when they'd gone to the beach.

Claudette knew her kidnapper. She'd let him into her bedroom. She'd gone willingly.

'She say why she called him "The Orange Man"?'

'She didn't call him that,' Caspar answered. 'I did. She brought home one of these pictures one day. I asked her who it was of and she said it was her friend. That's what she called him – *mon ami* – my friend. I thought she meant a school friend. So I said, "Hey, you're friends with an orange man", and it stuck.'

'I see,' Max said. 'What about her friends? Did they ever talk about the Orange Man?'

'No, I don't think so,' replied Mathilde. She looked at Caspar who shrugged his shoulders.

'Did any other children go missing from Claudette's school?'

'No. Not that we know of.'

Max looked at his notes.

'What happened the day of the – when you noticed Claudette was gone? What did you do?'

'We went looking,' Caspar said. 'We went house to house. Pretty soon we had a posse out helping us – neighbourhood people, all canvassing, stopping people in the street, asking questions. I think, by the end of the day, between us, we'd covered every inch of two square miles. Nobody saw nothing. Nobody knew nothing. That was the Tuesday, the day she went missing. We spent the next two weeks just looking for her. One of the guys here, Tony – he's a printer. He made these wanted posters which we put up all over. Nothing.'

Max scribbled a few notes and read back a couple of pages.

'Were any ransom demands made?' Chantale asked.

'No. Nothing. We didn't have much, outside Claudette and each other,' Caspar said, his voice slipping on a tear, a wobble going through his tough exterior. Mathilde took his hand and he clasped it back.

'Are you two gonna find her for us?' he asked Chantale.

'I promised your brother I'd look into it,' Max said, giving both of them an impassive look that was meant to flatline any hope they had.

'How are you coming along with the Charlie Carver case?' Mathilde asked.

'What do you mean?'

'Any leads?'

'I'm not at liberty to discuss that, Mrs Thodore. Client confidentiality. I'm sorry.'

'So you think it's the same people?' Caspar asked.

'There are similarities but there are differences,' Max replied. 'It's too soon to say.'

'Vincent Paul thinks it's the same people,' Caspar said, matter of factly.

Max stopped scribbling and stared blankly at the paper in front of him.

'*Vincent Paul?*' Max said, as casually as possible. He looked, briefly, to Chantale who caught his eye and directed his gaze to a set of photographs hung on the upper left-hand corner.

'Yes. You know him?' asked Caspar.

'Only by reputation,' Max said and stood up. He pretended to stretch his arms and neck. He walked around the table to the photographs on the wall, shaking imaginary pins out of his hands.

There it was, in a corner, second in from the edge of the wall, a family photograph – Claudette, aged about three, Mathilde and Caspar, looking happier and an age younger, Alexandre Thodore in priest's collar, and, in the middle of them, sitting down, probably so he could fit into the shot, Vincent Paul, bald and beaming. The priest had his arm around part of his huge back.

Max guessed what it meant – Vincent Paul had been donating some of his drug millions to Little Haiti – but he'd keep it to himself.

He returned to his place.

'After we'd searched as much we could we asked the Marines for help,' said Mathilde. 'I mean, we're both American citizens, so's Claudette, but you know what happened? We saw a Captain and all he wanted to know was why we'd left the US for a "shithole like this" – that's what he called it. Then he told us the soldiers "were too busy to help", that they had "democracy to restore". On our way back to our car we walked by a bar and there was a whole bunch of Marines in there "busy" restoring "democracy" by getting loaded on beer and dope.'

'What happened with Vincent Paul?'

'We went to him after the US army turned us down.'

'Why didn't you go to him first?'

'I –' Mathilde began, but Caspar cut her off.

'How much do you know about him?'

'I've heard good and bad, mostly bad,' Max answered.

'Same as Mathilde. She didn't want us going to him.'

'It wasn't that –' Mathilde began, but caught the don't-try-and-deny-it-*again* look her husband was giving her. 'OK. With the troops here and everything I didn't want it known that someone like *him* was out looking for our daughter. I didn't want us getting arrested as accessories or sympathizers.'

'Sympathizers?'

'Vincent was tight with Raoul Cedras – the head of the junta the invasion overthrew. They were good buddies,' Caspar explained.

'I thought Aristide would be more Paul's type?' Max said.

'It started out that way, for sure. Aristide was a good guy once, when he was a priest, helping the poor in the slums. He did a lot for them. But the day he got elected President was the day he started turning into Papa Doc. Corrupt too. Pocketed millions in foreign aid. Two weeks into his term Vincent wanted to cap his ass.'

'I never thought people like Paul had principles.'

'He's a compassionate man,' Mathilde said.

'So he helped you?'

'A lot,' she said. 'He spent a month searching the whole island for her. He had people looking for her in New York, Miami, the Dominican Republic, the other islands. He even got the UN to help.'

'Everything but hire a private investigator,' Max said.

'He said if he couldn't find her nobody could.'

'And you believed him?'

'We would if he'd found her,' Mathilde said.

'Anyone else get in touch with you? The Carvers had other guys looking for their son before me. Any of them talk to you?'

'No,' Caspar said.

Max jotted down a few more notes. There was one more thing he needed to know from the Thodores. 'From what I've heard, loads of kids go missing here every day. Vincent Paul must have a lot of people coming to him for help. Why did he help you?'

The couple looked at each other, unsure of what to say next.

Max made it easy on them:

'Look. I know what Vincent Paul's up to, and I truly do not give a flying fuck. I'm here to find Charlie Carver and

Claudette too, if I can. So, please, level with me. Why did Vincent help you out?'

'He's a friend of the family – *my* family,' Caspar said. 'My brother and him go back a ways.'

'Paul gives your brother's church in Little Haiti money, right?'

'Not just that,' said Caspar. 'My brother runs this shelter for Haitian boat people in Miami. Vincent pays for it. He's invested a lot of money in Little Haiti, helped a lot of people get on their feet. He's a good man.'

'Some people might beg to differ,' Max pointed out and left it hanging right there. He stopped himself from saying that down the road from Haiti, in Liberty City, there were ten-year-old kids selling Vincent Paul's dope while one or more of their parents were probably smoking their lives to hell with the same shit. The Thodores wouldn't give a good damn about any of that right now, and why should they?

'Some people could beg to differ about you too, Mr Mingus,' Mathilde retorted, gently, making a point as opposed to driving one home.

'They usually do,' Max said. He smiled at them both. They were decent people: honest, hard-working and basically good; the very same kind of people he'd sworn to protect. 'Thanks for all your help. Please don't blame yourselves for what happened to Claudette. There's nothing you could've done. Nothing at all. You can stop burglars and murderers and rapists, but people like the Orange Man, they're invisible. They're like you and me on the outside, usually the last people you'd suspect.'

'Find her for us, please,' Mathilde said. 'I don't care about the people who took her. I just want our daughter back.'

41

'Do you still think Vincent Paul took Charlie?' Chantale asked in the car. They were driving to the first of the Faustin addresses on the page from the phonebook.

'I ain't rulin' nothin' out. Fact he helped look for Claudette doesn't mean a damn thing. I'll know when I talk to him,' Max said, putting two of the wire figurines he'd taken away with him under the dashboard with a couple of pictures of the Orange Man. He was going to send the figurines to Joe for fingerprinting.

'Do you know how to reach him?'

'I've a feeling *he'll* find *me*,' Max said.

'It's your gig,' Chantale sighed. She hadn't mentioned the temple and she didn't seem to be mad at him either. She was behaving normally, flashing her easy smile and occasionally laughing her filthy laugh, all affectionate professionalism. She was a tough one to read, a consummate politician, mistress of on-tap pleasantness. A lot of white-collar types were like her – sincere in their insincerity.

'Did your husband discuss his cases with you?' Max asked.

'No. We had a rule about not bringing our work home with us. You?'

'I wasn't married when I was a cop. But, yeah, me and Sandra used to talk about what I was workin' on.'

'She ever crack a case for you?'

'Yeah, a couple of times.'

'Didn't that piss you off? Make you doubt your abilities?'

'No,' Max laughed and smiled at the memory. 'Never. I

was proud of her – *real* proud. I was always proud of her.'

They stopped in traffic. Chantale studied him as they waited. Max caught her at it and tried to read what conclusions she was coming to. She gave nothing away.

All of the first five Faustin houses on Max's list had been destroyed by fire, mobs, the army, a hurricane and a UN helicopter crash. No one nearby knew who Eddie Faustin was.

The next house they went to was at the edge of the Carrefour slum. It was the only intact structure on a road otherwise made up of ruins converted into hovels. The house was set a little away from the street, with steps leading up to the front door. All the windows were bare. Max noted that the panes, while filthy, were all intact. No one answered the door when they knocked. They checked the windows but the place appeared deserted, despite the furniture in the front rooms and the white sheets Chantale reported hanging on the clothes line in the back yard, when Max had lifted her up so she could see over the wall.

They asked a couple of passers-by who it was who lived in the house. They said they didn't know, that the house had been that way for a long time. No one entering, no one leaving.

'How come no one's moved in – from off the street?' Max asked.

They couldn't say.

Max decided he'd come back at night to take a closer look. He didn't want Chantale there when he broke in. He'd put her through enough.

Travelling down the rest of the list took them to houses whose owners had long gone, leaving their shells to the poor. The former home of Jerome Faustin was overflowing with famine kids with bellies so bloated they had to walk with their legs wide apart to keep their balance. It was a variation of the same picture in the next house, only these children were sitting down to eat with their parents – dried leaves, mud cakes and a bucket of greenish water. Max didn't believe they were going to put any of it in their mouths until he saw a little girl of about five bite off a piece of the baked dirt and put it in her mouth. He felt fit to gag, but he held it in – partly out of respect for these poor souls who hadn't eaten what he could easily lose and not miss, and partly out of fear that his vomit would make it into their food chain. He wanted to give their parents all the money in his pocket but Chantale advised him against it, telling him to buy them food instead.

They found a store and bought a few sacks of maize, rice, beans and plantain. They came back and left it in the fore-court. The children and adults looked at them curiously and carried on eating their meal.

Max and Chantale moved on. By late afternoon they'd finished. They'd talked to two old ladies who'd offered them lemonade and stale cookies, a man on his porch looking at a year-old newspaper, a mechanic and his son, a woman who asked them to read to her from a German Bible, another who recognized Max from the TV and told him he was a good man. Although he couldn't yet prove it, Max was now sure the house in Carrefour belonged – or had at some point belonged – to Eddie Faustin.

After he'd driven Chantale home he drove back there.

42

Max waited until nightfall, then he went round the back of the house, climbed over the wall and dropped down into a garden of dead grass and withered bushes.

He picked the two back-door locks and let himself in.

He turned on his flashlight. Inside the dust lay so thick and soft it looked like Christmas card snow. No one had been here in a long while.

There were two floors and a basement.

He went upstairs. Large rooms with plenty of good-quality furniture – cupboards, closets, chests of drawers, tables and chairs all in mahogany, clawed brass feet on everything. Marble or glass coffee tables. Brass beds with still hard mattresses, well-upholstered armchairs and sofas.

The place had barely been lived in, but whoever had owned the house must have felt safe enough here, at the edge of the slum, a few feet away from a cauldron of poverty, desperation and violence. There were no bars on any of the windows. The house hadn't been broken into. Max guessed the owners were locals, well-known in the slum; the sort of people you didn't mess with, the sort of people whose property you respected more than your own.

He went down to the basement. It was hot and humid, a rancid accent in the air. His flashlight picked out the damp on the walls, the bricks greasy with moisture. There was something on the ground.

He found a lightswitch. A single bulb on a flex lit up the large black kite-shaped *vévé* on the ground. It had been drawn in blood. The *vévé* was divided into four sections, a different symbol in the first three, a photograph in the last. The photograph was of Charlie, sitting in the back of a car – possibly an SUV – looking straight at the camera.

He read the *vévé* clockwise – first the Mr Clarinet symbol, followed by an eye, a circle with four crosses and a skull in it and, lastly, the photograph. There was a corolla of purple wax in the centre of the *vévé*. Assuming this was Eddie Faustin's place, he'd most likely performed the ceremony before he'd kidnapped Charlie.

Max slipped the picture into his wallet.

The basement was otherwise empty.

He was about to leave the house when he remembered there were things he'd left unchecked. He went back upstairs. The dust was so thick it muffled his steps. He sneezed twice.

He found nothing.

He tapped the walls. Solid. He looked under the chairs. He moved the furniture. He popped sweat shifting the heavy cupboards.

He shifted an oak closet.

He heard something fall on the floor.

It was a videotape.

Back in Pétionville, Max played the tape.

It began with a boy walking down a street. He was dressed in the Noah's Ark uniform – blue shorts and a short-sleeved white shirt – and carrying a satchel on his back. Max put his age at between six and eight years old.

He was being filmed from inside a car.

The screen fizzled into black and a new image cut in: a group of about twenty children, all in uniform, gathering in front of the gates of Noah's Ark. The camcorder panned across the crowd, laughing and playing, some chasing each other, some paired off, others grouped together talking, until it found the boy from the first shot, chatting to two friends. It zoomed in on his face – cute rather than pretty – and then on his mouth, wide, smiling – and then it pulled away, capturing the boy's head and torso and a little of the background. Next it moved to the boy's right, just above his shoulder, and settled on a little girl, bending over to tie her shoes. A boy had lifted her skirt all the way up her back and he and his friends were laughing. The girl was as oblivious to the boys as she was to the cameraman recording her humiliation. When she stood up and her skirt fell back into place the boys ran away laughing.

The next image was of the boy in class, from outside, the cameraman standing somewhere on the left, hidden by bushes which blew in and out of shot. The boy was listening to the teacher, making notes, often raising his hand. His face lit up whenever he knew an answer, a mixture of pride and happiness stealing into his features. If he was picked to answer he'd smile as he spoke and carry on smiling afterwards, savouring his triumph. He was a front-of-the-class kid, one mature and disciplined enough to understand the importance of studies and the value of education, one who probably never got into trouble and would have made his parents proud – if they were around to see him. He had lively, clever, inquisitive eyes; eyes that wanted to know about all they could see.

Static suddenly filled the screen and then it went black again. It stayed that way for an age.

Max let the tape run. His heart was pounding and he was getting a familiar fluttering in the pit of his belly, something he hadn't had since his early days as a detective when he was on the verge of making a grim discovery; one part anticipating the find, one part fearing it, one part knowing it would be worse than before. At the start it had always been more horrific than anything he'd imagined, the lengths one human being would go to to ensure the utmost suffering of another. Before he'd gone to jail he was numb to it, immune, the limits of his imagination ending at the pit of hell. If he'd found someone dead of a single gunshot to the head he'd consider the murderer a crucible of mercy and compassion – of all the things they could have done, they'd chosen the quickest, simplest way of taking life.

Prison had returned those first-time feelings to him, intact, as if all those years of going through the leftovers of monsters' feasts had happened to another.

The screen went white for a few seconds, then, briefly, blue, before a completely different place appeared – a concrete building the size of an aircraft hangar set in the middle of lush vegetation. Max paused the tape and studied the frozen, flickering image. It didn't look like anywhere in Haiti. There were trees all around the structure, an abundance of green, a health and vitality to the surrounding land.

He hit play.

The next image was taken inside the building – a spacious hall with sunlight streaming in through high windows.

A line of children, alternating between boys and girls, all aged under ten, were walking up to a table draped in a red and black silk cloth. The children were immaculately dressed in black and white – black skirts and white blouses for the girls, black suits and white shirts for the boys. They approached the table and drank from a large, gleaming gold chalice, exactly as they would have done at holy communion, except there was no host to chew on and no priest officiating, only a man stepping up to the table after every child had been and, with a gold ladle, topping up the receptacle with a thin greenish liquid.

The boy he'd seen at the beginning of the tape stepped up to the chalice, took it between his hands and drained it. Then he put the chalice back exactly where he'd found it and stared right into the camcorder. His eyes were dead space, twin vacuums sealed in a skull; every ounce of life, thought and personality they'd possessed in the earlier shots was gone for good. The boy left the table and followed the line of children leaving the hall, his walk slow and laboured, as if he had someone inside him pulling levers to make him move. All the children moved the same way, with old steps.

Max knew what the liquid was. He'd had it. He knew what it did. It was a potion – zombie juice.

Like in the movies, voodoo zombies are technically the living dead – only they're not really dead at all, but in a deep catatonic state. They're normal people who have been poisoned with a potion which completely incapacitates them. Their minds are working. They're fully conscious, but they can neither move nor speak. They don't even appear to be breathing. They've got neither a heartbeat nor a discernible pulse. After they've been buried the *houngan* or *bokor* – usually the person responsible for their condition – will dig them up and give them an antidote. They will regain consciousness, only not as the people they were before, but as near vegetables. The priest hypnotizes the zombies and makes them his slaves – either for himself or whoever's paying him. They do whatever they're told.

Boukman had used zombies.

Max pressed play.

The boy was back in the front row of another classroom, only this time his eyes were barely moving and his face was expressionless, his features not registering that he was taking in a single thing about the proceedings. The camera pulled away and showed someone addressing the class from the left.

It was Eloise Krolak, the principal of Noah's Ark.

'You fucken' *bitch*,' Max whispered, freezing the tape as her face came clearly into view. Her features were pointed and severe, almost rodent-like in their alignment.

He knew from then on that the rest of the tape would only get worse.

He hit play.

He was right.

When it was finished, Max sat there watching the static on the screen, unable to move. He stayed where he was for a long time, shaking.

43

Max considered telling Allain about the tape, but he held off. He'd gather his evidence first.

He copied the tape, packed the original up with the figurines and drove to the FedEx office in Port-au-Prince.

He let Joe know what was coming. He also asked him to see what he could find on Boris Gaspésie.

He drove to Noah's Ark. He parked up the road and fixed his mirror so he could see the gate.

He walked in and checked to make sure Eloise Krolak was there. He saw her addressing her pupils the same way she was talking to the zombie kids in the video. He thought back to the video, to the things he'd seen being done to those children. He felt suddenly sick.

He went back to his car and waited for her to come out.

In the afternoon it rained.

Max had never known rain like it. In Miami it poured – sometimes all day, all week, sometimes all goddamn month – but the rain fell and dribbled away into puddles or disappeared into the ground and back into the air.

In Haiti rain *attacked*.

The sky went near black as rain swarmed out of dense storm clouds and swooped down on Port-au-Prince, drenching the city to its foundations, turning bone-dry earth to running mud within seconds.

The sewers in the street quickly flooded and belched waste back up on the streets, which ran black and brown. In the houses around him rooftop reservoirs filled up to the brim and spilled over or broke clean off their rusted fittings and crashed to the ground; power went and came and went again; pipes burst; trees were stripped of leaves, fruit and even bark; a roof caved in. Confused and panicked people ran into equally dazed and terrified pets, cattle and strays, all of them collapsing into struggling, thrashing, conjoined heaps. Then came the rats, hundreds of them, flooded out of their holes, scuttling downhill towards the harbour in a great wave of rank, diseased fur, squealing in panic and fear. Great blasts of thunder blew holes in the atmosphere and sheets of lightning followed, quickly flashing up every detail of the damaged, drowning streets, awash with mud and shit and teeming with vermin, before snatching the vision back into darkness as if it had been an illusion.

The rain stopped. Max watched the storm move out to sea.

Eloise Krolak didn't leave Noah's Ark until after 6.30, when she was picked up in a silver Mercedes SUV with blacked-out windows.

Max tailed the car out through the city and along the mountain road to Pétionville. It was dark now. Traffic was heavy.

They slowed to a crawl at the end of a long thick red-neon streak of stalled tail lights. Max was four cars behind.

The opposite side of the road was mostly free. Barely anyone seemed to be heading into the capital at this hour.

Except for the UN.

A convoy passed the traffic jam – two jeeps followed by a truck, then, moving slower, another jeep, whose occupant was shining a flashlight into each of the stalled cars.

The beam passed Max. He looked straight ahead and kept his hands on the wheel.

He heard the jeep stop.

Someone knocked on his window.

Max didn't have his passport on him, only his AMEX card in his wallet.

'*Bonsoir, monsieur,*' the UN soldier said. Blue helmet, uniform, young white face. He addressed Max in French.

'Do you speak English?' Max asked.

The soldier caught his breath.

'Name?' he asked Max.

Max told him. He'd hardly finished saying his surname before the soldier had pulled a pistol and was aiming it at his head.

He was made to get out of the car. When he did he was immediately surrounded by half a dozen men aiming rifles at his head. He put his hands up. They frisked him, took his gun and frog-marched him off the road to where the truck and three jeeps were parked. Max protested his innocence, yelled at them to call Allain Carver or the American Embassy.

He felt something prick his left forearm and saw the syringe sticking out of his arm, the plunger going down, clear fluid going in, someone counting down in his ear.

Then he understood: he was finally going to meet Vincent Paul.

He wondered what part of him Paul would take away or fix so it didn't work the way it once had.

He should have been worried but the dope they'd given him took care of that. He had no fear. Whatever it was they'd given him was beautiful shit.

PART FOUR

44

'How are you feeling?' Vincent Paul asked Max, after he'd pointed for him to take a seat in an armchair facing his desk. They were in Paul's study – discreet air-conditioning, walls lined with bookcases, framed photographs, flags.

'Where am I?' Max asked back, his voice croaky.

He'd been in a room with no windows for two days. That was where he'd come to when the injection had worn off. His first feeling was panic: he'd checked himself all over for missing parts, scars and bandages. Nothing had been done to him. Yet.

He'd had regular visits. A doctor and a nurse – plus three armed guards – had come to check him out. The doctor had asked him a bunch of questions. He'd spoken his English with a German accent. He hadn't answered any of Max's questions. On day two he stopped coming.

Max had been fed three times a day and given a daily American newspaper where nothing was ever reported about Haiti. He'd watched cable TV on the set at the foot of his bed. The morning they'd taken him to meet Vincent Paul they'd shaved his face and head and given him his clothes back – washed and pressed.

'You should relax. If I wanted you dead I could have let those little kids rip you to pieces,' Paul said in a low deep voice Max felt in his gut. Paul was very dark, with eyes set so far back in his skull they were reduced to two moving gleaming pinpoints of reflected light, as if he had fireflies buzzing around in his sockets. His face was barely lined. He looked mature but nowhere near the age Max guessed him to be – early fifties. Bald dome, long fine nose, huge jaw, thick eyebrows, short stout neck, no fat, all muscle, making Max think all at once of Mike Tyson, a *mapou* trunk and a bust of a cruel tyrant with pretensions to greatness. Even seated he was imposing, everything about him exaggerated and monumental.

'It's not dying that concerns me,' Max said. 'It's how much of me you'd leave alive.'

Max wasn't outwardly nervous, but inside he was wired with anticipation. Very little in his life had prepared him for a moment like this – captured, utterly at the mercy of a foe. He didn't know what was around the next corner. If Paul carved him up and turned him into Beeson, he thought, he'd blow his brains out first chance he got.

'I don't follow.' Paul frowned. The hands that had crushed and torn a man's testicles from his body were folded across his lower chest, abnormal in their girth, intimidating in their size, hands nature had made so large it seemed aesthetically normal that they had the two extra pinkies they did. And he'd had a manicure. His nails glowed.

'You carved up one of my predecessors so he can't hold his shit,' Max said.

'I don't follow,' Paul repeated, slower.

'Didn't you – or one of your guys – split Clyde Beeson in two and rearrange his insides?'

'No.'

'What about that Haitian who was working the case? Emmanuel Michaels?'

'*Michel*-Ange –' Paul corrected him.

'Yeah.'

'– who was found by the docks with his penis stuffed down his throat and his balls in his cheeks?'

'Was that you?'

'No.' Paul shook his head. 'Michelange was fucking some-body's wife. The husband had him taken care of.'

'*Bullshit*!' Max reacted instinctively.

'If you ask around you'll see that it's not. It happened two weeks into his investigation.'

'The Carvers know about this?'

'They would if they asked around,' Paul said.

'How did they know it was the husband?'

'He confessed to it. He did it in his bedroom, with his wife watching.'

'Who'd he confess to?' Max asked.

'The UN.'

'And?'

'And *what*?'

'They take him in?'

'Sure. For as long as it took him to tell them what he'd done. Then they let him go. He runs a hotel and casino near Pétionville. Doing well. You can talk to him, if you want. The place is called El Rodeo. His name is Frederick Davi.'

'What about his wife?'

'She left him,' Paul answered, face deadpan, his eyes laughing. Max carried on his questioning.

'OK. Darwen Medd? Where is he? Did you kill him?'

'No.' Paul shook his head, looking surprised. 'I don't know where he is. Why would I want to kill him?'

'A warning. Like the one you sent out to the UN rapists,' Max said through a dry mouth.

'*That* wasn't a warning. That was *punishment*. And there hasn't been another rape by the occupiers since,' Paul said and smiled. 'I knew you were following me that time. You weren't hard to miss. Good cars stand out here.'

'Why didn't you do anything?'

'I've got nothing to hide from you,' Paul said. 'Tell me more about your predecessors.'

Max explained. Paul listened, his face solemn.

'It wasn't me. I assure you. Although I can't say I'm sorry to hear about Clyde Beeson.' Close up, Paul's accent favoured English over French. 'Pathetic little toe rag. A lump of greed waddling on those two stumps he calls legs.'

Max managed a smile. 'So you met him?'

'I had them both brought here for questioning.'

'Shouldn't it have been the other way round?'

Paul smiled but didn't answer. He had a mouth of bright white teeth. He suddenly looked disarming and pleasant, almost boyish, the kind of person you could imagine doing good deeds and meaning them.

'What did they tell you?'

'What you're going to tell me: how the investigation is progressing.'

'You're not my client,' Max said.

'How much do you know about me, Mingus?'

'That you'll torture the information out of me.'

'Something we have in common,' Paul laughed, picking up a file from his desk and holding it up. It had Max's name on it in bold capitals. 'What else?'

'You're a major suspect in the kidnapping of Charlie Carver.'

'Certain people think my name's a euphemism for everything that goes wrong here.'

'Witnesses placed you at the scene.'

'I was there.' Paul nodded. 'But I'll get to that.'

'You were seen running away with the kid in your arms.'

'Who told you that? That old woman outside the shoe place?' Paul chuckled. 'She's blind. She told Beeson and Medd the same thing. If you don't believe me, go and check when we're done. And you might want to look in the shop too. She keeps her dead husband's skeleton in there in a glass case, opposite the door. You swear someone's watching you.'

'Why would she have lied to me?'

'We lie to white people here. Don't take it personally. It's in the DNA.' Paul smiled. 'What else do you think you know about me?'

'You're a suspected drug baron, you're wanted in connection with a missing person in England and you hate the Carvers. How am I doing so far?'

'Better than your predecessors. They didn't know about England. I take it you got that from your friend' – Paul flicked through some pages in the file until he came to the one he wanted – 'Joe Liston. You two have a lot of history, don't you? The MTF, "Born to Run", Eldon Burns, Solomon Boukman. And that's *just* when you were in the police. I have a lot more information on you.'

'I bet you got everything there is to get.' Max wasn't surprised that Paul had looked into him, but hearing him mention Joe got him worried.

Paul put the file down and looked across at the pictures arranged in front of his desk. The frames were large and thick, but they were in proportion to the desk, which was a wide and thick slab of highly polished, solid dark wood. Almost everything on it appeared a size or two larger than normal: a black fountain pen the size of a fat cigar tube, an oversized telephone that could have been mistaken for a young child's toy with its large receiver and big round keys, a china coffee cup the size of a soup bowl, the biggest angle-poise lamp he'd ever seen – like a scale model of a street lamp built for a baby elephant's playpen.

Neither said a word. They studied each other, Paul leaning

right back in his chair so even the reflection vanished from his eyes and left Max looking deep into two barrels.

The silence widened and then congealed around them. Max couldn't hear anything going on outside. The room was probably soundproofed. There was a long couch with cushions piled up on one side, a book beside it on the floor, open, face down. The couch was as wide as a single bed. He imagined Paul lying there and reading, engrossed in one of the many bound volumes on his shelf.

The room was closer to a museum than an office or a study. A framed Haitian flag hung on one of the walls – tattered and dirty, with a burn hole in the white centre. Facing it was a blown-up black-and-white photograph of a tall, bald man in a dark pinstriped suit holding a young child's hand. They were looking at the world with level, questioning stares – especially the child. Behind them, blurred, was the Presidential Palace.

'Your father?' Max motioned to the picture. He'd guessed from the eyes that they were related, although he was a lot lighter than his son. He could have passed for Mediterranean.

'Yes. A great man. He had a vision for this country,' Paul said, fixing Max with a stare he could feel but barely see.

Max got out of his chair and went over to the photograph for a closer look. There was something very very familiar in the father's face. Vincent was wearing the same clothes as his father. Neither were smiling. They looked like they'd been stopped hurrying somewhere important, and had posed out of politeness.

Max was sure he'd seen Perry Paul before – no, *certain* of it. But *where*?

He returned to his seat. A thought began to form in his mind. He dismissed it as impossible but it came right back at him.

Vincent Paul sat forward, smiling like he'd read Max's mind. The light finally reached his eyes and revealed them to be a pale hazel colour with a hint of orange about them – surprisingly delicate, pretty eyes.

'I'm going to tell you something I never told the other two,' Vincent said quietly.

'What?' Max asked, as a cold wave of anticipation began to build up around his shoulders.

'I'm Charlie Carver's father.'

45

'The woman you know as Francesca Carver was once called Josephine Latimer,' Vincent began. 'Francesca is her middle name. The rest of it came later.'

'I first met her in Cambridge, England, in the very early seventies. I was a student at the university there. Josie lived there with her parents. I met her in a pub one night. I heard her before I saw her – laughing, filling the place with laughter. I looked for her across the room and found her staring right at me. She was *stupendously* good looking.'

Vincent smiled warmly as he spoke through his memory, his head leaning back a little, staring more towards the ceiling than at Max.

'And you helped her skip the country so she didn't have to go to jail for killing someone in a hit and run. I know,' Max broke in. 'Question is: where d'he go? That damsel-in-distress rescuing guy? The one who threw his life away for love?'

The question caught Paul off guard.

'I didn't throw my life away,' he countered.

'So you'd've done the same thing all over?'

'Wouldn't you?' Paul smiled.

'A little regret's always healthy,' Max said. 'Why do you hate the Carvers?'

'Only Gustav.'

'What's Allain doing right?'

'He's not his father,' Paul answered. 'When Josie and I arrived in Haiti, we went to my family home in Pétionville.

My family lived on a large estate on top of a hill. I hadn't told anyone I was coming, just to be on the safe side.

'When we got there we found that the whole place – that's five big houses, one of which I remember my father building practically with his bare hands – the whole lot had been bulldozed by order of Gustav Carver. My father owed him money. He collected – and *how*.'

'That's pretty extreme,' Max said.

'Carver has an *extreme* dislike of competition. If it had been a straight business debt, I could just about have accepted it as "fair". That kind of thing happens in business all the time. But this wasn't business, this was personal. And when it's personal Carver *always* plays to the *absolute* finish.'

'So what happened?'

'The short version: my family had two very successful businesses – import-export and construction. We were undercutting Carver on certain products, sometimes by up to fifty per cent, sometimes more. People stopped buying from him and came to us. We also had a project to build a hotel for pilgrims going to Saut d'Eau, the sacred waterfalls. It was going to be low-budget, but with the volume of business it was going to attract, we would have made a fortune. Gustav Carver was furious. He was losing face and a lot of money – and the only thing that man hates more than losing money is the people he's losing it to.

'He secretly bought the Banque Dessalines. We'd taken out a loan for some business expansion. Gustav bought our debt and called it in. We didn't have the cash to hand so he shut us down, made us bankrupt. He took over the Saut d'Eau project and then he killed us financially, ruined my family's reputation, smeared the Paul name.

'Then, to cap it all, after he'd literally reduced our world to rubble – do you know what he did? He used the *bricks* from our estate to build *his* bank. That was all too much for my father. He was a very proud man but he wasn't a fighter. He shot himself.'

'Jesus!' Max gasped. If Paul wasn't exaggerating – which Max doubted he was – he understood his hatred of Carver. 'What about the rest of your family?'

'Two sisters and a brother, no longer in the country or ever likely to come back.'

'Your mother?'

'She died in Miami the day we arrived. Pancreatic cancer. I didn't even know she was ill. Nobody told me.'

'Aunts, uncles, cousins?'

'I have no family in Haiti. Outside of my son – *if* he's here.'

'What about your friends?'

'True ones are a rare commodity at the best of times, but in Haiti, unless they've known you all your life, "friends" in the monied circles we used to move in have the habit of becoming scarce when you hit a lean patch and extinct if you're ruined. To them, the only thing worse than not having any money is having had it and lost it. They shun you like your misfortune's contagious. I asked one of my father's "friends" of long standing for some help – somewhere to stay and a small loan to tide me over until I got myself back on my feet. This was someone my father had helped out a lot in the past. He turned me down flat, said I wasn't a viable risk,' Paul said bitterly. Max could virtually see the loathing coming off him. Paul was someone who collected grudges and thrived on his hatreds; it was the dark heavy fuel that drove him. People like him – betrayed, kicked in the teeth, stabbed in the back, written off – made for the highest achievers and the worst human beings.

'So what did you do after you saw what had happened to your estate? Did you have any money?'

'No. Not a cent,' laughed Paul. 'What I *did* have was Anaïs, my nanny. I was a virtual son to her. She'd cared for me ever since I was born. In fact, she'd helped deliver me. We were so close I swore she was my real mother. Knowing my father, I wouldn't have been too surprised. He and my grandfather weren't exactly advocates of monogamy.

'Anaïs took us in. She lived in a tiny little house in La Saline. We all slept and ate in the same room, washed at an outdoor tap. It was a life I'd seen but never thought I'd know, and as for Josie, well, she got a serious culture shock, but she used to say English prison was worse.'

'You never thought of going back to England, facing the music?'

'No.'

'What about her?'

Paul sat up and pulled his chair in closer to the desk. 'I wasn't going to let the woman I loved go back to hell, not when I had the power to stop it.'

'So you did wrong to do right? At least you're consistent.'

'What else could I have done, Mingus?'

'Do the crime you do the time.'

'Sorry I asked. Once a cop . . .'

'*No*,' Max cut him off. 'She *killed* somebody because she was *drunk* behind the wheel. She was *no* saint. She *wasn't* in the right. And you know that, same as me. Think about the victim's family: flip the picture and it's *her* getting killed in a drunk hit and run, and you're left with the grieving. You'd see things *very* differently, *believe* me.'

'Those three kids you killed, do you think about *their* families?' Vincent asked icily.

'No, I don't,' Max spoke through gritted teeth. 'Know why? Because those three "kids" raped and tortured a little girl for fun. I know they were fucked-up on crack, but most

407

crackheads don't do that to people. Those shitheels didn't deserve their lives. The guy Francesca killed is a whole different ballgame and you know it.'

Vincent pulled himself right in to the desk, cupped his massive fist in his palm and fingers and leant over. Max saw his disarmingly pretty eyes again.

Neither of them spoke. Max held Vincent's stare for the longest time. The big man finally broke the stand-off. Max resumed his questioning.

'Anyone come out here looking for you? Cops?'

'Not that I knew of then, but it was only a matter of time before our trail led to here. We lived in La Saline for a year and a half. We were safe there. It's the kind of place where you don't go to unless you live there, or know someone, or have a well-armed military escort – or want to commit suicide. It's exactly the same now.'

'How were the people towards you?'

'Fine. They accepted us. Obviously Josie might as well have come from outer space, but we never had a single problem all the time we were there.

'For a living we worked at a local petrol station, and then we ended up managing it. We did something quite innovative at the time here. We added a diner, a carwash, a garage and a small shop. Anaïs ran the diner and Josie ran the shops. She dyed her hair brown. I only employed people from La Saline. We had to pay off a couple of Macoutes for protection – Eddie Faustin and his teenage brother, Salazar.

'I could tell Eddie had a serious thing for Josie. He'd be round there every day, bringing her something, always when I was out getting supplies. She always refused to take it, but in the nicest way, so as not to offend him.'

'What did you do about it?'

'What could I do? He was a Macoute – and one of the most feared ones in the country.'

'Must have pissed you off, being that *weak?*'

'Of course it did.' Vincent looked at him quizzically, trying to determine his angle.

Max didn't have one. He'd wanted to get a rise out of Paul, deliberately unsettle him.

'Go on.'

'Business was good. Two years after we'd arrived, we moved out of La Saline and bought a small house in town. I thought we were pretty much safe. No one had come after us. We could relax a little. Josie had taken well to life in Haiti. She took to the people and they to her. She never really got homesick, but obviously she missed her parents. She couldn't even send them a postcard to let them know she was OK, but she accepted that that was the price to pay for her freedom.

'Things went wrong the morning Gustav Carver stopped for petrol. I refused to serve him. His driver got out, pulled a gun on me and ordered me to pump gas. Of course, the minute he did *that* he and his car were suddenly surrounded by anybody who was around – some twenty people, some of them had guns, others machetes and knives. They would have killed him and old man Carver if I'd given the word, but what better punishment than to humiliate a proud man in front of the son of the man whose life he'd destroyed? I tell you it was *sweet.*

'I took the gun off the driver and told him and his boss to clear off my property. The driver had to push the car three miles in the hot sun to the next petrol station – because there were no cellphones then, car phones didn't work out here, and we don't exactly have emergency breakdown services to come and bail you out if you break down.

'Carver was looking at me through the back window like he wanted to kill me. Then he saw Josie and his expression changed. He smiled, at her, but – mostly – at *me*.

'I'm not sure if things would have been different if I'd let Carver fill his car up and drive away. It's not the way I really live my life. I can't imagine a situation where I'd *ever* kowtow to that evil bastard. If I did that, I might as well have driven those bulldozers through my family estate myself.

'But, all that day and the next, I kept expecting the worst, that a couple of carloads of Macoutes would come for me.'

Vincent broke off and looked away at the photograph of him and his father. His face was rigid, his lips pinched tight, his jaw clamped shut. He was trying hard not to explode – whether in anger or sadness, Max couldn't tell. He doubted Paul had opened up to anyone in many many years, so that all the emotions he'd felt at the time had been bottled up, sealed away and never given the space to dissipate.

'It's all right, Vincent,' Max said quietly.

Paul took a few deep breaths, regained his composure and continued.

'A few weeks later Josie went missing. Someone told me she'd gone off in a car with Eddie Faustin. I sent people out looking for her, but they couldn't find her. I went to Faustin's house. They weren't there. I carried on looking. I combed the city, I went to all the spots Faustin hung out. She was nowhere to be found.

'When I got back home there was Gustav Carver, waiting for me indoors. After the petrol incident, Carver had done some digging. He had two Scotland Yard detectives with him, as well as a copy of Josie's police record, and a whole bunch of English newspapers with headlines about her case and how she'd skipped the country. Some papers even claimed I'd kidnapped her and had cartoons showing me as King Kong. Carver said it was a good likeness.

'He told me he'd had a long chat with Josie and that she'd understood her predicament and agreed to his terms. But it all hinged on me saying yes – or so he said. If I said no the detectives would take Josie and me back to England. If I gave my consent they'd go away and say we weren't in Haiti.'

'What did he want you to agree to – giving up Josie?'

'Yes. He wanted her for his son, Allain. She was to remain with him for the rest of her life, bear him children and have absolutely no contact with me whatsoever. That was it. As for me, well, I was free, as long as I never made any attempt to see her or contact her ever again. Oh, and I had to *personally* pump Carver's gas whenever he stopped by.'

'And you agreed?'

'I had no choice. I reckoned he would have sent me back to England and kept Josie in Haiti. At least, me staying in the country meant that I was *close* to her.'

'I don't get it,' Max said. 'Carver destroyed your father and everything your family had built up. Why not go the whole way and get rid of you too?'

'You obviously don't understand the man, Mingus,' Vincent chuckled sourly. 'You've been to his house? You've seen the Psalm, haven't you – in gold, near that picture of his dead wife? Psalm 23, Verse 5?'

'Yeah, I've seen it.'

'Did you read it?'

'Yeah, I know it: "*Thou preparest a table before me in the presence of mine enemies: thou anointest my head with oil; my cup runneth over.*" It's from the famous *The Lord is my Shepherd* Psalm. And?'

'I take it you didn't do too well in R.E.'

'R.E?'

'Religious Education — sorry, you probably call it "Bible study".'

'I did OK.'

'The meaning of Psalm 23, Verse 5 is this: in ancient times, the best form of revenge on your enemies wasn't death or imprisonment, but for them to watch you living it up and having a good time. After all, isn't success the greatest triumph over those who've hated you and wished you ill?'

Max was struggling to stay objective, neutral, even on his client's side, but what Paul was saying, coupled with the things he'd heard and read about Gustav Carver, were tempting him out of his professional shell.

'So he kept you here so you could watch Allain step out with the love of your life?'

'Technically, yes,' Vincent chuckled. 'But . . . theoretically, *no*.'

'What do you mean?'

'She wasn't stepping out with *Allain*.'

'But I thought . . .' Max stopped. He was lost.

'What kind of detective *are* you? I thought you were supposed to be good — no, the *best*.'

Max didn't say anything.

'You mean you *really* didn't notice anything *at all*?' Vincent was on the verge of laughing. 'About *Allain*?'

'No, *should* I?'

'You've lived in Miami all your life, you've just spent *seven years* in prison, and you *still* can't tell a *queer* a mile away!'

'*Allain*?!' Max was shocked all over again. Something else he hadn't expected or seen coming. He could normally tell people's sexual orientation, not that it was too hard to spot in America — especially Miami — where people tended to be more open and upfront about which way they swung. Had his skills deteriorated *that* much?

'Yes, Allain Carver is a homosexual – G-A-Y – a *massissi*, as we call them here. Actually, Mingus, I'm not so surprised you missed it. Allain's very discreet and straight-acting.

'There had been rumours about him for years, but no proof. Allain's never shat on his own doorstep. He just goes for long weekends in Miami, San Francisco, New York. Does his thing there, bottles it up over here.'

'How do you know?'

'I've got photographic proof – videos too. Clyde Beeson took them for me. I employed him – anonymously, through a second party – about ten years ago. In fact it was you who recommended me to him.'

'*Me?*'

'You don't remember . . . ? Well, why should you? I offered you the job first, but your exact words were: "I don't fish for shit in toilets. Go to Clyde Beeson. He might do it for free."'

'Sounds like the kind of thing I would've said. I was offered a lot of that sleazy stuff – divorces – but that's not my line,' Max said. His head was still spinning. 'So I guess coming out here is a big no-no?'

'*Squared.* You know what they say about gays? They say: "There aren't any in Haiti – they're all married with kids." It's like that all over the Caribbean. Homosexuality is viewed as a perversion, a sin.'

'Poor Allain,' Max said. 'All his money, influence, status, position – and he has to sneak around pretending he's something he isn't.'

'He's not a bad guy,' Vincent said. 'Quite the opposite, in fact.'

'So why did you get those pictures taken?'

'To smear him. I was going to plant the pictures in the Haitian press.'

'Why?'

'Yin and yang. The yin, to liberate Allain, free him of his secret. The yang – revenge on Gustav, to embarrass him. The timing would have been perfect: the old man was in poor shape. Baby Doc had fallen from power, his wife was dying, his health wasn't good – I thought a little public humiliation would push him over the edge – you know, *kill* him with natural causes.'

'Why didn't you see it through?'

'I couldn't do that to Allain, exploit the poor guy's sexuality, trample over him so I could get to his father.'

'How *honourable*,' Max sneered sarcastically. 'I can see where you're coming from and God knows you've got as good a motive as any, but if you hate him that much why don't you just shoot the bastard?'

'Once bitten, twice shy.'

'You tried that?'

'Eddie Faustin stopped the bullet.'

'That was you? Figures,' Max nodded. 'So, Gustav married Allain to Francesca to put an end to the rumours?'

'Yes,' nodded Vincent. 'And . . .'

'And?'

'That wasn't *all* Gustav wanted her for. He also wanted her for himself – not just for sex, but for *breeding*. He desperately wanted a grandson. All he has is granddaughters and he's backward enough to believe that men make better leaders.

'He spent most of a decade trying to get her pregnant. He referred to their sessions as "making a deposit,"' Vincent laughed bitterly. 'Josie had two miscarriages, a stillbirth, a daughter who only lived for six months, but no son.

'We got involved again in the late eighties. When she got pregnant with Charlie, Gustav thought it was *his*, the country thought it was *Allain's* and *I* knew it was mine and Josie's.

Besides, I've got the results of a paternity test. She was barely sleeping with Gustav by then. She'd managed to limit him to the days when she was ovulating – although she'd lied to him about which days those were, so he was basically too early or too late.

'She had Charlie in Miami. Allain was with her. They're actually very good friends, you know. He helped her get through the early years in that family. As far as he saw it, he and Josie were in the same boat – obviously at opposite ends.'

Max let out a deep breath.

'Why are you telling me this now? Why not earlier?'

'Because I'm telling you now. The time and place are right.'

'Why didn't you tell Beeson or Medd?'

'Beeson I didn't trust. Medd . . . I didn't think he was good enough.'

'So I meet your standards?'

'Up to a point.'

'Thanks,' Max mumbled sarcastically, although he agreed with Paul. He wasn't as good as he used to be. Or maybe he'd never been that good in the first place; or maybe he'd just got very lucky for a very long time, because a lot of breakthroughs were little more than that – luck, and the carelessness of the criminals who made it happen. Or maybe he was pointing the wrong set of fingers at the problem: maybe he just didn't *want* to do this kind of shit any more. He wasn't sure.

He put his doubts to one side. He'd go back to them later, sometime.

'What was your relationship with your son like?'

'I used to see Charlie once a week.'

'Who chose his name?'

'I had no say in it,' Paul said sadly.

415

Max took advantage of Paul's moment of fragility to clear up something that had been bugging him since his first night in the country.

'What's wrong with Charlie?' he asked.

'He's autistic,' Paul replied quietly.

'Is that *it*?' Max was incredulous.

'*It's* a big deal to us – and to him.' Paul sounded hurt.

'But why the secrecy?'

'Gustav Carver doesn't know. And *we* didn't know if we could trust you with the information.'

'Did Beeson or Medd know?'

'No.' Paul shook his head.

'When did you find out he was autistic?'

'We both knew something was wrong, pretty much from the time he started walking. He wasn't communicative like a normal baby.'

'How did that make you feel, when you found out? When you were told?'

'We were both shocked and confused at first, but –'

'No, I asked how *you* felt.'

'Bad, at first. Because I knew there were things that I'd never be able to do with my son,' Paul said, his voice cracking a touch. 'But, you know, that's life. It isn't *all* yours. Charlie's my boy, my *son*. I love him. That's all there is to it.'

'How did you keep all that from Gustav Carver?'

'A lot of luck and a little cunning. He's also not the man he once was. The stroke left him a bit soft in the head. But I'll say this about him. He loves my boy with every *ounce* of his wretched body. Obviously he doesn't *know* Charlie isn't his, let alone about the autism – but, take it out of that context and watching them together was really quite touching. The old man helped Charlie take his first steps. Josie showed me the video she shot, said it was *almost* a shame the child wasn't his. She said the kid made him *nicer*. I don't believe her. If he'd known the truth about my boy he would have beaten his brains out with his bare hands.'

'If that's the case, why didn't Francesca – Josie – and Charlie move in with you?'

'Josie didn't want Charlie growing up in an environment like mine. And she's right. Someone will probably punch my clock one day, Mingus. I know that. I wouldn't want the two people I love most in the world getting caught in the crossfire.'

'Why don't you quit, walk away?'

'You never quit this life of mine. It quits you.'

'That *is* true,' Max agreed. 'Why d'you do it in the first place?'

'To get Josie back. I picked the fastest route to the kind of money and power I'd need to take on Carver if I had to. I took a look at how the Haitian military were smuggling Colombian cartel cocaine in and out of the country and I saw ways it could be improved. That's all I'm going to say.'

'Wasn't there another way?'

'To make a billion dollars in twenty years – *in Haiti*? No.'

'Your motive's original – the reason you got started – I'll give you that. Twenty times outta ten all you hear is some wannabe Scarface say, you know, he got into it 'cause of his neighbourhood, 'cause he had no opportunity, 'cause his mom's never loved his arse as much as her boyfriend did. Peer pressure this, socio-economic conditions that. Blah-blah-blah. That's all you ever hear. But *you* – out of everything you could've said, you tell me you turned to drug dealing for *love*,' Max snickered. 'That is some *unbelievable* shit, Vincent. And you know what is even more unbeliev-able? I *believe* you!'

'I'm glad you see the funny side.' Vincent fixed Max from

417

the bottom of his sunken stare, the beginnings of a smile on his lips. 'I'm putting you back in circulation this evening. When Allain asks where you were, you weren't with me, understood?'

'Yeah.'

'Good. Now, let's talk a little more.'

46

Max was blindfolded and put in the back of an SUV. The trip to Pétionville took a good while, a lot of it uphill over bumpy ground, leading Max to think that Paul's hideout was in the mountains. There were two other people in the car with him, Vincent Paul and the driver. There was plenty of talking in Kreyol, some laughter.

Max reviewed the conversation he'd had with Paul, starting with the truth about Charlie's parentage, the shock of which still reverberated through him. He hadn't doubted it was the truth when he'd studied the photograph of Vincent with his father. Charlie looked something like the younger Vincent had, but he took strongly after his paternal grandfather – same eyes, same expression, same stance. Paul had shown him an album of family photographs going back to the late 1890s, every face in it containing a trace element of the missing boy's physiognomy; all of Paul's relatives had been white or high yellow – right up until his black grandmother. He explained that Charlie turning out the colour he had wasn't really that uncommon in Haiti, given the nation's mixed bloodline. Max thought about Eloise Krolak and the blue-eyed, near-Caucasian descendants of Polish soldiers in the town of Jérémie. As a formality, Paul had shown Max a copy of Charlie's paternity test.

They talked about the investigation. Paul told him he'd been in the area when Charlie had been kidnapped. He'd rushed to the scene, arriving in time to see the mob pull Faustin out of the car and stab and beat him to death, before cutting off his head, sticking it on a spiked pole and dancing it away into the slum. Charlie was gone. Nobody had seen him being taken out of the car, but then nobody had seen how Francesca had managed to end up halfway down the road either. Paul guessed that Francesca had held on to Charlie so tightly, the kidnappers had had to carry or drag them both away with them until they'd broken her grip. He had no witnesses to this, only people who'd seen Francesca coming to in the road.

Paul had checked out Faustin. He'd been to Saut d'Eau and spoken to Mercedes Leballec, and he'd checked out the house in Port-au-Prince. He'd found the *vévé*, but nothing else. The trail had gone cold from then. Paul was sure Charlie was dead. He thought the boy had been kidnapped by one of Gustav's many enemies and smuggled out of the country via the Dominican Republic. He'd searched there too, but drawn a blank.

They'd discussed Claudette Thodore. Paul didn't think the kidnappings were related.

Max revealed some but not all of what he'd uncovered. He didn't mention the tape he'd found nor the potential Noah's Ark connection. He didn't mention what it told him – that Haitian children were being stolen, brainwashed and turned into sex toys for foreign paedophiles.

Paul knew he'd been following someone from Noah's Ark but he didn't know who. Max refused to tell him because he didn't have the evidence he needed. Paul agreed to let him complete his investigation and offered to help him in whatever way he could.

The blindfold came off on the outskirts of Pétionville. The SUV they'd been riding in was wedged between a military jeep with UN markings and Max's Landcruiser.

Max stared out at the passing streets in the near evening, right before the end of daylight. Christmas was coming but there was no sign of the impending holiday – no Santas, no trees, no tinsel. It could have been any time of the year. He wondered what Haiti had been like before its troubles, in more peaceful times. Had those ever existed here? He was starting to care a little about the place, to want to know more about it, to want to know how it could produce people like Paul, who he had to admit a repulsed admiration for – loathing his methods but lauding his intentions, and even understanding his reasons for getting into the business he was in. Would he have gone the same way if he'd had Paul's life? Possibly, if he hadn't fallen apart first. Would Paul have gone the way Max had? Probably not, but if he had he'd have steered a clearer, quicker course and never fallen down the way Max had. Would Max have liked Paul better had he been a law-abiding mogul? They probably never would have met.

'We didn't talk payment,' Paul said, as they rolled into the Impasse Carver.

'Payment?'

'You don't work for free.'

'You didn't hire me, so you don't owe me,' Max said.

'I'll give you something anyway – for your troubles.'

'I don't want anything.'

'You'll want this.'

'Try me.'

'Peace of mind.'

Max gave him a quizzical look.

'Solomon Boukman.'

'*Boukman*?' Max started. 'You *got* him?'

'Yes.'

'How long have you had him?' Max kept his tone and

posture as even as he could, riding out the shock waves, stifling any signs of anger or excitement in his voice.

'Since your country returned him to us. The *really* dangerous ones – the killers, the rapists, the gang leaders – I have picked up at the airport.'

'What do you do with them?'

'Lock them up and let them rot.'

'Why don't you just kill them?'

'They didn't commit their crimes here.'

'What about the rest? Do you give 'em jobs in your HQ?'

'I don't employ criminals. Bad for business, especially my line of work.'

Max had to laugh. They pulled up outside the gate of his house.

'Find out what happened to my son and I'll bring you and your nemesis together. Just you, him, four walls, no windows. He won't be armed and you won't be searched,' Vincent said.

Max thought about it for a while. He'd wanted Boukman dead in America, and when he'd heard they'd let him go he'd wanted him dead too. But now he wasn't sure he could shoot him in cold blood. In fact, he *knew* he couldn't do it. Boukman might've been a monster, the worst criminal he'd ever encountered, but killing him would make Max no better than him.

'I can't accept that, Vincent. Not that way,' Max said, and got out of the car.

Paul wound down the window.

'Your country had him and they let him go.'

'That was their business. I'm not a cop any more, Vincent. You seem to forget.'

'You too,' Vincent smiled, and handed Max back his Beretta and holster. 'I didn't think you'd accept.'

Paul nodded to his driver. The car started up.

'Oh, and by the way – remember I told you how Gustav Carver bulldozed our family estate? This is what he built over it. Enjoy your stay,' Paul said, and smiled bitterly before raising the blacked-out window and driving off.

47

There were five telephone messages waiting for him – Joe, Allain and three from Chantale.

He called Allain first. He stuck to the script he'd formulated in the car on his way back: act like nothing had happened and everything was the same as before. He didn't say anything about Eloise Krolak for now. It was still early days and he only had the videotape to go on. Instead he explained that he'd spent the last few days chasing up a lead that had turned into a dead end. Allain thanked him for his dedication and hard work.

Max phoned Joe. The big man was out on a case. He wouldn't be contactable for the rest of the night.

He had a shower and made a pot of coffee. He was halfway through his first cup when the phone rang. It was Chantale.

She sounded relieved when she heard his voice. They had a long talk. Max told her the same lie he'd told Allain. He didn't know how much he could trust her. How much did she know about Charlie? And what about Allain? Had she guessed he was gay? Women were supposed to be able to spot that kind of thing.

Chantale told him that her mother's condition was deteriorating. She didn't think she'd last until Christmas. Max used that as an excuse to tell her not to come by the next day. He didn't want her around while he tailed Eloise. He said he'd cover for her with Allain. She said OK, but her voice said it wasn't.

After they were done he went and sat out on the porch.

The dark air was alive with the chatter of the nocturnal insects. A light wind was blowing behind the house, caressing the leaves and carrying with it the sweet fragrance of jasmine and burning trash.

He thought things through:

Vincent Paul didn't kidnap Charlie.

So who did?

Was it one of Paul's enemies or one of Carver's?

If it was the last, did they know the truth about Charlie's parentage?

What about Beeson and Medd?

They must have come a lot closer than he had and they'd paid for it.

The thought of Beeson getting to something before him stirred up the dormant vestiges of his competitive pride. He got close to angry imagining the sweaty little ferret almost cracking the case when he couldn't seem to get to first base.

Then he remembered what had happened to his old rival and he let the thought go.

He needed to talk to Beeson again, find out what he knew. He'd ask Joe to bring him in.

Until then, all he had to go on was Eloise Krolak.

Whether or not she was connected to Charlie's disappearance was something he'd soon find out.

48

The following evening Max watched Eloise being picked up outside Noah's Ark by the silver SUV. It had just gone 6.00 pm. He tailed the car to Pétionville, where it pulled into the driveway of a two-floor house on a tree-lined residential street near the town centre.

Max drove down the road, got his bearings on the house and parked at the end.

After an hour he took a walk to check the place out. It was pitch black outside. Not only was the street completely deserted, but no one seemed to be living in any of the other houses either. There wasn't a single light coming from any of them. And neither did he pick up a single sound, other than the song of the cicadas and the branches creaking above his head. It was eerily quiet. He didn't even hear the mountain drums.

He inspected the house from the opposite side of the road. A TV was on in an upstairs room. He wondered if Eloise was watching a video like the one he'd found.

He returned to the Landcruiser.

The SUV pulled out of the house just after 7.00 am. They were almost immediately held up in traffic. Pétionville was already teeming with people milling around the indoor market – a wide mustard-coloured building with a rusted brown tin roof. The streets were already open for business, men and women of all ages selling fish, eggs, live chickens, dead chickens – plucked and unplucked – mounds of questionable-looking red meat, homemade sweets, potato chips, soft drinks, cigarettes and booze. The country might have been limping and crawling through the ages, but there was a vibrancy about the people in the early morning Max hadn't ever felt in any American city.

It took them twenty minutes to get on the road to Port-au-Prince and another fifty to make it to the capital. Eloise got out in front of Noah's Ark and waved to the SUV as it drove away to the Boulevard Harry Truman with a honk of the horn.

Max followed the vehicle along the coastal road. As the Banque Populaire came into view, the SUV indicated that it was turning right into the entrance reserved for staff and VIPs.

Max sped past as the SUV entered through the gates, then he did a U-turn and headed back towards the bank. He drove around the building until he found the customer entrance.

As he was rolling into the public car park he saw someone he recognized walking towards the main doors. The person stopped in mid-step, turned around and started heading back in the direction they'd come from.

There was only a medium-sized hedge separating the two car parks, staff and general public. Max could clearly see the SUV and the figure hurrying towards it.

It all made so much sense.

He suddenly understood why Claudette had drawn her kidnapper orange:

It was his hair – that ginger afro.

The Orange Man:

Maurice Codada, the Head of Security.

That evening Max called Vincent Paul and told him everything he'd found out. Paul listened in silence.

'We'll go get them in a few hours' time – early tomorrow morning,' Paul said quietly. 'I want you to interrogate them. Get everything you can out of them. Do whatever you have to to get them to talk.'

49

Max was collected by Paul's men shortly after 3.00 am and driven to the Codada–Krolak house. The couple were being held separately in the basement.

Max checked on both of them before going to inspect their house.

Max crossed a red-and-black tiled foyer that led into an open-plan living room area, furnished with a huge TV, a video recorder, a sofa, several armchairs and a few potted palms.

On the right was a well-stocked bar, complete with uphol-stered stools. Max went and checked behind it. He opened the till. It was stuffed with banknotes and coins. The notes were gourdes with Papa and Baby Doc's faces on them. He found a loaded .38 under the bar, as well as a small stack of CDs of Haitian and South American music. Hanging on the wall next to the bar was a Papa Doc-era Haitian flag, black and red instead of blue and red. He understood then that it corresponded to the design of the tiles.

The Duvalier theme continued upstairs. Dozens of black-and-white photographs hung in the corridors – a younger Papa Doc in a white coat, smiling from the middle of a group of poor people, all of them abject and miserable in their clothes and surroundings, yet smiling quite happily. Many, Max noticed, were missing limbs, hands and feet. It must have been taken at the time of the yaws epidemic. At Duvalier's feet sat a group of tough-faced young children, all of them black except for one – a light-skinned boy with freckles. It was Codada.

Max followed Codada's evolution from child thug to man thug. He posed with Bedouin Désyr and the Faustin brothers, now in Macoute uniforms – navy-blue shirts and pants, bandanas around their necks, guns in their belts, eyes hidden behind thick wraparound shades, booted feet on dead bodies, all smiles.

He stopped at a series of photographs showing Codada supervising a construction site. His mouth dropped open. Clarinette's temple was somewhere in the background of almost every shot.

He looked in the master bedroom. Codada and Eloise Krolak slept in a four-poster bed with a huge TV at the foot of it.

A small framed painting of a boy in a blue uniform with red trousers playing a flute hung on one wall. Max instantly recognized it as the same painting that had been hanging on the wall of the Manhattan club he'd first met Allain Carver in, right near where they'd been sitting. He'd seen it elsewhere too – Codada's office in the bank.

He took the painting down and turned it over. There was a label on the back:

'*Le Fifre*; Édouard Manet.'

Max heard voices in the corridor. Two of Vincent's men were coming out of a room at the end.

He walked down to it. It was a large study, furnished with a desk and computer nearest the door, a library of bound books at the far end and, in between, a dark-green leather armchair and another big television set. A woman was there, working at the computer.

The drawers had all been opened, their contents piled on top of the desk: five bricks of used $100 bills, stacks of photographs, half a dozen CDs – each a different colour – and two trays of floppy disks labelled 1961 through to 1995.

Max went over to the bookcase, pausing at another portrait of Papa Doc, this one very different from the ones he'd already seen in the house. Here the dictator, dressed like Baron Samedi, in a top hat, tails and white gloves, sat at the head of a long table in a blood-red room, staring straight at the viewer. Others sat around him, but their faces weren't shown. They were shadowy, ambiguously human forms, rendered in a shade of brown so sombre it was practically black. In the middle of the table was a white bundle of some sort. He looked closer at the canvas and recognized a baby.

He looked away and moved over to the bookshelves. The books were arranged in blocks of colour – blue, green, red, maroon, brown and black – and had their titles stamped on the spines in gold letters. He homed in on a title: *Georgina A*. The next book along was called *Georgina B*, the one after *Georgina C*. He pulled it out and opened it.

No pages. The 'book' was really a video case in disguise, like the kind of hollowed-out Bible he'd known junkies to stash their works and supplies in. Max took out the plain black cassette. A photograph of a scared-looking pre-teen girl was underneath. He opened cases *A* and *B* and found a different photograph in each. In the first she was smiling at the camera, in the second she looked confused.

He went through the rest of the shelves. Tapes everywhere, all of them stored in cases branded with girls' names. There were no boys anywhere, no *Charlie* or *Charles A–C*.

But he found *Claudette T*.

And he found *Eloise*.

'What've you got?' the woman asked from behind the desk. New York accent.

'Videotapes. What about you? What's on the computer?'

'Sales records – everything up to 1985 has been scanned from ledgers. And there's a database on the machine. This couple have been selling kids to men,' she said.

'I'll come and look in a minute,' Max said, going back to the television. He turned it on and fed *Eloise A* into the video player.

It was impossible to put a date on the footage, but there were only hints of the adult Eloise in the child whose face filled the screen for at least two solid minutes. She couldn't have been more than five or six then.

Max stopped the tape when the abuse started.

The woman at the desk had stopped working. Her expression, teetering between disgust and despair, told him she'd seen what he had.

'Let's see what you're working on?' Max asked, quickly going over to her.

She showed him her screen – an image of a blank sheet of paper, divided into six vertical columns headed *Nom, Age, Prix, Client, Date de Vente* and *Adresse*. It was from August 1977, and showed which child had been sold to which client and where they'd been taken to.

He quickly scanned this last column: of the thirteen children listed, four had gone either to the US or Canada, two had been taken to Venezuela, one apiece to France, Germany and Switzerland, three to Japan, one to Australia. The buyers were identified by their full names.

They looked at the database.

It was quite a history.

The database was divided into years, and then subdivided into countries.

Apart from their names, addresses, dates of birth, occupations and places of employment, there was also a record of the buyers' (called 'clients' on the database) salaries, sexual orientation, marital status, number of children, and the names and addresses of their contacts in business, politics, media, entertainment and other areas.

The first recorded transaction was dated 24 November 1959, when Patterson Brewster III, Managing Director of the Pickle and Preservatives Company, 'adopted' a Haitian boy called Gesner César.

The adoption cost $575.00.

The most recent adoption recorded was that of Ismaëlle Cloué by Gregson Pepper, a banker from Santa Monica, California.

The cost was $37,500 (S).

(S) signified Standard service – no frills, no benefits, no short cuts, no special favours; the buyer chose his 'Product' (as the children were referred to in the database section listing their details), paid and left with him or her. The price remained constant and there was no competition for the product.

If one or more other buyers were interested in the same child then the sale went to Auction (A), with the price starting at its current Standard rate.

The highest paid for a child at auction was $500,000 for a six-year-old girl by the Canadian chief executive of an oil company in Kuwait. That was in March 1992.

Other service categories were:

(B) – which stood for Bon Ami (good friend), or a buyer who could reserve a child of his choice from the menu, without facing competition. The cost was higher – between $75 and $100,000 – depending on the child's popularity and the buyer's 'additional value' (found in a separate box on the database, below the contacts section: this signified a buyer's clout – his links with governments; someone of high value was charged at the lower end of the scale).

(M) – Meilleur Ami (best friend), or a buyer who ordered *à la carte*. He got almost anything he wanted, brought to him from anywhere. For that privilege he could pay anything between $250,000 and $1,000,000.

Many buyers were graded (R) – recurrent purchasers – with numbers indicating the amount of times they had used the service. Most were R3 or R4, but several hit double figures, the highest being an R19.

There were 2,479 buyer names on the database. Three hundred and seventeen came from North America. They included senators, congressmen, bankers, diplomats, stockbrokers, senior cops, senior clergy, senior military personnel, doctors, lawyers, high-level businessmen, actors, rock stars, movie producers and directors, a press baron and one former talk show host. Max recognized only a handful of the names, but most of the organizations, establishments and companies they were attached to were household names.

The 'menus' consisted of files of photographs of individual children – a head shot and three full body shots – clothed, in underwear, and naked – which were sent to buyers via email. The buyers would reply with their choice.

In the days before the internet the buyers had met up at private clubs and had been given the files in paper form. Many preferred this method because they said emails were vulnerable to hackers. The clubs were also good for networking.

Max next studied a photograph file showing children and their corresponding buyers. The buyers had either been snapped unawares from a distance, or their images had been lifted straight from video footage.

One whole file was devoted to pictures of buyers in or around the place where they kept the children, which Max recognized from the tape he'd found at the Faustin house.

They had been photographed meeting and greeting each other, and inspecting the mouths of children standing on what looked like auction blocks. The buyers never looked at the camera, which led Max to think that they were being photographed in secret.

The final photos in the series showed them boarding boats bound for a nearby coastline.

'Do you know where that is?' Max asked.

'Looks like they were taken on La Gonâve. It's an island off the coast.'

'Could you look up a name for me on the database. First name Claudette – two "t"s – last name Thodore.'

The woman brought up her details and printed them out. Claudette had been sold to a John Saxby in February 1995. He lived in Fort Lauderdale, Florida.

Max thought of the rest of the North American buyers and how he could set all those enslaved children free. He'd give Joe a copy of all the evidence. His friend would be a hero: when it was all over and the indictments had been handed down they'd make him Chief of Police.

But first things first.

He returned to the basement.

50

'Can we get you anything, Mr Co-da-da? Water? Coffee? Something like that?' Max offered, starting things off on a co-operative note. He had an interpreter with him – a short, sweaty man with Oriental features and brilliantine in his hair.

Codada sat with his hands tied behind his back, ankles chained together, bare lightbulb burning right above his head. Eloise Krolak was locked in the next room.

'Yes. You can get out of my house and then go fuck yourself.' Codada surprised Max by replying in English, his French accent as strong as his defiance.

'I thought you couldn't speak English.'

'You think wrong.'

'Obviously,' Max said.

Codada had on sharkskin pants and black pinstriped socks that matched the silk shirt he wore open three buttons down to his pale milk chest. Max counted four gold chains around his neck. He also reeked of a musky aftershave he'd applied with complete disregard for subtlety. On his way over to the house Max had been told that the Codadas had been surprised coming back from a nightclub in the mountains.

'Why d'you think you're here?' Max asked.

'You think I have the boy – Charlie?' he answered, pronouncing Charlie '*Tssharlie*'.

'Correct. So let's not waste each other's time. Do you have him?'

'No.'

'Who does?'

'God.' He looked skywards.

'You saying he's dead?'

Codada agreed with a nod. Max looked at his eyes. Codada was looking straight at him, not a hint of a lie, voice steady, truth telling. It meant nothing of course, for now. Codada probably hadn't worked out that he was a dead man either way.

'Who killed him?' Max asked.

'The people – dey *keel* Eddie Faustin – *en même temps* –?'

'So, you're telling me the mobs who attacked Eddie Faustin killed Charlie too? That what you're sayin'?'

'*Oui.*'

'How do you know this?'

'I – *investiger?*'

'You *investigated it?*'

Codada nodded.

'Who told you?'

'In the street where it happen. *Témoins.* Wit-ness. The people talk to me.'

'So you had witnesses, who *saw* this happen?' Max pointed to his eyes. 'How many? One? Two?'

'More. *En pille moune.* Many. Ten. Twenty. It was big big *scandale* here. Like if the daughter of Clinton kidnappe.' Codada flashed a smile. His gold tooth caught the light and an instant warm yellow light poured out of his mouth. 'Charlie dead. I say dis to him father very many times. "Your son he dead," I say but him not listen.'

'You told Allain Carver this?' Max played dumb.

'*Non.* I tell him *father.*' Codada smiled more intensely, ready to drop the bomb on him. 'Gustav. Gustav father of Charlie.'

Max wasn't going to tear the ground away from Codada's feet just yet. He returned Codada's smile with one of his

437

own. A bolt of panic pierced the confidence in the head of security's face.

'Tell me about Eddie Faustin. Were you good friends?'

'Not friend.'

'You didn't like him?'

'Him and him brother, Salazar, they work for me in the police.'

'You mean the Ton-ton Mackooots?'

'Yes, we was Macoutes.' Codada tried to straighten himself up in his chair, failed, resigned himself to a slump.

'Did Eddie work for you afterwards – when the Mackooots finished?'

'*Non.*'

'Did you see Eddie at all afterwards?'

'Only when he drive Monsieur Carver.'

'You didn't talk to him?'

'I say hello, how you do.'

'Did you meet up? Go for a drink?'

'A drink? With *Eddie?*' Codada looked at Max like he was suggesting something not only impossible but utterly absurd.

'Yeah, why not? Talk about old times?'

'Old time?' Codada laughed. 'When we *Macoutes*, Eddie Faustin work for *me*. I his *boss.*'

'So you don't mix with the help either. You do some of the worst things imaginable, but you *won't* spend quality time with some guy because he was your subordinate back in the glory days of Doc? You people have some fucked-up standards, let me tell you.' Max shook his head and looked Codada straight on. 'Anyway, Eddie Faustin was going to kidnap Charlie. Did you know that?'

'*Non.* No true,' he insisted.

'*Yes*, true. Yes, *very* true.'

'I say *no* true.'

'Why is that?'

'Eddie' – Codada pulled a proud face – 'a *good* man. He never do bad to Monsieur Carver. He *love* Monsieur Carver like . . . like him *father.*'

'Eddie tell you that?'

'No. I see. I *know*. I feel.'

'Is that right? You see, you know, you feel? OK. *I know* Eddie was working for Charlie's kidnappers. That was why he drove the car to that road that day. He was waiting for them to come and take the boy.'

'*Non!*'

'Yes!'

'Who tell you dis – dis shit?'

'I *investigay* too,' Max said. 'And it's *not* shit.'

Codada's face said he didn't believe him, told his interrogator he thought he was bluffing.

Max decided to switch lanes and ask him about other things. He went over to a corner of the room and picked up one of the prompts he'd brought from Codada's house – Claudette's videotape.

'Tell me about your business?'

'"Business"?' Codada searched him.

'That's what I said.'

'I no 'ave "business".'

Max glanced at the door. An armed man was guarding it. His interpreter was standing against the wall behind Codada.

'You ever steal children?'

'I *no* steal children.'

'*Bullshit!*' Max thundered. 'You and your crew stole children to sell to rich perverts. *That* is your business!'

'*Non!*' Codada snapped back and tried to stand, but he fell flat on his face.

Max put one foot on Codada's back and pushed down

hard until he heard the vertebrae cracking.

'*YES!* You did, you lying cocksucker!' Max seethed as he ground his foot down harder on Codada's spine, making him gasp in pain. 'You stole those kids and you took them to La Go-Nav and sold them to kiddie rapers like yourself. I bet that's what we're gonna find when we go there – we're gonna find your latest batch of merchandise. You sack full of fucking shit!'

Max stamped on him hard and Codada cried out.

'Pick him up!' Max snapped at the soldiers.

They set him back in the chair.

Max opened Claudette's videotape box and showed him her photograph.

'You know her?'

Codada didn't answer, just winced in pain.

'John Saxby – the guy who bought her? Tell me about him: what does he do? And don't talk shit because we've got your accounts – your *business* accounts. Answer me.'

'I no more want speak,' Codada said, looking past Max, his eyes going matt dull as he focussed on the door.

'Oh, you "no more want speak"? Well, *fuck you*, Maurice, because I'm as good as it fucking gets for you. Think I'm giving you a hard time, *now*? This is *easy* time, Maurice, because you either speak to me *now*, or Vincent Paul will *make* you speak. Do you understand?'

'Good kop, bad kop?' Codada sneered.

'There are no cops here, Maurice. And there's no *good* either. You're *through*. You hear me? You're *over*. You know why? I'm going to talk to Eloise. I'm going to *make* her tell me what you won't. You understand me?' Max said, mouth close to Codada's ear. 'You still "no more want speak"?'

Codada didn't reply.

Max turned and walked out of the room.

51

Eloise shot Max a furtive look when he walked into the room, then stared down at the plain white handkerchief in her cuffed hands.

'Eloise? My name is Max Mingus. I'm investigating the kidnapping of Charlie Carver.'

No reply.

'I know you speak English as well as I do,' Max said. She stayed silent, kept her eyes on the handkerchief, her body slightly hunched forward, as if she would have drawn her knees up to her chest if she could.

'Let me paint the picture for you. This is going to go very *very* badly for you both.' Max kept his voice low and soft, his tone non-threatening, one of shared intimacy. 'You know who Vincent Paul is. I've seen what he does to people and trust me, it is *not* pretty.'

She didn't even move.

'Eloise, I'm not like him. I want to help you. I've seen the videotapes of you when you were a little girl. I've seen what that man in the next room did to you. If you help me, I promise you that I will talk to Vincent about you. I'll explain to him that it wasn't really your fault you got involved in the things you did. You might have a good chance of getting out of this alive.'

Silence.

Then Max heard the unmistakable boom of Vincent Paul's voice outside the house.

'Eloise. Save yourself. *Please*,' Max implored. 'If you don't help me, Vincent Paul *will* kill you. He's *not* going to take your past into account. He's *not* going to care that you were once a little girl, that that evil bastard out there snatched you from your home and raped you and abused you. He's just going to see what he's looking at – a teacher, someone responsible for the lives of young vulnerable children, orphans, who let evil men abuse them and even participated in it. I won't blame him for his actions, Eloise. Think about it. Think about it hard. I'm offering you a way out. That sack of shit in the next room isn't worth it.'

Max walked out and saw Paul standing in the corridor. He greeted Max with a half-smile and slight nod.

'Give her this.' Vincent put something small and wet into Max's palm.

Max looked at it and went back in to Eloise.

'Recognize this?' he asked her.

Her eyes widened and teared up when she recognized what the bloody gleaming chunk of metal between Max's fingers was.

'*You leave him alone!*' she screeched.

'If you don't tell us what we want to know, Eloise, we are going to take him apart, piece by piece.' He grabbed her hand and pressed her lover's gold front tooth into her palm.

She stared at Max, her eyes poisoned darts. He knew then that she wasn't the warped innocent he was almost sure she'd be. She wasn't any kind of victim at all. She was every bit as guilty as Codada.

'You're still going to kill us whatever,' she sneered, French accent smothering American inflections.

Paul walked in, dragging Codada behind him by his cuffed legs.

Eloise cried out when she saw him. She tried to stand.

'*Sit down!*' Max thundered. 'You *will* answer my questions or that child-raping scumbag over there will lose a lot more than his teeth. *Understand?*'

Max didn't wait for an answer.

'Charlie Carver? What did you do with him?'

'Nothing. We *don't* have him. We *never* had him. We *never* *would* have had him. You've come to the *wrong people*, detective.'

'Have I?' Max got in her face. He'd come back to Charlie later. 'Where is Claudette Thodore?'

'I don't know who she is.'

Max pulled the picture out of his wallet and showed her. She glanced at it for a second.

'She wasn't one of mine.'

'What do you mean?'

'I didn't work with her.'

'"*Work with her*"? What do you mean?'

'I didn't groom her.'

'"Groom her"?'

'Teach her etiquette – table manners – the things you need to know in polite society.'

Max was about to ask her to expand on what she'd said, but Codada gurgled something from the floor.

'He says he'll talk now,' Paul translated.

'Yeah? Well, I don't want to listen to him right now. Take him back.'

Vincent dragged Codada out.

Max turned back to Eloise.

'Grooming – go on, tell me.'

'You mean you can't figure it out?' Eloise sniggered.

'Oh, I know what it *is*,' Max sneered. 'I just want to hear it from *you*.'

'Our clients are all very wealthy men, people who move in high-society circles. They like their product to be of a certain standard.'

'Their "*product*" being these children?'

'Yes. Before selling them we teach them table manners, and the correct way to behave around adults.'

'As in saying please and thank you when they're getting raped?'

Eloise didn't answer.

'Answer me.'

'It's more than just *that*.' She got defensive.

'Oh?'

'Ill-mannered people get nowhere in life.'

'And you're *what* – doing them a *favour*, teaching them how to hold a knife and fork at some paedophile's dinner table? Give me a *motherfucking break*, Eloise!' Max shouted. 'Why d'you *do* it, Eloise? I saw those tapes. I saw what happened to you.'

'You saw, but you didn't *see*,' she countered, boring into Max with hard eyes. 'You should look *again*.'

'Why don't you just fill me in on what I'm missing?'

'Maurice loves me.'

'*Bull-shit!*' Max spat.

'Why?' she countered, calmly. 'What did you expect to find? A *victim*? A helpless, weeping adult-child? Someone right out of your training manual? Someone to placate with some monosyllabic psychobabble, some reassuring grunt?' She was defiant and angry, her voice falling just outside a shout. Yet, in spite of this, her delivery was completely devoid of passion, as if she had been rehearsing this speech all her life and the words had lost their meaning to her, become a row of audio dots she had to follow until they stopped.

'It's easy for you to paint us all as innocent, vulnerable little victims, but we're not all the same. Some of us *beat* the system. Some of us come out on *top*.'

'You call *this* coming out on top?' Max threw his hands around the room. 'You're gonna die and you're gonna die *bad*.'

'No one has ever treated me as well as him. Ever. In my whole life. I have no regrets. If I could change anything, I really wouldn't,' she said, calmly.

'Tell me about Maurice. How did he steal you? What was his technique?'

'He didn't "steal me",' she said, impatiently. 'He *rescued* me.'

'Whatever,' Max sighed. 'Just tell me how he did it.'

'The first thing I remember about him was his camera – he had a Super 8 then. It covered half his face. I used to see him in the mornings. Me and my friends would wave to him. He'd talk to us, give us things – candy, these little wire figurines he made of us. He paid me the most attention. He made me laugh. My friends were so *jealous*.' Eloise smiled. 'One day he asked me if I wanted to go away with him – go on a trip to a magical place. I said yes. And the next thing I knew, I was sitting next to him in a car. Best decision I ever made.'

Max tried to swallow but his mouth was arid. She was right. She wasn't what he was expecting. He knew all about Stockholm Syndrome, where kidnap victims fall in love with their captors, but he'd never encountered that in a child abuse case before.

He was deeply confused – and lost and horrified – and the worst part was he couldn't help himself from showing it, letting her see into him, letting her have the edge on him, the authority.

'But – what about your family?'

She let out a sour laugh, her face rigid, her eyes cold and fixed.

'My family? You mean my "apple-pie mom and dad", like you have in America? Is that what you think when you speak of *my* "family"?'

Max looked at her blankly. He'd let her talk until he could think of a way to come back in and impose himself.

'Well, it wasn't like that, let me tell you. The little I can remember I'd give *anything* to forget. Eight to a tiny one-room house, so poor the only thing I had to eat was dirt cake. Do you know what dirt cake is? It's a little cornmeal and a lot of dirt mixed together with sewer water and left outside to dry into a cake. *That's* what I ate every day.'

She stopped and looked at him defiantly, goading him to come back at her with something bigger, to try and net her with some homespun morality.

When she saw he wasn't going there, something in her changed and became unsure. Then she breathed deeply through her nose, held in the air, closed her eyes and lowered her head.

She held her breath for well over a minute, her eyeballs squirming back and forth behind her eyelids, her fingers screwing up the corners of her handkerchief and her lips moving fast but soundlessly, either in prayer or conflict with her conscience. Then, one by one, the neurotic motions timed out: she put the handkerchief down on her lap and rested her hands, palms down, her lips froze and her eyes rolled to a stop.

Finally she exhaled through her mouth, opened her eyes and addressed Max.

'I'll tell you everything you need to know. I'll tell you where we keep the children and who we sell them to. I'll tell you who is involved, and who we work for.'

'Who you work *for*?'

She opened her eyes and met his.

'You didn't think *Maurice* ran this all by himself, did you?' she laughed.

Paul came back in.

'Maurice is many things, but clever isn't one of them,' she giggled fondly, and then almost immediately flipped into business mode. 'I'll tell you *absolutely everything* – but on one condition.'

'Try me,' Max said.

'You let Maurice go.'

'*What*? Absolutely no fucking way!'

'You let Maurice go and I'll tell you. He was just a cog in a very big wheel. We both were. If you don't let him go, I *won't* talk. You might as well turn your guns on us now.'

'*Done*,' Paul suddenly interrupted, making Eloise start. 'As long as we verify whatever information you give us, I'll let him go.'

'Give me your word,' Eloise said.

'I give you my word.'

Eloise bowed her head solemnly to indicate they had a deal.

Max didn't know if he believed Paul would let Codada walk, but he put that to the back of his mind.

Paul put his hand on Max's shoulder and tapped him, which Max understood as a sign to resume the interrogation.

'Tell me who you're working for.'

'Can't you guess?'

'Eloise, you've got a deal. We ain't going to play cat and mouse no more. We ain't going to play clever. I ask you a question, you give me an answer – and you tell me the truth. Simple as that. Understood?'

447

'Yes.'

'Good. Who are you working for?'

'Gustav Carver,' she said.

'No fucking *shit*, Eloise!' Max yelled. 'I *know* he's your fucking boss already! He runs Noah's Ark. He runs the bank where your motherfucker child-rapist lover works!'

'But you asked who we're wor –'

'Don't get fucking *cute* with me!' Max leant all the way over to her. 'You hold out on me any more, I swear to God I'm going over and capping Maurice myself.'

'But I'm *telling you* it's Gustav Carver! He is our *boss*. He is behind this. He runs this. He *owns* this. He *started* it! He *invented* it!' Eloise insisted, her voice trembling. 'Gustav Carver. It's him. He's been doing it for almost forty years. Stealing children, turning them out, selling them for sex. Gustav Carver *is Tonton Clarinette*.'

52

'Maurice first met Monsieur Carver – Gustav – in the 1940s. He lived in a village in the southwest, about fifteen miles out of Port-au-Prince. At that time one of the most widespread diseases in Haiti was yaws. Maurice's area was the most heavily infected.

'Maurice told me these stories about how it attacked his parents. His mother was the first to get it. First her arms withered, then her lips fell off, then her nose was eaten away. They were driven out of the village. They lived in a clapboard shack, Maurice and what was left of his parents. He watched them fall apart, literally.'

'How come he didn't get it?' Max asked.

'Le Docteur Duvalier – François Duvalier – Papa Doc – saved him.'

'Was that how they met?'

'Yes. The shack was on the way to the village. The doctor was setting up a hospital nearby and he found Maurice sitting there between the bodies of his parents. Maurice was the first person he inoculated.'

'I see,' Max said. So far so the usual 'victim of his upbringing' defence.

'They had a problem with protecting their medical supplies. They were always getting raided by the locals. So Maurice organized a gang to act as security. Kids his age, some younger. They watched over Le Docteur Duvalier while he was working, and they watched over the hospital at night. They were very effective. They used catapults, knives and clubs. They carried their weapons around in *macoutes* – these straw satchels you see the peasants carrying. Duvalier called them *"mes petits tontons macoutes"* – my little men with bags. The name stuck.'

'That's *so* cute,' Max laughed sarcastically. 'What about Gustav Carver? Where does he come in?'

'Monsieur Carver was always around. He was the first white man Maurice had ever seen. Medical supplies were impossible to get hold of. It was Monsieur Carver, with his business contacts, who brought the supplies from America.

'Maurice loved Le Docteur Duvalier, but they weren't ever lovers – if that's what you are thinking.' Eloise spoke to Max as she scrutinized his face.

'I wasn't thinking that,' Max said.

'But you suspected it?'

Of course he had, but he was back in control now and staying that way.

'Remember our deal? I ask, you answer. What happened next?'

'Maurice went to work for Le Docteur Duvalier. He was responsible for Le Docteur Duvalier's safety during his Presidential campaign.'

'When did they start stealing children?'

'Le Docteur Duvalier, as well as being a doctor, was also a *bokor* – you know what that is?' she asked him, condescendingly.

'I've been here long enough, lady,' Max responded, giving her a hard look. She smiled at him, for the first time, very nervously, showing crooked yellowed front teeth. She reminded Max of an old rat. All she needed were stick-on whiskers. 'I also know that there's voodoo and there's black magic. I know enough about one to tell it from the other.

450

So, stop me if I'm wrong, but Papa Doc was practising black magic, wasn't he?'

'He dealt with the dead, the spirits. That's why he needed children.'

'How?'

'The only thing that separates us from the spirit world are our bodies. When they go we become spirit. Spirits used to be people and like people they can be fooled,' Eloise said, stretching her fingers, which were short and thin, like broken brown pencil stubs held together with sellotape.

'So what's the point of being a ghost – a spirit – if you can't see what a mortal's up to?'

'This is where you have black magic. Le Docteur Duvalier used the souls of children – the purest, untainted souls you can find, the ones the spirits will always speak to and help out.'

'How did he get their souls?'

'How do you think?'

'He killed the children?'

'He *sacrificed* them,' Eloise replied again, condescendingly.

'So Maurice and his crew used to steal children for Papa Doc?'

'Yes. He stole to order, because Le Docteur Duvalier wouldn't take just *any* child off the street. He was very specific about who he wanted. It was different every time. Sometimes he'd need a boy, sometimes a girl. They had to be born on a certain date, they had to come from a certain region. They had to be under a certain age. Never over ten. Their souls became less pure at that age. They started developing into adults then. They knew more.'

'And the spirits wouldn't talk to them as much,' Max concluded.

'Yes.'

'So Maurice stole these children and Gustav Carver knew all about it?'

'Yes, he did – and more than that: he was in charge of procuring the children. Le Docteur Duvalier would specify what he wanted to Monsieur Carver. Monsieur Carver and Maurice would look around the country, photographing likely subjects. They would present the photographs to Le Docteur Duvalier, who'd choose the one he wanted.'

Max's blood ran cold. Her eyes weren't lying and her body language wasn't deceptive or panicked. She *was* telling the truth. It figured. It fit. Everyone knew Gustav Carver was close to Papa Doc, that they went back a long way. Gustav was an opportunist. He probably saw in Duvalier an identical ruthlessness to his own – and the same will to act without conscience or remorse.

'What did Papa Doc use these children – these children's souls – what did he use them for?'

'To trick his enemies.'

'How?'

'We all have a guarding spirit – a guardian angel, I suppose. They watch over us, protect us. When he'd captured a child's spirit, Le Docteur Duvalier made it do his bidding. He used them to fool the guardians who watched over his enemies into giving away their secrets, see if they were plotting to get rid of him.'

'And for that he got – what did Baron Samedi give him? The Presidency?'

'Yes. And once he'd got it, Baron Samedi kept him in power, gave him dominion over all his enemies – as long as he made the offerings and continued to do his *loas's* bidding.'

'And you believe this?'

'Maurice said Baron Samedi used to appear in the room, during the ceremony.'

'Yeah? Sure it wasn't the same guy was in that James Bond movie?'

'You can mock all you want, Mr Mingus, but Le Docteur Duvalier was a very powerful man –'

'– who killed children – defenceless, innocent children. I don't call that *"powerful"*, Eloise. I call that weak, and cowardly and evil,' Max interrupted.

'Call it what you want,' she bristled. 'But it *worked*. No one killed him. No one overthrew him – and your people *never* invaded our homeland.'

'I'm sure there are more earthly reasons for that, and your Doc is dead,' Max said. 'Talk to me about Carver and Codada. The child kidnapping. At what point did it become a business?'

'Once Le Docteur Duvalier was in power, he rewarded Monsieur Carver with business contracts and monopolies. Maurice became security adviser. Many people who had originally backed the President fell out of favour with him, but this never happened to Monsieur Carver or Maurice. They were at his bedside when he died.'

'Touching,' Max quipped. 'So Carver built his modern business empire on the backs of kidnapped children?'

'Not to begin with. It was just expansion, growth, like they cut down forests to build roads and towns. Le Docteur Duvalier needed to make his offerings to keep going.

'Maurice told me Monsieur Carver saw the business potential when a CEO from a bauxite mining company came to Haiti. The island is naturally rich in bauxite. Monsieur Carver got involved in a potential deal, but he was up against a mining conglomerate from the Dominican Republic. He hired a private detective to do some research into the company, investigate its management. The managing director was a paedophile. He liked little Haitian boys.

'He kept a young boy in a house in Port-au-Prince. During the week the boy went to a private school. He was taught etiquette – table manners, the correct way of conducting yourself in civilized company –'

'Just like you taught?' Max interrupted.

'Yes.'

Max could see more pieces of the awful jigsaw coming together. It suited Carver's MO: he wasn't a creator, he was a parasite. He'd been born into wealth and had set about acquiring more, not through entrepreneurialism but by buying or bulldozing his way into ownership of businesses others had devoted their lives to setting up and running.

He thought of the old man, his house, his bank, his money. He felt suddenly irrelevant, cancelled out. What was he now? – a man who did good things for bad people?

'Go on,' he murmured.

'The managing director was a family man, old money, with good connections in the Dominican government. A scandal like that would have ruined him.'

'So – don't tell me – Gustav Carver presented the man with the evidence and made him pull out of the deal?'

'Yes, sort of, but not quite,' Eloise said. 'Monsieur Carver didn't know anything about bauxite mining, so he brought the Dominicans in as partners anyway.'

'And, seeing the success he'd had, and probably working out that paedophiles are an elite little group who tend to know each other, he started providing the Dominican or his "*friends*" with fresh "supplies"?' Max followed on.

'That's correct.'

'And these "*friends*" were either businessmen who Carver could cut deals with or connected to the kinds of people who could help him expand his empire?'

'That's it.'

'So, he got them children and they gave him contracts and money in exchange?' Max asked.

'And, most importantly, more connections – others like them, or others not like them – very very powerful people. Monsieur Carver *acquires* people. It's how he built his business empire into what it is – and not just here, in Haiti. He has interests all over the world.'

She stopped talking and opened up the handkerchief in her lap and folded it, very neatly, from left to right, into a triangle, which she doubled up to make another. She smoothed out the surface of the shape, admired it and undid it, working backwards.

'But there's more to it than just money and clout, isn't there?' he resumed. 'The sweet dirt he has on them, these high up, powerful people? He must have enough to bury them ten times over. He *owns* them. He has power over them. They're his slaves. He tells them to jump, they ask "how high?" Right?'

Eloise nodded.

'What about Allain Carver?' Paul looked at Eloise. 'Is he involved in this?'

'*Allain*? No. *Never!*' She smirked and then sniggered.

'What's so funny?' Max stared at her. Her smirk was irritating the hell out of him – it was the I-know-better look teachers had.

'Monsieur Carver called Allain his "dickter – daughter with a dick". He said if he'd known Allain would turn out a faggot, he would have given him away to one of his clients – for free,' she laughed.

'Fancy that,' Paul cut her off. 'He thinks gays are perverts but paedophiles aren't.'

She tried and failed to hold his look. She went back to her handkerchief, which she rolled, like pastry, into a cylinder.

'So Allain didn't know *anything*?' Max picked up again.

'*I* didn't know anything about it, Max,' Paul said.

'You're not Gustav's *son*.'

'A son he's all but disowned,' Paul reminded him. 'I believe her. I know Allain. He doesn't even know about most of his father's *legitimate* businesses. I've got the inside track, remember? Gustav kept this one *really* secret. To be doing something like that in a place this small – and *still* keep it secret. That takes some doing. And to keep it so hidden that even *I* haven't heard about it . . .'

'Everyone was implicated,' Eloise said. 'That's why no one spoke about it. And with his connections, if something ever did look like it was going to get out . . .'

'He'd crush it into nothing,' Paul finished.

Max thought about Allain. Unless he found evidence which completely exonerated him, Max decided he'd interrogate him about what he did and didn't know, all the same, just to be sure.

'Tell me about Noah's Ark.'

'No one suspected a thing. Everyone thought it was just a simple charity – and it was, for the *wrong* children.'

'What do you mean by "wrong children"?'

'The surplus – and the ones that didn't get sold.'

'Where did they end up?'

'Monsieur Carver found jobs for them.'

'Nothing wasted.' Max looked at Paul. Paul's face was rigid, his jaws clamped shut, his lips pressed tightly together. From the way he was standing, six-fingered hands half formed into fists, Max knew he was getting ready to blow. He hoped he'd have time to get everything out of Eloise before Paul tore her head off.

'When did you start "grooming" the children?'

'I must have been fifteen or sixteen. Monsieur Carver was

very proud of me. He called me. I was his favourite,' she smiled, her eyes tearing up and at the same time glowing with a cold, burning pride.

'Monsieur Carver already knew something about *vodou* potions, the ingredients that go into making the serum they give to turn people into zombies. He'd studied up on all that kind of stuff. He's a trained hypnotist, you know. He told me he'd always worked on children – poor slum kids.'

'How? Sexually?'

'He taught them manners.'

'So was it Carver's idea to take these rough kids and shape them – "groom them" – into obedient sex slaves with perfect table manners, so they'd pass in those upper circles?'

'Yes. No one buys a half-finished car.'

'Is he still doing it? Hypnotizing kids?'

'Once in a while, yes, but he's passed his skills on to people in La Gonâve.'

Max stared at a long thin crack running down the length of the wall in front of him, breaking his concentration and letting his mind wander. He was feeling angry now, bitterly sick to the stomach. He was seeing himself back at Gustav's side, looking at Mrs Carver's portrait, empathizing with the old man because they were both widowers who'd lost what they'd loved the most. He'd cherished the image, held it up as proof that Gustav Carver wasn't a monster, but a man . . . still a human being. Not even the things Vincent had told him about the old man had completely destroyed the image. But this – what he'd heard now, what he was listening to – had dissolved his fondness for the old man in acid. He wished she was lying. But she wasn't.

He had to go on, finish it.

'With the adopted kids: what happened if something went

457

wrong, say they tried to escape or tried to tell someone what's happening?'

'They're conditioned not to. Their new owners are supplied with serum, which keeps them in a —' she broke off and searched for the word, smiling when she'd landed on it '— "co-operative" state. We also have people on hand to help. If anything goes wrong, the owner calls a number and we take care of it.'

'Like an after-care service for a — a washing machine.'

'Yes,' she smiled condescendingly. 'An "after-care" service, as you put it. It covers everything from re-orientating a child — that means hypnotizing them again — to, if the matter is serious, removing him or her from circulation.'

'You mean killing them?'

'That has been necessary, yes,' she nodded. 'But seldom.'

'What about when these kids get older, d'you kill 'em too?'

'That has been sometimes necessary also,' Eloise agreed. 'But seldom. Usually they grow up and move on. Sometimes they stay with their owner.'

'Like you did?'

'Yes.'

'What about if I was a client with special desires. Say I wanted an Asian kid.'

'That can easily be arranged. We have branches all over the world. We'd just fly one in for you.'

Max switched back to Charlie.

'What about a handicapped child?'

'It hasn't been done before, that I know of. But there are no limits, no extremes, no places we won't go — but that has never been requested,' she said.

Max gave Paul a quick look and shook his head. *They didn't have Charlie. They didn't take him.*

'Who kidnapped Charlie Carver?' he asked her.

'No one. He is dead. I'm sure of it, Maurice is sure of it. He spoke to a lot of witnesses who were there when the mob attacked the car. They all said they saw the boy being trampled and kicked around on the ground by people running at Eddie Faustin.'

'What about his body?' Max asked Eloise.

'He was a three-year-old *child*. Easy to miss.'

'But wouldn't the mob have left it behind?'

'Why? A mother or father could have taken his clothes for their own child.'

Paul breathed deep through his nostrils. Although his face was rigid and emotionless, Max heard the hurt echo deep within him in the way the air passed into his lungs with staccato rhythms. Paul believed her. His son was dead.

Max studied Eloise to see if she'd heard or noticed anything, but she was keeping her eyes down, worrying the ends of her handkerchief.

Max couldn't be sure Charlie was dead. Something screamed at him that it wasn't so.

What about Filius Dufour? What about Francesca's certainty that he was still alive?

The voice of reason countered:

You believe an old fortune teller and a grieving mother? Come on!

Max was almost done with Eloise.

'And how involved was Gustav Carver in the day-to-day running of this business?'

'Up until his stroke he was *very* involved in it. Like I said to you before, he is Tonton Clarinette.'

'How?'

'He played his part in hypnotizing the children.'

'How?'

'Did you find the CDs in the study?'

Max nodded.

'Did you listen to them?'

'Not yet. What'll I hear?'

'*Do-Re-Mi-Fa-So* – each individual note, played on a clarinet, with a short gap in between. On each CD an individual note is held longer. For example, on the blue one it's *Re*, on the red one it's *Fa*, and so on. They're codes,' Eloise explained. 'They get implanted into the children's minds when they're being hypnotized.

'There are six stages to our hypnosis process. The first three strip away what you know and the last three replace it with what we want you to know. For example: a lot of the children – say ninety per cent of them – were off the streets. They didn't know anything about table manners, using a knife and fork. They ate like monkeys, with their hands. Under hypnosis, they'd be conditioned not to do that, to lose the association of consuming food with their fingers, to *forget* they ever ate food like that – to *unlearn*, if you will.'

'But they could learn that anyway?' Max said.

'Of course. Most people learn through repetition, trial and error. But that's time consuming,' she explained.

'So their minds associated a certain behavioural pattern with a certain code? Like a reaction – like that dog that got taught to sit up and wag its tail whenever it heard a bell ringing – Pavlov's dog?'

'That's exactly it – conditioning,' Eloise said.

'And let me guess: the perverts used the codes to keep the kids in line?'

'Yes,' Eloise nodded. 'The *Clarinette* codes induced Pavlovian reactions. The clients play a certain set of codes to get what they wanted out of their child. For example, if they want full sexual compliance, they play a disc where the codes run backwards. If they want the child to be on his or her best behaviour in front of adult company, they'd play a

460

disc where *Re* is the dominant note. You get the picture?'

'In Technicolor,' Max mumbled disgustedly. He looked at Paul and felt his gaze buried deep behind the shadows in his sockets. He sensed waves of rage coming off him. He turned back to Eloise. 'You used that zombie potion too, didn't you?'

'How did you know?'

'Got it all on tape,' Max said.

'Tape? Where did you find it?' She looked worried.

'It doesn't matter. Answer my questions: zombie juice – why was it used?'

'To keep the children docile and receptive to conditioning. It's easier to manipulate a stupefied mind.'

Max shook his head and then rubbed his temples. He needed to stop – stop hearing this, stop being here.

'So you're telling me that's Gustav Carver on those CDs, right? Playing the clarinet?'

'He used to participate in the hypnosis. He'd sit and play his clarinet to condition the children. When you get to the headquarters on La Gonâve you'll find the video vault – there are plenty of tapes and photographs of him sitting in the middle of groups of children,' Eloise said. 'Maurice told me he once asked him why he participated, why he didn't just record the notes once. Monsieur Carver said it was the closest he came to having *"absolute power"*.'

'When did he stop playing?'

'Some time in the mid-eighties – because of his illness. *He* might have retired, but his myth didn't.'

'Mr Clarinet – Ton-ton Clarinet?'

'Yes, like I keep saying, Tonton Clarinette is real. Tonton Clarinette is Monsieur Carver – Gustav Carver.'

'But if it's all supposed to be a secret, how did the myth get out?'

'A few of the children escaped over the years,' she said quietly. 'Not from us, but from their masters. Three are still at large.'

'Was one called Boris Gaspésie?'

'Yes. How did you know?'

'I ask, you answer. What about the others?'

'The boy and two girls – Lita Ravix and Noëlle Perrin.'

Max wrote down the two names. He was done with her. He gave a long hard look, searching those rat-like features for something close to regret or shame for what she'd done. There was nothing of the sort there. There never had been.

He nodded to Paul to indicate that he was through, then he got up and left the room.

53

Max paced around in the street outside the house, his head churning with all the revelations.

He'd need to see all the evidence and, above all, confront Gustav Carver to be sure – even if he believed Eloise was telling the truth. She didn't have a lying way about her because all the self-preservation instincts had been brutalized out of her. Liars tripped themselves up with inconsistencies and improbabilities, often in the smallest details, the loose threads that when tugged unravelled the whole tapestry. What Eloise had told him all fitted, all flowed in one direction.

What he couldn't understand was what Gustav had been thinking, getting outsiders in to investigate Charlie's disappearance. Hadn't he thought that they might find out about his business along the way? Hadn't he at least considered it a risk?

Of course he had, Max concluded. You don't stay on top of your game for as long as Gustav had by flying close to the sun. People like Gustav never took blind risks, they took informed risks. They didn't just look before they leapt, they knew every single millimetre of the ground they'd land on.

But then, like all absolute tyrants, Carver had always had his own way. He'd never met a challenge he hadn't flattened. So what if he got found out? What could one person do against Carver and his network of contacts who, even if they were a fraction as powerful as Eloise had suggested, would wipe that person clean off the face of the planet?

Carver considered himself untouchable, and with good reason.

Had Gustav Carver been behind what had happened to Beeson and Medd? Had they got too close? No. Max didn't think so. At least definitely not Beeson. Beeson would have tried to blackmail Carver and Carver would have had him killed. Why leave him alive so he could tell people what he knew?

So what about the reason he'd originally come here? Charlie Carver? What *had* happened to him?

He didn't know for sure, but he suspected he was dead.

What about Eddie Faustin? What part did he play? He'd *definitely* been trying to kidnap the boy the day he was killed. That was beyond doubt. Faustin had been waiting for the kidnappers to come and get Charlie at a pre-arranged rendezvous, and then the mob had turned up and things had gone badly wrong.

Or had they?

Maybe Eddie *had* been set up, double-crossed by the kidnappers. It was possible. They'd paid the mob to start a riot around the car and kill the ex-Macoute. It would make sense if the kidnappers wanted to avoid being identified – or suspected.

Yet Codada had said that Faustin was loyal to Gustav Carver, that he loved him like a father. Why would he betray him? What had the kidnappers offered him? Or maybe they hadn't offered him anything at all – maybe they had something on him. That wasn't hard – an ex-Macoute with bloody hands, now working for the head of a child sex ring.

How much had Faustin known about Gustav's business? Was the kidnapping related to it?

But that still left Charlie unaccounted for and unexplained.

What was there to go on?

He didn't know. He'd hit a dead end.

Where to now?

Half an hour later, Paul came out to join him in the street.

'She's given me the location of the place in La Gonâve. They've got about twenty kids in there now. They used a cargo boat to get them over there. Every month they fill the hold up with new kids,' Paul said. 'We'll be getting them out tomorrow evening.'

'What about the military here?'

'It'll be a joint operation with the UN. I have a good friend there,' Paul explained.

'What about Gustav?' Max asked.

'You bring him in.'

'*Me?*'

'Yes, you, Max. Tomorrow. I want to avoid casualties. If we go up to the Carver estate his people will start shooting. The Americans are stationed quite close by and they'll come to investigate. Knowing them they'll kill all of us and tell Carver to have a nice day.'

'He's got a *lot* of security.'

'You'll have plenty of back-up, if you need it. Our guys will follow you up to the estate and wait close by. You'll have radio contact with them.'

'Assuming I get him out, where do I take him?'

'Get him out on the main road. We'll take him from there.'

Max didn't want to do it. He'd never had to bring a client in, and he remembered the affection he'd had for Gustav, the one and only time they'd met before.

'Make sure you tell Francesca so she's out of the way. Allain too.'

'It's in hand,' Vincent said and started heading back to the house.

'What about them – Codada and Eloise?' Max asked. 'You gonna let them live?'

'Would *you?*'

54

The next morning Max woke up with the phone ringing in his ears.

It was Joe. He was all apologies. He said he'd been too busy to work on the stuff Max had asked for.

Max told him he needed to talk to Clyde Beeson. Joe said that was the main reason he was calling.

Beeson had been found dead in his trailer. Forensics estimated he'd been there at least two weeks. His pitbull had eaten away one leg and was working on the second when the cops had broken down the door. Although the postmortem report had yet to confirm it, it looked like suicide. Beeson had opted out with his Magnum.

Max took the news quietly, bitterly disappointed that he hadn't had a chance to have a detailed talk with Beeson about the case that had ruined his life.

That Beeson had died bad, he wasn't surprised. He'd had it coming. He'd scored impressive results and made a small fortune off the back of them, but he'd pissed off a lot of people along the way; Max had been one of them, Joe another. He'd come within a hair of ruining their lives. They'd come within a hair of killing him.

Sadness and even a sense of pity didn't orbit his thoughts. Max had loathed and despised him.

'Anything you want to say about the late Clyde Beeson?' Joe asked,

'Yeah. *Adios, motherfucker.*'

55

Gustav Carver smiled warmly when he saw Max walk into the living room, his great gargoyle face turning into something straight out of a horror cartoon as it registered, processed and displayed his pleasure: his eyebrows creased into upward arrowheads, his brow furrowed disjointedly like the spring bands on a collapsed chest expander, and his lips thinned to pale pink rubber bands as they stretched and curved towards his earlobes.

'Max! Welcome!' Gustav shouted to Max across the empty space.

They shook hands when they met. Carver over-applied his grip and accidentally pulled Max forward into him. They bumped shoulders, awkwardly, jock-style by default, neither knowing the drill. Carver, who had been using his other hand to balance himself on his silver-topped black cane, staggered back and threatened to keel over but Max grabbed hold of him and steadied him. Gustav righted himself with Max's help, took in the remains of the minor panic in Max's expression and giggled almost coquettishly. He smelled strongly of booze, cigarettes and musky cologne.

Max noticed a tall Christmas tree in the corner of the room, not too far from Judith Carver's portrait. It had fibre-optic lights, hidden among the pines, which morphed continuously into shades of red, purple and blue before stopping at a steady all-white and then repeating the colour changes. The rest of the tree was decorated with twinkling gold and silver streamers, hanging baubles and a golden star at the top. It was surprising to find something so tacky in Carver's tasteful surroundings.

Gustav seemed to read Max's thoughts.

'That's for the servants. Those damn lights fascinate them, simpletons that they are. One night of the year I let them use the room. I buy presents for them and their children and they go and find them. Do you like Christmas, Max?'

'I'm not sure any more, Mr Carver,' Max said, quietly.

'I *hate* it. It's when I lost Judith.'

Max stayed silent – not out of awkwardness, but because nothing in him was moving in the old man's favour.

Gustav looked at him curiously, brow tensing, eyes narrowing and crinkling at the corners, a hostile wariness about his expression. Max met his gaze with a blank look, giving nothing away except his indifference.

'How's about a drink?' Carver insisted rather than offered. He wafted his cane over the armchairs and sofas. 'Let's sit.'

He sunk into the armchair one haunch at a time, his bones creaking and popping with the strain. Max didn't offer to help him.

Gustav clapped his hands and barked for a servant. A black-and-white-uniformed maid stepped out from the darkness surrounding the doorway, where she had probably been standing the entire time. Max had neither seen nor sensed her until she appeared. Carver asked for whiskey.

Max sat close to the armchair.

Carver leant across to the coffee table and picked up a silver box filled with untipped cigarettes. He took one out, put the box back and picked up a smoked-glass ashtray with a silver lighter inside it. He lit up, took a deep drag and held on to the smoke for a few seconds before letting it out slowly.

'From the Dominican Republic, these,' Carver said,

holding up the cigarette. 'They used to make them here. Hand-rolled. There was a shop in Port-au-Prince run by two women – ex-nuns. Tiny place called *Le Tabac*. All they did all day was sit in the window and roll cigarettes. I watched them once for about an hour. I just sat in the back of my car and observed them at it. Pure concentration, pure dedication. Such craft, such skill. Customers would come in all the time and interrupt them to buy a couple of cigarettes. One would serve while the other carried on. Me? I'd buy two hundred. The amazing thing is that each one of those cigarettes was identical. You couldn't tell them apart. *Amazing.* Such precision, dedication. You know, I used to make all my employees sit outside the shop to watch those ladies work – to teach them to adopt virtues like diligence and attention to detail in their work for me.

'Those cigarettes were wonderful. A deep, rich and very *satisfying* smoke. The best I've ever had, I think. These aren't too bad, but there's nothing like the original.'

'What happened to the shop?' Max asked out of politeness rather than interest. He had to cough and clear his throat to make his voice heard – not that there was a blockage. He was getting nervous, dark energy coursing through him, muscles tightening, his heart pumping ever harder and louder.

'Oh, one of them got Parkinson's Disease and couldn't work any more, and the other closed up the shop to look after her. Or so I heard.'

'At least it wasn't cancer.'

'They didn't smoke,' laughed Carver, as the maid reappeared with a bottle of whiskey, water, ice and two glasses on a tray. 'I always drink and smoke at this time of year. Damn the doctors! What about you? Care to indulge?'

Max said no with a shake of his head.

'But you *will* join me for a drink?'

An order not an offer: Max nodded and tried a smile, but the insincerity made his lips coagulate into a crumpled pout. Carver shot him another curious look, this one laced with suspicion.

The maid deflected attention off him by pouring the drinks. Carver took his whiskey neat. Max took it with ice and water almost to the brim. When she was gone they clinked glasses and toasted each other's health, the coming year and a happy conclusion to Max's investigation. Max pretended to take a sip.

He'd sat at home trying to work out the best way to tell Carver that he was taking him in. He'd contemplated just walking in and confronting him with what he knew and then marching him out to his car. But he'd nixed that because he wasn't a cop.

He'd decided to get Carver to confess to what he'd done, own up to having masterminded the sex ring and even explain his actions and justify them. He'd spent the entire day planning it, how he'd lure Carver further and further into implicating himself, all the while shutting off every escape route until the old man's admission of guilt became a formality, the symbolic toppling of the chessboard king.

All day in the house he'd worked up his strategy, anticipating the many possible turns the confrontation would take and preparing the response he'd have waiting at every corner. He rehearsed his questions and worked on his voice until he reached the light, conversational, friendly, open, seemingly unguarded tone he was looking for: all bait and no hook.

Paul had called in the afternoon, told him to go get the old man after they'd taken the house in La Gonâve. He'd arranged for Allain to phone him on the pretext of inviting him up to the house for an update. Paul said that Allain was pretty broken up at having to make the call. To him it was his father he was betraying, not a criminal he was setting up for the fall.

By nightfall everything was straight in his head. He'd showered, shaved, and changed into a loose shirt and pants. At around nine Allain had called. Max guessed Paul's operation had been a success.

As he was driving out of the house he'd been stopped by some of Paul's men in a jeep. They'd handed him an unsealed envelope and told him he was to give it to Gustav when the time was right.

Then they told him he'd have to wear a wire when he saw Gustav.

That had upset everything – at least in his head.

He'd never worn a snitch socket in his life. He'd been on the other end, listening in. They were leads you put on vermin to take you to bigger vermin.

He was told it was for his own protection, that he couldn't go in there carrying a walkie-talkie.

Yes, sure, *that* made perfect sense, but it was the rest he objected to – being Paul's stoolie, getting Gustav Carver to incriminate himself on tape, to confess and sign his death warrant.

He'd thought about it – not long, because he didn't have much time and he really didn't have any option but to accept what he couldn't refuse.

They'd all gone back to the house. He'd shaved his chest and they'd taped the mic just above the nipple, the lead running down his torso and curling around his back like an elongated leech, stopping at a receiver and battery clipped to his trousers.

They ran a test. He heard his voice loud and clear.

They walked back to their cars. He asked how things had gone in La Gonâve. He was told they'd gone very well.

On his way driving up to the Carver estate he decided that the thing he wanted most of all for Christmas was to be done with this, with Haiti, with Carver, with this case.

He accepted that his case was over: Charlie Carver was dead and his body would most likely never be recovered. The mob that had killed Eddie Faustin had trampled him to death.

That fit, that made sense and added up quite tidily, at least on paper.

It would do, but it wasn't really enough. Not for him, not if he wanted to sleep easy for the rest of his life.

He needed more proof that the boy was dead.

But how would he get it? And why?

But who was he kidding with *that* bullshit now? He wasn't a private detective any more, remember? That was all over. He was finished. Hell, he'd been finished from the moment he'd shot those kids in New York. He'd crossed a line you didn't come back from. He was a convicted murderer; he'd taken three young lives in cold blood. That cancelled out everything he'd once been and much of what he'd stood for.

And now he was setting up his former client. He'd never ratted out a client before and he'd never known an investigator who had – not even Beeson. It was something you didn't ever do, part of a long code of inviolable ethics, all of it unwritten, all of it handed down in whispers and winks.

Carver was, not surprisingly, drinking a very good whiskey. Max could smell the quality coming out of his glass, even under all the water it had been doused with.

'Allain and Francesca will be down shortly,' Gustav said.

No they won't, thought Max. He had passed them both on his way up, being driven away by Paul's men.

'So? How's the investigation going?' Gustav asked.

'Not too well, Mr Carver. I think I've hit a dead end.'

'It happens in your profession, I'm sure, as it happens in most professions that require brains and drive, no? Go down a road and hit a block, what do you do? You go back to the start and find another way around.'

Carver drilled Max with a fierce look from his practically black eyes. The old man was dressed as Max remembered him from the last time they'd met – beige suit, white shirt, black shoes buffed to a dazzle.

'Is this constipation of yours a very recent thing? Allain told me, not a few days ago, that you were on to something – close to a breakthrough?' Carver's voice had an undertow of contempt about it now. He crushed out his cigarette and put the ashtray on the table. A maid came almost immediately and replaced the ashtray with an identical, clean one.

'I *was* on to something,' Max confirmed.

'And?'

'It wasn't what I was expecting.'

Gustav studied Max's face, looked it over like he'd seen something about it he hadn't seen before, then he smiled very slightly.

'You *will* find my grandson. I know you will.' He slung back his drink.

Max thought of three possible responses to that – witty, sarcastic and bubble-bursting confrontational. He used none, merely smiled and lowered his eyes to make Carver think he was flattered.

'Are you all right?' Carver asked, scrutinizing him. 'You don't seem yourself.'

'What self would that be?' Max asked, only it wasn't a question, it was a statement.

'The man who was here last. The one I admired – the

gung-ho-shitkicker – John Wayne-Mingus. Sure you're not coming down with something? You haven't been with one of the local whores, have you? Open those legs and you'll find an encyclopedia of venereal disease.' Carver chuckled, missing what was happening right next to him. Max had taken his gloves off. The interrogation was about to start.

Max shook his head.

'So what's the *matter* with you, eh?' Carver swiftly leant over, clapped Max hard on the back and laughed. 'You haven't even touched your damn drink!'

Max stared hard at Carver, who stopped laughing. He was still smiling but it was only wrinkles and teeth; all merriment had fled his face.

'It's Vincent Paul, isn't it?' Gustav sat back. 'You've spoken to him. He told you things about me, didn't he?'

Max didn't reply, didn't let it rattle him. He just carried on giving Gustav his spotlight beams, his face a mask of indifference.

'I'm sure he told you some terrible things about me. Terrible things. The sort that would make you question what you're doing working for me – "monster" that I am. But you have to bear in mind that Vincent Paul hates me – and a man who hates *that* hard is always going to work overtime to justify that hatred and – especially – to convert others to his way of thinking.' Carver chuckled but he didn't meet Max's eye. He leant over the table and took another cigarette out of the box. He tapped either end on his palm before putting it in his mouth and lighting it. 'You, of all people, I'm sure, don't need *that* pointed out to him.'

'He didn't take Charlie,' Max said.

'Oh, what utter *blasted rubbish!*' Carver thundered, making a fist of his cigarette hand.

'He *was* there the day Charlie was kidnapped, but he wasn't

475

the kidnapper,' Max insisted, raising his voice, but staying calm.

'What is *the matter* with you, Mingus?' Carver said, wheezing a little. 'I *tell* you, it's him.'

'And I tell you, quite clearly, it isn't him. He *didn't* do it. Kidnapping children isn't his style, Mr Carver,' Max said pointedly.

'But he's a drug dealer.'

'Drug *baron*, actually,' Max corrected.

'What's the difference – do they live a year longer?'

'Something like that, yeah.'

'So what did he *say* to you, Vincent Paul?'

'Many things, Mr Carver. Many *many* things.'

'Such as . . . ?' Carver threw his arms open in mock invitation. 'Did he tell you what I did to his father?'

'Yeah. You ruined his career, and –'

'I didn't "ruin his career". The poor sap was going out of business anyway. I just put him out of his misery.'

'You destroyed their estate. You didn't have to do that.'

'They owed me money. I collected. All's fair in love and war, Mr Mingus. And business is war – and I *love* it.'

Carver laughed acidly. He poured himself more whiskey.

'How did you feel, after the Paul sob story?'

'I could understand why he would hate you, Mr Carver,' Max answered. 'I could even sympathize with someone like him, in a place like this, where you're only as powerful as you make yourself, and that old school eye for eye and tooth for tooth revenge is the only way you get even.

'And I understand how someone like you, who knows the true meaning of hatred and hating, would see the point of view of someone like Vincent Paul – a man who hates another man because of some bad stuff one did to the other. You wouldn't have it any other way, Mr Carver. Because for you, there *is* no other way. Hatred begets hatred and you're all right with that. Suits you fine.'

'So you think I'm a "monster"? Join the club!'

'I wouldn't call you a monster, Mr Carver. You're just a man. Most men are good, some are bad – and then some are *real* bad, Mr Carver,' Max said, keeping his voice low, but clear, his eyes two blade points.

Carver sighed, sunk his whiskey and dropped his cigarette in the glass where it fizzled out in the residue.

'You take the word of a drug dealer – no, a "drug *aristocrat*", as you put it, over mine. You're a policeman, Mr Mingus – a *disgraced loser* of a policeman – but once a policeman *always* a policeman. You *know* the damage that man's poison does to your countrymen, to their children. You've seen it. Your friends and colleagues have seen it. Drugs are the single biggest menace to western society. And yet you are quite happy to take the side of one of its major suppliers.'

'I *know* what Vincent Paul does, Mr Carver. And – as of a few hours ago – I *know* what you do.'

'I don't follow.'

'Well. At this very moment your property in La Go-Nav is under new ownership. Your business there has been closed down.'

That hit Carver so quick and hard he had no time to cover up his shock. For a fraction of a second Max saw him exposed and looking as close to scared as he imagined a man ever could be without screaming.

Carver reached slowly for his cigarette box. As a precaution Max unclipped the trigger guard on his gun holster, even though he doubted the old man was packing or anywhere near a firearm.

The maid appeared silently out of the shadows, replaced

the whiskey glass and ashtray with clean ones and hurried out, head bowed.

Max wasn't going to force anything out of the old man because he didn't think he'd have to. Carver would talk when he was good and ready.

The old man poured himself another whiskey, this one almost to the brim. Then he fired up another cigarette and settled back in his chair.

'I assume you already know what Paul's men will find there in La Gonâve?' Carver asked, a little wearily.

'Children?'

'Twenty or so,' Carver confirmed with a calm and openness that disconcerted Max.

'You've got records there too, right? Details of each and every sale – who, what, where.'

'Yes,' Carver nodded. 'Filmed and photographic evidence too. But those aren't the crown jewels. By going into that house, the way you people have . . . Do you have the slightest *idea* what you're opening up?'

'Tell me.'

'This will make Pandora's Box look like a tin of peanuts.'

'I understand you're well connected, Mr Carver,' Max deadpanned.

'*Well connected*!' he laughed. 'Well connected? I'm plugged into the fucking *grid*, Mingus! Do you know I am one phone call from having you killed and two calls from making you disappear without trace, make it like you never existed. Do you know that? *That's* the kind of power I wield – THAT is how "well connected" I am.'

'I don't doubt that, Mr Carver. But those one or two phone numbers ain't gonna help you now.'

'Oh? Why not?'

'The phone lines have been cut. Try it.' Max pointed to

a telephone he spied on the other side of the room.

When he'd driven up the mountain road, he'd seen people working on the telegraph poles.

Carver snorted contemptuously and pulled hard on his cigarette.

'What do you want from me, Mingus? *Money?*'

'No,' Max shook his head. 'I have questions I need answers to.'

'Let me guess: why did I do this?'

'That's a good enough place to start.'

'Do you know that in Greek or Roman times it was common for adults to have sex with children? It was commonplace. It was accepted. Today, in the non-Western world, girls are married off to grown men at the age of twelve, sometimes. And in your country, teenage pregnancies are *legion!* Underage sex, Mr Mingus, is *everywhere* – always was, always will be.'

'Those weren't no *teenagers.*'

'Oh, damn you and your *stupid* morality, Mingus!' Carver spluttered, stabbing out his cigarette and swallowing a good gulp of whiskey. 'People like you with your self-righteous codes of conduct and ethics, with your secular notions of right and wrong, you always end up working for people like *me* – people unencumbered by things like "feelings" and "consideration for others" – the very things that hold you back. I do things you wouldn't even think about doing. You think you're tough, Mingus? You've got *nothing* on me.'

'Some of those kids looked no more than six years old,' Max said.

'Yeah? You know what? I've had a *freshly born baby* stolen from right under its mother's nose, because that was what one of my clients *desired.* It cost him two million dollars and bought me a lifetime's influence. It was *worth* it.'

479

Carver was raging on whiskey fumes, but this wasn't the drunk bragging of a man who didn't give a fuck until the hangover kicked in. He would have said the same thing and had the same attitude in identical circumstances if he'd been sober. He meant every word he said.

The maid reappeared, replaced the whiskey tumbler and ashtray and quickly left with the used ones.

'What's the matter, Mingus? You look ill. This too much for you to *handle*?' Carver sneered, slapping the armrest. 'What were you expecting – a *mea culpa*? *FROM ME*?! *FUCK THAT!*'

Max doubted the old man really understood his predicament. Decades of having everything his own way had blinded him to the obvious and the certain. He'd never faced someone he couldn't bribe, corrupt or destroy. Nothing had stood in his way that he hadn't bulldozed or bought out. Right now, he was probably thinking that all of his paedophile clients would come to his aid, that the pervert cavalry would come riding over the hill to rescue him. Maybe he was thinking of bribing Max out of taking him in. Or maybe he had something else up his sleeve, some trap door that would suddenly open beneath his feet and drop him to freedom.

From outside the room Max heard a short cry and the sound of breaking glass. He looked at the doorway and saw nothing.

'But you're a father yourself . . .' Max began.

'That never stopped *anyone* and *you* know it!' Carver snapped. 'What do you take me for? I'm a professional: I keep an emotional distance from everything I do. It allows me to perform unpleasant tasks with impunity.'

'So you admit that what you've been doing is –'

'*Unpleasant*? Of course it is! I *hate* the people I deal with. I *despise* them.'

'But you've done business with them for –'

'Close to forty years, yes. You know why? I have no conscience. I eradicated that from my way of thinking a long time ago. Having a conscience is an overrated pastime.' Carver edged closer to him. 'I may hate them, but I *understand* paedophiles. Not what they do – that's not for me. But who they *are*, where they're coming from. They're all the same. They never change: they're all ashamed of what they do, of what they like, of what they are. And most of all they're all *terrified* of being found out.'

'And you exploited that?'

'*Absolutely!*' Carver exclaimed, clapping his big hands together for emphasis. 'I'm a businessman, Mingus, an entrepreneur. I saw a market with a potentially loyal customer base and plenty of repeat trade.'

'You also saw people you could blackmail . . .'

'I never "blackmailed" anyone, as you put it. I've never had to threaten a single one of my clients into opening doors for me.'

'Because they already know the score?'

'Exactly. These are people who move on higher planes. People whose reputations are *everything*. I've never abused our relationship, never asked for more than, maybe, *two* favours from any *one* person in all the time I've known them.'

'And these "favours"?' Max asked. 'What did they give you? Trade monopolies? Access to confidential US government files?'

Carver shook his head, smirking.

'Contacts.'

'More paedophiles? Ones on even *higher* planes?'

'Absolutely! You know the maxim that you're only six people away from any one person? When you have the *esoteric* interests my clients do, Mr Mingus, you're more like *two* people away.'

'Everybody knows everybody else?'

'Yes. To a degree. I don't deal with *any* everybody.'

'Only the ones you can get something out of?'

'I'm a businessman, not a charity worker. There has to be something in it for me. Risk versus reward.' Carver reached for another cigarette. 'How do you think we got to you, in prison? All those calls? Did you ever think of that?'

'I guessed you had juice.'

'"*Joose*"!' Carver erupted in laughter, mimicking Max's accent. '"*Joose*", you call it? Ha, ha! You damn Yankee Doodlers and your slang! Sure I've got "*Joose*", Mingus! I've got the whole fucking *orchard* – *and* the pickers *and* the pressers *and* the damn packagers! How about a prominent East Coast senator who's very good friends with someone on the damn Rikers board? How's that for "*Joose*"?'

Carver lit his cigarette.

'Why me?' Max asked.

'You were – in your prime – one of the best private detectives in the country, if not *the* best, if your ratio of solved to unsolved cases was anything to go by. Friends of mine sung your praises till they were blue in the face. You even came *damn* close to uncovering us once or twice in your earlier career. *Damn* close. Do you know that? I was suitably impressed.'

'When?'

'That's for me to know and you to find out.' Carver smiled as he blew pale blue tusks of smoke through his nose. 'How did you find out about me? Who broke? Who cracked? Who betrayed me?'

Max didn't reply.

'Oh, come on, Mingus! Tell me! What does it fucking matter?'

Max shook his head.

Carver's face dropped to an ungainly angry heap some-where past his nose. His eyes narrowed to slits and blazed behind them.

'I *order* you to tell me the name!' he yelled, grabbing his cane from the back of the chair and pushing himself up.

'Sit down, Carver!' Max shot up from his chair, snatched the cane and pushed the old man roughly back on his seat. Carver looked at him, surprised and afraid. Then he glanced at the cigarette burning in his ashtray and crushed it out.

'You're outnumbered here,' he leered up at Max. 'You could beat me to death with that' – he nodded at the cane – 'but you wouldn't get out of here alive.'

'I'm not here to kill you,' Max said, glancing over his shoulder, expecting to see the maid coming for the ashtray and maybe others with her, rushing to their master's defence. There was no one there.

He dropped the cane on the couch and sat down.

Then heavy footsteps entered the room. Max turned around and saw two of Paul's men standing near the entrance. He held his hand up for them to stay put.

Carver saw them and snorted contemptuously.

'Looks like the odds just changed,' Max said.

'Not really,' Carver said.

'Your servants? You got them from Noah's Ark, didn't you?'

'Of course.'

'They weren't good enough for your "clients"?'

'That's right.'

'They were lucky.'

'Really? You call their life "lucky"?'

'Yeah. They didn't spend their childhood getting raped.'

Carver gave him a long look, scrutiny that gradually turned to amusement.

'How long have you been here, Mingus, in this country? Three, four weeks? Do you know why people have children here? The poor, the masses? It's not for the same cutesy reasons you have them back in America: you know, because you want to – most of the time.

'The poor don't *plan* to start families here. It just *happens*. They just *breed*. That's all there is to it. They fuck, they multiply. They're human *amoebas*. And when the babies are old enough to walk their parents put them to work, doing what they do. Most of the people in this country are born on their knees – born slaves, born to serve, no better off than their *pathetic* ancestors.'

Carver paused for breath and another cigarette.

'You see – what I do, what I've done – I've given these kids a life they couldn't possibly hope to have, a life that their dumb, illiterate, no-hoper parents couldn't even have *dreamt* about because they weren't born with brains *big* enough. Not all of them suffer. I've educated almost all the ones I couldn't sell, and all those who made the grade I've given jobs to. A lot of them have gone on to do very well for themselves. Do you know what I've helped create here? Something we didn't have before – a middle class. Not rich, not poor, but in the middle, with aspirations to do better. I've helped this country become that little bit normal, that little bit Western, in line with other places.

'And as for those I sold. Well, do you know how some of them end up, Mingus? The clever ones, the tough ones, the survivors? When they get old enough, they wise up and they play their sugar daddies like big fat pianos. They end up wealthy, set for life. Most of them go on to lead perfectly normal lives in civilized countries – new names, new identities – the past just a bad blurry memory – if *that*.

'You think of me as evil, I know, but I have given *thousands* of people honour, dignity, money and a home. I've given them someone they can respect when they look in the mirror. Hell – I gave them the damn mirror too. In short, Mr Mingus, I've given them *life!*'

'You're *not* God, Carver.'

'Oh no? Well then, I'm the next best thing in a place like this – a white man with money!' he thundered. 'Servitude and kowtowing to the white man is in this country's DNA.'

'I beg to differ, Mr Carver,' Max said. 'I don't know too much about this place, true. But from what I can see, it's been royally fucked over by people like you – you rich folk with your big houses and servants to wipe your asses. Take, take, take – never give a damn thing back. You're not helping anyone but yourself, Mr Carver. Your charity's just a lie you tell people like me to make us look the other way.'

'You're sounding just like Vincent Paul. How much is he paying you?'

'He's not paying me *anything*, Mr Carver. You never did tell me why you insisted on bringing *me* in to look for Charlie, seeing as I'd almost caught you once.'

'The operative word is "almost".' Carver managed to smile, despite the snarl in his voice. 'You only saw what you could prove, what you could believe. You were interested in the pixels, not the whole picture.'

'You thought I'd stick to looking for Charlie and ignore the rest?'

'By and large, yes.'

'You got me wrong, by and large, didn't you?' Max chuckled.

Carver glowered at him.

'I have a question for you,' Max said.

'Shoot.'

'Who do you think has Charlie?'

'That's *still* your job,' Carver murmured and looked away.

He clenched his paw into a fist. Max watched him crying very quietly and gently, in small shakes and smaller sips of air. Max looked at the open cigarette box and a mad craving suddenly leapt out of nowhere and jumped on his shoulders. He suddenly wanted a smoke, something to do with his hands, something to take the edge off what he was sitting through. Then he spied his glass of diluted whiskey and considered downing that for a while, but he shook off the temptation.

'I knew about little Charlie, you know,' Carver said, without turning back to Max, addressing the bookshelves. 'I knew the first time I saw him. I knew that he wasn't mine. She tried to keep it from me. But I *knew*. I knew he wasn't mine.'

'How?' Max asked. He hadn't expected this.

'Not *completely* mine,' Carver continued in the same tone, as if he hadn't heard Max's question. 'Autism. It's a possessive illness. It keeps a little of the person for itself and never *ever* relinquishes what it has.'

'How did you know?'

'Oh, different things,' Carver said. 'Behavioural patterns not quite right. I know about children, remember?'

Max reached into his pocket and took out the envelope Paul's men had given him. He slipped out the two photocopied sheets of paper that were inside and handed them to the old man.

Then he stood up and stepped away.

Gustav Carver sniffed and wiped the tears from his eyes. He opened the sheets of paper and looked at the first. He blinked and snuffled. He looked a little closer, his mouth half opening in a bemused grin, but still heavy with sadness. He shuffled the pages – first, second, second, first – scrutinizing each. Then he held a page in each hand and looked from one to the other, back and forth, his eyes growing tinier and tinier as they disappeared behind ever more finely slitted lids. The loose folds of drooping flesh on his face began to shake, going bright red at the edges, starting around his jaw, moving up to under his eyes. He stiffened and took a deep breath.

And then he looked right at Max and screwed up the pages in his hands, chewing down the paper with his fingers. When he dropped them on the floor they were crushed and compressed into tiny pellets.

When Max had opened the envelope he'd found copies of the results of the paternity test proving Vincent Paul was Charlie Carver's father. Paul had attached a scribbled card with it:

'Max – Hand these to Gustav Carver when the time is right.'

Carver slumped back in his chair, his complexion ashen, his eyes vacant, the fight gone out of him, a monument brought crashing down to earth. If he hadn't heard what he had from the old man's lips, Max might have felt sorry for him.

They remained there in silence, one in front of the other, for a very long and slow moving moment. Gustav Carver's eyes were pointed right at him, but their stare was weightless and empty, like a dead man's.

'What do you mean to do with me, Mingus?' Carver asked, his voice sucked clean of its authority and thunder, little more than a rattle in his throat.

'Take you in.'

'Take me in?' Carver frowned. 'Take me in *where*? There are no *jails* here.'

'Vincent Paul wants to talk to you.'

'*Talk to me!*' laughed Carver. 'He wants to *kill* me, Mingus! Besides, I won't say a word to that . . . that *peasant*!'

487

'Suit yourself, Mr Carver.' Max took the cuffs off his belt.

'Wait a moment.' Carver raised his hand. 'Can I have one last drink and cigarette before you do that?'

'Go ahead,' Max said.

Carver poured out another large whiskey and lit one of his untipped cigarettes.

Max sat back down in his place.

'Mr Carver? One thing I can't understand is, with all your contacts, how come you never took Vincent Paul out?'

'Because I'm the only person who could. Everyone would have known it was me. There would have been a civil war,' he explained.

He drew on his cigarette and sipped his drink.

'I never did like filters. Killed the taste.' Carver blew on the orange coal and laughed. 'Do you think they've got cigarettes in hell, Mingus?'

'I wouldn't know, Mr Carver. I don't smoke.'

'Think you can do a little something for me?' Carver asked.

'What?'

'Let me walk out of my house? On my own? Not between those . . . goons.' He flicked his eyes at the men by the doorway.

'Yeah, but I'll have to cuff you. Precaution.'

Carver finished smoking and drinking and offered Max his wrists for the cuffs. Max made him stand up, turn around and put his hands behind his back. Carver groaned as the cuffs locked on tight.

'Let's go.' Max started leading him out towards the door, holding him tight because Carver was staggering and limping heavily.

They hadn't gone five paces before Carver stopped.

'Max, please, not like this,' he slurred, gasping booze and stale tobacco in Max's face. 'I have a pistol in my office. A revolver. Let me finish it myself. You can empty the chamber, leave me the one bullet. I'm an old man. I don't have long.'

'Mr Carver. You stole hundreds of children and ruined not just their lives, but their families' lives too. Most of all you stole their souls. You destroyed them. You took their futures. There isn't punishment enough for you.'

'You self-righteous little prick,' Carver spat at him. 'A *cold-blooded killer* lecturing *me* on morality, you —'

'You done now?' Max interrupted him.

Carver dropped his gaze. Max started dragging him towards the door. Paul's men came forward. Carver stumbled along for a few steps and then stopped again.

'I want to say goodbye to Judith.'

'Who?'

'Judith — my wife. Let me look at her painting just one more time. It was such a good painting, so lifelike, so much like her,' Carver said, his voice breaking.

'It's not her. She's dead. And you're sure to see her soon.'

'What if I don't? What if there's nothing? Just one more look, please, Mingus.'

Max thought of Sandra and relented. He waved the men back and took him to the portrait.

He propped up the old man as he gazed at the picture of his wife and mumbled to her in a mix of French and English.

Max looked at the Hall of Fame — the mantelpiece and all the framed photographs of the Carvers pressing flesh with the great and the good. He wondered if he'd find any of those famous names in the records.

Carver stopped his babbling and leered at Max.

'None of them are clients, don't worry,' he slurred. 'But they're no more than two people away. Remember that. *Two people.*'

'OK, let's go.' Max took Gustav's arm.

'Get your hands off me!' Carver jerked himself roughly out of Max's grip and tried to step back, but he lost his already precarious balance and fell heavily to the floor, landing on his back, his cuffed wrists taking the brunt of his weight.

Max didn't move to help him.

'Get up, Carver.'

The old man rolled over on his side, painfully, gasping and groaning. Then he was on his front. He tilted to his right side, pulled up his left leg, and tried to push himself up, but it was his bad side, the one he needed the cane to support, and his leg only executed a quarter move before it froze up and he rolled back on to his chest. Carver caught his breath and blinked. Then he scraped and wriggled and budged forward along the floor towards Max, wincing and snorting in agony.

When his face was at Max's toes, the old man looked up as far as he could.

'Shoot me, Max,' he pleaded. 'I don't mind dying. Shoot me here, in front of my Judith. Please!'

'You're getting up, Carver,' Max said impassively, stepping behind the old man and grabbing him roughly up by the cuff chains. He pulled him back to his feet.

'Don't hand me over to Vincent Paul, please, Max, *please*. He'll do unspeakable things to me. Please shoot me, *please*. I can accept it from you.'

'You make a lousy beggar, Carver,' Max said into his ear.

'Shoot me, Max.'

'Carver, at least try and have some *dignity*. See this?' Max unbuttoned three buttons on his shirt and showed Carver the microphone taped to his chest. 'You don't want Vincent Paul's people coming and carrying you out of here, do you?'

'Isn't that called "entrapment"?'

'Not here.'

With an expression halfway defeated and all the way disgusted, Carver nodded solemnly to the door.

'Let's go.'

Max led him out of the house.

There were three jeeploads of Paul's men outside.

All the servants and security had been rounded up and stood in the middle of the grass, guarded by four people with rifles.

'In America I'd get a fair trial,' Carver said, as he eyed the scene.

'In America you'd get the best defence lawyer your money could buy. Justice may be blind, but it sure ain't deaf, and you know same as me – ain't nothin' talks louder than cold hard cash.'

A few of the servants called out to Carver, their voices plaintive and confused, sounding like they were asking what was wrong, what was going on.

'You know what he's going to do to me, Max? That animal will rip me up and throw me to the savages. Do you want that on your conscience? Do you?'

Max gave the cuff keys to one of Paul's men, as another took hold of Carver.

'Maybe I'll do like you then,' Max said.

'How so?' Carver asked.

'Bypass my conscience.'

'Bastard!' Carver spat.

'*Me?*' Max almost laughed. 'What does that make *you?*'

'A man at peace with himself,' Carver sneered.

Max signalled to the men to take Carver.

That was when the old man erupted:

'*Damn you*, Max Mingus! *Damn you*! And *damn* Vincent

491

Paul! And *damn* each and every one of you gun-toting monkeys! *DAMN YOU!* And . . . and *damn* that little *bastard* runt and the *treacherous bitch* that hatched him! I hope you *never* find him! I hope he's *dead!*'

He glared at Max with a beady intense loathing, his breath heavy and tired, a wounded dying bull contemplating one last angry charge.

A total silence hung over the front of the house, as if Carver's roar had sucked in every immediate noise in its wake.

All eyes were on Max, waiting on his riposte.

A short time later it came:

'Adios, motherfucker.'

Then, looking at the men whose hands were clamped on Carver's arms and shoulders:

'Get this sack of shit out of here and bury him *deep.*'

56

On his way back, Max stopped off at La Coupole, where a party was in full swing. The Christmas decorations were out. The place had been decked out in tinsel and streamers and there were flashing multicoloured lights in the shape of pine trees, stuck to the walls.

The music was hideous – a medley of Christmas carols set over an unchanging pumping techno beat, sung in English by a Germanic female vocalist with an approximate grasp of the language, which rendered her pronunciation comic; 'holy night' was sung as '*holly nit*', 'Bethlehem' became a place called '*Bed-ahem*', 'Hark the herald angels sing' turned into '*Hard Gerald ankles sin*'. The atmosphere, however, was jubilant and friendly, people out having a good time. Everyone was smiling and dancing – outside, inside, behind the bar, probably in the bathroom too. Plenty of jokes and laughter were breaking up the music. The American soldiers were mixing with the UN peacekeepers, and both, in turn, were mixing with the locals. Max noticed that there were a lot more Haitians there – men and women. To his dismay, when he looked that little bit closer he noticed that the women, all of them, were whores – dresses too tight, make-up on too thick, all wearing wigs and those shop-window stares that pulled you in – and the men were their pimps; hanging back but clocking any man who came within glancing radius of their walking ATMs.

Max bought a double rum and moved out of the bar to watch the dancers in the courtyard. A drunk Marine asked him if he was Military Police, someone else asked him if he was CIA. A red-faced girl with gold studs in her ears held plastic mistletoe over his head and kissed him with lips wet with beer. She asked him if he wanted to dance and he said no thanks, maybe later. Her voice was pure Oklahoma. He watched her go off and do the same thing to a Haitian standing by the DJ booth. Seconds later they were dancing close.

He couldn't help himself. He felt bitter about what had happened, bitter about Carver, bitter about working for him. He didn't care if he'd helped bring down the old man, he didn't care that the old man was now sitting somewhere waiting for Vincent Paul to come and pass sentence. It wasn't what he'd come here for.

The horror of what he'd seen on those tapes danced dervish-like in his head.

Before he'd shot the three kids who'd tortured Manuela he'd felt an endless hollowness in his stomach, a sense of utter futility sandwiched between layers of despair; a feeling of nothing making any difference ever again, of everything just getting worse and worse until today's sickest crime became tomorrow's cat-scratch. Then he remembered what he was doing there, why he'd taken the case, why he'd devoted almost two years of his life to solving it. Manuela had smiled at him. Just the once. It was when they were on the beach – him, Sandra and Manuela. He was setting up the parasol and deckchairs. A black and white couple had strolled by hand in hand, and the woman had told them how cute their child was. She was pregnant. Max had looked at Sandra and Manuela sitting there together, and at that moment, for the first time, he'd wanted a family. Manuela might have read his mind because she caught his eye, looked right into him and smiled.

494

He'd thought of her and only her as he'd shot her killers. The last of them – Cyrus Newbury – hadn't gone quietly. He'd screamed and cried, pleaded for his life, recited half-remembered prayers and hymns. Max had let him beg himself weak, beg until he lost his voice. Then he'd blown him away.

The rum had a calming effect on him. It smothered his troubles, floated them away to some place where nothing really mattered for a while. It was good stuff, sweet painkiller.

A couple of whores in straight black wigs sidled over to him and sandwiched him, smiling. They were near-identical twins. Max shook his head and looked away. One of the girls whispered something in his ear. He didn't understand what she was saying, the music muffled her words to all but the sharpest sounds. When he shrugged his shoulders and pulled an 'I don't understand' expression she laughed and pointed to somewhere in the middle of the crowd. Max looked over at the clump of moving bodies – jeans, sneakers, T-shirts, beach shirts, vests – not seeing what he was meant to see. Then a camera flash went off. A few of the dancers were surprised and turned around to look for the source of the flash, then went back to their moves.

Max searched for the photographer from where he was, but he didn't see anyone. The girls walked away. He stepped down on the dancefloor and picked his way through the crowd to where the flash had come from. He asked the nearest dancers if they'd seen the photographer. They said, no, like him they'd only seen the light.

Max went back inside the bar to look for the girls. They were talking to two Marines. Max went up to them and was about to ask about the flash, but when he looked at them he realized that they weren't the two girls who'd accosted him. He mumbled an apology and continued looking around the bar, but he never saw them. He asked the barman, but he just shrugged. He checked the bathroom area; no one. He went outside and looked up and down; the streets were deserted.

He had a few more drinks inside. He got talking to a Sergeant Alejandro Diaz, a Miami resident. Diaz was sure Max was CIA. Max played him along for quiet laughs, neither confirming nor rubbishing the sarge's suspicions. They talked about Miami and how much they both missed the place. Diaz told him many of the places Max referred to – clubs, restaurants, record stores, dancehalls – were long gone. He recommended a new members-only place to Max called TWLM – Three Writers Losing Money – whose lapdancers, he claimed, all had masters' degrees. He gave Max a card bearing the club's name and logo – a cartoon alligator, all smiles, wearing wraparound shades and a bowler hat, holding a quill in one paw, a champagne bottle in the other – and a phone number at the bottom. Diaz told him they'd ask him for a password when he called. When Max asked him what the password was, Diaz couldn't remember it.

Max went off home at around 3.00 am, reaching his gate twenty minutes later.

He went to the living room, took off his gun holster and slumped down on the chair. He saw that the trigger guard was unfastened. He never left it open – ever – not since the time when he was a rookie and some kid had grabbed his gun.

He took the Beretta out and checked it. The bullets were all there. It hadn't been fired.

Maybe he was getting forgetful. He'd had a long day, a *momentous* day.

He considered getting up and completing the journey to bed, but he couldn't be bothered. It was too far.

He closed his eyes and fell asleep.

57

The next day he got a call from Allain. He wanted to see him that afternoon.

Allain was pale – waxy-looking, with a slight bluey tinge to his ghostly skin. A rash of stubble had advanced across the lower half of his face, and there were deep shadows under his eyes, spreading to the start of his cheeks. Max could tell he'd slept in his clothes. He was wearing his jacket to conceal a badly crumpled shirt, whose collar was crushed and whose cuffs he hadn't bothered to roll down. His tie was on crookedly, his top button undone. He'd combed his hair back, but the style was running low on brilliantine; clumps of hair were already starting to pull away from the main, leaning off to the side and pointing in different directions. It was as if someone had taken the old Allain, the first one Max had met, and gone over him with a wire scrubber; he was still recognizably all there, but much of the gloss had come off, the creases were flattened and all the edges were blunt.

They were in a meeting room on the top floor, sitting on opposite sides of a round table. They had a great view of the sea through smoked grey glass. Max thought there was water in the carafe in front of them, but when he poured himself out a glass alcohol fumes wafted out. Max tasted it. Neat vodka. Allain was almost through the glass he'd poured himself. It was 3.00 in the afternoon.

'Sorry,' Allain said sheepishly. 'I forgot.'

He wasn't drunk.

Max wanted to know how aware Allain had been of his father's activities. When he talked to him he went for the soft-track approach cops used on suspects they were engaging in seemingly casual or informal talk. It consisted of asking the same questions in different ways over the course of the conversation.

Allain had Max's plane ticket waiting for him on the table. He'd be leaving on the 11.30 flight back to Miami the following day.

'Chantale'll take you,' Allain said.

'Where is she?'

'Her mother died on Tuesday. She took her ashes back to her hometown.'

'I'm sorry to hear that,' Max said. 'Does she know what happened?'

'Yes. Some,' Allain said. 'I haven't told her the full details. I'd appreciate it if you kept those to yourself.'

'Sure.'

Max turned the subject to the raid in La Gonâve. Allain told Max what they'd found, looking absolutely horrified as he reeled off the details. When he'd said as much as he could he broke down and wept.

After he'd recovered Max resumed his questioning. Had his father never mentioned Go-Nav to him? No, never. Had his father ever played him the clarinet? No, but he knew he played. He was also a fairly gifted trumpeter. Had he ever been suspicious of why it was his father had such a vast array of business contacts? No. Why should he? The Carvers were important people in Haiti. He remembered meeting Jimmy Carter before he'd run for President. In Haiti? No, Georgia. His father had done a deal to import Carter's peanuts after the Haitian crop had failed. Carter had even

come by to say hello when he was in the country negotiating for the junta's peaceful surrender. Max went back and
forth like this, and the more he asked and the more Allain
answered, looking Max in the eye with sad, bloodshot eyes,
vision slowly steaming up with alcohol and heartbreak, the
more he convinced Max that he really didn't have a clue
about what had been going on around him.

'He hated me you know,' Allain blurted. 'He hated me for
what I was and he hated me for what I wasn't.'

He ran his hands back over his hair to smooth it down.
He wasn't wearing his watch. Max noticed a thick pink scar
over his left wrist.

'What about you, Allain? Did you hate him?'

'No,' he replied tearfully. 'I would have forgiven him if
he'd asked me.'

'Even now? With all you know?'

'He's my father,' Allain replied. 'It doesn't excuse what
he's done. That still stands. But he's my father all the same.
All we have here is ourselves and our families.'

'Did he ever use any of those psychological techniques
on you?'

'What? Hypnosis? No. He wanted to get a shrink to
straighten me out, but Mother wouldn't let me. She always
stuck up for me.' Allain looked at his blurred reflection on
the table. He finished his glass and wiped his mouth with
the back of his hand.

Then he suddenly clicked his fingers and patted at his
jacket.

'This is for you.' He pulled out a crumpled but sealed
envelope, which he held out to Max between his fingers.

Max opened it. Inside was a receipt for a money transfer
into his account in Miami.

$5,000,000.

Five million dollars.

Max was speechless.

A big pile of money on a plate.

Tomorrow he was going back to Miami. He had his life to restart. The money in his hand would be a great big help, maybe all the help he'd ever need.

Then a shadow stole up and chilled the vision.

'But . . .' Max started, looking up from the zeros.

He remembered Claudette Thodore, sold for the money that went into the Carver empire, an empire made out of the flesh and bones of children. Some of that money was in his hands, and that money was his future.

'Isn't it enough?' Allain looked suddenly frightened. 'I'll gladly pay you more. Name it.'

Max shook his head.

'I've never been paid for a job I didn't finish,' he said, finally. 'I can't even tell you for sure what happened to Charlie.'

'Vincent's back on the case again,' Allain said. 'He liked you, you know, my father. He said you were an honourable man.'

'Yeah? Well, I don't like him,' Max answered. 'And I can't accept this money.'

He put the receipt on the table.

'But it's in your account. It's yours.' Allain shrugged. 'Besides, the money doesn't know where it's come from.'

'But *I* do. And that's a big problem,' Max said. 'I'll wire it back to you as soon as I get the chance. So long, Allain.'

They shook hands, then Max walked out of the boardroom and headed for the elevator.

He parked his car near the pastel pink Roman Catholic Cathedral and walked off into downtown Port-au-Prince.

Close to the Iron Market he stopped by a building that claimed it was a church, despite looking like a warehouse from the outside.

He pushed the door open and went into what was, quite simply, the most extraordinary, beautiful chapel he'd ever seen.

At the end of the aisle, behind the altar, covering the entire wall from the ground up to three shuttered windows under the vault, was a mural, some twenty-one feet tall. He walked down between the plain-looking wooden pews and took a seat in the second row from the front. A dozen or more people – mostly women – were sitting or kneeling in various places.

The Virgin Mary, in a yellow dress and blue cape, dominated the Nativity panel. She came towards the viewer with her hands clasped over her heart and two angels behind her, holding up the ends of her cape. Behind her was an open, thatched structure, like a hut with a roof but no walls, very similar to ones he remembered seeing from his car window on rides in and out of Pétionville.

The mural panels were capped and linked by angels, playing music or bringing down garlands to the scenes below, suggesting that Jesus's life, from beginning to rebirth, was one act.

He'd sometimes cracked cases after a solo brainstorm in a church; an hour or so sitting contemplating eyeless icons and stained-glass windows, breathing in stale candle fumes, and feeling the weight of all that humbled silence around him. That had helped him get his head straight and his thoughts in line.

What now? Where was he going after this?

In the immediate, there were the same old problems he was facing before he went away: he'd have to go back to the house and face all its happy memories, massed behind the door, ready to engulf him the minute he walked in, a welcoming party of ghosts. He thought of Sandra all over again and sorrow mounted up in hot damp pressure behind his eyes and his nose.

When he got back to Miami, his career as a private detective would be over; the end of everything he knew how to do and still, somehow, *wanted* to do – despite the things he'd seen, all the danger he'd been in; despite fearing that he wasn't as good any more, that there were things here he might have missed.

What was he going to take away from Haiti? What was he going to gain? Not money, not the satisfaction of a job well done because – and for the very first time in his career – he hadn't solved the case. He was leaving unfinished business behind. The little boy's face would haunt him for the rest of his life. He was still really none the wiser about what had happened to him. It was all speculation, conjecture, rumour. Poor kid. A double innocent.

He'd helped bring down an international paedophile ring – or at least started the process of its collapse. He'd saved the lives of countless children and spared their parents a taste of death in life, of having to carry on with a loved one gone. But what of the children they'd find and free? Could they be cured? Could the process be reversed, could they put back what had been taken away? He'd have to wait and see.

Wait and see: that was the best and worst he could expect from his life now. The thought spooked and then depressed him.

He left the church an hour later, stopping a woman coming through the front door to ask her the name of the place.

'La Cathédrale Sainte-Trinité,' came the reply.

Outside the sun dazzled him and the heat and noise disorientated him for a while, as he walked through the streets, further and further from the cool, quiet, innate sombreness of the church.

He got his bearings again and walked back to where he'd parked the car. It was gone. Shards of broken glass on the sidewalk told him what had happened.

He didn't mind. In fact he really didn't care.

He retraced his steps and found the Iron Market. Opposite was a long row of parked *tap-taps* waiting for custom: 1960s hearses, coupés and sedans, and the voodoo-psychedelia of their painted exteriors. He asked the driver at the head of the queue if he was going to Pétionville. He nodded and told him to get in.

They waited for a full forty minutes for the car to fill up with people coming in off the streets with baskets of vegetables, rice and beans, live chickens, and dead wet fish. Max found himself wedged tightly in the corner, a large woman sitting on his lap, almost buried beneath the half a dozen bodies crammed in the back.

When the driver was good and ready they left. He took the back streets out of the capital, where the only competing traffic consisted of people and livestock. Inside the car it was lively, everyone seeming to know everyone else, everyone talking to one another – everyone, that is, except Max, who couldn't understand a damn word.

He packed his case and had dinner at a restaurant near La Coupole.

He ate rice, fish and fried plantain and left a good tip before he walked out of the door with a wave and a smile to the pretty young girl who'd served him.

As he walked back home he watched the children,

bedraggled, skinny, bloated bellies, filthy, dressed in rags, many in tight packs, scavenging through rubbish heaps, some playing games, some hanging around on street corners, a few stumbling barefoot behind their parents. He wondered what he'd saved them from.

58

'I'm sorry about your mother, Chantale,' Max said, as they drove to the airport. They were halfway there and they'd barely spoken.

'In a way I'm not,' she said. 'Her last days were really bad for her. She was in a lot of pain. No one should have to go through that kind of suffering. I really hope she's gone to a better place. All her life she believed in the one after this.'

Max didn't have anything to say to that, anything that would sound sincere and comforting in its conviction. He'd gone through the same thing right after Sandra had died. Her death had felt final, a sudden full stop and nothing coming after. Life had felt utterly worthless to him.

'What are you going to do?' he asked her.

'I'll see. For now, Allain wants me to stay on and help him out. He's in charge of everything at the moment. I don't think he can cope. It hit him real hard.'

'Yeah, I know. I appreciate you driving me here. You didn't have to.'

'I couldn't let you leave without saying goodbye.'

'It doesn't have to be goodbye,' Max said. 'It could be "see you later" or "see you soon". Why don't you give me a call when you get back to Miami?' He started writing down his number, got past the area code and then realized he'd forgotten it. 'I'll have to call you.'

She looked at him, met his eye and let him stare straight right at her sadness, a pain so deep she'd lost sight of it, so intense it was on the verge of overwhelming her. He felt clumsy and stupid. Wrong move at the wrong time in the wrong place.

'I'm sorry.'

She shook her head, whether in forgiveness or disbelief he couldn't tell.

They pulled up opposite the airport.

Chantale took his arm.

'Max, don't call me. You're not ready. Not for me, not for anyone,' she said, doing her best to smile with her quivering lips. 'You know what you need to do when you get home? You need to bury your wife. Mourn her, cry, let it out, wash her ghost right out of your heart. Then you can move on.'

PART FIVE

59

Back in Miami, back at the Dadeland Radisson Hotel. They hadn't given him the same room as he had had before, but they might as well have done because it was identical to his memory of the last one – two single beds with brown and yellow tartan bedspreads, a bedside table with a Gideon's Bible inside, a writing desk and chair with a hazy mirror that needed a more vigorous polish, a medium-sized TV, and an armchair and table by the window. The view wasn't any different either – Starbucks, Barnes & Noble, an ice cream parlour, a carpet warehouse and a cheap Chinese eaterie, beyond that some of Kendall's quiet houses, set away from the road, drowned in trees and shrubbery. The weather was good, the sky a deep liquid blue, the sun nowhere near as intense as he had become used to in Haiti.

When he'd got out of the airport he hadn't even bothered trying to take the route home, just told the cab driver to bring him straight here. He'd made the decision on the plane, right after lift-off when the wheels had left the runway and his guts had dropped through his seat. He didn't want to spend Christmas or see 1997 in at the house, the museum to his past life, his past happiness. He'd return there the day after, 2 January, when he was set to check out.

It wasn't over.
He couldn't get Charlie Carver out of his head.
Where was the kid?
What had happened to him?

He'd never left unfinished business for this very reason – it kept him up nights, it haunted him, it wouldn't let him be.

He hit Little Haiti. The shops, the bars, the market, the clubs. He was the only white face there. No one bothered him, plenty of people spoke to him. He often thought he recognized faces he'd seen in Port-au-Prince and Pétionville, but they were no one he'd met.

He ate dinner every night at a Haitian restaurant called *Tap-Tap*. The food was great, the service temperamental, the atmosphere warm and raucous. He sat at the same table – facing a noticeboard with a missing persons poster of Charlie stuck in the middle.

He chewed over the case in his head. He went through it chronologically. He laid out the evidence. He added it up. Then he worked in other detail – background, history, people.

Something wasn't right.

There was something he hadn't seen, or something he'd overlooked, or something he wasn't *meant* to see.

But what, he didn't know.

It wasn't over.

He *had* to know what had happened to Charlie Carver.

60

Twenty-first of December. Joe called him just after 8.00 am to tell him they'd rescued Claudette Thodore and arrested Saxby. Saxby had started spilling his guts the minute they'd slapped the cuffs on him, trying to cut a deal with everyone from the arresting officer to the medic, promising to tell them about a private club in Miami, and bodies dumped in the Everglades, in return for a reduced sentence.

Father Thodore was on his way to Fort Lauderdale to see his niece.

Joe asked Max what he was doing staying at the Radisson. Max couldn't think of anything remotely intelligent to say so he told his friend the truth. To his surprise Joe told him he knew where he was at and he should take all the time he needed. No sense in rushing into what you've got the rest of your life to work out and get over.

They made arrangements to meet at the L Bar the next night. It was the first chance they'd had to meet since Max's return. Joe had been busy: Christmas always brought out the crazies.

'Buy you a drink, Lieutenant?' Max asked Joe's reflection in the booth window.

Joe stood up with his hand out, face a big ear to ear grin.

They hugged.

'You look good *now*, Max,' Joe commented. 'Not like you spent the last ten years hangin' upside down in a *cave*.'

'You lost weight, Joe?' Max asked. Next to Vincent Paul, no man would ever be big again, but Joe had definitely lost more than just his place in Max's league table. His eyes were wider, there was a hint of cheekbone, a finer edge to his jaw and his neck was somewhat slimmer.

'Yeah, dropped a few pounds.'

They sat down. The barman came over. Max ordered a double Barbancourt rum neat, Joe the same with Coke.

The two old friends talked. It was easy and unhurried. They started small and built up to big. The drinks kept coming. Max told his whole story pretty much straight down the line, unravelling everything piece by piece, as it happened, starting with when he met Allain Carver in New York and ending with Vincent Paul in Pétionville. Joe said nothing the whole way through, but Max watched the light slowly dying out of his friend's expression as he gave a detailed account of what he'd discovered. Joe wanted to know what would happen to Gustav Carver.

'I guess he'll be turned over to some of the parents whose children he stole.'

'Good. I hope they each gets a slice of him. One for every child,' Joe growled. 'I *hate* them motherfuckers, man! *Hate* them!'

'What's happening with the organization?'

'The Florida perverts we can handle. We've put together a squad to take them down. That's happening in the next few days,' he said. 'The rest I'm in the process of giving to friends of mine in the other states. Feebs will get their piece too. It's gonna be a big job. Expect to be hearin' about this for a long while to come.'

They clicked glasses.

'Now, I got somethin' for you. It ain't gonna be of no use now, but you asked for it so I brought it along anyway,'

Joe said, handing Max a brown envelope. 'First up: Darwen Medd. He's dead.'

'What? When?'

'April this year. Coastguard boarded a boat from Haiti, looking for illegals. Found Medd in the cargo hold. Naked, hands and feet tied, tongue cut out, sealed in a barrel. Autopsy report said he'd been in there at least two months before they found him. Also said he was alive when they took his tongue, still alive when they sealed him up.'

'Jesus!'

'This may not have been the same people who cut Clyde Beeson open. I did a little digging. When Medd went off to Haiti to work this case he was on the verge of being arrested by the Feebs for drug trafficking. He was helping an ex-client of his bring stuff in from Venezuela. A lot of people I talked to think this was their work. The barrel had Venezuelan markings on it, and the boat had stopped off there before going to Haiti.'

'How clean was the cut to his tongue?'

'Scalpel. Professional — well, except for the way they let him bleed.'

Max took a long pull on his drink.

'Same person did Beeson,' Max said.

'Not necessarily . . .' Joe began.

'What else you got?' Max cut in.

'Remember that evidence you couriered me? Print on that videotape helped us solve an old case.'

'Yeah?'

'You remember before you went out there you asked me to look into the Carver family? The only thing I could find on file was a B & E on their house here, where nothing got taken *but* the burglar took a king-size dump on one of their fancy plates?' Joe laughed. 'Get this – the prints the lab took off the videotape was the *same* as the prints they found on the turd plate.'

'*Yeah?*'

'Uh-huh. Gets better – *much* better.' Joe leaned closer, with a smile. 'Now, we still don't have a file on the perp, just the match. Not here in the US anyhow. *If* we'd bothered to run the plate prints with the Mounties we would've known *exactly* who Turdman was.'

'And . . . ?'

'That *other* guy you asked me to look into – Boris Gaspésie,' Joe said.

Max felt his pulse quicken as a cold jolt passed down his spine.

'Tell me.'

'Wanted for two homicides in Canada.'

'What happened?'

'Boris must've been one of those Carver kids, 'cause he was adopted by this man, Jean-Albert LeBoeuf, a surgeon. Leboeuf was also a paedophile. Went to Haiti all the time.

'Boris killed him when he was twelve. Stabbed him more than fifty times. They found pieces of the guy splashed all over the place. The kid had split him open from his neck to his guts. Real precise cuts too. He told the detectives who interviewed him that his so-called adoptive dad made him watch videotapes of his operations. Used to tell him that he'd do the same thing to him if he told anyone what was going on between them.

'Boris also told the cops his real surname was Gaspésie, and that he'd been kidnapped and brainwashed in Haiti. They bought the first part, but not the second. The adoption papers were all in order.

'Court was real lenient on the kid. They put him in a hospital outside of Vancouver. He was there for about six months, doin' real well, no complaints, model patient. Then, one day, out of the blue he gets into a fight with one of the other kids in there. Witnesses say the kid pulled a knife on Boris and Boris defended himself. Only he *over*-defended himself, knowwhumsayin'? Put his attacker in a coma.

'Now things roll into Strangeville. Boris gets put in the hospital's secure wing. He gets attacked again, only this time it's one of the staff – this male nurse who'd been on the job a month, goin' at him with a syringe full of adrenalin.'

'Carver had sent people to kill Boris,' Max said.

'That's what it looks like now, yeah. Back then, who knew? Only Boris, I guess, because the next thing that happened was he escaped, went on the run. They had a manhunt but they never found him.'

'When did all of this happen?'

'Nineteen seventy to seventy-one,' Joe said.

The waiter came over. They ordered refills.

'Like I said, Boris is wanted by Canadian police for two homicides. One's a banker called Shawn Michaels, the other a businessman called Frank Huxley –'

'*Again*? Those names?' Max said, pulse quickening.

'Shawn Michaels and Frank Huxley,' Joe said. 'Mean anything to you?'

'Some,' Max said. 'Carry on.'

'Boris's bloody prints were all over their dead bodies. He'd tortured them for at least three days before he killed 'em.'

'How d'he kill 'em?'

'Cut their windpipes with a scalpel.'

'Figures,' Max said. He opened the envelope and took out a sheaf of photocopied pages held together with a thick clip. The first page was the report on the murder. Max looked through the pages Joe had given him, turning back one after the other until, clipped somewhere in the middle, he found a copy of Boris Gaspésie's mugshot. It wasn't a good copy, but he clearly recognized the unsmiling teenage face as an early draft of the man he'd known as Shawn Huxley.

Huxley was Boris Gaspésie.

Huxley had handled the tape he'd found at Faustin's house.

He'd found Faustin's house because of the page from the phone book in the box handed to him by Dreadlocks/ Darwen Medd at Saut d'Eau.

He hadn't seen Dreadlocks's face.

Boris Gaspésie was Dreadlocks too?

Why had he gone to Saut d'Eau in the first place?

Huxley had told him Beeson and Medd had gone there.

Huxley had been guiding him all along.

Huxley had kidnapped Charlie.

The world fell out from under Max's feet and he stood suspended over one great big void.

'There's another thing, Max,' Joe said. 'You and Boris got something in common.'

'What?'

'A person: Allain Carver. Around the time of the shit on the plate incident, a "Shawn Huxley" got caught drunk driving on US 1. He got booked and put in the drunk tank. Gave his profession as journalist. Made one phone call. To Allain Carver, who came and bailed him out in two hours.

'You know, I almost missed it. It was late in the day and I thought I'd better try cross-referencing the names of Gaspésie's vics in case he was using their ID. I typed in "Shawn Huxley" by accident.'

'You can be the luckiest person in the world and the worst cop in the history of law enforcement, but that good luck'll get you through every time. When it's the other way round you get blamed and fired,' Max said.

'Ain't that the truth.' Joe chuckled, then his face got serious. 'Whatchu gonna do, Max?'

'Makes you think I'll do anythin'?'

'I thought you'd *do* nothing, I woulda told you nothing.'

61

'Vincent? It's Max Mingus.' The line wasn't good, a lot of static and squeals.

'How are you, Max?'

'I'm good, Vincent, thanks. I think I know who took Charlie.'

'*Who?*'

'I'm coming back tomorrow.'

'You're coming *back*?' He sounded surprised. 'What? *Here*? To *Haiti*?'

'Yeah. Tomorrow. First flight I can get.'

'You don't need to do that, Max,' Vincent said. 'I can handle it from here. Really. Just tell me.'

'Negative,' Max said.

'What do you propose?' Vincent asked.

'Let me finish my job. Give me a week tops, from touch-down. If I don't get anywhere then I'll tell you what I know and haul ass back here. Anything happens to me on the search and I don't make it, I've left all the information you need with Joe Liston. He's got your number. He doesn't hear from me a week from tomorrow, he'll tell you everything.'

'OK. It's a deal.'

'Here's what I need from you: first up, I want to make as little noise as possible coming back. No one outside your most trusted can know I'm in the country.'

'I'll have some people meet you on the runway, take you out through the military exit.'

'Good. Next: I'll need a good car.'

'OK.'

'And a gun.'

The morning of his departure he'd taken the Beretta apart and dropped its components in Pétionville's open sewer holes.

'Consider it done.'

'Thanks. I'll call you before I leave.'

'OK.'

'And another thing, Vincent – same as before, this is *still* my gig. You let *me* run things.'

'Understood,' he said.

'See you very soon.'

'Indeed,' Vincent said. 'Oh, Max?'

'Yeah?'

'Thank you.'

PART SIX

62

Chantale had just finished loading two cases into the back of her Fiat Panda and locking the door to her house when he crept up and tapped her shoulder.

'Max!' She jumped with shock and gasped when she saw him, a confused smile tripping across her lips. She was dressed in jeans and a light-blue blouse, small gold studs in her ears, a thin chain around her neck and minimal make-up, the look one of formal informality. She took travelling seriously.

'Where's Allain?'

'He's gone. Left the country,' she said, worry creeping into her face. He was blocking her way to the car. 'I'm going too. My plane's leaving in a couple of hours and I really want to beat the traffic, so . . .'

'You ain't goin' nowhere, Chantale.' Max pulled out the Glock Vincent Paul had handed him when he'd picked him up at the airport.

She panicked.

'Look, I didn't know anything was wrong until yesterday,' she said. 'Allain came by early in the morning. I'd just woken up. He told me not to go back to the bank because he was letting me go. He said something had gone wrong and he had to go talk to the family lawyers in New York. He didn't know when he'd be back. He gave me a receipt for a money transfer to my Miami bank account. Said it was my golden handshake.'

'Did you try and find out what had happened?'

'Sure. I called a couple of friends in the bank, but they didn't know anything. They didn't even know I wasn't coming back.'

'How much did he give you?'

'Not as much as you.'

'How *much*?' he insisted.

'A million.'

'That's a lot of money, Chantale.'

'Allain's a generous guy.'

'What else did you do for him apart from be his PA?'

'*Nothing!*' she snapped. 'How *dare* you –'

'Where's Charlie?'

'*Charlie?* I don't know.'

She looked scared, but she didn't seem to be lying. Had she even guessed Allain was gay?

'How much *do* you know?' Max asked. 'What's Allain been up to since I've been gone?'

She scrutinized him, trying to read him, work out his angle. He tapped the gun against his leg impatiently.

'He's been doing a lot of money transfers. I overheard him yelling at someone down the phone about the time some of them were taking. I took a couple of calls from banks in the Caymans, Monaco, Luxemburg . . .'

'Do you know how much money?'

'No. What is going *on*, Max?' she said.

Max handed her a copy of Gaspésie's teenage mug shot. 'Ever see him with Allain?'

'He's a boy,' she said.

'He grew up. Look hard. His name might be –'

'Shawn Huxley?' she offered.

'You know him?'

'Yeah. He said he was a journalist, and an old friend of Allain's.'

'How many times did you see them together?'

'Two, three times at the most. He always came to see Allain at the bank. He was there just last week. He asked me if I wanted to come waterskiing with him that weekend. He's been renting Allain's beach house.'

'Where's that?' Max asked.

She told him. It was three hours away. He asked her to write down the directions.

'Do you know anything else about Huxley? Did you ever hear what they talked about?'

'No. I know they laughed a lot the last time they met,' she said, then her expression darkened. 'Did they kidnap Charlie?'

'Why d'you think I'm back?'

'That's *impossible!*' she said.

'How well d'you know Allain?' he asked. When she didn't reply he told her what he knew for sure, watching her face as first surprise (Allain's sexuality, Huxley's true identity), then disbelief (that Vincent was Charlie's father), then complete bewilderment (all of it at once) took over.

She leant against the wall, unsteadily, as if about to faint. Max gave her time to settle herself.

'I don't know *anything* about *any* of that, Max. I promise you.'

Their eyes met.

'I want to believe you,' he said. He'd been taken in by Allain, Huxley and Gustav. He didn't want to add her to the list.

'I've told you all I know. I just want to get out of here. I just want to get my plane. *Please.*'

'No.' He shook his head and took hold of her arm. 'You're missing that plane – and every other plane until this gets cleared up.'

'But I don't *know* anything.'

He took her on to the sidewalk and beckoned to the car parked behind his. A man and a woman got out of the back and came over.

'Keep her in the house until you hear otherwise,' Max said. 'Treat her well. *Don't* hurt her.'

63

Carver's beach house overlooked a tiny scrap of paradise — a small but utterly beautiful white sand beach, hidden away deep in a cove of dark rock, surrounded by mountains on one side and postcard-perfect blue ocean on the other.

Max had watched from above as Huxley and two women had gotten into a speedboat moored off a jetty and gone off waterskiing. Then he'd walked over to the house.

The house — a Spanish-style villa of the kind semi-wealthy expats bought as retirement or holiday homes in Miami — was surrounded by a thick twenty-foot-high cement wall, topped with spikes, broken glass and razor wire. Yet when Max pushed the metal double gate, it opened wide on to a paved courtyard, swimming pool and sun loungers. Under normal circumstances there was no need to close it. They were perfectly isolated amid an area of small white chalky rocks, tufts of wild grass, cacti and barren coconut trees with yellowy green leaves.

He stepped inside and pushed the gate shut.

There was one other person Allain Carver loved as much as, or possibly even a little more than, himself — his mother. There was a shrine to her in the corner of the living room, a slab of gleaming polished granite inlaid with her black-and-white photograph — a professionally shot studio portrait making her look glamorous and distant, a star in her own universe. Her name and lifespan were stamped below her image and gone over in gold leaf. The shrine was completed with a small pool in which several round purple candles floated.

All the other pictures in the house – hung on the walls or placed on furniture – were of Allain from his late teens upwards. Max was surprised to see snaps of a man who looked like the most strenuous physical activity he'd ever undertaken was walking to and from his car, surfing, white water rafting, hang-gliding, mountain climbing, parachuting, bungee jumping and abseiling. Carver was grinning broadly in every photograph, clearly in his element in each of them, living life to the full and as close to the edge as he could take it.

Max recognized how little he'd known his employer, how much he'd been taken in by him, and who he'd been up against. This was a side of him people didn't know or even suspect he had. Here, alone, Allain Carver had truly been himself.

The rest of the living room was minimally furnished. A dining table was placed near the back window, overlooking a veranda and then the sea, no doubt perfect for intimate sunset dinners. There were only two chairs, facing each other at either end of the table. At the opposite end of the room, facing the gate and pool, was a leather sofa and a wall-mounted TV screen, with a chrome and wood coffee table in between. A four-shelf bookcase, lined with everything from leather-bound encyclopedias to gay erotic fiction, took up an entire wall, while a solitary island of two reclining easy chairs, a lamp and another table stood in the middle of the room. There was a CD player with a curving rack filled with music, most of it classical.

The house reeked of stale cigarettes, cold reefer and perfume.

Max weapons-checked and found an eight-shot Smith & Wesson revolver taped under the dining table. He emptied the shells into his pocket.

He checked out the kitchen, which was to the left. There was a fridge and freezer, both well stocked with food, the fridge full of fresh produce – plenty of salad and fruit. He found a bottle of water and drank half of it down. There were stacks of well-thumbed cookbooks and a folder of recipes cut from magazines in a corner on the shelves. The dishwasher was on.

He found another revolver on top of the fridge. He removed the shells.

He crossed back out through the living room. The bathroom was spacious, with a sunken tub and a shower, plenty of toiletries, both male and female. Next he went to the master bedroom – dominated by a kingsize bed with a brass rail bedstead. It had the same great view of the sea and the horizon as the living room. He could see the speedboat pulling a skier. The bed was unmade. Clothes were strewn on the floor – mostly women's.

There was a revolver in the bedside cabinet. He added the shells to his collection.

He went into the first guest bedroom and found it completely empty except for a blue Globetrotter suitcase and matching overnight bag placed side by side near the door. The suitcase was padlocked shut. Max opened the bag and found a British Airways one-way first-class ticket to London from Santo Domingo, dated 3 January – the next day. In a side pocket he found a British passport belonging to Stuart Boyle.

The photograph inside was of the man he'd known as Shawn Huxley.

Huxley's appearance had changed a little – he'd lost the

moustache and his hair had grown out to a short afro. He looked mature. He was smiling at the camera.

The house felt empty. It was quiet. He couldn't even hear the waves.

The second room had two overnight bags in it, which belonged to the women Huxley was with. It was also home to a dirty-looking photocopier and a box of paper. The machine had been unplugged. Max opened the copier lid. Nothing. He opened the box. Empty.

He looked around the rest of the room. Nothing to see.

He stared at the copier. He moved it away from the wall. A layer of dust and two dead insects.

No weapons in either room.

Max went to the master bedroom and watched the boat in the middle of the window.

After an hour of waterskiing they turned back towards land.

64

The girls came in first. Kreyol, laughter.

Then Huxley, shutting the door, talking.

More laughter.

Max was in the first guest room, sharing space with Huxley's suitcase and phoney ID.

He suddenly remembered the bottle of water he'd drunk from. It was a new bottle he'd uncapped. If they went to the kitchen they'd know someone was in the house.

Shit!

There was a bump next door, in the master bedroom, followed by voices, then short laughter.

One set of feet – flip-flops – outside, right by the door.

The door handle budged and moved down.

Max stepped back from the door, gun cocked.

Silence.

The air-conditioning went on.

Max waited.

The flip-flops retreated.

Another set of feet – bare – padded across the corridor and headed for the living room.

The toilet flushed. Flip-flops followed the feet.

A woman's playful scream, Huxley growling, then a moan.

The second woman's voice, talking from the bedroom, then laughing.

Max listened. He heard nothing. He thought of the water. He had to move in.

His palm was sweating up around the butt of the Glock.

He wiped his hand on his shirt. Glocks weren't his favourite pistols. His preferred weapons had more heft and stature, like Berettas and Colts did. Glocks felt and looked like toys. Vincent Paul had given him a new .45 Glock 21 with a 13-shot clip. Joe had the same weapon. He loved Glocks, said he hardly sensed they were there when he had one on.

Flip-flops followed by bare feet came back and went into the bedroom.

Talking, giggling.

Max moved near the door and waited.

He heard Huxley talking low. Moving around on the bedsprings.

Max opened the door a crack. Silence.

Max stepped out on tiptoe.

Huxley spoke again.

More gasping, moaning, climbing in pitch.

Max braced himself. His head was clear. He was here for Charlie, to find out where they were keeping him or where they'd buried him. He wasn't here for revenge. He was just finishing his job and closing out his career. He had the element of surprise on his side. They wouldn't be expecting him.

Huxley said something else.

Now's the time.

Max stepped silently into the room.

Some scene.

All three were so into it they didn't realize he was in the room.

The two women were on the bed, naked, heads buried between each other's thighs. Huxley was sat in a chair opposite, yellow Triumph T-shirt, powder-blue flip-flops, shorts around his ankles, mouth agape, his erection in his hand, stroking slowly.

Max aimed the Glock at his head.

Huxley was so lost in his show he didn't notice Max standing in front of him, at point-blank range.

Max cleared his throat.

The girl on the bottom looked up at him, freed her head and screamed.

Huxley stared at Max like he was a hallucination, his expression normal and relaxed as if he was waiting for his brain to flip his sanity switch back on and make the vision disappear.

When it didn't he panicked. He tried to keep it from showing overall, but the colour left his skin, his nostrils flared, his eyes opened up more and his lips parted and stayed half open.

The second girl screamed. They both sat up and grabbed the sheets to cover themselves. Dark skinned, high cheek-bones, full plump lips, beautiful. Huxley had great taste.

Max put his fingers to his lips for them to be quiet and stepped away from the bed in case they tried to lunge at him.

'Charlie Carver,' he said to Huxley. 'Dead or alive?'

Huxley cracked a smile.

'I told Allain you'd be back,' he said, sounding almost pleased. '*Especially* when you wired him his money back. He couldn't believe it. I *knew* you were on to us then. I *knew* it was only a matter of time before you came to finish your job. *I knew it.* I've never seen someone cut and run so fast. Allain ran away like his asshole was on fire.'

'*Answer me.*'

'Charlie's alive.'

'Where've you got him?'

'He's safe. Near the Dominican Republic border.'

'Who's got him?'

'A couple,' Huxley stammered. 'They haven't harmed him at all. He's virtually like a son to them.'

'Let's go get him,' Max said.

65

Huxley drove. Max sat next to him with the gun trained on his waist.

'When was the last time you saw the kid?' Max asked.

'Three months ago.'

'How was he?'

'Very well. Healthy.'

'Any speech?'

'What?'

'Can he talk?'

'No. He won't.'

It was mid afternoon. Huxley explained that they would be driving back to Pétionville, then up the mountain road, past the Carver estate, stopping close enough to see the lights in the houses in the Dominican Republic. He hoped to reach the place where Charlie was being held by late evening.

'Tell me about the people who've got the kid.'

'Carl and Ertha. Old folk, in their seventies. The most dangerous object they've got in the house is a machete – and that's for coconuts. Carl's an ex-priest –'

'*Another one,*' Max quipped.

'– originally from Wales. He knew Allain's mother very well. He helped Allain in his teens, when he discovered he was gay.'

'Carl gay?'

'No. Women and the spirit you buy in bottles are his thing.'

'That why he got kicked out of the church?'

'He fell in love with Ertha, his housemaid, and left of his own accord. Mrs Carver supported them. She bought them the farmhouse near the border. Allain made sure they never wanted for anything. They're good people, Max. They've treated Charlie as their own. He's been very happy there, really blossomed. It could have been much worse.'

'Why wasn't it? Why didn't you kill him? Why go through all this trouble, this risk of getting caught, by keeping the kid alive?'

'We're not monsters, Max. That was *never* part of the plan. Besides we *like* Charlie – what he represented. Gustav Carver, with all his power and money and contacts – the old fool didn't even *know* the kid wasn't his – let alone that it was *Vincent Paul's* – his *sworn enemy.*'

Huxley halved his speed when they entered Pétionville, and then slowed to a creep once they got into the densely populated centre, where the distinction between street and sidewalk was buried under masses of moving and stationary bodies. They drove up the hill past La Coupole.

'How did you find us out?'

'It's what I do,' Max said. 'Remember that videotape you planted in Faustin's house? You fucked up. You left your prints on it. One loose thread's usually all it takes to catch the big fat fish.'

'So, if it hadn't been for that –?'

'That's right,' Max said. 'You coulda spent the rest of your sorry ass life pullin' your pud – or whatever life you had left. See, with Allain running off the way he did, it would only have been a matter of time before Vincent Paul caught up with you.'

'I was planning to leave tomorrow,' Huxley said, bitterly, tightening his grip on the wheel, all four knuckles popping out. Fighter's hands, Max thought. 'Vincent Paul wouldn't have known about me. Hardly anyone saw us together. Only Chantale knew my name – well, *one* of them.'

'Was she in on this?'

'No,' Huxley said. 'Absolutely not. Allain debriefed her on where you'd been and who you'd seen every day, but she didn't know what was really goin' on – any more than you did.'

'Why don't you tell me 'bout that, what was "really goin' on" – right from the start?'

'How much do you know?' Huxley asked. They were heading up the precarious mountain road. They passed a Suzuki jeep in a ditch. Children were playing on it.

'Broad strokes – this: you and Allain kidnapped Charlie. Motive: to bring down Gustav Carver. Allain was in it for money first, then revenge. You were in it for payback then greenback, but payback before all else. How am I doin'?'

'Not bad,' Huxley smirked. 'Now, where do you want me to start?'

'Wherever you want.'

'OK. Why don't I tell you all about Tonton Clarinette – Mr Clarinet?'

'Go ahead. I'm all ears.'

66

'My sister Patrice – I used to call her "Treese". She had these beautiful eyes – green – like Smokey Robinson's. Cat's eyes on dark skin. People used to stop and stare at her she was so beautiful.' Huxley smiled.

'How old was she?'

'No more than seven. It was hard to tell things like age and dates and stuff, because we were illiterate and innumerate, like our parents and their parents before them, like everyone we knew. We grew up in Clarinette, dirt poor. As soon as we could walk we were helping our parents with whatever they were doing to put food on the table. I helped my mother pick fruit. I'd put mangoes and genip in baskets, then we'd go down to the roadside and sell them to pilgrims going to Saut d'Eau.'

'What about your dad?' Max asked.

'I was scared of him. He was a real bad-tempered guy. Beat you over nothing. I'd look at him the wrong way and he'd get this thin stick and whip my little ass. He wasn't like that to Treese though. No. He worshipped her. Made me jealous.

'I remember the day the trucks came to the village – big trucks, cement mixers. I thought monsters had come to eat us up. My dad told us the men driving them said they were going to put up huge buildings and make everyone in the town rich. He went to work on the site. Perry Paul owned it then. I think the idea was to build some sort of cheap accommodation for the pilgrims who come to Saut d'Eau.

Most come from very far and they've got nowhere to stay. He built the temple too. I guess he wanted to create some kind of voodoo Mecca.

'After Gustav Carver put Paul out of business, he took over the project. There was a management change. Things were different. This man arrived one day – strangest looking man I'd ever seen – a white man with orange hair. You never saw him working. All he ever seemed to do was play with kids. He became our friend. We used to play soccer. He bought us a ball.

'He was a fun guy. He made all the kids laugh. He told us stories, gave us presents – candy, clothes. He was like a great dad and a big kid brother all rolled into one. He used to film us too with this Super 8 camera he had. It made him look like half his face was this black ugly machine with a protruding round glass eye – kind of creepy and funny at the same time. He filmed Treese most of all.

'One day he took me and Treese to one side and told us he was going away. We were real sad. My sister started to cry. And he said not to worry, he'd take us with him if we wanted to come. We said yes. He told us to promise not to tell our parents anything otherwise he couldn't take us.

'We agreed. We left the village without telling anyone that afternoon. We met our friend in a car all the way down the road. There was another man with him. We'd never seen him before. Treese started saying maybe we should go back. The stranger got out of the car, grabbed her and threw her inside. He did the same to me. We both started crying as they drove off. Then they injected us with something, and I don't remember much else that happened after that – how we got to the house on La Gonâve or anything.'

They'd passed the Carver estate and were heading uphill along a bumpy, potholed stretch of road. They'd had to stop once for a broken-down truck and another time for a man coming down the mountainside with his herd of skeletal goats.

'You saw the tape, right? The one I left for you? You watched it?'

'Where d'you get it?' Max changed gun hands.

'I'll tell you later. You saw what was on it – the potion they gave us?'

'Yeah,' Max nodded.

'My memory's pretty fucked up from that whole "indoctrination process". You couldn't put me on a witness stand because whatever I've got up here' – Huxley tapped his cranium – 'my brain is like spaghetti. I remember things like they were in a dream. I don't know how much of it is dis-association and how much is down to the zombie juice they fed us.

'It wasn't as strong as the stuff the voodoo priests make people catatonic with, but it was enough to make you lose all control of your senses. They used to feed us it every day. Like communion. We'd go up, receive this green liquid in a cup, drink it.

'Then there was the hypnosis with music notes. Gustav Carver would sit in the middle of this all-white room and we'd stand around him in a circle, holding hands. He played his clarinet to us. And while he was playing we'd get our "instructions".'

'What about your sister? Where was she in all this?' Max asked.

'I don't know. The last time I remember seeing her was in the back of the car when we were kidnapped.' Huxley shook his head. 'She's most likely dead. We weren't allowed to grow up.'

'How do you know this?'

'I'll come to that too,' Huxley answered, and then resumed his story. 'I was sold to a Canadian plastic surgeon called LeBoeuf. He always looked at me like he was stripping me down to the bone. He made me watch him doing his operations. I learnt how to cut people up. I got handy with knives. I taught myself to read out of medical books.

'Justice was on my side when I killed him, but it was also in Gustav Carver's pocket because they never tied LeBoeuf in with him. No one believed what I told them about being kidnapped in Haiti, about being brainwashed, about Tonton Clarinette, about my sister. Why should they? I'd just cut a man up into little pieces and redecorated the house with his insides.'

'What about when the cops searched the house for evidence, right after they'd found the body?'

'They didn't find anything linked to Carver — or if they did, it never found its way out into the open. The old man had tentacles *everywhere*,' Huxley said. 'I busted out of the hospital they had me in because Gustav tried to have me killed in there. No one believed a damn word I said. It was a nuthouse. I wasn't surprised. By the time they *did* start thinking that maybe there was something in it, I was gone, a fugitive, on the run, a wanted man.

'I lived on the street. I hustled. I did what I had to do. I didn't like some of it, but that's the life I was handed. All the while I was on the run I started putting it together — what had happened, who was behind it. I remembered a person LeBoeuf had known — not someone from the surgery, a friend of his. Shawn Michaels. He was a banker.

'I tracked him down. I made him tell me about Carver's business — how it worked, everything.'

'Then you killed him?' Max said.

'Yeah,' Huxley nodded. 'I took his address book. He knew

other paedophiles, people he'd recommended Carver's service to.'

'You went after them?'

'I only got to one.'

'Frank Huxley?'

'That's right. He had a stack of videotapes of what went on in La Gonâve and Noah's Ark. The tape you found was a compilation I made – you know, a preview of forthcoming horrors.'

'What about the rest of the people in the address book?'

'They were too hard to get to.'

'What about Allain, when did he come into the picture?' Max asked.

'In Canada I lived out on the street most of the time. I knew a lot of hustlers,' Huxley said. 'So did Allain. He went in for rough trade. We had mutual acquaintances. These two guys I knew were always bragging about this wealthy Haitian they were bangin'. I got curious. I found out who he was.

'I went to this bar Allain always went to to meet his pick-ups. We got talking. When I found out he hated his old man almost as much as I did, we were in business.'

'So you put together a plan to bring down the old man?'

'Essentially, yes. Our motives were very different. Allain was just this poor spoilt little rich boy whose daddy didn't give him any love on account of his sexuality. He could've lived with this if one of his lovers hadn't worked for the family's law firm in Miami. He told Allain the old man had completely cut him out of his will. He'd left it all to his in-laws and closest lieutenants.

'The way the Carver business is set up is that if the old man is taken ill or has to go away somewhere urgently, responsibility for running things falls to the next most senior Carver in Haiti. Allain had covered for his father while he was away before, so he knew the ropes. He'd found out there was over half a billion dollars in various "rainy day" cash accounts. As head of the Carver empire he could do what he wanted with the money —'

'But he needed the old man out of the way first,' Max finished.

'That's right,' Huxley said. 'Allain didn't have the first fucking clue how to get at the money. The guy's got cunning but no street smarts — and *waaaay* too many feelings. Mine are pretty much dead.'

'So it was your idea to kidnap the boy?'

'Absolutely,' Huxley agreed proudly. 'Most of it was. We'd kidnap the boy, hole him up somewhere very safe, bring in an outside investigator and steer them towards discovering Gustav.'

'By "steer" you mean plant a trail of clues?'

'That's right.'

'Or literally hand them to me like you did —'

'— out by the waterfalls? Yeah. That was me under that wig.'

'Suited you,' Max said sourly.

It was now dark. Huxley had killed his speed. They were the only people out on the road. Max had checked behind him to see if Vincent Paul's escort had kept up. Max had been followed to the beach house, and then back to Pétionville. He couldn't see anyone behind them.

'Of course it was important you got on with Vincent Paul too. He had to trust you, open up to you. He didn't do that with Beeson and Medd.'

'Is that why you killed 'em?'

'I didn't *kill* either of them,' Huxley began. 'I made *examples* of them.'

'You cut Medd's tongue out and stuffed him into a *barrel* — some fuckin' *example*!'

'He *choked* to death,' Huxley corrected. 'Look, I admit what I did was a bit – extreme – *barbaric*, even. But with reward money that big, we couldn't afford to have every arsehole and chancer coming out here and trying their luck. It acted as a deterrent. People got wind of what had happened to Beeson and suddenly they had better offers for jobs out in Alaska. Yours is a small world, Max. All you private eyes all know each other.'

'But what did they *do wrong*?'

'Beeson was too close to the old man. He was reporting directly to him, bypassing Allain. Plus he fucked up with Vincent Paul. They didn't hit it off. He was next to useless to us,' Huxley explained. 'And Medd – he was almost there, but then he got suspicious about the clues he was getting. He told Allain it was all too obvious, too easy. It was only a matter of time before he found us out. I took pre-emptive action.'

'What about the Haitian guy?'

'Emmanuel? Emmanuel was a lazy motherfucker. Too busy fucking around to do any serious work. I would have cut his dick off myself, someone hadn't thought of it first.'

'And then you got me?' Max said.

The road had flattened out. The surface was unusually smooth and the wheels seemed to glide along it, the car's engine emitting a soothing hum. The stars had begun to appear in the sky, twinkling low, the galaxies so close they resembled rhinestone clouds. The whole way there Huxley had been calm and assured. Not once had he even asked Max what he planned to do with him. It had occurred to Max that they weren't going to find Charlie Carver at all, that Huxley was taking him to the place where he'd cut up Beeson and Medd. If that's what it was, it wouldn't happen to him. He wouldn't let it. He'd kill Huxley at the slightest hint of something going wrong. Not that he really believed Huxley had that in mind at all. Huxley had lived most of his life seeking revenge for his sister and for himself. Now he had it he didn't really care what came next.

'You were the one I always wanted for this job,' Huxley said. 'I'd followed your trial, every day. I read up about you. I really respected what you did. I felt like you were on my side, like if we'd ever meet up one day you'd be one person who'd at least understand where I was coming from, what I'd been through.'

'People feel the same way about their favourite rock stars,' Max punctured the bubble. 'Take it a little further and it's called stalking.'

'Guess your life's made you a hardarse too, huh?' Huxley laughed.

'My life's been a failure,' Max said. 'Anyway you look at it. Doing what I did made no difference – except to me. It didn't bring back the victims, it didn't turn back the clock and give them back their innocence. It didn't help their parents, their families. Not in the long run. Closure's bullshit. You never recover from that kind of loss. You take your tears with you to the grave.

'But I'm glad you think my life helped you – 'cause it sure as shit didn't help me. I lost the only genuinely good thing I ever had. My wife. She died when I was in prison. I never got to hold her again, touch her, kiss her, be with her – never got to tell her how much I loved her – all because of the life I'd led. All that "good" I thought I was doing, it added up to one big zero. It put me in jail. If that ain't failure, I don't know what is.'

Max looked through the windshield, into the darkness.

'Yeah? How come Gustav let Allain do the hiring?' he asked.

'He didn't. That dinner you went to? That was your inter-view with Gustav. If he hadn't liked you, you would've been on the next plane back to Miami,' Huxley said.

'That ever happen?'

'No. Allain and I chose well.'

They drove on in silence for a while. Max holstered the Glock. He wouldn't need it for now.

'Tell me about Eddie Faustin?'

'Using him was my idea too,' Huxley said.

'How did you turn him? I thought he was loyal to the old man.'

'Everyone has their price.'

'What was Eddie's?'

'Francesca. She was Faustin's wet-dream girl. I told him he could have her if he helped us out – through his *bokor* – Madame Leballec. She was a good friend of my mother's,' Huxley explained.

'Hold up,' Max said. 'You *told* Mrs Leballec to tell Eddie he could "have" Francesca? So she was a fake?'

'Yes and no. She *has* some powers, but she's a black magi-cian – a witch. Lying's part of their repertoire,' Huxley said. 'She has many believers.'

'So, when we went to see her and Eddie's "spirit" told us to go to the temple –'

'– where you met me, and I gave you the box that had Eddie's address in it, where you found the videotape . . . ?'

'You'd paid her to show us the way?'

'Yes. And, by the way, she's no cripple either – and Philippe's her lover, not her son. And please don't ask me how she tricked the séance out, 'cause I don't know,' Huxley said and then he laughed.

'*Shit!*' Max said. 'OK – back to Faustin.'

'Eddie was deeply troubled. Paranoid that all the bad stuff

he and his brother did when they were Macoutes was catching up with him. He was visiting Madame Leballec on a monthly basis to get his fortune read.

'And that's where we came in. Allain paid Madame Leballec a lot of money to give Faustin a tailor-made fortune – one where he got the girl of his dreams and lived happily ever after.

'She told Faustin that a man he'd never met was going to approach him about a top-secret job. She told him he had to do it if he wanted his dreams to come true.'

'So you met him?'

'Yeah, one night outside the taffia shack where he went. When he heard what I was proposing he didn't want to go along with it. He rushed off back to Madame Leballec. We'd anticipated that. She upped the ante. She persuaded Faustin that Charlie Carver was really a spirit who had escaped from Baron Samedi and had possessed the boy. The boy needed to be handed back to Baron Samedi's envoy – namely me.'

'*Bullshit*!'

'He fell for it.'

'Christ!'

'Faustin was *so* stupid it was practically a talent. Factor in the superstition that everything that goes bump in the night is some madcap spirit and you've got the perfect fanatic.'

'OK, tell me about the kidnapping. Things didn't go to plan, did they?'

'In what way?' Huxley asked.

'The riot,' Max replied.

'No, that *was* planned. Faustin had a lot of enemies. We paid some of them to be where we told Faustin to be. He thought I was going to walk up to the car and take the child away.'

'The nanny – Rose – died.'

'Faustin killed her, not us.'

'Did you intend for Faustin to die?'

'Yes.'

'Who took Charlie?'

'I did. I was in disguise, among the crowd attacking the car. I grabbed the boy, disappeared with him.'

They went through a small village of thatched huts. Max saw no signs of life whatsoever except for a small tethered goat, caught in the headlights, munching on a bush.

'So, who was Mr Clarinet? Carver or Codada?'

'They both were. Codada filmed the kids and stole them to order. Carver stole their souls and sold their bodies.'

'What about that symbol? That bent cross with the broken-off arm?'

'You didn't recognize that?'

'No.' Max shook his head.

'Manet's *Le Fire*. Remember that painting? The soldier boy with the flute? It was the organization's badge, how they recognized each other. There was one hanging in the club you met Allain in. He sat you where you'd notice it. There was one in Codada's office, when Allain took you to meet him. There was another in Noah's Ark, right outside Eloise Krolak's classroom. There's one hanging in every club. The symbol is an outline of the painting. It was meant to be subliminal,' Huxley said and chuckled. 'Maybe it was *too* subliminal.'

'You could've made this easier, just left me an anonymous note telling me who to look for.'

'No,' Huxley said. 'It couldn't be that easy. You'd have wanted to know who was behind the note. You would have found us.'

'But couldn't you have just blown the whistle on the Carvers?'

'Here? You'd have better luck whispering to the deaf. And you know what happened in Canada. That wasn't the way it was going to happen,' Huxley said.

They continued in silence. Max tried not to think about the way he'd been played from the very beginning to the very end, and tried to focus instead on the positive outcome, that he would soon be freeing Charlie from his captors and reuniting him with his real parents. That was the main thing, the important thing, the *only* thing. *That* was why he'd come here.

He didn't know what he was going to do about Huxley.

'What about Allain?' Max asked. 'Where d'he go?'

'Your guess is as good as mine. He never told me. We settled up and that was the last I saw of him. I don't expect he'll ever be found.'

'So you *did* get money out of it?'

'Yeah, sure. I didn't want to go back to preying on horny faggots,' Huxley said. 'We're not too far now.'

Max checked his watch. It had gone 8.00 pm. In the distance he could see the lights of a town. He guessed they were close to the Dominican Republic.

'Unlike you, Max, I have no regrets. Mine might have been a poor life, a miserable life even – *but* it was *my* life. Not theirs – *mine*. And it was my sister's life too. Our lives. Ours to keep, ours to live. They took them from us. They took her from me. So, I took it *all* from them.

'Allain didn't give a shit about those kids. He was horrified and disgusted by what his father was doing, sure, but you know, it was always really just about him. Not anyone else. He just wanted to rip his dad off, piss in his face and steal his money. He used to say the only things worth doing in life are worth doing for money. I never understood that mentality.

'You say you made no difference, that you're a failure? You shouldn't think that way, Max. You killed monsters and saved the lives of the children they would have fed on. Just like I did.'

The road was taking them downhill, closer to the border. Gaining on his left, on top of a nearby mountain, Max saw the lights of a house.

'Charlie's in there,' Huxley said and turned off the road.

67

Carl and Ertha were waiting for them by the door. Ertha, dressed in a loose brown dress and sandals, was a voluminous Creole woman of indeterminate age, with the sort of kind and gentle face it was impossible to imagine angry. Carl was half her height and next to her appeared close to skeletal. His head was way too big for his body, a pumpkin speared on a dressed-up broomstick, and he made it even larger by wearing what was left of his hair – thick chestnut-tinged grey manes sprouting out from the sides – down to his shoulders. His face – heavily lined, weathered, pocked, bloated, boiled red – was as classic a lush mug as Max had ever seen, home to a million stories with ordinary beginnings, extraordinary middles and forgotten endings. His eyes, however, were a remarkably clear and brittle blue, making Max think that he'd kicked the bottle quite recently, cleaned up in time for the rest of his life.

They were both smiling at the car and at Huxley as he got out. Then they saw his face and their features drooped and sadness filled their expressions and bodies, changing their posture from welcoming to edgy.

Max stepped out and they stared at him with contempt, already knowing what – or who – he'd come for. They looked him over, sizing him up as he came forward. They weren't impressed.

Huxley picked up on what was going on and didn't bother introducing them.

The couple walked into the house and led them to a room

where the door was open. They stepped aside. Huxley gave Max a nod to go ahead in.

Sitting on his haunches, threading ring pulls through a long bootlace, Charlie, now aged five, was sitting on the floor. The first thing Max noticed about him were his eyes, which were essentially the same as they were in his pictures, except that they were a little larger and sparkled with intelligence and mistrust. He was a beautiful child, a cherub whose innocence was shaded with a capacity for mischief, his features leaning more to his father than his mother. Max had expected Charlie to be sitting on his hair, or at least for it to be plaited and placed in a wound-up coil on top of his skull, but Charlie had since surrendered it to scissors and styling. It was trimmed short and combed neatly, with a part in the middle. He was dressed in blue shorts, white socks, shiny black shoes and a red and white striped sailor T-shirt with an anchor on the right breast. He looked happy, healthy and very well – even lovingly looked after, about as far removed from any kidnap victim Max had ever found and freed.

Max crouched down and introduced himself to Charlie. Charlie looked, confused, for help, to Huxley, standing behind Max. Huxley crouched down and spoke to the boy in French – Max heard his name repeated twice – and then he tousled his hair, picked him up and spun him around. Charlie's eyes lit up and he laughed, but formed no words. He was beyond speech.

After Huxley had set him down Charlie fixed his mussed hair until it was exactly back to the way it had been when they'd first seen him. Then he resumed threading his ring pulls, selecting one from a pile on the floor and adding it to the chain he was working on. He completely ignored Max, didn't even act like they were in the same room.

Huxley left the room and went next door to talk to Carl

and Ertha, who were standing close to the doorway, looking in. He took them away, one arm around each, out of earshot.

Max stepped out to look. Ertha was turned away, facing a wall and a framed black-and-white picture of priests in black cassocks, one of whom must have been a younger Carl. She was biting her hand to stifle her crying.

Carl tugged Huxley away from her, back towards the door and spoke close to his ear, looking over at Ertha as he did, who was now leaning against the wall for support.

Huxley came back to Max and whispered to him.

'Carl's just told me we'd best take Charlie now, while we can. If we stay much longer Ertha will be too upset to let him leave.'

Huxley went into the room and picked Charlie up off the ground, so suddenly the boy let go of his necklace and all the ring pulls slipped off the lace and fell on the floor. Charlie's face suddenly went bright red and he looked very angry as he was carried out of the room. He made low moaning sounds, as if he was imitating a trapped and wounded animal's cry for help.

Charlie's expression turned from anger to confusion as he passed Ertha and Carl, now together. Ertha's head was buried in Carl's shoulder and she was holding on to him tightly, arms overlapping across his narrow back, refusing to see what was happening. Carl wasn't looking their way either as he stroked the back of Ertha's head, the two of them right then about the saddest, most broken two people Max had ever seen.

Charlie reached out for them both as Huxley carried him out through the door. The boy's mouth opened and his eyes darted from Max to Carl and Ertha in panic and bewilderment. Max braced himself for the kid's notorious screaming. It didn't come. Instead Charlie started bawling like any other small child – loudly and hysterically – but no differently to any normal child.

They left the house and Max shut the door behind him. No sooner had he done so than he heard Ertha release her grief, and even the little of her pain he heard as he walked away pierced him to the quick and made him very briefly question what the hell he thought he was doing taking the boy away from here – a healthy atmosphere, and these good, loving people – and taking him to the outskirts of an open sewer and his father, the drug baron.

Max opened the car door and told Huxley to put Charlie in the back.

Huxley settled Charlie in the car and closed the door.

'What now?'

Max held out his hand. Huxley shook it.

'Stay off the roads,' Max said. 'Vincent Paul ain't too far behind.'

'Thanks, Max,' Huxley said.

'So long Shawn . . . Boris – whatever.'

'Take care of yourself, Max Mingus,' Huxley said as he stepped away from the car and into the darkness, the night quickly engulfing him.

Max got in the car, started the engine and drove down the hill without looking back.

He turned on to the road and drove away.

He knew he wouldn't have to wait long before he met Vincent Paul on the road.

And sure enough, not five minutes later, he saw the head-lights of an approaching convoy.

68

Early the next morning Vincent Paul, Francesca and Charlie came to collect him.

Paul drove, Max in the passenger seat, Francesca and Charlie in the back. They made smalltalk, most of it inconsequential, words spoken for the sake of passing from one moment to the next and beating back the silence in between – the weather, political rumours, jokes about Hillary Clinton's eyesore pink suits.

Charlie ignored them all. He had his forehead pressed to the window and spent the whole drive staring at the parched landscape whizzing by in a wiry sandy blur. He was dressed in new jeans, a blue T-shirt and sneakers. Max noticed how long his legs were. He'd take after his father. He'd be a tall man.

Francesca stroked her boy's shoulder and back with long soft caresses. From time to time, as she spoke, she'd glance at him and let her eyes rest on him. The smile never left her face.

Max would be flying out in a UN plane bound for Miami airport. Once there he'd be escorted out, bypassing customs. He suddenly thought Vincent would ask him to carry drugs through for him, but just as suddenly as the thought entered his mind the voice of sober reason cut it in two: Paul would hardly need a *mule* when he had the UN at his disposal.

They drove through a side entrance, away from the main terminal, which took him on to the patched runway where a military-green DC10 was parked. The passenger door was open and steps had been wheeled up to it. The runway was otherwise empty.

'Am I the only cargo?' Max asked.

'No. You're the only *passenger*,' Paul corrected him, shutting off the engine. They both sat together looking at the plane.

'What about Chantale?'

'I've let her go. She'll be leaving for Miami in a few hours' time.'

'Gustav Carver, Co-dada, Eloise Krolak? What's happened to them?'

'What do you *think*?' Paul said, his face impassive. 'The world has to balance, wrongs have to be righted. You know how it is.'

Max nodded. He did.

'What are you going to do with yourself, back in Miami?' Paul asked.

'I've got things to balance in my world, things to make right,' Max said.

'Well, Gaspésie got away.' Paul stared at Max from the bottom of his sunken sockets. 'And, of course, Allain Carver's on the run too. Want the job?'

'No.' Max shook his head. 'You know, Vincent, you should let it go. It's worked out good for the three of you. You both got Charlie back – safe and sound. You've all got each other. You should be thankful. Most of the time it doesn't end that way.'

Paul made no comment, just stared out at the runway.

'What about you?' Max asked. 'What are you going to do?'

'I'm thinking of changing the way I do a few things.' Paul looked back at his family and smiled.

'Well, the Carver empire's all yours now,' said Max. 'Pity the old fucker didn't live to see that.'

'Do you believe in God, Max?'

'Yeah, I guess.'

'Then Gustav *is* seeing all of this happen – from his house in hell.'

They both laughed as one. Francesca didn't join in. Charlie kept staring out of the window.

They all got out of the car.

Two jeeploads of Paul's bodyguards, which had been following them on the way to the airport, pulled up nearby. Paul walked over to them, leaving Max alone with Francesca and Charlie.

Max realized that he hadn't spoken to Francesca since that night she'd come to see him in the house. He guessed now that Vincent Paul had dropped her off there right before he'd saved his life in the street.

'And what about you?' he asked her.

'What *about* me?'

'Is this it? Are you gonna stay here?'

'Why not? It's home. For better *and* for worse,' she laughed and put her hands loosely around Charlie's shoulders. Then a shadow crossed her face. 'Will you say anything? About me?'

'Don't worry about that,' Max said.

He looked at Charlie. Charlie looked back at him, his eyes focussing on Max's chin. Max crouched down to get to eye level with him.

'So long, Charlie Carver,' Max said.

'Say bye-bye to Max,' Francesca said, waving Charlie's hand.

Max smiled at him.

Charlie smiled back.

'Be safe.' Max ruffled Charlie's hair. Charlie immediately put his hands up and rearranged it the way it had been.

Francesca hugged him and kissed his cheek.

'Thank you, Max.'

Max walked over towards the plane, where Paul was stood watching two of his men each carrying a heavy army kitbag up the passenger steps.

'Is that what I think it is?' Max asked Paul.

'No,' Paul said. 'Wouldn't dream of it. That *is* for you though.'

'What is it?'

'Twenty million dollars – ten on behalf of the Thodores for the safe return of Claudette, and the rest is from us for bringing Charlie back.'

Max was stunned.

'The reason you initially came here was for money. The reason you came *back* was for our son – and for that they can never print enough money.'

'I don't know what to say,' Max said, finally.

'Say *au revoir*.'

'*Au revoir*.'

'*Au revoir, mon ami*.'

They shook hands.

Paul turned and went back to where Francesca and Charlie were standing.

Max climbed the passenger steps. When he reached the top he turned around and waved at the three of them once more. Then he homed in on Charlie and waved just to him. The boy raised his arm slightly but then changed his mind and let it drop.

Max looked out at Haiti one last time – low-lying mountains, low-hanging sky, bone-dry landscape, sparse vegetation. He wished it well, the very best. He didn't think he'd ever see it again. A lot of him hoped he never would.

Epilogue

In the air he checked out the money:

$20,000,000 US in $100 bills.

He couldn't resist it. He had to look.

He took out a stack of bills. He split the paper band containing them and they spilled on the floor.

He was still too numb to react. He'd never ever seen this kind of money before, not even on a drug bust.

He slipped a couple of hundreds into his wallet and scooped the rest up and put it away in the bag. He checked the other one.

More money – and a white envelope with his name on it. He opened it.

It was a Polaroid. He barely recognized it – the where and when it had been taken – then he remembered the last time he was in La Coupole: the photographer's flash.

He was standing staring straight at the camera, rum glass in hand, looking tired and drunk. One of the two whores who'd accosted him was standing close to his left, the other was mostly out of the frame.

In her place, pointing a gun at his head, with a huge smile on his face was Solomon Boukman.

Max turned the photograph over.

'*YOU GIVE ME REASON TO LIVE*' was written on the back in Boukman's unique capitals, same as the note they'd found in his prison cell.

Max's heart began to race.

He remembered how he'd been surprised to find the

trigger guard of his holster undone. He looked at the photograph again. Boukman was holding his Beretta to his head. He could have pulled the trigger. Why didn't he?

'*YOU GIVE ME REASON TO LIVE*'

A chill swept through Max, right then. His insides turned ice cold.

There was a note from Paul inside the envelope.

'*Max – We found this in the villa you were staying in. On the pillow. He got away from us. I didn't tell you then, because of what was happening. We're looking for him. Don't worry. He won't get away again. Take care. VP.*'

No, you won't. You won't get him, thought Max. *You should've killed him when you had the chance.*

Max looked back at the photograph and studied Boukman's face. They'd meet again, he knew it – not tomorrow, not even soon, but sometime down the line. It was inevitable, the way some things simply are. They had unfinished business.

Christmas Eve.

Max walked out of Miami airport and found a cab. He put the bags in the back and got in.

'Where to?' the driver asked.

Max hadn't given his next move any thought. He considered going back to the Radisson Kendall again, maybe for a week, to get his head together and a few things straight.

Then he thought the better of it.

'Home,' Max said, giving the driver the address of his house in Key Biscayne. 'Take me home.'

Acknowledgements

With very special thanks to my agent, Lesley Thorne, for her incredible commitment and support, and to Beverley Cousins, my inspiring editor.

And to those without whom . . .

Dad; The Mighty Bromfields: Cecil, Lucy, Gregory, David, Sonia, Colin, Janice, Brian and Lynette; Novlyn, Errol and Dwayne Thompson; Tim Heath, Suzanne Lovell, Angie Robinson, Rupert Stone, Jan and Vi, Sally and Dick Gallagher, Lloyd Strickland, Pauli and Tiina Toivola, Rick Saba, Christine Stone, Robert and Sonia Philipps, Al and Pedro Diaz, Janet Clarke, Tomas Carruthers, Chas Cook, Clare Oxborrow, Michael und die Familie Schmidt, Georg und die Familie Bischof, Haarm van Maanen, Bill Pearson, Lindsay Leslie-Miller, Claire Harvey, Emma Riddington, Lisa Godwin, Big T, Max Allen, Alex Walsh, Steve Purdom, Nadine Radford, Simon Baron-Cohen, Marcella Edwards, Mike Mastrangelo, Torr, Seamus 'The Legend' and Cal de Grammont, Scottish John, Anthony Armstrong Burns of E2, Shahid Iqbal, Abdul Moquith, Khoi Quan-Khio, mon frère Fouad, Whittards and Wrigley's.

. . . thank you!

The author is also deeply indebted to the management and staff of Tres Escritores Que Pierden Dinero, Calle Ocho, Miami, Fl. Thanks, guys, it's good to be home.